The Speed of Life

THE SPEED OF LIFE

Yanina Gotsulsky

VOX NOVA
A NUMINA PRESS BOOK

SAN RAFAEL, CALIFORNIA

Library of Congress Cataloging-in-Publication Data

Gotsulsky, Yanina, 1968-
 The speed of life : a novel / Yanina Gotsulsky.
     pages cm
"A Vox Nova Book."
 ISBN 978-0-9842600-3-4
  1. Karenina, Anna (Fictitious character)--Fiction. 2. Tolstoy, Leo, graf, 1828-1910--Fiction. 3. Authorship--Fiction. I. Title.
 PR9199.4.G673S64 2012
 813'.6--dc23

                          2012000135

Cover design by Glen Edelstein
Cover Image Copyright © 2012 by Kristina Oboznaya
Used under license from Shutterstock.com

A Vox Nova Book
Published by NUMINA PRESS
www.numinapress.com
Printed in U.S.A.

for my grandmother

from the author

In the late 1980s I was working in Moscow. One day, while foraging through a used bookstore, I came across what would become my personal treasure—a volume of excerpts from Tolstoy's journals. "Tolstoy on Art and Literature" humanized the great master for me, with entries like: "Do I have any talent compared to modern literary masters? Absolutely not." The struggles of the man behind the mask of genius served as a springboard for this novel. Everything spoken by Tolstoy on these pages is my translation of his actual words.

I have also used passages from the poetry of Anna Akhmatova and Boris Pasternak. Full texts of these can be found on my site: www.yaninagotsulsky.com

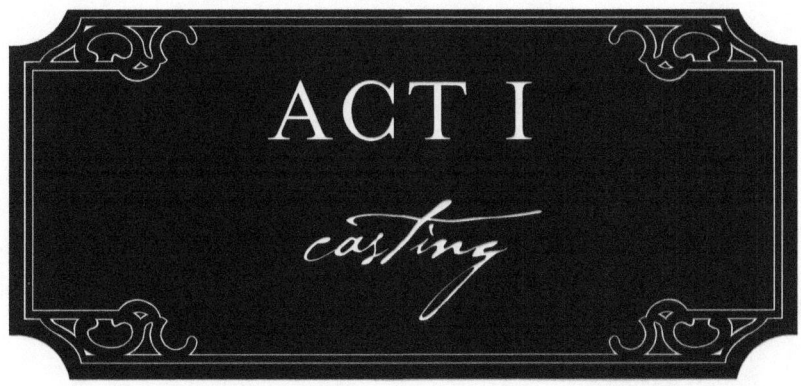

ACT I

casting

cobblestones

To L.N.T.

OUR FIRST MEETING. Do you remember?

Moscow, 1989. My temporal bookmark. What was yours? How old were you that spring? Sixty? For you it must have been 1889.

So…

Moscow, 1989. Perestroika. Glasnost. We in the West are in love with Gorbachev. In Russia they don't understand our love affair with a Communist apparatchik whose provincial accent is comical and whose deeds are abrasive. He has dared to wage war on the country's favourite pastime—vodka. His worth is clear to me. The Gorbachev era has allowed me to return. Again I am in this land that retains traces of my previous life. A foreigner in my once home.

Moscow. Lermontov Theatre. Rehearsing a play that I wrote. My first big success. Soon forever married to tragedy. Almost at the end of one love. Almost ready to meet another. Between men, between certainty and doubt. A time of youth when possibilities outnumber failures.

I walk out of the theatre. It is our lunch break and I like to wander through the streets of central Moscow. Time-steeped names: Sretenka, Taganka, Kitai-gorod, Arbat—I love the inscrutability of the faces and the sincerity of the scars in these historical neighbourhoods. The very Russianness of them, or, I should say, what I associate with Russianness. History and disdain, grandeur and squalor, solidity and uncertainty.

Would anything have changed in my life had I not walked out that day; had I accepted Luke Garson's proposition to dine at the "Chez Margarita" co-operative (new code word for private) restaurant, his favourite haunt for lunch-time *borscht*, vodka and cabbage *pirozhki*? We had had another fight that morning. I did not feel like talking. I wanted to wrap myself in Russia, to free myself from him.

So… Moscow, 1989. Spring.

~~~

I leave the theatre through the stage door, tighten the belt of my raincoat and lift the collar. It is cooler than the April sun rending the clouds would intimate. The cracked asphalt before me is dotted with puddles. Glancing down at my new lace-up granny boots, I navigate around the murky water. Luke hates this outfit I'm wearing. He calls it my "Anna Karenina get-up"—long skirt, ruffled blouse, and these boots that look like they come from the 19th century. He doesn't care that this is fashionable. I don't care to appease him. A mini skirt and fishnets just don't rhyme with my mood. I pass the time-battered church in the theatre's backyard, wondering whether it will ever be renovated. I have heard that there are plans in the making. Along with shedding communism, the country is once again feverishly donning the ill-fitting dusty cloak of Christianity.

I approach the back fence and, thinking about the dilapidated beauty of the chapel, lift the heavy latch on the iron gate. As I step out onto Bolshaya Bronnaya Street I hear the bell toll once in the belfry. This startles me and I look back. That's impossible! The windows are boarded up and the bell tower is empty. Surely. It must have been one of the hundreds of Moscow's gold-domed churches somewhere close by. It is a momentary jolt but it brings with it a whiff of the unexpected, a flicker of excitement.

I turn my attention to the street but something feels different. Details reach my awareness in slow motion, as if the atmosphere has acquired a levity and images are having a difficulty solidifying in it. Cobblestones. Why have I never noticed the quaintness of cobblestones on one of Moscow's oldest streets? Some writer I am! As I roll my eyes at my own ineptitude, I hear the neighing of a horse, and an elegant calèche rolls by, the liveried coachman giddy-yapping the horse with gusto and apparent disregard for the spectacle his anachronistic get-up is producing. Then I note the second peculiarity. Uncharacteristically for Moscow, a city of over ten million people, this street is almost deserted. A few buildings away an old bearded man dressed as a peasant—sashed tunic, woven birch-bark *lapti* on his feet—crouches in the doorway of a building, feeding a mangy dog. A woman with a parasol is strolling down the opposite sidewalk. Otherwise the street appears deserted.

My brain auditions the only logical explanation—Mosfilm is shooting a period movie. But I see no crews, no lights, none of the bustle usually associated with a film set.

Is it their lunch break? Are the trappings of movie-making hidden away when Russian filming pauses? Would this have anything to do with the fact that stealing state property is the casual hobby of almost every Russian citizen? If so, why are the actors still here in their costumes? Are they getting into the mood by utilizing Stanislavsky's method? Something is not adding up. Why would Russians need to practice The Method? Their lives are one big experiment in method acting.

A third oddity emerges: the air is unusually clean for Moscow, no scent of gasoline, exhaust fumes, perspiration, cigarette smoke. It must have rained while we were rehearsing, but... I don't have a chance to complete my thought because at this moment I see the store.

How had I missed it before? My entertainment on this trip has been scouring the used bookstores of Moscow. A dollar on the black market can be exchanged for 10 rubles. Considering that 100 rubles is an average monthly salary, I am deliriously rich. Rare works that would cost Russians many months of savings, I buy by the suitcase-full and ship back to Canada. Yet somehow I have overlooked a bookstore across the street from my theatre!

The name is delicious. *"Knizhnaya Lavka Sorokina."* Before me is "Sorokin's Book Shoppe"—the slightly archaic wording, the slowness of another time when pride of ownership connoted quality of merchandise. A foreshadowing of great treasures inside. Perestroika, indeed, is wonderful! Here is an alternative to the faceless "DOM KNIGI"—"House of Books" or, more precisely, "House of A Book." One lonely monolithic gargantuan book. A volume filled, no doubt, with the wisdom of Lenin, Marx and Brezhnev combined.

I glance in both directions, making certain once again that I am not interfering with some scene being filmed, and cross the street.

As I push open the door, triggering the tinkling of a brass bell, I realize what final brush stroke had been missing from the portrait of the prevailing strangeness—the texture of sound. There is no growling of un-mufflered automobiles that always slaps one in the face in Moscow.

But who can contemplate minutiae when one is about to enter the temple of thought?

I must admit that I don't recognize you at first when I cross the threshold of the shop and take in the delectable eccentricity of my discovery. A long, narrow room at the back of which, in lieu of the usual counter with a bored peroxided saleswoman, there is an ornate large desk. A kerosene lamp exudes a glow onto two seated men. One of them, you, holds a cup half lifted—a gesture frozen between doing and being.

I will learn later that it is tea you are drinking. A strong Ceylon tea with cherry preserves that your business partners always bring out for your visits.

Both of you stand up as I make the first steps into the store. You set your cup down.

"Good day," I smile and look around. At that moment the sun again breaks through the clouds, invades the glass storefront and lays its ochre fingers onto the floor-to-ceiling shelves lined with the most astounding book collection! The volumes are in several languages, all in perfectly preserved old bindings. As if awakened by warmth, dust dances around in the sunrays like the souls of the authors and all the readers who have ever perused these books, inviting me to touch, to explore, to sample.

There is a slight dizziness. I attribute it to excitement. A slight sense of the almost-dream.

"May I be of service, *baryshnya*?" says one of the men. Not you. The younger one. The proprietor, Sorokin.

He calls me *baryshnya*—young lady. A strange word to hear. One encounters it on the pages of prerevolutionary Russian literature. One hears it from the lips of geriatric White Army officers and exiled princesses living out their final days in Paris, Toronto, Buenos Aires or other moored dinghies of the sunken Russian Empire. *Baryshnya* is an archaeological artefact on the 1989 streets of Moscow. At most I expect *devushka*, young woman. Often just *grazhdanka*. Citizen. A pale form of address. Bled dry of any noble meaning. They never look at you when they address you as citizen. Always away from you into themselves. I am a citizen of a very different land, I inevitably reply. That wakes them up.

Something stirs in them: bewilderment, disbelief, hatred, amusement. They awaken into Life. My contribution to the snowball of Perestroika.

But here I am facing a man who is already alive. Smiling. Calling me *baryshnya*.

"I would like to look around," I lay my hand on the nearest volume. Anchoring myself to its wonderful pace, when books were made with love, every letter handwritten, then rewritten, then set in type and bound in leather.

Your outfits too look as if they are from another century. Why doesn't that galvanize me into a speeding curiosity? Do I assume you are actors who also wandered in? Am I too spellbound by books to give much weight to the idiosyncratic fashion sense of two Russians? Or maybe I don't rationalize, for in the middle of a dream we don't think to find explanations for everything that is happening around us. We fly over our sorrows and forget to ask who has given us wings.

That's right, I don't question. My mind accepts your reality because it is not out of tune with my desire. Theatre training plus emotional tribulation now result in an instinctive suspension of disbelief.

Your muffled voices re-engage in a conversation that I must have interrupted. I am not looking at you but I know your eyes are upon me. My hand senselessly traces the book bindings. I feel your gaze on my cheek, my neck. Your eyes do not question. They possess. But I have just left a man with eyes so similar to yours. He is now in the theatre, sharing a stale salami sandwich with the production manager. I am here, not wishing to enter another gaze full of this maddening power. This assuredness is too much too soon. That you are somebody I am certain. That you are you, I will not know until later. That we will be together twenty years ago and twenty years hence will be established in the next few minutes.

With every breath I inch closer to your table. The dance of destinies has begun. I have heeded your call. Why are you summoning me from your reality, slowing down the speed of my atoms to perceive a time layer that is not mine?

You place a top-hat on your head. Lift a parcel wrapped in thick paper and twine. Make a few steps towards the door. Sorokin follows you.

I turn to the books. They will save me. Will they? Did they save you? I open a volume of La Fontaine's fables, translated by Ivan Krylov.

"So if Rachinsky is wrong," says Sorokin as he passes me, "what then is most important?"

You place your parcel on one of the shelves and lean on your walking stick. Perhaps it is my imagination, perhaps my vanity, but I think you raise your voice. "What's most important in fiction is an element of novelty, originality. It has nothing to do with how something should be written. It's not that you'd read the 'Kreutzer Sonata' and have an epiphany, oh that's how one must write... No, in some aspect you must go further than others; chip off a fragment of uniqueness, no matter how small. That's why Dostoyevsky's 'Crime and Punishment' is wonderful in its first part and weaker in the second. Dostoyevsky was never a particularly good writer precisely because he always had too many thoughts and always needed to say too much."

"But, Your Excellency, Lev Nikolaevich..." Sorokin is indignant. You raise your hand, silencing him and continue:

"Nevertheless, Dostoyevsky is true art. As opposed to my good friend Fet[1], who at sixteen wrote: 'the stream gurgles, the moon shines, and she loves me.' He kept writing, writing, writing and at sixty he writes: 'she loves me, the stream gurgles, and the moon shines.'"

You tip your hat to Sorokin, to me. You leave the store. Sorokin walks back to his desk, now himself entangled in thought. Then I realize that your parcel is still on the shelf. I have to talk to you again! I am already trapped but I don't know it yet. I grab the package and run out the door. I think that I see the flap of your grey coat turn the corner. I rush after this clue.

I rush. I speed up. Something's wrong.

A bell tolls again but it is moving, moving further away as if it is another person's memory being carried beyond the boundary of my perception. A spinning heaviness descends upon me. The unbearable velocity of car engines, jostling crowds, sirens, stench, music. The rain that is beginning to fall is already a different rain. Its tempo is jarring. I don't see you.

---

1   Afanasy Fet—one of the most influential Russian poets of the late 19th Century.

I turn around. I must go back to the store. I must learn who you are. But there are no more cobblestones on Bolshaya Bronnaya. Where the store had been I see a blinking sign of a café. I am standing by the theatre fence. Alone. Clutching in my hands the one connection to you. The one bridge that will eventually let me enter your world. You have left me your journals.

stage notes

Reality is circumscribed only by the limits of our imagination. My world, my real world, the one inside my head, I envision as a play. On the stage of my imagination there is no set, no backdrop. The back wall of my theatre is exposed. Bricks painted black. Everything is black and bare. Barren. Except for empty picture frames, large and small, plain and ornate, hanging from the flies like raindrops suspended in space.

I never see the audience. Sometimes I wonder if they're there.

Today's scene starts with an acoustic guitar strumming a plaintive Russian melody in a blackout. Low at first, it builds, as a spotlight comes up on a table, centre stage. The legs of the table are made of stacked books. I am sitting cross-legged on top of it. I see myself from afar, a mere character in that play. I am no longer "I" but KARINA. I observe Karina's face as if it belongs to a stranger—its lines are angular, its planes are pale. One of your journals is in front of her. It's a thick worn notebook with pages warped by time and frequent fingering. But she's not looking at it. Her eyes are focused far away.

The music volume continues to increase, becoming unbearably loud for a couple of beats. It stops abruptly. The stage is flooded by lights. YOU enter.

In my mind's eye you are not the solemn, grey-haired maître we're used to seeing in portraits, but a man at the pinnacle of his creative and physical prowess—around the age of forty. You are dressed in a black kosovorotka, black pants and tall black boots. You stand behind the table on the stage, but Karina doesn't notice you just yet. She begins a soliloquy.

KARINA: So many years have passed since that day in Moscow. Today is September 9, your birthday. I can finally address you as an equal. My manuscript is done. Written, rewritten, polished and ready to be sent out into the world. There, literary agents, editors will have to judge my novel. Of course I should say, *our* novel. Your Anna Karenina provided the seed.

How surprised you would be to learn that "Anna Karenina" is counted among the greatest works of world literature. Only I know the truth. It is your greatest cry for help. After spending all these years studying your Anna, dissecting every phrase, pondering every paragraph for its structure and meanings, I can finally voice what you weren't able to: you didn't mean to kill her. You suspected that a fundamental part of you might die should that character perish. You simply didn't know how to stop the train wheels.

(Karina flips through your journal. The rustling pages sigh. She finds an entry from 1856 and reads your words out loud. Her voice is measured, like an incantation.)

KARINA: Novels teach us to understand people and to love them with all their shortcomings.

(You place a hand on her shoulder. Your lips move, repeating these same words.)

KARINA: More than that. (She sets the journal down.) A novel is an intimate conversation. We love writers for daring spiritual nudity. Had it not been for your attempt to create the Modern Woman in Anna, I would not have been able to see you at your moment of collapse. At the end of your first draft Anna lived. Then for four years darkness intensified, swirling around you, drawing you in. You yielded, and you took Anna with you. I resolved what you could not. It should bring us both peace.

extra

To L.N.T.

Your journals were, as usual, my bedtime reading last night. The more I delve into them, the more I become certain that they don't just mirror your truths. There is something alive in your words. Alive, so many years after you yourself no longer are. As if to confirm this, as I was drifting off into sleep I heard a voice: "No genius can emerge in isolation. External stimuli—a good book, a conversation—evolve one's reflection more than years of secluded labour. A thought's birth must take place in public, whereas its refinement and expression have to be conducted in solitude."

I know it was you.

Once, in Moscow, I went to your house. It's a museum now, every item lovingly preserved by your wife. Among its treasures is a phonograph recording of you talking to local children. Thomas Edison, an admirer of your work, had given you "the sound recording machine" and you delighted in tinkering with it. When I first heard your voice it was no surprise—deep, measured, self-assured, the drawn-out lilt of old Russia quite unmistakable in your pronunciation. A voice I have never forgotten.

However, I think you have the wrong idea. All these years while I was writing the novel, and even before, I hadn't lived my life as a hermit. It is quite impossible to be one in a city like Los Angeles. It is easy to be invisible though. A perfect choice for one running away. Memories don't follow people here.

It must be difficult for you to imagine that this arid little town —a chicken farm on the shores of the Pacific in your time—has become such a metropolis. You'd hate it here, I think. Time plays tricks here. The days rush on, enslaved by strict business cycles, yet they all seem like one long day. Here fantasy has become an industry. Here randomly intersecting fates pass for friendships. Here, make-believe is the prevalent reality, and here, my self-imposed solitude has grown quite full of people.

"Where are you from?"

"Canada," I say usually.

"Oh, that's why you have a slight accent."

"Russia," I reply when I am in a talkative mood.

"My, you don't have any accent at all!"

Americans are so intrigued with the concept of Russia. It's as if they've been told their whole lives not to play with matches and suddenly they are confronted with a blazing torch. But I'm not going to embark on a diatribe against Americans or America. There is no point hating a country, just like there is no point loving one. A country is just a congregation of people, speaking, more or less, the same language, adhering, more or less, to the same set of rules. Innately, however, people are alike no matter where you go. Differences are in the weather, food preference, and indoctrination. Differences are irrelevant to a nomad, like me.

"What do you do?" ask my American friends.

"I'm an extra."

"You mean you're an actress?"

"No. I'm an extra."

Perfect word to describe me, don't you think? Extra, superfluous.

Few understand this lack of ambition. All are comforted by it. I am no competition for the inhabitants of this city, most of whom are trying to claw their way up the cinematic ladder. I am willing to dissolve in a crowd. I am popular because of it.

When I first moved down here, I briefly entertained the idea of working in a theatre. Of course not as a playwright. I couldn't bear to look at paper, to think of the black tracery of letters marking white. But theatre was the only life I knew. However, the more I considered the naked vulnerability of a theatre space lit by house lights, the more I realized that I couldn't handle it. It was too intimate a world.

One day, waiting for a restaurant manager to interview me for a waitressing job, I was leafing through a copy of the Hollywood Reporter left by someone on the bar. An ad caught my attention. "Casting Call! Extras needed for major Hollywood productions. Experience a plus but not necessary. Excellent pay. Flexible schedule. Bring a headshot…"

Movies. An art form totally foreign to me. A world so saturated with egos that I could easily survive there unnoticed. I walked out of the restaurant without seeing the manager.

In my apartment I jotted down a fake résumé, listing American films and TV series that had filmed in Toronto over the past several years. I threw in a couple of Canadian productions as well, for authenticity's sake. I had seen hundreds of acting résumés so the format was easy—year, film, director, role. 1987, 1988, 1989… Police Academy. Moonstruck. Anne of Green Gables. Directors? I couldn't remember, nor did I care, nor would anyone else. I crossed that column out. Role—Extra, Extra, Extra, Extra. Under Education I listed my unfinished BFA—a background in Theatre looked convincing for a twenty-six-year-old looking for a job in film. Under special skills I listed everything I could imagine, short of marathon running and scalping.

Satisfied with the content and format I pulled out a black-and-white 8x10. I had it done in Toronto a couple of years before, when my career had been on the rise. It was a splurge. It was worth it. The photographer, Marcella Petri, a woman a few years older than me, was being hailed as Toronto's next great artist. Her name frequently mentioned along Canada's other photographic great—Yousuf Karsh. I now stared at this photo. The face, my face, looked lit from within. Serene and intense at the same time. I supposed that it still looked the same. Nobody would know that the inside of this young shell had been so badly mangled.

A week later at the extras cattle call in Universal Studios I handed this photo with the résumé to the casting agent. He looked me over as one would look over a piece of furniture, deciding whether it would fit into some allotted space. I could read his thoughts clearly—young, average height, slim, long hair, can be moulded into any average costume and fit any period. He glanced at my list of imaginary credits, "Oh yeah? Police Academy filmed in Toronto?"

"Yeah," I echoed him. "Mostly around the Saint Lawrence Market."

I was hired. One production led to another. Then another. I showed up dutifully. I never tried to gesticulate wildly behind the actors' heads to be able to whisper some day in a darkened movie theatre, "Hey, there I am, right there!" I never tried to convince the assistant directors that if I could have just one line, the scene with Mr. and Miss Superstar would be so much more realistic. I never complained about the long hours or the cold or the heat when winter scenes inevitably were filmed in the summer and summer scenes were filmed in the winter. I never bragged loudly about walk-on roles on Star Trek. I slept with many men.

Inside the stars' "honey wagons" and behind the sets in the tall yellowing grass of the California countryside. In their cars and in their homes. After fancy dinners in Malibu and after a few shared glasses of wine on the Sunset Strip. It wasn't lust and it wasn't depravity. Simply when memory got too intense, the only way I could drive the demons away was to focus acutely on my body.

Finding men on movie sets was easy. It was just as easy to keep them out of my life.

When a man asked, "Can I pick you up at your apartment?"

I responded with, "I'll meet you at the restaurant."

"What do you like to do in your spare time?"

"Walk along the beach."

"I just finished reading this book…"

"I hate talking about books."

"What do you want to do with your life?"

"I'm doing it."

"Being an actress?"

"Being an extra."

So you see, I haven't at all lived like a hermit. I have only sealed my heart hermetically.

stage notes

THE THEATRE IS *dark except one spotlight, stage left. KARINA is standing in the circle of illumination. I am standing. Every writer is the character. No character is conscious of the writer. Thus in one body we both stand. One aware fully, facing the unfaceable in third person. Another, not even an inkling that her life is a staged version of somebody's memory.*

A second spotlight comes up on TOLSTOY leaning over the table where he is installing a toy train track. The middle of the table-top is piled with figurines, miniature buildings, train cars. KARINA walks up and begins setting the decorations around the track. TOLSTOY picks up an antique-looking bright red train engine.

TOLSTOY: Can one ever regain that sense of novelty, that carelessness, that need for love and that power of faith one had as a child? I recall how I would go upstairs, and stand before the icons in my thick quilted housecoat, and say with rapture, "God bless Papa and Mama!" and recite a prayer I had learned from my beloved mother so that my love for God and for her blended strangely into a single emotion! After my evening prayers I would cuddle up under my blanket. Light, peace, and happiness filled my soul. I would surrender to ever-shifting reveries.

KARINA: Reveries of what?

TOLSTOY: They were always vague and always filled with pure love and expectations of brilliant happiness.

(TOLSTOY places the toy engine on the train track, pushes it, and watches it roll to the edge of the table)

KARINA: I remember going to bed and pulling out my history book with the portrait of Lenin in the front and making a solemn promise to him that I would win the city-wide poetry contest. I think I too had light and happiness fill my soul as I looked in his eyes. But carelessness... I don't recall a feeling of carelessness.

(KARINA pushes the toy train and it rolls off the table and shatters. TOLSTOY kneels and picks up one broken piece.)

TOLSTOY: I would take some favourite toy, a porcelain bunny or puppy, tuck it into the corner of my down pillow and revel in the thought of how warm and comfortable it is. Eventually thoughts would become jumbled and entangled until at last I would fall asleep. Could it be that life has left such heavy tracks in my heart that those simple ecstasies have vanished forever? Have I only memories left to console me?

KARINA: Life leaves no tracks in the heart. Life rends the heart into a million fragments, each embossed with characters once known.

in third person

To L.N.T.

"WHAT HAPPENED?" ASKED my grandmother. "Don't be scared. If it's easier, tell it in third person."

Third person? The words hewed into the ice of shock.

First person—*I*. Second person—*you*. Points of view. Literature class. School. Mishka.

Third person—*he*. That image. That sound…

My grandmother mistook silence for lack of understanding and embraced me. A rare gesture of affection.

"Just pretend that it didn't happen to you," she said. "Imagine someone else in your place. Do you want to try that?"

I nodded.

"In some ways, she is quite like you," my grandmother prompted.

Indeed. That other non-Karina was also nine years old. Hair neatly braided. School uniform always pressed. She had the same beige-and-brown plaid coat with its sleeves already too short and the white lace of the school uniform's cuffs peeking out.

"Now tell me what happened to her, little bird."

Hesitantly, I cleared my throat, tested the sound it emitted: "I… She…" My voice felt detached as I did this, "She was walking home from school with Mishka…"

It was hard, at first, picturing myself outside the scene. But liberating too. Because as I hovered beyond that other girl's skin I could observe at leisure. For example I noticed that as those two walked past the dirty grey piles of snow clinging to building corners, Mishka grabbed the girl's hand several times but then, pretending it was an accident or a game, he dropped it. The girl pretended not to notice at all.

Mishka always walked her home. Sometimes he carried her school bag, sometimes he bought ice-cream and they took turns licking it. Mishka was a brooding, skinny boy who was excellent at drawing dragons and telling stories of knights defeating them. He was also solemn and polite, unlike the other boys. Maybe it was because his mother drank too much, and he had never had a father, and, as the adults whispered, he had grown up too fast. Sometimes his mother disappeared for days and Mishka scrounged the neighbourhood, gathering empty bottles and exchanging them for a few coins at the liquor store.

Mishka dreamed of someday going off on a quest to fight a dragon. He said that dragons did exist in this world but that one had to be very pure of heart to fight them, and preferably English. He always sighed at that, and his voice cracked with longing. It was the voice of a boy who thought eating his fill of potatoes was a treat, and who wore hand-me-down rubber boots stuffed with newspaper for warmth and fit.

"Mishka and... and this girl had stayed late after school," I continued. "They'd been rehearsing for the Soviet Army Day variety show. It was getting dark so they took a shortcut through the train station."

~~~

The train station. An evening in late winter. The lights on the platform are on already. Their tired glow makes the melting snow and the rapidly melting daylight look more grimy than usual. There are hardly any people around—a few soldiers smoking; a drunkard on the bench slurring a gypsy song. Nobody pays attention to two kids walking slowly along the platform. "Can you keep a secret?" suddenly asks Mishka. As he says these words, he turns around, his face close to her face. His breath congeals into a cloud. Like a tiny ghost. Then he bends down and his lips touch hers. They are wind-chapped and scratchy. She has never been kissed by a boy before, so maybe this is normal.

"I will marry you when I grow up," he says.

She giggles, not knowing the proper behaviour in such circumstances.

"I will marry you," he repeats.

She laughs and runs past him. He chases her, first laughing too, then catches her, trying to kiss her again. She pushes him away. "But I don't love you," she says.

She isn't sure this is true. But they are standing under one of the glowing street lamps, painfully exposed to all the adults, especially the stationmaster who is making his rounds and is now heading in their direction. Surely if he notices them kissing he will summon the militia or even her parents.

Mishka doesn't care. He raises his voice and those words, that she will be his wife that she will love him, hack into the air, ring in the cement crevices of the train station. Now the drunkard starts laughing, "Hey kid, you should grow your hammer before you start nailing girls down." The soldiers laugh too. Mishka takes a step backwards. Then another. "Tell me you love me," he shouts, as he jumps down onto the train tracks. "Tell me, or I will stand here and not move!"

The world implodes into silence and is reborn into pandemonium.

Bells clang, announcing an approaching train. Voices yell for help. She runs to the edge of the platform. Mishka is standing in the middle of the tracks. So close. So dangerously far away.

She wants to scream, Mishka, get out! But her mouth is dry, her throat tight with fear. She kneels in the melting snow, her white tights becoming saturated at the knees with muddy slush. The stationmaster's shrill whistle sounds nearby.

She cannot tear her eyes away from Mishka. His body is frail on the bulky cross-ties. The railway has been transformed into a gigantic tongue of an approaching lizard.

Mishka never once looks back at the rushing monster. He stares only at her. He is saying something, but the train is too close, too loud. His words are but a puff of breath near his lips. Those lips that had pressed so daringly into hers. The tiny cloud, the voiceless good-bye dissolves. As metal frantically screeches against metal, orange-red sparks flare up—the embers on the breath of the looming beast. Its horn, a blast from a giant throat, howls piercingly. One more moment and…

A spray of warmth hits her cheek. Red droplets spread on the white cuff of her uniform. Like confetti. And then… frightened faces are all around. Snippets of conversation reach her: What happened? Where?

As a man picks her up off the ground she sees something shiny in the dirty snow beneath her knees. A golden button from Mishka's overcoat.

~~~

Now, as an adult, I no longer know how closely my story resembles those actual events. I'm certain there were two nine-year-olds, a train station, the red drops on white lace. I'm certain it was February. As for the rest... Dealing with pain in third person anaesthetizes memory.

But I do remember one thing—waking up in the middle of that night because there were quiet voices in the room. My grandmother's and my mother's. "Her first kiss," sighed my grandmother. "This is a bad omen."

I wanted to tell her that she shouldn't worry about omens because it all happened in third person, but when I opened my eyes, I saw a field of snow. And Mishka standing next to a slain dragon.

stage notes

Same setting as *before. The table is piled with envelopes. Most are crumpled. A few torn pieces are on the floor. KARINA and TOLSTOY sit back-to-back on the stage next to the table. Their laps are overflowing with papers.*

KARINA: This afternoon, finally, I pulled a stack of letters out of my mail box. Responses about my manuscript. I ripped the first one open. Then the second. Then the third. One after another they were all rejections… Most were form letters. Some were mere slivers of paper, a sheet cut in four or into strips the size of bookmarks with stamped rejection phrases. One was my own letter with "NO!" scribbled over it in a red marker. My only hand-written response… One after another they fell to the floor. Around my feet more and more paper, like long-forgotten snow, like meaninglessness… Have you felt this? How did you react?

(TOLSTOY picks up a letter, skims its contents and throws it away.)

TOLSTOY: I was very upset, but now I have calmed down. I know that I have something to say and that I have the power to say it effectively. Afterwards, let the public pronounce what it will. I must work wholeheartedly; give it everything that I have. Afterwards let them spit on the altar.

KARINA: I envy you. Over the years your faith had stumbled and regained its footing but you had never lost a sense of identity. In it you always found support. You phrased it once so…

TOLSTOY: I must be true to myself...

KARINA: ...so succinctly!

TOLSTOY: ... a writer by ability; an aristocrat by birth.

KARINA: *(echoing him)* A writer by ability; an aristocrat by birth. That's it! I, on the other hand, have no such wellspring. My belief system begins with Scene One and always has an ending. My identity is wrapped up in words. What if they fail?

(TOLSTOY gets up, walks over to the table and begins clearing it off)

No, no, no, mustn't think of that. I have stepped into a wrong reality, that's all. I need to find my way back to that other path where at least my words mattered. But relinquished realities are not as easily regained as an abandoned room or a recanted allegiance.

(KARINA forces herself up, as if the weight of the paper is too much for her to remove. She walks downstage, to the very edge of the proscenium, reaches her arm out towards the audience.)

Once, success came easily. My plays were staged in some of the best theatres of Moscow and Toronto. Then came, as Pasternak wrote, "death and sulphurous fire and sorrow." I stopped writing. Was I wrong? Can talent be lost and found and lost again like a sock? Yes, I write again but does that make me a writer? Millions of people write. They write letters, declarations, notes, denunciations, even poetry. How am I different from the masses? Am I?

(The table is now clear of paper. The only object visible on it is an oversized malachite inkwell and a quill. TOLSTOY joins KARINA downstage. He stands next to her)

TOLSTOY: About forty years ago, a not terribly bright but very cultured lady summoned me to listen to a novel she had just composed. This novel began with the heroine sitting by a pond in a poetic forest. She was dressed in poetic white robes, had poetically loose flowing hair, and was reading poetry. The action was set in Russia, where all of a sudden the hero appeared from behind some bushes, wearing a hat with a plume à la William Tell. Of course he was accompanied by two poetically white dogs. The author was certain that this whole set-up was very poetic. But that would all be fine if the hero did not have to open his mouth and speak. Alas, as soon as this gentleman with the plume à la William Tell began talking to this maiden in white robes, it became obvious that the author had nothing to say, that she was under the influence of previously read stories, and thought that by rehashing old memories, she herself could evoke a semblance of art. Art cannot be produced on demand or on a whim. It has to be born in the artist…

KARINA: Or stillborn. *(She scoops up a handful of letters now in a pile next to the desk, and throws it up into the air.)* Thank you very much… there are a number of reasons… not to… not to … not…not right…perhaps… it is also possible…and certainly… unfortunately… nor do we feel… we apologize… the very best of luck and success.

Do literary abortions merit a tombstone in an artist's universe? I am ready. Let's analyze where I went wrong. I promise that by the end of our conversation we will be elbow-deep in gutted words. I will hide nothing. You be the judge.

The all-important caveat: in an autobiography a writer is masked; in fiction naked; in memory delusional.

TOLSTOY: So what is this?

KARINA: This is where the past is born. My version of "All happy families are alike. Every unhappy family is unhappy in a unique way."

trains, sausages, and bridges

July, 1979. Karina is standing on a platform of a train station. She hasn't been here since…

But no time to reflect. A high-pitched sound ruffles the crowd. The first boarding whistle. She is finally getting her wish. She is going on a journey.

~~~

Her life was defined by the train station. That other life. It was a million thoughts and a thousand fears ago, for the "old she" is lost in the labyrinths of time and can only be glimpsed through the fragmented, muted glass of memory. It was a minute ago and a step away, for the "new she" is a direct, defiant response to the essence of her old persona. The persona who innocently tethered her security to the rhythmic rattle of train wheels.

The train station was two blocks away from her home—a two-room, one fireplace, zero bathroom, reincarnated shack. It might have sheltered sheep or pigs before the Communist Liberation, but a little human ingenuity slapped clay on the wooden walls, covered them with whitewash, waived the magic ramrod of socialist reality, and—voilà—the perfect abode of the proletariat; the hovel where two generations of her family grew up.

Beyond these walls lay a fenced-in yard, a cherry tree, a chicken roost, a water pump—a source of neighbourhood envy and a rarity, which afforded her family the luxury of almost never having to go to the crowded communal well. And in the background, permeating all the fibres of her childhood was the metal-clanging, conductor-whistling, engine-sighing, ground-reverberating, heaving and crawling kaleidoscope of faces, suitcases, parallel tracks and intersecting fates.

Her mother's work was down the street from the train station. Every morning before going to the office she took Karina and her brother to their kindergarten. The road to their first educational Oz was lined with uneven rows of houses that leaned on either side of an unpaved street like idle drunken sailors. Beyond them, a rusted bridge straddled the train tracks.

Every morning and every evening she climbed up the rickety structure and traversed the most mysterious and exciting place in her yet unencumbered existence. Ascending high over the human beehive of the station she always felt excitement. She was growing gigantic, and under her feet the scheduled and patterned bustling of grey adult crowds diminished with every step. Even the imposing machines were assuming more toy-like proportions. On the top step she carried out a secret ritual, turning her head to the right and the left, making a wish in each direction.

Her wish was to travel.

There in the distance, to either side of her, the parallel steel tracks converged on the horizon, their vanishing points delineating her world. Somewhere beyond were the Kremlin's crimson stars, and Lenin's hallowed tomb, and the Aurora—the battleship that valiantly stormed the tsar's Winter Palace during the Revolution and with a mighty wallop of its cannons announced the birth of this heaven on earth, the Union of Soviet Socialist Republics.

She was certain that her path would take her into some thrilling future that would encompass all these marvels. A path that began now, with these steps.

Some planks from the wooden covering of the bridge were missing, and through the holes under her feet she kept an eye on the roofs of the trains below, surrendering to daydreams of impending grandeur.

But about halfway across the gaping planks, a gurgling fear would overtake her. She would become convinced that one more step, and she would slip into one of these holes. Fantasies squelched. She became aware of being a small body yanked through these moments by forces beyond her control.

To avoid imminent disaster she clutched her mother's hand, shut her eyes and held her breath until the clanking of heels on the metal steps announced the end of the crossing.

Why was she afraid? Her mother's grip was strong. And even if she did go down, the mother, dragged after her was too big and wouldn't fit through. Years later while reading Anna Karenina, its leitmotif of the train would strike her as a bittersweet déjà vu. Perhaps, like in the book, her fear was a foreshadow of the impending death of her world, and of that particular "her" who was cheerfully marching along to absorb the first lessons of canonical Communism.

But at that point there were no bad associations with trains. Not yet. In awe she looked at these long green metal sausage links, with bright gold-and-red USSR coats of arms proudly embossed on the sides of each car. Their windows, at one time or another, had reflected the ever-changing panoramas, like flickering postcards in the family album of Mother Russia—from the sparkling, serene snows of Siberia to the balmy, bright beaches of the Black Sea; from majestic Moscow to the proud peaks of Georgia. She longed to be a part of their world.

~~~

Now, she is no longer a dream-filled toddler crossing the tracks. On this day she is eleven years, one month and five days old and her first wish is about to come true. Finally she isn't merely an observer in the train station. She is here with a purpose, with a ticket and a destination. Her family has their worldly possessions in four suitcases— three mustard-yellow ones for the parents and Grandma Irina and a smaller red one shared by her and her brother. They are leaving their familiar world behind.

A tight circle of relatives encloses them. They are all talking simultaneously. She sees their mouths moving, but the deafening pounding in her temples drowns out all other noises of that summer morning. Their mouths are smiling, but their eyes are sad. The juxtaposition makes them seem like grimacing players in a movie. In fact, everything is surrealistically cinematic. Except this time she is playing one of the leading roles.

What do their faces express, she wonders? Happiness for their bright prospective future? Sadness at the distance that is about to intervene between them irrevocably? Envy that it is not they, who are leaving Russia? In each of the people saying good-bye to their family the feelings are probably a combination of all three. Purity of emotion happens only in brief flashes in the course of a human life.

Every so often one of the adults bends down to her and smothers her in a hug. Some are warm, some are obligatory and therefore cold, and most are accompanied by kisses. As their faces descend closer to her level she can see their red eyes and can feel the dampness of tears as their cheeks touch hers. It is immensely frightening for a child to see adults cry. This only adds to the feeling of doom, which squeezes her heart like a corpulent attendant at the public baths wringing a sponge.

She also begins to cry. But not because she shares their sentiment. No, her tears are flowing because she will never again see a portrait of the Great Lenin.

~~~

She is a good little communist. A true product of a country that for sixty years has prohibited religion. It is taught in schools that there is no God. That He is an old wives' tale. That the concept of God had been born of man's inability to explain certain natural phenomena in the forgotten antiquity of pre-communist enlightenment. According to the Soviet philosophy, since there are now scientific advancements, there is no longer a need for religion. It makes sense, and she believes her teachers. Millions of children believe them.

Millions lay their souls open to a much more insidious creed. When pondering her childhood, her future self will often dead-end into a "why". Why would a whole nation discard the yoke of one religion only to don, willingly, the noose of another?

Eventually she will understand what the founding fathers of the Soviet state understood in 1917—man's quest for meaning and spirituality cannot be assuaged by logic. So they imbued Soviet dogma with the best traditions of religious orthodoxy. Their banners blazed with the holy trinity of communism—Marx, Engels and Lenin. Marx and Engels had set out the rules and the tenets, but were largely ephemeral, vague entities—Marx the Father, Engels the Holy Spirit. But Lenin was the Son—he had come from the people and died in the height of his reign, having planted the seeds of the new religion.

His life was documented in numerous allegorical, deifying accounts—the gospels of communism. He was depicted as a saint, a perfect invincible being from birth to his death. His portraits hung on every official wall—from baby Lenin, to proselytizing Lenin, to Lenin with his apostles, to close-ups of Lenin peacefully, or lovingly, or sternly (depending on the institution) gazing onto his future followers. His statues obligatorily graced every city in his empire. And from early childhood his faithful followers sang hymns and swore their undying allegiance to Him. After Lenin came a long line of Soviet saints and martyrs—but Lenin with his eternal gaze towered over them all. The idol, at whose feet her childhood was spent.

Then one day a conversation took place in her perfectly ordered and familiar world. Her father was sitting at their kitchen table, his fingers tapping the checkered vinyl tablecloth. "Karina, I have to tell you something," he said.

She looked at him with expectation, but he continued tapping, avoiding her eyes. Pale pink square (once red) tap-tap; beige square (formerly white) tap-tap-tap; pink, tap. At last he stopped and lifting his head from his cup of tea he said: "Karinushka, we're leaving."

"Where to?" she inquired, "Moscow or Leningrad?" Where else could a person go but to the great Meccas of Communism?

"To Canada."

Canada. Her brain processed the information, feverishly pulling out relevant facts from her knowledge deposits. Canada: the second largest country in the world, after the USSR of course. Canada: they attempt to appropriate hockey as their national game. It's Russian of course. Canada: languages spoken—English (impossible to pronounce) and French (its only saving grace). Canada: they have Niagara Falls, one of the Seven Wonders of the modern world. Hard to imagine. The exclusion of Lenin's

Mausoleum from this list—a clear indication of a capitalist conspiracy or plain ignorance. Canada: deeply entrenched on the wrong side of the political divide. Canada. As it sank in, her father's calm announcement shook her to the core.

She knew what her reply had to be. She had read it in books about young Communist heroes. Her teachers had taught her, when in doubt, think of what Pavlik Morozov[1] would say.

"Traitor to the Communist Party! Enemy of the People!" The ideal and disciplined Soviet child that she was erupted with the most horrible epithets that she could fathom for her father's turncoat decision. Tears singed her eyes, threatening to unravel her perfect tirade. Surely Pavlik Morozov didn't cry.

"You're trading in your Motherland for a washing machine!" she added, stomping her foot. This was a reference to a letter written from Canada by Aunt Sonya—her dad's cousin. In it she had described—surely plagiarizing a paragraph out of a science fiction novel at the prodding of capitalist agents provocateurs—a machine that washed clothes without a woman having to constantly crank its handle, and then another machine that dried clothes in one hour! That couldn't be. There wasn't even a word for this second contraption in Russian. And as every school child knew, Russian scientists were in the forefront of scientific advancements. If they hadn't come up with a gadget like that, nobody else could have!

She was disgusted, furious. But instead of punishing her for her disrespect, her father waited with a bittersweet smile until venom gave way to wordless sobbing. He must have known that her rose-colored glasses would soon be knocked off her face.

~~~

Now. The time is now. They board the train. Karina's once beloved machine has turned into a missile that is about to eject her from her native soil.

As scenery changes rapidly beyond the windows, she tries to commit every wooden hut, every birch tree to memory. And all the while tears flow. She cries because never again will she see her best friend Nata;

---

1   Pavlik Morozov—young Communist martyr who denounced his own father to the secret police and was murdered by relatives in retaliation.

never again will the neighbourhood mutt Urka lick her hand as she feeds him a filched piece of bread. She cries because she is leaving a country that is in her blood, in every atom of her being.

They reach the border around midnight. It appears at first glance like any provincial train station—a wooden barrack with official insignia. Except this one is swarming with soldiers in greatcoats, brass buttons glittering like ensnared stars in the light of surrounding projectors. Except this one has sprawled gossamer wings of barbed wire, unfurling them far into the endless night.

The station house is composed of two rooms. All passengers get off the train and are told to gather their belongings in the first room—a barren, windowless space. Soldiers are circulating in pairs amid the huddling anxious groups of the soon-to-be expatriates. The door to the second room is shielded by two sullen guards.

"That's border patrol and customs. They will examine our property in there." A slim woman whispers and smiles, with what she probably hopes resembles certainty, at an old man who is sitting on top of his suitcase, an extinguished pipe grasped in his blue-veined hands. One of the passing soldiers hears her statement. "Yes," he laughs ominously "your last chance to change your mind in there. After that, well, don't say we didn't warn you." The other soldiers find this incredibly amusing and burst into laughter.

Meanwhile people are being herded through the customs door, a few at a time. Before long her family's turn comes. One of the guards examines their travel documents.

"Enter," he hisses through his teeth. Suddenly she remembers the opening lines of a poem entitled "The Verdict," from an Akhmatova book her parents hid in their nightstand. She un-hid that slim, typewritten, hand-bound volume as often as she could, memorizing the often perplexing lines. Now one of them comes into focus:

> And it fell, this word, this slab of stone,
> Onto my still heaving, living breast

The second room. A spotlight on a huge bust of Lenin. He seems sombre, frowning. Along the opposite wall is a counter, behind which stand five exhausted border patrolmen.

She feels somewhat relieved seeing a couple, who had been called in before them, locking up their suitcase and turning towards… another door! Several soldiers around it, guns poised, snarling dogs straining leashes. That must be the exit, she realizes. Beyond it stretches foreignness. She turns away from it. She will taste it all too soon, for all too long. Now she concentrates on everything that is dear and Soviet and about to be snatched from her.

Her mom tells her to watch her brother as the adults take the suitcases to one of the guards at the counter. What are these men in the Red Army uniforms thinking as they rummage through the luggage of traitors such as them? Their job is to make certain nobody smuggles any national treasures or classified materials out of the country. She peers into their emotionless faces, certain that the stony masks hide deep loathing for every owner of every bag.

Bang!!! Yes she is right. The hatred explodes.

A tiny old lady had shuffled in right after them. Her huge round glasses hide half her face and make her eyes look like blue saucers. A sad old woman. Very few people travel alone.

Now the guard who is checking her suitcase has discovered a shoebox filled with photographs. Bang! His fist descends on the counter again, and with a swift movement of his arm he sends the box flying to the filthy floor. A halo of memories, a spray of smiles spills out and lies under everyone's feet, mixing with the cigarette butts, shreds of newspapers and streaks of mud.

"You're not allowed to take any signed photos with you!" shouts the guard, spattering the infidel before him with saliva and disdain. "For all I know, you have something encoded in these words. Pick out only the ones without any writing on them!" Disciplined by her proletarian life into unquestioning obedience, the woman—someone's mother, someone's grandmother—gets down on all fours and complies with the command to the accompaniment of jeering from the sentinels of this, her last, Soviet citadel.

A child's whimper is cut off by somebody's hand clasped over its mouth. All eyes are averted. Nobody dares to help.

Karina's brother clings to her, fingers turning white with strain, eyes glossing over with liquid panic. "Don't cry," she whispers and caresses the boy's hair. "Don't cry. I will give you a chocolate bar when we're done." Minutes stretch out; condense; jumble into an incomprehensibility. She is only aware of her wildly beating heart. Its loud staccato surely about to leak into the auditory arena of observant Soviet warriors.

But their family's inspection goes by without incident. The final suitcase lid falls closed. Documents are stamped and pass from hand to hand. They are steered out of the second door and step into Poland.

In retrospect, shedding one's country turns out to be quite prosaic. Enter a building. Exit a building. Don't look back. Don't.

~~~

Officially they have become refugees. With other outcasts they board a commuter train. Her father pays for their passage with two bottles of Russian vodka, which, as they discover, is more coveted by Polish train conductors than currency. Not that they have a zloty to spare. Only two hundred US dollars per family is allowed out of the Soviet Union.

They arrive at an international station at three o'clock in the morning. Their band of vagabonds drips into a vast square room, dark and abandoned. The men in their group gather their vodka supply and go to make arrangements for further passage. The women and children spread out on the benches and most soon surrender to a heavy slumber.

Her mother and grandmother lean their heads against each other. Their breathing slow, synchronized. Her brother curls up, head in their mother's lap.

But Karina cannot sleep. She notices a patch of light in the hushed darkness. To occupy herself, she slides off the bench. Looking over her shoulder and making sure that the adults do not notice her disappearance, she approaches the blue-tinged illumination.

It is a small shop, closed for the night, but inside a fluorescent light glows. Grabbing the metal bars on the window, she pulls her face as close to the glass as possible, peers inside and … She sinks into a stupefying numbness. She has never seen so much food in one place!

Superimposed on the background of succulent Polish sausages, hams, breads, and Technicolor mountains of fruits and vegetables, images of her life flash in front of her eyes. She can hear the slogans blaring in her head.

"The Soviet Union is the greatest country in the world!"

"Soviet children are the happiest and most cared for children in history!"

"You kids should thank Uncle Lenin for your limitless possibilities in this land of the free workers and peasants."

And at the same time she sees herself in the middle of winter, one tiny link in a long queue of bodies encircling their local market. She is seven years old and has to help her mother with the household chores. So there she is, standing in the snow for three hours to get milk. She has almost outgrown her coat, which was bought only the year before. It and the two scarves wrapped around her head are poor protection against the ravenous jaws of Russian wind. Yet she waits. And when there are only four people left in front of her, the milk runs out and they are told that there will be no more until next week. A regular instalment of a Soviet existence. But in front of the Polish prosperity her thoughts begin curdling into a scream. All she can identify at the moment is the word "Why?"

Later she will disentangle the emotional knot of this single question: Why had she been fed the empty calories of dogma? And why had she found those words satisfactory?

How many moments does it take, this crumbling of a religion? How long does it take to convince a child that her god fell off the cross, wiped away his greasepaint, packed up his travelling troupe and took his carnival act to the next town? Is it for better or for worse that as she kneels and grabs at his still moist footprints, she discovers that the blood had been all too real?

The mirage of a Bolshevik Utopia begins evaporating in the sombre light of insight: everything she had believed in, every communist dictum had been a grotesque lie! Her whole world had been a lie! Her life had been a lie! Only one thought plays over and over in her mind—she, herself, had been a lie. Revulsion tugs at her heart. Her unhinged unbridged soul gapes for a new identity.

the legacy of ghosts

Her memory of the train ride that crossed Poland, Czechoslovakia and deposited them on the banks of the West is all but erased. Only two brief scenes remain. One is arriving in Austria.

~~~

Night. The train slows down on its approach to the station. Streetlamps appear. They emit an eerie orange glow. She has never seen orange streetlamps and their light looks ominous against the starless blind sky. "The orange light cuts through fog," says her father. "It increases visibility." Then the train stops. Sounds begin. Guttural screams in German that make her skin crawl. Confused, sleepy refugees shuffle out of the train. On the platform soldiers in strange uniforms are holding growling guard dogs. And this detached voice screams out in a language she has always associated with fear and death. She shivers, waiting to hear "Achtung! Hände hoch! Schnell!"

~~~

The second memory is meeting the ghost. It happened on the train one night before they arrived in Austria but she's not sure which Eastern European frontier they were crossing at the time.

~~~

She cannot sleep. Everyone is resting in the compartment and if she turns on the light she will wake them up. She climbs down from the upper bunk she's sharing with her brother and slides the door open just enough to sneak out.

"Where are you going?" her mother's voice is weighed down by sleep.

"To the restroom."

"Do you want me to come with you?"

"No, I'll be fine."

The hallway of the train car is awash in a hard fluorescent glow. She shuts her eyes momentarily against the onslaught of brightness and when she opens them she jumps. There is a girl standing just in front of her. In the next moment she realizes that it's her own reflection in the black square of the window. She presses her face to the glass, trying to see in the darkness. It's futile, however she is fascinated that her face reflected in this foreign glass of this foreign train in this foreign blackness is still her own.

She is so absorbed in studying what makes her *her,* that she only becomes aware of another presence when she hears a sigh. Several paces away on one of the fold-down metal seats that are positioned between the windows there is a hunched shape wrapped in a grey shawl. Karina recognizes her. It's that old woman with the forbidden photographs.

"I cannot sleep either," says the woman, but when Karina wants to formulate that more than sleep is evading her, that she cannot grasp who she is anymore, she suddenly bursts into tears.

"I wanted to be a writer," she squeezes out between sobbing, "and now…"

"And now what?"

"Everything will be foreign… the language…"

"Is that all?" the woman smiles. "Language can be learned, especially by one as young as you. But if you're meant to write, you will. What's your name?" the woman inquires.

"Karina. Karina Razumovskaya," she approaches the woman and crouches down next her. The floor is too dirty to sit on. The other seats are too far away. Karina wants to know whether her own fear at the border station had been shared by this adult who took on the contempt of the soldiers with quiet resolution, but she doesn't want to evoke the painful, embarrassing incident, so she asks instead, "And how can I know if I'm meant to write?"

"Let me tell you a tale Karina," says the woman, ignoring the question, staring past the girl, down the length of the train car. "Once, many years ago two men met at a train station. It was November 7 by the old calendar, in the year of our Lord 1910. The day was drab. Wind snuck under clothing and licked vulnerable flesh with icy wetness. The sky was overcast, a blanket of high white clouds stretching as far as the eyes could see. The air smelled of frost but the ground was barren—all blackness, greyness and rot.

"One of the men was a peasant. Elderly, he shivered in his threadbare coat, a cloth sack slung over his shoulder. The other was young, tall, elegantly dressed. His hands were laden with gifts for his young wife who was soon to be delivered of their first child. He wouldn't have noticed the peasant had it not been for a gust of wind carrying his quiet words clear across the platform. The old man was talking to a woman of indeterminable age and pedigree. Leaning on her, as if testing her solidity he said these words overheard by the young man: 'One must not accept without criticism the thoughts of famous authors, just as one must not ignore the thoughts of obscure, not-famous people.'

"This idea was so unbefitting a peasant that the young man moved closer. The conversation between the old man and the woman was indeed about literature. Furthermore, this ancient country bumpkin was belittling the publishing world, putting down all great contemporary writers, most of the dead ones and praising some obscure figures of antiquity.

"Finally, unable to contain himself, the young man asked, 'So what would you recommend, old man, to someone who is serious about a literary career? Forget about it? Quit writing altogether?'

"For the first time their eyes met and the young man was amazed at the depth of intelligence he saw in this weathered face. 'Of course! That is my usual advice to all beginning writers. We do not live in the right time for writing. Abandon literature, if you want to heed the advice of an old man. It's too late for me! I'm going to die soon… but as for you, there is no reason to idle away your time.'

"'And if I don't? If I can't because that is what God put me on this planet to do, what do you propose then?'

"'Give me a piece of paper,' said the old man. 'If you must write I will give you the only advice a writer needs.'

"The young man pulled a pencil and a small notebook from his coat pocket. It was leather bound, purchased in Moscow several months before. He had been carrying it around since, dreaming of all the tales and lives that he was going to plant in there, but he was yet to trespass the stern whiteness of the page.

"The peasant ran his calloused hand over the edges of the notebook, flipped through its untouched heart, opened it to the first page, and wrote something down. 'If you insist on writing, this is the one indispensable attribute for a writer in order to survive.'

"Suddenly the spark that had lit up his eyes went out.

"The young man looked in dismay at the one word scrawled across the page: VERA. He and his wife had decided to call their child Vera, if it would be a girl. How did this man know? Then he realized that the peasant had intended the literal meaning of the word—Faith.

"At that moment he heard the woman shriek: 'Lev Nikolaevich, get up! Lev Nikolaevich! Help, somebody help me!' The old man had collapsed onto the platform...'"

The train lurches, and Karina is yanked out of the story. She tries grabbing onto the woman to avoid falling down but somehow misses her and hits her shoulder on the compartment door. The vision of the chilly sky and the grey train platform dissipates.

"She called the peasant Lev Nikolaevich?" Karina asks, regaining her balance. "Wasn't that Tolstoy's name?"

The woman nods. Her blue eyes behind thick spectacles seem huge and vacant. "It was Tolstoy. And the young man was my father. Let me show you something." She disappears into her compartment and comes out with a small leather notebook. The cover is cracked from age and a few specks of gilt allude to a long-gone inscription.

Karina's night-time friend opens the notebook to the first page. Yellowed paper, frail and brittle like an old person's skin. Faded handwriting, unsteady hand. One word in capital letters—VERA.

Karina finally forgets her misery. She stretches her fingers over the page. For a few blissful moments she contemplates her proximity to another hand, years away, that had written this. The hand of a Writer.

"Keep this notebook," she hears the woman say. "I've no use for it now. My father never wrote in it. Neither did I. A true writer should carry on the tradition started by Lev Nikolaevich."

Karina glances through the pages. Indeed not a single word. Except the first one. Vera. Faith.

When she looks up, the woman is gone. She retreats to her compartment too, hugging her gift, finally sleepy.

In the morning she wakes up because of a strange stillness. The train is not moving. There is commotion in the hallway. She hears whispers "How long has she been dead? They say two days. Must have been a heart attack after that ordeal at the border station. Poor old woman. Can you believe nobody noticed?"

Karina slides her hand under the pillow. The notebook is still there. She goes back to sleep.

stage notes

THE TABLE IS *gone. The empty frames, as in the previous scenes, remain. There is an allusion to railways: mangled train tracks resemble the anti-tank "hedgehogs"—a monument to the defenders of Moscow that stands some twenty kilometres outside the Russian capital, marking the spot where in World War II German troops were halted. KARINA emerges from this tangled metal. In her hands is a small, weathered notebook.*

KARINA: I filled that little notebook frenetically, words catching up with words without rhyme or reason, slogans mixing with lines of poetry. Phrases that led nowhere. It was my life raft through the emigration to Canada. Having it made me feel as if I belonged. My nation was small, leather-bound, but it existed.

(TOLSTOY, following KARINA's trajectory through the tracks slowly approaches her as she speaks. He stands directly behind her, towering over her.)

Afterwards there were so many other notebooks. I preferred the plain cheap ones. They were unpretentious instruments. In them, my blue, black and sometimes purple patches of staked-out real-estate, I wrote poems, short stories, essays, and plays, plays, plays. Finally years later I even have completed the one task all writers aspire to—a novel. So where is my sense of accomplishment, of controlling my destiny? Where is my happy ending?

(KARINA places her notebook onto a protruding part of the metal jumble.)

TOLSTOY: Novels end with the hero and heroine getting married. That's where they should begin. They should end with them getting un-married. Otherwise, describing people's lives in a way that ends the narrative in marriage, is the same as describing a person's travelling adventures and stopping the tale in the very spot where he is taken hostage by highway robbers.

KARINA: Highway robbers. Funny, that's the precise image I get when I tell people where I was born and spent my childhood. They inevitably affect a look of boundless pity, as if I had been taken hostage by highway robbers for the first eleven years of my life. Over and over I am beset by the same question, "Wow, growing up in the Soviet Union! You must have hated it?"

"No. No I quite loved it."

This always warrants an explanation.

I was a child. I played. I had friends. I excelled in school. I had a roof over my head, my mother's cooking on the table, clothes that looked no worse than my friends', and often better because my grandmother sewed.

True, very few people in the Soviet Union of my generation reached adulthood while still singing paeans to the State. The disillusionment, however, came gradually. The veils fell away with every passing year, accelerating during the teenage years, until, usually by the age of sixteen or seventeen, the mis-shapen monster of the society dropped all guises and stood completely naked.

I left long before that. Probably at the height of my infatuation with my homeland.

So why did I love thee, the land of my youth? Let me count the whys:

Theatre. An indispensable part of our lives. We went to the theatre more often than the movies. Revisiting our favourite shows over and over, our minds were allowed to rhyme with the familiar lines and roam through the nuances of each night's variations. Puppet theatres, children's theatres, youth theatres, adult theatres, ballet, opera—again and again and again we waited with baited breaths for the curtain to rise, for the magic to begin, for the actors to believe so ardently in the reality of their stage lives that we were swept along in the force of their beliefs. We were even invited to participate in some productions—"No, prince, no!" we screamed in delicious horror. "The witch is in the forest, don't go there!"

Algebra. In the first grade. Reading Turgenev and Lermontov in the second. Schools were geared towards the best students. Everyone else had to aim high and catch up with the best. No pandering to the lowest common denominator. No pacification of the average. Children's brains were presumed to be malleable and expandable. Demands were put on us, results were achieved. Every school day was an intellectual challenge. And an adventure. It was pure delight for me. Admittedly, not for everyone.

Holidays. May Day. The world streaming with red banners. Multi-coloured ribbons woven into girls' hair, culminating in huge blooming bows. The weather already warm. The citrusy sweet scent of linden flowers. The air filled with balloons and songs. The New Year. A tree carried into the house by dad and uncle Kolya, still dripping melted snow. Frost and pine aromas spicing up the moods. The box of decorations being pulled from the cellar. Lifting layers of cotton from clip-on skiing bunnies, fragile silver icicles, transparent purple-yellow-orange balls. Dad winding a garland of lights around the tree. The star topping it off. The lamp being turned off in the room. Snow outside lit by the moon. Tree lights glittering, reflecting in the tinsel. Trying to fall asleep, because the sooner I did, the sooner the gifts appeared.

Books. Everyone had a personal library. Books were a status symbol and a currency. Books were discussed, yearned for, collected. Books were so necessary that even forbidden works were circulated in a *samizdat* format—people retyped, copied by hand and distributed great novels, poetry, essays under the threat of imprisonment. Books were the bloodline of the culture.

Pride. Pride in the history of a land that had withstood the invasions of Napoleon and Hitler and driven both out. Pride that in World War II, the Great Patriotic War as it is known in Russia, we spared no woman, no child, no old person. We fought ferociously for every desecrated patch of the Motherland. Armed with sticks and knives and bare teeth against a technological Superman, we won. Every classroom in every school had a wall of portraits of young heroes: the seventeen-year-old hung by the Nazis because, though raped and tortured, she didn't reveal where her partisan troop hid out; the ten-year-old who crawled through a mine field to deliver a message to the headquarters and didn't make it back... the fourteen year old... the nine year old... There was not a family in the eleven time zones of the Soviet Union that was not scarred by the War, that did not hear its echoes daily.

(Blackout. Distant echoes of explosions. Mixed in them is the sound of Shostakovich's 7th "Leningrad" Symphony. It grows louder, more defiant, after every explosion. The music is a bridge into the next scene.)

stage notes

RED LIGHTS COME *up on the metal knot of train tracks. KARINA is alone on the stage.*

KARINA: We each took one memento out of Russia. Mine was a book of Pushkin's fairy tales that some day I planned to read to my children. I never imagined that soon I would will myself to forget my native land. My brother's keepsake was Lusik, a toy panda bear. He was named after our favourite cat. The bear had the same colouring as the unfortunate feline, whom I, aged seven, found one day outside our gate, his skull flattened by the wheels of some car. My grandmother ran out of the house when she heard my screaming. Without a word she disengaged my hands clutching the black-and-white body, pulled me out of the pool of my vomit and Lusik's blood, and carried me to the water pump. My brother was too young to be introduced to death. That was the only thing she said as she washed my face in cold water. When Timur woke up from his nap we told him that Lusik the Cat went to live in the village with our relatives. A few days later the panda bear appeared. From then on my brother believed that if he hugged Lusik the Bear, then someone in the village would hug and love Lusik the Cat. *(pause)* My grandmother's memento was a photograph that had been the only decoration in her room. A glossy patch tacked to a wall. For years I asked her what it was a picture of. For years her reply consisted of only one word… "Frames."

frames

A BLACK AND white photograph—an image of a great hall. Sunlight streaming in through the tall arched windows illuminates the ceiling then bounces onto the walls, which are tiled with picture frames and... It takes a moment, perhaps two, to notice that the paintings are missing from the frames. As if some eccentric billionaire decided to exhibit rectangles of ornate mouldings in his mansion.

"Where is this, grandma?"

"Leningrad. The Hermitage. 1944."

"Why are the picture frames empty?" Karina's "whys" rarely land into palatable explanations.

"Why, why, why... Why should I always tell you stories, little bird? You tell me why you think they are empty."

"I don't know."

"Perhaps the answer will come to you, if you stare long enough into the image. Examine it carefully. Use your imagination."

Ah, imagination! It can meander through so many vistas, and sometimes even cross paths with truth.

She studies the photograph. Allows her imagination to enter that faraway hall, to fly wide and saturate deep into a reality embedded in a glossy patch of paper. She considers the abandoned walls. They are much darker within the frames. Outside them the paint is faded by the constant caressing of daylight. High above the walls is the intricate plasterwork of the vaulted ceiling—a remnant of last century's fairy tale. How lonely the ceiling is. Its friends are gone. Those dreamlike, kaleidoscopic canvases are all gone. But why? Did they get stolen? Were they removed because they contained anti-Soviet propaganda? Grandma said "1944."

"The War! Were they hidden from the Nazis?"

The grandmother nods. Barely perceptible signs of satisfaction in her unsmiling face. Now Karina knows that if she sits quietly, her grandmother will catch memories in the swirling silence. She knows that those memories will pour out. All she has to do is be attentive and prod them on in a half-whisper.

~~~

Why did the paintings leave? It began when the Guardians of Art heard the whistling of the first falling bombs. Then mothers, clutching the torn bodies of their children, shrieked in the listless sunlight beyond the walls. Sirens wailed in the souls of the Guardians. The loss of their precious wards would be a loss for all humanity. They had to move fast to preserve them. Tick-tock, tick-tock—the urging of antique clocks accompanied their efforts. Tick-tock, tick-tock—they did not know when the next angel of death would fly over the city. Tick-tock, tick-tock—six days later, over two million masterpieces were removed from their frames and packed away in crates, to be carried to a haven deep in the impenetrable heart of Russia. How long would these treasures be in exile? The Guardians did not know, but they committed to memory every detail of every painting and their precise positions on each wall. They left the frames in place as a symbol of their hope that someday the paintings would return. Finally, exhausted, they descended into a dungeon deep beneath the museum to await the end of the dark horror.

Tick-tock... They waited... Tick-tock... The food supply in the blockaded city was bombed in the first days of the siege. Again and again rations were reduced until hundreds of thousands of civilians faced starvation. But the vault of the Hermitage had huge vats of carpenter's glue for making frames. The Guardians concocted a jelly out of the glue. Those who forced their stomachs to believe that this jelly was food lived. And waited. Tick-tock...

For nine hundred days they waited. Half of them lived to breathe the air of liberation. When they emerged, the first thing they saw were the empty frames on their beloved walls. One of them took a snapshot.

As they stepped outside, they saw more empty frames, more dark, gaping reminders of savagery masquerading as human progress. The constant shelling, and shaking, and shuddering shattered the glass panes in the architectural monuments of the once exquisite city. Now they stared at the desolation below through the blind sockets of empty window frames.

Corpses—the frames of those who once had been people—were the macabre decorations of the streets. They fell from stray shell shards, they fell from pain, they fell from disease, famine and exhaustion. They fell dead, and nobody had the strength to pick them up and haul them away. So they lay there. Mouths gaping. Frozen, empty frames of unfulfilled laughter.

And those who still shuffled through the streets differed little from the ones no longer moving. Tock-tick, Tock-tick. The clocks moved backwards. The empty frames demanded to be possessed by their ghosts.

"Ghosts, grandma?"

"Imagine a woman. Trudging through the snow banks pulling a sleigh. Her gloves are ripped to shreds. Her fingers, red from the unyielding Baltic winds, seem to be frozen onto the rope. But she moves on and on, pulling her sleigh and a rusted bucket filled with water from the river. A man's coat seems too heavy for her frail frame. A thick belt with a brass buckle cinches her waist. How old would you say she is? Her back is hunched. The wind has blown the scarf from her head but she doesn't notice. Her hair is all white. She must be at least sixty. But look closer. Her face is unfurrowed by wrinkles. It is bloodless, passionless, smooth as a marble statue's. She cannot be more than twenty-five years old."

"Is her hair covered with snow?"

"Some of it. But in the strands framing her face, frozen flakes mingle with the ice of tragedy. And no amount of heat will melt away this whiteness. No amount of heat will bring back her sons." Again she settles into the quiet tempo of the tale.

The woman's sons withered away slowly. The older one, Alyosha, first asked for food, then cried softly under his blanket, hoping she would not hear. The younger, Pasha, did not emit a sound. Hunger stifled his cries. Only his eyes begged and accused her.

She implored the boys to hold on. In a daze she stumbled through the familiar avenues and alleys of the city. Searching for a way out of the nightmare. Searching for anything edible. There were no rats, mice, cats, dogs, birds left. Searching…

While all around her there were symphonies in that bitter December of 1942. There was no public transportation, no fuel, no heat, no electricity. Nourishment consisted of a rationed 125 grams of black bread—two mouthfuls of flour and sawdust—and whatever human ingenuity could disguise as food: tooth paste, soups from leather belts and tree bark, tea from pine cones and dirt. Yet there were symphonies.

The symphonies of hissing howling showering bombs. Usually, as she had no strength to run to the nearest shelter, she hugged a building and listened to the thumping applause of earth chunks and bricks around her.

The symphonies of trust. Nobody locked their apartments anymore. Infants, often the last to die, had to be located amid the corpses of siblings and parents and brought into orphanages for a chance at survival. Day and night social workers scoured the city, arranging the harmonies of apprehensive knocking, creaking doors, dead bodies dragged along ice-encrusted parquet floors and piled on balconies, faint heartbeats inside tiny rib cages.

The symphonies of small gratitudes. Thank goodness for the food convoy that did not fall through the ice of Lake Ladoga. One more week of bread. Thank Mother Russia for snow. Now tea would not taste of decomposing flesh, the flavour that had irrevocably seeped into the city's water supply.

Yet despite Death's non-stop concert, there was actual music in Leningrad every day and every night. In the deep basements by bonfires, in the arches and the churches, in the emptied stores and in the snow-filled parks. For over a fortnight as she haunted the decimated streets, she had stopped in front of the Russian Museum to listen to a string quartet. There were always other listeners. Two of them—the corpses of a woman and a girl, frozen in an embrace on a bench. Notes of Tchaikovsky wove through the crystalline December air, which carried these melodic filaments and plaited them into the strands of Prokofiev, Glinka, Mussorgsky wafting up from the defiant city on the banks of the Neva. The symphony of man's determination to survive.

Survival. She had to find a way. By the locked doorway of St. Isaac's Cathedral, she dropped to her knees, turned her eyes to heaven and begged a long-forgotten God for an answer. A wisp of a prayer flitted through her memory and condensed on her lips. "Our Father who art in heaven, hallowed be Thy name..." She did not know the rest.

Her grandparents had been too afraid to insist on religion. Mutely she traced the bas-reliefs on the bronze doors. Imposing, bearded men she did not recognize. Who were they? Saints? Apostles? Only one figure was familiar. There in the top image, riding a donkey entering a crowd of worshipping people. Down below, surrounded by guards. Whipped and tortured. Jesus. The son of God. The prayers of the old women were always addressed to him. He might provide the answer. All she had to do was remember. Remember those summers spent in the village when hushed stories of old Russia were gulped down along with warm freshly squeezed milk. What was it that the old women said? "Thou hast forsaken me, he told his Father..." But that was not it. Not forsaken. There was a purpose.

The answer came to her. God sacrificed his son. To save humanity. She knew what she must do. Finally there was a calmness in her steps.

For seven days she fed her youngest son Pasha her ration of bread. For seven days she replayed in detail the lessons of her childhood spent in the village. Look here, the calf must not suffer. The knife must be sharp. Use one rapid, decisive stroke.

On day eight the New Year came. 1943. Alyosha woke up to the dizzying aroma of cooking meat: "Mama! We have food?" he ran into the kitchen. "Where is Pasha?"

"He's gone to the village to live with Aunt Lena. Here, eat, my tiny bird, eat."

She did not taste a morsel. It was all for Alyosha. He had to exist. Surely this horror could not continue much longer.

It continued for three hundred and ninety-two more days. Too long for her older son to withstand. She held him close to her breast, and kissed him and pleaded with him, but her sacrifice had not been enough. She watched him fade until he was no more. Then her spirit seeped out in a cascade of teardrops and a barren darkness descended into the empty frames that used to be her eyes.

Her grandmother's voice is even, as if reciting not revisiting those distant frozen months.

"Who was she, grandma? A friend?"

"No," the grandmother stands up. Runs her hand through a loosened strand of hair. Hair that she dyes with henna monthly because it has been all white since the War.

stage notes

A LARGE PROJECTOR *screen dominates the stage. On it is a still image—a close-up of a shrapnel gouge in a building wall. Above it a sign in Russian and English: "Damage from one of 250 thousand German shells and bombs dropped on Leningrad during the Blockade." KARINA and TOLSTOY are sitting on a bench, stage left. As KARINA speaks the picture slowly zooms out, until we see that the damaged structure is a column of St. Isaac's Cathedral.*

KARINA: "Fictions and realities live in different compartments of the mind," my grandmother said once. "The easiest way to deal with tragedy is to store it with your fictions."

"So in that case, can you take a beautiful fiction, store it with your realities and become happy?" I asked.

She shook her head. "If you believe that a fiction is your reality," she said, "you are either insane or you're a writer. In neither case are you happy."

I didn't agree with my grandmother. I rarely agreed with her. Her world was too black-and-white and I was determined to inhabit a world of colour.

I think that the only time she allowed herself to be happy was when she worked. She worked hard, long hours, driving her body to exhaustion, past the point where thought or memory was possible. My grandmother became a nurse after the war. Dealing with other people's pain was her way of not facing her own.

She also had someone who needed her again. She had adopted a girl. It was just after the siege ended in the viciously cold winter of 1944. She was walking from the Palace Embankment, pulling a sleigh with a bucket of water, every few steps reminding herself that she didn't have to huddle close to the walls, that there would be no more shelling. She walked aimlessly, knowing that her feet would eventually bring her to her building. She turned a corner. She would never remember which. There was a girl sobbing over a corpse on a frozen street. "Mama, wake up," wailed the child in a quiet, exhausted voice. My grandmother stopped. Pulled a crust of bread from her pocket and extended it to the crying child. The girl looked up with eyes grey and huge, filling up half the emaciated face. Eyes grey like those of the ghosts who haunted her.

"What is your name, little one?"

"Nastia." Such a vulnerable voice. A slight lisp.

"Come," said my grandmother embracing her. "Let your mama rest now."

The girl didn't question it. She bit into the crust and soon fell asleep, cradled in my grandmother's arms. She placed the sleeping child on the sleigh, spilling the water into the snow. The full bucket would have been impossible for her emaciated arms to carry. Nastia. Anastasia. My mother.

(*A rapid slide show of images from the siege of Leningrad— boarded up palaces; dark crosses of airplanes in a white sky over the Kazan Cathedral; a spindly-legged child dragging the corpse of an infant on a sleigh; women hacking ice on the Neva River; people sprawled on the snow of Nevsky Prospect as plumes of smoke from explosions obscure the Admiralty's needle; a starving man, taught skin over bones, holding his ration of bread in one hand, as his eyes beg from under his ushanka; the snow-dusted body of a woman wearing valenki—only these worn felt boots are seen, because someone has covered the body with a jacket—but passersby have no strength to move it. The slide show stops on an image of a little girl. A tendril of blond hair has escaped the scarf covering her head, falling over her eyes. Her eyes are huge, made more so by the gauntness of her face and the rim of dark circles.)*

KARINA: Can you begin to empathize with these characters? Can you even envision the foreignness of their existence?

TOLSTOY: In describing characters or settings which are unusual for the majority of readers, never let slip your mind characters or settings which are familiar. Take these common ones for your basis, and then, comparing them with the unusual, describe the latter.

KARINA: So you are willing to listen on? You don't mind my sharing stark intimacies with you?

TOLSTOY: I understand you, and have experienced it myself, fearing the work of writing lest it be egotistical and idle but I know that in it, when it is earnest, is my greatest bliss, and therefore it is my calling.

KARINA: Let's change the topic. We are growing serious, and then we are in great danger of being dull. Let's talk about you. But since we began with a photograph…

(The stage is flooded by lights for an instant. When they are turned down there is a different slide show on the rear screen— images of Tolstoy.)

A little over five thousand photographs of you are extant. You are smiling on only ten of them.

The rest show a man with a frown, an angry impatience in his eyes. An assessment of your personality based on these photos would be unjust. You were not stern at all. Serious, yes. Pensive. Intelligent. But also mischievous, energetic, witty, sentimental and passionate. You simply hated having your photograph taken.

So where were the photographers when you were just a friend, a father, a husband? Like that day of your oldest son's engagement party at your Moscow estate. About thirty people gathered in the grand salon, including Sergei's future in-laws, who were meeting you for the first time. They were shy and tongue-tied around the renowned Count Tolstoy. The evening's rhythms were faltering, the tone of the gathering was uncomfortable, the conversation kept stumbling, the cook had burned the stew and the meal was late. Your wife, Sofia Andreyevna, left the room to supervise the mayhem in the kitchen. Without her gracious social manner the atmosphere around the table quickly disintegrated.

"Let's play a joke on Sofia Andreyevna," you suddenly suggested with a roguish grin that immediately melted the ice of discomfort. You had all the guests—the future in-laws, your friends, the younger children, the English governess—hide under the table. Its ample ivory tablecloth descended to the floor, easily concealing everyone. All waited, suppressing giggles, for the rustling of Sofia Andreyevna's silk skirts. When, a few minutes later, your wife came into the room, she discovered the table settings undisturbed, everyone gone, total silence. "Dunechka!" she screamed out in amazement to the maid, "what happened to Lev Nikolaevich and the guests?" That's when you gave the command and everyone jumped out giving her a "royal fright." She immediately forgave you, of course, because everyone was laughing, the party relaxed and enjoyable at last.

"You always invent some foolishness, Levochka," she squinted up at you, succumbing to the mirth in the room. She always forgave you all your pranks and whims.

This side of your personality has not been recorded in photographs. Instead, day after day, your world increasingly becoming as "private as a goldfish bowl," strangers, acquaintances, reporters and disciples dropped by your house and asked you to pose, so that they would have a memento of the minutes spent with the great man. You absolutely detested the exercise of arresting the progress of your life and standing still for a photo. But because you went out of your way never to hurt another person's feelings you complied. You posed. And frowned.

I don't like photographs either. I never display them. Empty frames are much more evocative markers of life's passage. I collect frames.

However, there is one photo on the title page of my copy of Anna Karenina that has drawn me time and again. On it you must be no older than thirty. A debonair young officer, clean shaven, a solemn ember in your eyes. You sense the weight of your destiny and you are determined to take it on. You're still strong. Do you remember what you confessed to your journal at that time?

TOLSTOY: *(Laughing, affecting a pompous voice)* My goal is literary fame and the good that my works may bring.

KARINA: *(Nodding.)* But in your last novel, "Resurrection," there is a different face. No longer noble. A peasant with a long beard. The glow is gone, replaced by weariness and weight.

TOLSTOY: The faces of writers are never their own…

KARINA: The faces of writers are never their own. They are mutable, muted. Mutilated by countless others invading their skin and bones, spilling from them, talking for them.

first

A TORN-OUT MEMORY. The fourth year of her life. The hovel on Pioneer Street. Pure white light pouring into the room from a square window over the only table. The walls, thick with plaster and lime wash. The windowpane hovering like a frozen whisper trapped in a rough-hewn wooden collar.

The table up against the wall. Only three chairs around it. There are other chairs in the room but her memory's eyes don't see them. Her memory's eyes are selective. They register the room as black and white. White walls, white light, white window, black outlines of furniture. A bed pushed up to the other wall.

Her grandmother's bed. She, Karina, is sitting on it. Absorbed by the light falling through the window. The light introduces colour, as if colour could only live within its blessing. It washes over the tall woman in a blue housecoat and a man's slippers—her grandmother.

Her grandmother is seated at the table, hair pulled up into a soft amber bun, face dipping into the light.

The only object in front of her is a white piece of paper. Made more white, more blinding, more alluring by the light that seems to have entered the room only to illuminate it.

Her grandmother is moving a pen over the paper. A magical rite, for this movement produces that which Karina most loves—words, tales, worlds.

"Grandma, read what you wrote."

"Dear Lenochka, it has been almost three months since…"

Suddenly an idea! A brilliant idea. A breath-scorching idea.

"Grandma, may I too have a piece of paper and a pen?"

She sits at the table across from her grandmother. Observes the action. Hand up, hand down. Studies the tip of the pen. Up, down, forward, backward, swirl around, hop up, land again. Carefully, movements unpractised, awkward, she follows her grandmother's example. Her page too is beginning to be filled with almost neat rows of a blue-coloured heartbeat.

"Grandma, read what I wrote."

The thrill of revelation!

"Nothing, dear."

The collapse, deflation. It cannot be!

Through tears she begs now: "Grandma, try! Try, please. I did it just like you."

It has to make sense! She has tried so hard in her first effort to master this magic.

"Little bird, I cannot read this. It is just scribbles."

It's too early for tears, little bird, she will think years later, remembering this scene. It is only the first time you have written nothingness.

stage notes

KARINA AND TOLSTOY *are still on the bench. The rest of the stage is dark. Sound of thunder, then soft rapping of rain on glass.*

KARINA: I designed a logo for my letterhead. A fountain pen tip. A heavy drop about to slip off it, another breath and they will be separated. The uninitiated will think it is a drop of ink. We know better, don't we? It is blood.

TOLSTOY: This work of ours is quite distressing, gruesome. Nobody knows it but us.

KARINA: *(gets up and begins walking away)* I've reread the manuscript. I see flaws now. Fatal gaps. I'm afraid I've committed a beautiful mistake.

TOLSTOY: An artist is in a terrible predicament when he does not believe in the importance of expressing his thoughts.

(Blackout.)

muza

Wᴇɴ ᴅɪᴅ Kᴀʀɪɴᴀ decide that she would become a writer? One night comes to mind. A night so distant, so infinitesimally hidden beyond other nights and dreams that she has to recreate it layer by layer, nesting the memories inside one another like a matryoshka doll.

It starts with a single image—the sour cherry tree in their front yard is dropping its blossoms. A carpet of faint pink petals around its trunk, but in the night-light it looks like a lace throw.

Early May. Karina is sitting on the front porch steps. It is unusually warm, the breath of early summer soft against her skin. A large black-and-white tomcat is sprawled half in her lap, half on the wooden planks of the porch. The sky seems very close with its millions of billions of stars. Perhaps, if she squints just so, she can reach out and touch that inky blue silk; grasp a star in her hand. She sighs. No, that dream belonged to a much younger Karina. Now she knows the impossible distance of these sparkling mysterious suns. Some of them she can already identify. There is Polaris, the North Star. And the constellations of Ursa Major and Ursa Minor. Ursus—a bear. Ursa—a she-bear. Latin. She wonders if there was ever a Papa Bear constellation.

Inside their house, the adults enjoying one of their adult parties. Between bursts of laughter she sometimes hears the whooping call of the owl, the barking of the neighbourhood dogs, the shrieks of the tomcats fighting for territory and the female cats' high-pitched yowls egging them on. The cat in Karina's lap doesn't stir. He is content with the girl's hand stroking his neck and head. Besides, he knows that if he stays put, he might get more delicious scraps from the party table. He's already tasted the smoked sturgeon and the roasted chicken stuffed with apples.

Karina wants to go to bed. Not to sleep, no. In bed she can again open her new favourite bedtime book—The Little Prince. But bedtime is still far off. The room where she and Timur sleep is the larger of the two rooms in their house and therefore the centre of the party. The fold-out armchairs that are their beds are folded up to their daytime positions and are now occupied by eating and drinking guests. The last time Karina was in the house Aunt Vera was sitting in one chair. Her husband Maksim was sitting in the other one, with Lera in his lap.

Lera is the only woman who doesn't have a husband. For some reason the men think it is very funny to put her in their laps. Lera is her mother's best friend. Yet they're so different—Karina's mother is a tall blonde woman with wide hips, strong muscular legs and arms, and an ample bosom that she accentuates with tight bright-coloured sweaters. Lera is small and dark, waiflike. She doesn't have a sense of style, says Karina's mother, while shaking her head disapprovingly at Lera's starched white blouse with a spinster's lace collar and a plain grey skirt. Her only skirt. She begs Lera to show up at least to one party without her glasses; she argues with her to invest in some make-up. But Lera laughs this off, "Some Lancome-shmancom lipstick that would cost me two-months' wages is a ridiculous waste, and if I take off my glasses I'm liable to end up with a frog not a prince," and squints her myopic eyes, and kisses Karina's mother on the cheek. Karina doesn't think Lera needs any improvements. Her beauty is translucent, magical. Well, maybe the glasses do hide a tad too much.

Lera is one of Karina's favourite adults. She is quiet, always smiling, always bringing little gifts for Karina and Timur when she comes to visit—rock candy for him and lemon jellies for her; a colouring book for him and a fairy tale for her. Always two gifts, always acknowledging that the two children are individuals. The best ones are her "story-spark" gifts, a bottle cap for Timur and a ribbon for Karina; a shoelace for Timur and a gilt candy wrapper for Karina. Lera has a special look on her face when she brings those: biting her lower lip, flaring her nostrils, straightening her back as if giving a speech before the Party Presidium, she announces, "I think I've found something very unique for you this time." Then they all sit in a circle with their eyes closed, touching the "story-spark" objects, listening for them to reveal how they came to exist and how they came to belong to Karina and Timur. Sometimes the stories are silly and they all laugh heartily; other times the stories are quite like Hans Christian Andersen's, making them all sad and wistful.

Lera likes the sad tales best, she gets lost in them, taking off her glasses. Tears glisten in her blue eyes rimmed by dark lashes and serenity lights her face from within. Karina thinks that if a man ever saw Lera without her glasses he would surely fall in love with her.

It will be years before Karina would understand the stigma that kept Lera in her cocoon of loneliness. It was the stigma of her birthright and a shattered identity.

~~~

Loneliness passed into Lera's blood with her mother's milk. Perhaps even before, with her mother's thoughts as the child that would become Lera formed in her womb. Perhaps Nina Moiseevna Greenberg imprinted in the foetus the memories of a decimated band of partisans in the winter of 1943, and herself a twenty-year-old spurred on by hunger and exhaustion, no longer caring about danger, creeping out of the forest at dawn into a village just to find it abandoned; her own gaunt face reflected in a cracked window pane of a schoolhouse as a line of corpses swayed in the makeshift gallows across the square, the ice-rain rapping out a march on the placards dangling from their twisted necks. "Communist," said some of them. "Zionist pig," said others. She left that nameless village, taking the open road, no longer caring who might see her and at what moment her life might end. She didn't turn around when she heard a car engine approaching. She was deep behind German lines. The engine meant death.

But the engine caught up to her and slowed down and still no death came. And when a voice, kind, jocular, commanded from the car, "Halt," she did because it was just as easy to obey as not to. Then the same voice called out: "Wie heißen Sie?" She remembered the German she had studied with such enthusiasm in those all-but forgotten days before the war. *My name, my name. He just asked my name, like Sofia Leopoldovna in the classroom before the war.* Before the war, the apartment on Krivokolennyi Pereulok in Moscow. Moscow… no, stop. Halt!

"Wie heißen Sie?" the voice was gentler now.

"Ich heiße Nina," she replied with the careful pronunciation of a schoolgirl, not bothering to look up.

"Nina!" he laughed out loud. "Ninotchka! Greta Garbo hier in Rußland."

But when she heard "Ninotchka," the endearing softening of her name, the memories flooded back and she began sinking down into the snow. A small dark figure, swaddled in motley rags that used to be some other people's clothes, falling into the great endless blanket of whiteness over the battle-ravaged skin of Russia.

He didn't kill her and he didn't leave her to die on the frozen road. He took her with him to a small provincial town where his regiment was stationed, so far away from the theatre of war that life seemed almost normal. He nursed her back to health.

She tried to hate him. "Lassen Sie mich in Ruhe—leave me alone," she mumbled as her fever fell and rose.

He sat next to her, a handsome young officer in the middle of a war that he wanted no part of. His only desire in life was to create music. But he was a man of honour and honour demanded that he join the army.

He wiped her sweat, telling her she was beautiful, so beautiful that his heart nearly stopped when he saw her on the road, so beautiful that when his heart started beating again it resounded with melody.

"Don't touch me," she turned away, staring at a wall.

He said she was a Muse, sent by the gods to this frozen uncultured wasteland. As she drank hot tea, huddled in a corner of the bed in the large wooden *izba* he occupied, she listened to him play an upright piano with a white lace doily on top and a crystal vase filled with evergreen branches. This music transported them both to places where refinement once prevailed—the Prinzregententheater in Munich, the Great Hall of the Moscow Conservatory—places where beauty had been the norm; places that now seemed to exist only in their hearts.

One day, after playing a lovely Chopin etude, he began telling her about his childhood in Bavaria, about their family's castle, which sounded as unreal as Oz when all she had known was a communal apartment and one bathroom for ten families. But she wanted no words, just music, so she reached out to him and took his hand. "Bitte," she said, but instead of asking for an encore performance her body leaned into his. "Bitte," she repeated, and her chin tilted up. "Bitte," she whispered for the third time and closed her eyes.

"Ich liebe Dich," he whispered. *I love you.* She nodded.

Their love lasted almost a year. Then the advance of the Red Army forced his regiment to withdraw. Nina couldn't go with him. She couldn't stay. The people in town knew her as "the German's whore." Her love was high treason. If she waited for the arrival of the Russian soldiers at best she would have been sent to a labour camp in Siberia. Or, most likely, she would have been tortured and shot. A year ago she wouldn't have minded death. Now she carried her lover's child. Under the cover of night, she wrapped herself in loneliness and snuck out of town, taking the opposite road from the one that had swallowed Lera's father.

Seven months later, anonymous on a train station, as she hollered giving birth to her daughter, and two old women huddled next to her, Nina's guilt pummelled her. It had begun to swarm around her on the road, as she went from town to town, city to city, decimated by the enemy army. Disgust and fear filled her, as her belly grew. "Push, *milochka*," cooed the old women. "Push!"

Push, she thought. Push away the death camps, the murdered children. Push away the towns burned to the ground. Push away the rotting corpses swinging from tree branches. Push away the mass graves. Did her lover, her cultured gentle officer know of all these twisted bodies and glassy eyes staring into frozen skies as he cradled her in his arms? Would he have dragged her into the town square and hung a placard around her neck had she only once dared to whisper: Ich bin eine Jüdin?

Those questions besieged her again and again after her daughter was born. A daughter whose eyes were as blue and kind as her father's had been.

~~~

Lera's mother never found her answer. She bequeathed loneliness to a daughter who personified love and sacrifice and revulsion.

Loneliness, that's what Lera thought she deserved. Loneliness, but not solitude. She slept with men as long as they were married, safely unavailable. Her conquests, all but one, were artists. They fell for her vulnerability and her abandoned lust that demanded no reciprocity of affection. For her sex wasn't an act of intimacy but a force. She drew her power from their creative energies. And in return she nurtured their egos and nudged them to leap into great creations. For every lover she kept a journal, detailing intimacies, cataloguing compliments. She lined them up on a separate shelf, and when asked about these notebooks, she shrugged, "Oh, that? That's just my stars."

The only exception to the rule was Karina's father. He wasn't an artist—a mere engineer. Lera slept with him for years because he was available and always near. Slept with him while bringing gifts to his children and considering his wife her best friend. She slept with him and the others and when they threatened to leave their wives she dropped them, like the cherry tree dropping its blossoms, until a carpet of pale begging men sprawled at her feet.

But it will be years before the image of cherry blossoms and Lera's discarded lovers will meld in Karina's mind. Years before she will arrange pieces of information into a coherent elegance in a short story entitled "The Muse Ruse." On that, still innocent, night in May fallen flowers are just fallen flowers and stars are simply stars.

Karina sits on the porch, stroking the cat, listening for signs of the party slowing down. Is it time for the guests to leave yet?

But no, there is one more ritual left to this gathering—the music. Somebody always brings a bobbin of black magnetic tape that her father deftly weaves into their new "Yauza" reel-to-reel player. Usually it's fast-paced music with people singing in foreign languages. The adults then exchange knowing looks, and say short words like "jazz" and "rock" and "ABBA," and men invite other men's wives to dance.

But at other times there is no dancing. It's when the singers sing in Russian and the only musical instrument that is heard on the recording is an acoustic guitar. Then all the adults grow quiet, and draw their chairs as close to the spinning reels as possible and get a pensive look on their faces.

Tonight is one of those nights. A familiar gruff voice cuts into the guests' murmurs and everyone grows quiet inside the house. Now only this singer is heard. The universe coalesces into a point of pure sensuality —the sky filled with brilliant stars, the soft wind stirring up the fallen cherry blossoms, a purring cat in Karina's lap and a voice recorded onto a magnetic tape talking to an audience somewhere far away but also an audience right here.

His gravelly baritone is unmistakable. Of all the Russian singers with guitars that her parents and their friends like to listen to, this one is Karina's favourite. Some of his songs are funny in a way even she can understand. Like the one about Vanya and Zina watching clowns on television.

Karina picks up the cat and carries him into the house. The first song is about the war, about a soldier who perishes in battle and about his friend, who survives. This singer has many songs about the war. There are rumours that he is a war veteran himself. But Lera says that he is a young poet and actor from Moscow.

How magical, thinks Karina, *to invent something and to tell other people about it with such conviction that they too believe your invention.*

"And now," announces the singer, "to lift the mood a bit, I'll sing a song about plagiarism."

That's a new word and Karina memorizes it to ask her parents later.

> *I'm going to burst, like bundled TNT*
> *I'm tense and un-artistically bereft*
> *Today a Muse had come to visit me*
> *She came, she sat around, and then she left.[1]*

Russian nouns have no articles so Karina assumes that this "Muza," the Muse from the song, is a proper name. She imagines a sultry redhead who probably drank this poor man's tea, though he doesn't mention it, and then didn't even bother to thank him. *Plagiarism,* Karina thinks, *must be another word for bad manners.*

But the next verse talks about this same Muza hanging out with Blok for days on end, and practically living with Pushkin. Karina is startled. Blok lived at the beginning of the twentieth century and Pushkin at the beginning of the nineteenth. How could this same impertinent hussy visit all of them? Suddenly the image in her mind changes from a beautiful young woman to an ageless mean-spirited crag.

"Is Muza a witch?" she asks her mother as soon as the guests leave.

---

1   *A Plagiarizer's Song by Vladimir Vysotsky*

"She is a goddess who comes to artists," says her exhausted mother while piling dirty dishes in the kitchen sink.

"She really exists?"

"Yes, she does. An artist has to call her very hard and wait until she arrives. Then together they create paintings, or music."

"Or books?"

"Of course, books too."

"Can't artists create without her?"

"Yes, many don't have the patience to wait around until she shows up, so they start doing the work themselves."

Karina is so petrified of ever accidentally invoking Muza, that she determines that very night to work very hard without waiting for the awful hag to show up. She can't fall asleep. She is afraid that because she had thought so much about her, Muza might drop by for a visit. By the light of a flashlight under her blanket she writes her first short story about a little girl who doesn't believe in goddesses and as a good proletarian swears an oath to Lenin never to invoke supernatural powers.

From then on she writes every evening, because her fear grows in darkness—a fear that in idleness she might see a sallow lined face and the unkempt white hair of the goddess.

On a night in early December she wakes up with a start. There is a persistent phrase circling in her mind. It's about Ruslan, the new boy who has transferred into her class recently—he can draw wonderful flamingos, is the best student in math and has just asked Karina to be his girlfriend. The phrase repeats again and again. Two rhyming lines about Ruslan's green eyes. Karina climbs out of the warm bed, goes to her desk and writes them down. But no sooner does she cover her head with the blanket than the next phrase appears, and as she records it, another line of poetry floats in, then another. They flow freely, as if written down somewhere else before and she is just hearing and copying them.

She migrates between desk and bed the whole night, and by the morning has a long poem which she brings to the kitchen to show her mother. Karina is proud of this poem. It is beautiful and there is a warm satisfaction in knowing that this beauty was born in her.

"Well, what have we got here?" her mother sounds delighted. "It looks like the Muse visited you in the night, Karinushka."

stage notes

A FILM IS *being projected onto the backdrop: a pond surrounded by birch trees. Sun-kissed, emerald patches of grass. A duck gliding over the surface of the water. The audio, however, clashes with this idyll. It's a jumble of television sounds—infomercials for hair products, news reports on car chases and murders, canned sitcom laughter, televangelists. TOLSTOY is standing centre front, oblivious to the hubbub. KARINA enters, holding her hands over her ears, and crosses towards TOLSTOY. As she walks the noise dies down, so by the time she reaches him, all that can be heard is the rustle of leaves, water splashing, the odd buzz of a mosquito.*

KARINA: You know what I heard on the six o'clock news today? "We's foun' that chil'rens do better when they's put into small little groups." That was an elementary school teacher being interviewed. A teacher. Who am I writing for?

TOLSTOY: Any writer has a specific contingent of ideal readers in mind for his composition. One must clearly determine for oneself the demands of these ideal readers, and if in the whole wide world there are only two such readers, one must write just for them.

gods in bubblegum

To L.N.T.

W E WERE SHOOTING in West Hollywood today. When we wrapped, Simon Lottier, the extras' casting director suggested that we all head over to "Athena," the new bar that just opened on Sunset. It was practically around the corner from my apartment. Why not?

I stopped at home to shower and was the last to arrive. The interior struck an uncomfortable note in me. At first I couldn't quite pinpoint it. It was typical 21st Century LA chic—darkness barely diluted by amber and red Olympian torches; semi-nude statues, a nod to the Greeks but more reminiscent of strippers immortalized in plaster, stacked on top of one another to form columns; a dense crowd of beautiful natives resembling the animated version of these same white plaster bodies. At any given time, like fireflies in the night, several faces became illuminated by bluish light cast by cell-phone screens clutched before their eyes—dialling, texting, or reading messages. The music was a jazzy rendition of Bach.

I squeezed through the crowd and wedged myself between two bar stools, clutching my few inches of prime bar-top real-estate.

"What will you have?" asked an androgynous bartender. A magnificent creature with long black hair and sensuous lips.

As I looked up at the wall of liquor, I once again felt the chill of discomfort. But now I knew the source. A row of life-sized sculptures seemed to burst out of the wall over the bar. In continuation of the overall theme, these too were white plaster bodies. Both men and women. Not one the same but each a paragon of human beauty. But now I was seeing them close-up. Placed at a forty-five degree angle, chests straining forward, chins lifted up, they looked like they were taking flight, trying to emerge from torn, shredded rags that covered their skin.

"Vodka martini, straight up," I ordered, still spellbound by the frozen tense bodies. Their faces were obliterated by the thin plaster membrane they tried so desperately to shed. Like gods in bubblegum, I thought.

I viscerally felt their angst. Their frozen effort, their yearning was so familiar—don't we all feel this thin sticky substance covering our lives? If we could only burst through, if we could only shed it, would we not then embrace the light, the happiness, the warmth? Yet the more we struggle, the more we get entangled in the tacky, gooey mess. Are we not all gods in bubblegum?

"Hey, you made it." The voice's physical proximity startled me. The warm rush of breath on my ear. It was our second assistant director, Robert. "Come," he said, "we have a table." He grabbed my elbow and navigated me upstairs to a quieter loft area, where after exchanging greetings with my friends from the set, Robert and I sat down.

"Hey," he repeated, looking bashful. Robert had been eyeing me for a couple of days now, ever since we began shooting, but other than the usual greetings this was our first conversation. "I've been meaning to tell you...Don't take it the wrong way." I knew what he wanted. It was what every man wanted and his pick-up line would be as unoriginal as his desire.

He looked like such a stereotypical Californian—blonde hair, healthy tan, so ingenuous and at the same time so resilient in his innocence, that I didn't expect what came out of his mouth the next second, "You're like a visitor from another time," he said.

I was sideswiped; a snide remark that I had been preparing evaporated into silence.

"There is a sadness about you," he continued. "It makes you half present, but also it's as if it is driving you, helping you move through this time. It's as if our era is too..."

He paused, looking for the right word.

"Dense?" I offered, recovering.

"No," he said. "It's as if it's too fast for you. You struggle."

Maybe he said it differently, but that is the gist of it. And before he turned to talk to another person, yes, without even hinting at making a pass, he added: "You need a friend."

His words struck me with clarity. I realized that I haven't truly been alone for years. I've had a friend whose voice I've listened to daily but whose company I've taken for granted. You.

That film of sticky bubblegum suddenly froze and crumbled off.

With a giddy certainty I knew that a presence this strong could only emanate from one who exists. Exists right now. But how do I rationalize the fact of your death in 1910 with my sensing your existence a century away? From the perspective of linear time the dates of your life put you squarely in the past, not in the present.

The clue was in Robert's phrase about this time being too fast. That was it! Time is not a place you travel from and to. Time is innumerable currents of varied velocities. They exist concurrently, but we only tune into the one for which our receiver, our body, is naturally adjusted. So you too exist right now. Not in a different place in time but in a different pace of time!

If I learn to slow down, to tune into the speed of your time, your life, can I not reach you? Like you did many years ago in Moscow.

stage notes

KARINA IS STANDING *centre stage. The set is lit with countless candles. They flicker like stars in the surrounding darkness. Upstage there is a baby grand piano with an ornate candelabra on top. TOLSTOY is sitting at the keyboard. A soft melody is heard.*

KARINA: Nights are the hardest. My desire to speak with you overwhelms me. Once you publicly reproached Dostoyevsky for writing at night. You said that his dark, dank prose is the result of it; that visionary writing can only come in daylight. I don't agree with you. Moonlit thoughts are soothing. The boundaries of veracity are less tangible. In this murky light I can allow the deck of my mind to become crowded with phantoms and reality is finally pushed overboard.

(KARINA walks up to the piano and TOLSTOY stops playing.)

TOLSTOY: There is an element in fantasy that is better than reality. There is an element in reality that is better than fantasy. Indeed, full happiness might be in uniting both.

KARINA: *(lets her fingers touch the keyboard, striking three random notes)* Please, don't stop. You need that melody. Few remember now how well you played the piano. Fewer still know that you composed music. You never took your musical abilities seriously, all those plaintive wistful motifs so easily created and discarded, but when the world overwhelmed you with its problems, when words failed you, at least you could retreat to this wordless landscape.

(TOLSTOY begins playing again)

TOLSTOY: Music is more than an escape. It can teach us to separate great artists from great imitators. Take Mendelssohn for example. His music is beautiful, but it is no different from that of others. There is nothing unique. Beethoven, on the other hand, although I do not like him, he had the gift. You never know what he is going to say next. That's how it should be in literature and in all art forms.

KARINA: I don't understand. Mendelssohn or Beethoven—it's all a cacophony of notes jumping up and down an invisible stairwell of a scale. I cannot see their little hands connected in a circle of melody. Greatness or mediocrity—I feel them only in the music of language.

the rediscovery of words

First day in Canada. December 1979. Karina is convinced that she has arrived in the land of giants. Tall people, cars the size of steamboats, highways as wide as the Volga, the buildings of downtown Toronto propping up the sky, and one of them, an improbable needle out of science fiction, piercing the clouds and disappearing in them. She is astounded that there appears to be a government-imposed uniform—blue jeans.

Second day in Canada. Out of their ground level apartment's window in the monochromatic shades of a near-dawn she sees a squirrel for the first time in her life.

Third day in Canada. Her parents bring home groceries in the most colourful packaging! The taste, however, is horrible! The cured ham is bland and the bread has the consistency of cotton balls. A week later their social worker will explain to them that bacon needs to be cooked and that white bread is meant to be toasted in that silver machine that had been gathering dust on their kitchen counter.

Fourth day in Canada. She and her brother make a pact to speak nothing but English to each other. "Ok?" "Ok." That is the only word they know in English. An hour later she mimes an invitation to a game of hide-and-seek. "Ok?" Her brother nods, grinning. "Ok!" Finally, a game that matches their language skills.

Fifth day in Canada. Christmas. A whole nation celebrating a religious holiday. Amazing! It is similar to the Russian New Year festivities, except it commemorates the birth of a Jewish boy who would become the Christian messiah. Or a Christian God? Karina is not sure. Her confusion is further complicated by the symbolism. What does a reindeer with a red nose have to do with it all?

Sixth day in Canada. She is enthralled by a wildly imaginative cartoon series about a caveman and his friends. She has even isolated a word that is repeated with frequency—yabadabadu. Her dictionary, however, does not have a definition for this term.

Seventh day in Canada. A whole week in linguistic limbo is too long! She invades a library having made a resolution to learn English immediately. For this purpose she needs a familiar book. Marching up to the librarian, Russian-English dictionary clutched in hand, she delivers a well rehearsed phrase: "Fa-eerai ta-lei." Then she adds the word, which her father had taught her that very morning: "Pleez."

In reply the librarian says something unintelligible and smiles. So Karina tries again, louder and slower this time: "Fa-ee-rai ta-lei. Pleez." This time the librarian's answer is more lucid—shrugging shoulders, bulging eyes, shaking head.

Now humiliated, surely she had mixed something up, Karina opens the dictionary and checks the English wording opposite the Russian "skazka." No. She had been right. There it is, clear as day. She points it out to the librarian. Fairy tale.

"Oh," nods the woman with obvious relief, and then blurts out something that begins with the letter "f" but surely does not sound remotely like what Karina had been trying to say.

Then comes the desired walk through stacks of books, a big volume is pulled out, the woman leaves. The book falls open to an illustration—a debonair man, body encased in a suit of armour, sits on a white horse and through the opening of his shining helmet smiles at a damsel. A word flies out at Karina from the caption under the picture. A "knight." In Russian all letters are phonetic. Each one represents a sound in the language. What you see on the page is what you pronounce. Karina's oral muscles struggle with: K-NEE-G-H-T.

She cannot memorize a language like this. She cannot even pronounce it!

She sobs into the pillow that night, suddenly comprehending the full weight of emigration. For her it's the weight of lost books.

~~~

She remembers a winter night descending on a large provincial town. The fire crackling in the fireplace of a house. The adults sitting around a table in various stages of inebriation. Men have loosened their ties. Women have loosened their tongues. A four-year-old girl, in a white and blue plaid dress, climbs onto a chair. She stands up. With one dimpled little hand she holds the back of the chair for balance, and with the other she brushes the dark hair ringlets out of her eyes. Solemnly the child observes the adults and demands silence. She will tell them a story.

The girl begins reciting her pièce de résistance. A shocker to all grown-ups who firmly believe in the limitations of a child's mind. She is telling them a fairy tale. A long one. All in rhyme. Perfectly memorized. The adults watch with admiration as she dramatically changes voices, makes faces and gestures to punctuate the importance of words.

Ah! How she loves these perfect words. Their feel as they roll off her tongue. Their melody as they seem to rhyme so effortlessly, yet in their rhyme underscore the importance, the horror and the eventual triumph of goodness in the story. Of course she didn't make it up. It came from a big glossy book with wonderful colour pictures.

It is a tale of a fat ugly crocodile who lived in a forest swamp and one day ate the jolly sun, just because at sunset it had the unfortunate habit of rolling too close to the ground. The little girl was fascinated, moved to tears by the mayhem into which a sunless existence plunged the forest creatures. Little birds shivered, fluffy cute animals could not help but be afraid. They all went to the crocodile and begged him to release the sun. Of course the scaly arch-villain refused. Eventually, in the charming way of most children's stories, the bear beat the evil reptile to a pulp, pried his jaws open and made him puke up the much needed celestial torch.

Karina had read it and read it until it became a part of her.

From that moment on she began escaping into books, eventually learning to navigate the seas under Wolf Larsen's tutelage, walking the streets of sunken Atlantis alongside captain Nemo, helping D'Artagnan to save Madame Bonaceux and as a result winning the love of Athos. Yes, she improvised. She inserted scenes in which she met the protagonists and was invited along for the adventure. She extended the stories beyond the boundaries of THE END.

Mileposts of her childhood were marked by books.

Her fifth birthday. Her mother got her a stunning oversized volume— "The Golden Book of Fairy Tales" by Bozhena Nemtsova, a Czech writer.

Gift in hand Karina retired to her room. Unable to tear herself away from the familiar fairy tale format and the unfamiliar characters and twists that the Czech flavour afforded them, she read all night and finished it. The next morning, elated, she ran into the kitchen, kissed her parents and asked for another book.

Her mother burst into tears. It had cost her a week's pay, cashing in favours, procuring an impossible pair of Bulgarian shoes, which she had carried like a prize to the book store. There a friend of a friend's sister was the assistant manager. For the money, the shoes, plus the official cost of the book, she had pulled the coveted prize from under the counter. Karina's mother had hoped it would entertain her daughter for at least a month!

Third grade. Their family moved from their dilapidated shack into a brand new government-allotted apartment on the outskirts of town. In the USSR, citizens were assigned to libraries in accordance with the municipal region where they lived. Karina didn't like it.

Her old library had been in the center of the city, in a majestic 19th century building. The librarian knew her and indulged her precocious reading habits. The new library was in the basement of an apartment building—one of the monolithic faceless outcrops in fields of emptiness that was their new subdivision. The people moved in before the roads were finished and Karina had to trek through mud, getting lost a few times in the identical labyrinths of would-be playgrounds and potential driveways before she spotted the hand-painted sign for the library. Inside the librarian looked too young to know anything and too bored to ever expand her knowledge.

When Karina came up to register the librarian asked her in a monotone how old she was and what grade she was in. "Third grade," she said. "Nine years old, but…"

The librarian didn't wait to listen to her "but"—"Children's section through this door on the right. Literature suitable for first, second and third graders in the first four rows to the left of the door. Reading room straight ahead."

Karina looked around. There weren't many visitors in the late afternoon and the librarian was casually perusing a three-day-old "Pravda." Karina took a deep breath and dared to demand her attention again, "Excuse me, but I don't read books for third graders." The librarian began to frown. The girl hastened to explain. "I mean, I've read them all. Literally all of them."

The librarian squinted: "Have you read 'Dunno on the Moon'?"

"Yes, and 'Dunno in Sunny Town' and 'Dunno the Traveller'—I used to love Nosov when I was little, but he is for very young kids."

"How about 'Karlsson on the Roof'?"

"Astrid Lindgren?" Karina shrugged. "Yeah, all of her stuff too. Karlsson, Pippi, the Bullerby tales…"

For a moment the librarian considered the girl's neat school uniform and her bulging backpack. "Show me your school journal," she said.

A journal was a mandatory part of the Soviet scholastic arsenal. Every student kept one for the year. It was a daily record of one's academic progress. This was the place where homework was recorded, where teachers wrote comments about one's class conduct and chronicled the grades for tests and assignments. A concise summary of a student's future worth to the communist state.

Proudly Karina pulled her journal out. It had nothing but straight 5s—the equivalent of an "A" in the Russian grading system. It was also brimming with ecstatic comments—odes to her diligence, obedience, and exemplary communist spirit.

The librarian returned the journal and said that the girl could go pick a book and she'd decide whether it was appropriate for her. "You can go as far as the fifth grade, probably," she added.

Karina followed her instruction. Yet somebody must have misfiled a book, because when the girl brought Tolstoy's "Childhood" to the checkout counter the librarian dropped her newspaper in exasperation. "This is clearly marked for grade seven! Why can't you just go and pick out a nice book about Tom Sawyer, Huckleberry Finn and the oppressed Negroes in America or this wonderful new collection about young communist martyrs during the Great Patriotic War?"

Nothing could convince this woman that some children's intellects might be immune to the ideological poison in a book about a privileged boy's formative years in tsarist Russia. Karina had to go get her mother.

And then the three of them—Karina close to tears, her mother steadfast in defending her right to read, and the librarian, perplexed and distressed—engaged in a round of verbal duelling.

"Look, I cannot give a child in the third grade a book that is clearly marked for the seventh. I said she's welcome to the grade four and five level. Perhaps I'll consider some Sherlock Holmes books…"

"She has read them all."

"Then the Prince and the Pauper…"

"We have Mark Twain's collected works at home."

"The Count of Monte Cristo?"

"Dumas is her favourite, she knows it by heart."

"I'm not sure it is healthy for a young girl to read so much," said the librarian. "Now, how about this? We just got a new translation of Oliver Twist. I can see she is intelligent and she can handle it—it is a very vivid portrait of the capitalist exploitation…"

Tolstoy would have to wait, but that was Karina's introduction to Dickens. She fell in love with his world, its detailed rhythms. She had dreamt of some day reading him in the original.

~~~

Now, in Canada, when that dream should be so attainable, Karina realizes the impossibility of accomplishing it. That knight has dashed her dreams. For days she is inconsolable.

She goes to school, but being surrounded by peers does nothing to help her assimilate. Russia has just invaded Afghanistan, and she is held personally responsible for it. As if she rode in on the first tank. She wants so desperately to find understanding, to make friends! But all she can say, all she knows is: "Khelo, I don't spik Eenglish." How can she explain to them that the reason her family came to Canada was that her parents fled from that very same Communist regime that started this war? How can she challenge them on the stupidity of blaming a child for the military aspirations of politicians? Children have only one role to play in the wars of men—that of victims. Never mind the Soviet war classics, but have these kids not shuddered over the pages of Leon Uris' Exodus? Have they not cried when Gavroche was pierced by a bullet on the barricades of Paris? Have they not read? They must have, so why do they not like her?

Then, on a day in the middle of February, she walks into her home-room class to discover a world awash in red. From her desk in the back row she watches a bewildering pantomime. As each of her classmates enters, he or she carries a stack of red hearts. Large and small, simple and ornate, edged with filigreed doilies or sparkles. These cards are distributed according to no rule Karina can infer. It's not a birthday, all are partaking. It's not like the International Women's Day, for boys are receiving as well as giving. It soon seems to her that garlands of hearts stretch from student to student on the invisible strings of giggles and chatter. The whole room becomes a web of hearts. A web in which all but she are ensnared. Yet the only *raison d'être* of this ritual seems to be in exchanging cardboard cards.

Eventually the PA system checks the merriment. The Lord's Prayer is recited. As usual she refuses to stand up and talk to some god she has never been formally introduced to. Then the Canadian anthem is sung. Now she gladly contorts her tongue into sounds that, to her, approximate the lyrics. "Oh Canada! Arho maney tivlan…" She wants to prove to this country that she belongs. The bell rings. As they file out into the hallway she hears her homeroom teacher utter something at the end of which she recognizes her own name. Karina. Pronounced in that muddled Canadian way, that eradicates the first "a", and makes an almost-vowel out of the brittle Russian "r."

At lunchtime a boy comes up to her in the cafeteria. He is very handsome with his auburn hair, blue eyes and a roguish smile. She will always remember his name—Vince. Behind him, a group of the popular kids, watching. She grins, says "Khelo." He extends his hand and in it she sees a paper heart. Not red like the other kids' but a carefully ripped-out heart-shape bearing the blue lines of a notebook page. Something is written on it. She doesn't understand, points her finger to the writing and shrugs. He reads, each word chiselled into the air: "You dirty, fuckin' Russian."

She has no idea what that means, but it must be nice, judging from his smile. So she says the new word in her linguistic arsenal: "Senkyou."

But why are all the kids laughing? Slowly she examines her first paper heart. Flips it over. On the other side—a swastika.

She learns a lesson that day. Anger produces heat. Abandoning her coat and hat in school she runs the ten blocks to her apartment building. The ice rain singes her cheeks, drives her forward. Perhaps she slips and falls—that would explain her muddied torn tights and bloodied knee. She has no recollection of physical pain. Two images obliterate everything in her mind. The paper heart with the symbol she hates with every fibre of her body, and a photo of a grandfather she has never met, a Red Army soldier who died in Berlin three days before the War ended. That evening, armed with a dictionary, she composes her response. The next day she marches up to Vince, and declares in her loudest theatrical voice: "You are Canadian peeg!"

She walks away, head held high without waiting for his reaction. The laughter of the other kids is the only answer she needs.

Thus begins her real education in the language of her beloved Mark Twain and Dickens.

She resolves to write down her loneliness. To write away her pain. She decides that the gravity of her situation warrants the most sublime written form—the novel. Naturally, to stick it to all the Vinces of this world her novel will be written in English. She dives into the research. In this case, research into the language itself. She learns new words, she learns new ways of expressing herself: pariah, betrayal, angst, absolution, triumph.

She learns quickly. Now she is determined. Now she has proof that she can wield this new language. Two years later, at the Junior High graduation she receives the award as the best English student in the school.

And her first attempt at a novel? She only wrote its opening: a little girl gets off a train. In her hand she clutches a paper heart. The sun reflecting off the snow blinds her. She stops for a moment. "Schnell!" a voice shouts very close to her. She starts and drops the heart. There is no time to pick it up. She is pushed along by people behind her and as she looks back to the spot where she dropped it, she sees the guards in long coats, the growling dogs, the train station sign: Auschwitz.

stage notes

KARINA AND TOLSTOY *are on opposite ends of a large table. He holds a quill in his hand. She has a laptop in front of her. Between them are piles of neatly stacked papers. As the lights come up TOLSTOY glances over the page he has just finished writing and hands it to KARINA.*

TOLSTOY: Simplicity. That is the one quality, which I strive to obtain the most.

KARINA: How does one *simply* explain the next few uneventful years? Years, mind you, not months. Over three thousand days of gradually splicing my soul into the Canadian fabric. *(She turns her laptop so that it faces TOLSTOY)* I suppose I could simply skip over them, but that would make for bad literature. Characters, once introduced, must be dealt with, however many who played pivotal roles in my childhood simply have no place in the next act of my life.

(KARINA slides the laptop over to TOLSTOY'S side of the table, gets up and walks over to his chair.)

So what do I do? Tell the prosaic truth? The divorce of my parents? It's an all-too-common side effect of immigration. Couples cannot withstand the pressures of having to build lives all anew. Both remarried and both are unhappy. The Alzheimer disease that claimed my grandmother? At first I thought that it was a blessing, that she would finally forget the terrors that pursued her. Instead, she seemed to become trapped in a personal hell with all the ghosts, unable to escape, unable to explain herself out of it. The disappointment in my brother? He strove to become more Canadian than the Canadians themselves, changing his name to Tim, refusing to have anything to do with his Russian heritage, memorizing baseball stats instead of his school lessons. In his effort he erased a vital part of his self. He talks little and thinks even less. Handsome, egocentric, totally devoid of depth, he is all action—the perfect movie hero, who somehow has ended up on the pages of literature. What is the point of writing him as he is?

Of course I can invent something interesting for my family members to do, but that would take many volumes, a brief account of one life stretching into a long family saga. That is not my intent.

TOLSTOY: *(Tilting the computer screen so that he can read better.)* To write one good book in a lifetime is more than enough.

KARINA: I believed that I had written that one good book. I have obviously failed. This *(she points to the screen)* is just an explanation of its author. Perhaps after you understand me, you can identify what made my book flawed. Perhaps you can teach me how to fix it, how to make it better, make it true art.

TOLSTOY: *(shaking his head)* As soon as art became a profession, methods were immediately developed to teach this profession. Then, having chosen art as their profession, people began studying these methods, and soon professional schools were sprouting up. Writing classes in colleges, academies for painting, conservatories for music, theatrical schools for the dramatic arts… In writing classes they teach people to be able to write many pages of a composition without wanting to say anything, on a theme that they had never contemplated, and to write them in such a way that it would resemble the compositions of authors acknowledged as famous. But art is transferring an artist's unique feeling to other people. How can you teach that?

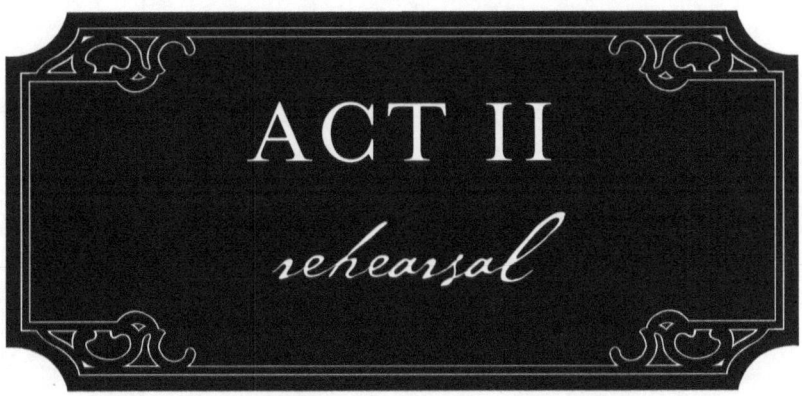

ACT II

rehearsal

beware the written word

Yesterday his photograph fell out of a book. Memory. Awakened by a piece of paper sighing to the floor. A photograph. A face. A gateway back to Russia. Not her Russia. Not her childhood. But a Russia she would reclaim as her own. Memory. A face. A man she had hoped never to remember.

~~~

Luke Garson. At the age of forty-five he is Canada's theatrical maharishi. An incarnation of Stanislavsky, salivate the critics. An incarnation of Bacchus, snicker the actresses and the usherettes, the prop girls and the set-designers. Luke Garson is the artistic director of The Dominion—the largest dramatic theatre company in Canada. He has an uncanny gift for discovering new talent, for galvanizing the 20th century into a two-thousand-year-old play, for attracting stars to the same boards as barely weaned students, for rearing a theatrical David who can withstand the Goliath to the South of the 49th parallel, with his ubiquitous rehashing of Oklahoma and a matinee of Grease.

There is not a person in Toronto's theatre circles who has not prayed at the altar of Luke Garson.

Enter our protagonist, aged twenty, about to start her third year of university, playwriting major with a minor in literature, now sitting on the patio of the Pickle Barrel on Yonge Street, sharing a Reuben sandwich with Stephen—a fellow theatre student. A portentous summer evening. The air is pregnant with a thunderstorm. The flow of downtown crowds accelerates from adagio to presto. Rivulets of pedestrians trickle into storefronts, subway entrances, streetcars, restaurants. Sam-the-Record-Man's gigantic red-orange LP blinks across the street. It frames Stephen's head like an infernal halo. Ordering another round of beer, he swerves the conversation into an unexpected direction: "My cousin is the stage manager at The Dominion. She told me that Luke Garson is looking for a new play, which must have a Russian flavour. He's got some upcoming deal in Moscow. You should submit your Fragments."

Fragments. The play had been triggered by an image—an old man in a train station. Waiting for a train he won't live to see. Forsaken by his muse. Possessed by his demons. Surrounded by plebeians, disciples, trivialities. Born Count Tolstoy, now a pauper and a drifter under an anaemic Russian sky.

Fragments. A classroom exercise turned into an obsession. Not letting her sleep at night. Demanding to exist. A manuscript that set itself down on a page in a form she barely controlled. Dialogue in her head steady, rapid, almost too rapid to record, and just when she'd think it was getting away from her, the spectral words would slow down, repeat themselves, repeat like a well-memorized poem, like lines already chiselled into some not too distant dimension. She could almost see the many faces whispering screaming mumbling them. Words recorded by her but not invented by her. What could she identify with in Tolstoy's reality? What could she understand about the price of genius, about its struggle with humanity? Not much back then. Not much even now, a year later. Yet Fragments became real. It became real through her. And it was good. But...

"Show it to Luke Garson? A lot of good that will do. He probably has Michel Tremblay, David French, Judith Thompson... Like I've got a chance."

"It can't hurt. Just give me a copy."

By the end of the week she surrenders a copy of the play. Fantasizes about what ifs for several days. Forgets about it soon after. Until one day the telephone rings.

"Hi, this is Luke Garson."

Yeah, right. She is certain it's Stephen, playing a prank. Well, the joke would be on him. Dashing through a mental list of Garson's known proclivities, she purrs: "I haven't forgotten Mr. Garson, your blow job is coming right up. Just can't decide—should I wear a red or a black garter belt for your viewing pleasure? "

She remembers two actresses in the lobby of The Dominion gossiping about the great man's famed distaste for pantyhose and his bedtime lectures on the allure of the garter: "Ease of access," the two women had giggled in unison.

Now, there is no giggling on the other end of the line. Just an awkward pause.

"Is this the… Razum-ov-skaya residence? Did you submit a play…?"

"Fragments? Are you serious?"

"Let's start again. This is Luke Garson. Can I presume I'm speaking with…?"

She cannot utter a sound. Her mind recoils, desperately trying to retrieve escaped words, escaped seconds of time. He presumes her silence is an assent.

"I've read your play…"

This is not happening!

"…and I would like…"

This is unreal! Sitting in a basement apartment on the outskirts of the city, talking to Luke Garson on a Saturday morning!

"Okay," she manages to squeeze out.

"How about lunch on Thursday? Do you know the pub on…?"

~~~

She has seen him from afar before. Like many theatre students, she has worked the concession stand at The Dominion to get into the plays for free. She has handed out coffee during intermissions and champagne during opening nights hoping to ensnare him in a witty phrase.

She has never dreamt that in a not too distant future he would set aside a whole hour, perhaps longer, just for her.

She has seen him from afar before, auditioning a million possible remarks that might bridge their two lives.

She could never have imagined his opening sentence: "It was you who wrote Fragments?"

"No, my uncle Anton Pavlovich." She knows that he will get the reference. He has just staged Chekhov's "The Seagull."

He assesses her body unabashedly. When his eyes finally return to her face he says just one word: "Beautiful." No sexual undercurrents in his voice, but a calmness tinged with annoyance.

"Oh, so beauty and brains can't mix?"

"My favourite cocktail. I usually take it in bed."

Her first inhalation of the rarefied bohemian air singes her cheeks. But she won't let on that she is a novice: "Look, that fellatio comment… you got the wrong idea."

"I always get right ideas. And I'm not flirting, just being honest. Besides, you're too young for my kind of favouritism. How old are you? Twenty-two? Twenty-three?"

"Twenty."

Again, a shadow of annoyance tugs his features: "Right. Let's get down to business."

She has seen him from afar before, but has never been brushed by more than a cursory glance in a crowd. Now across the table his whole energy is focused on her. She is not prepared for the sheer physical force, the entanglement of his gaze. For the first time she is in proximity of one who knows the weight of every moment, whose concentration rarely escapes the slippery "now," and she is unnerved by this intensity. Unnerved and something more. A feeling she will later identify as a sense of gratitude that this intoxicating attention has been—for a moment, a minute, a day—lifted from feeding his own ego and has settled generously in another's court.

But that afternoon: "Would you consider making a change or two to the play?"

Yes, Garson is a god, or at least the Theatre's highest priest, but she is wary of an attack on her work. Would she be able to discern where the improvements are constructive and where she is succumbing to the will of celebrity?

She doesn't like the beginning of this conversation. He doesn't notice.

"Not much of a change," he says. "Make the character of the disciple into a woman, or write it sexless, up to you, but there is an actress in Moscow I must use."

Immediate calculations in her head. Unexplored tension and nuances this might add. "Interesting. Perhaps. What else?"

It begins with lunch, slips into dinner, and ends with drinks at a jazz club. He drives her home. The subways have closed for the night.

As she is about to exit the car he grabs her wrist. Pulls her back in. The pressure of his fingers is a welcome pain. His face is inches away. He is too handsome… too intense… It hurts not to move, not to succumb. His skin gives off the scent of sandalwood mixed with the barely acidic musk of perspiration. Karina is still. He has to decide. He has to crave it. She prays for him to want her. He begins leaning toward her. She shuts her eyes. Ready for anything. Except…

His breath scorches her ear: "Don't do it," he whispers. "Please." In the next moment his lips press into her hand. Heavy velvet on her skin.

The bond lingers.

And then: "Go. I'll sit here until you get into the house safely."

For a week—more? less? she never will recollect—the telephone doesn't ring. Her life loses colour. The whirling seconds are filled with memorized words—his words; a remembered voice—his voice; imagined thoughts—his thoughts; the scrutiny in his eyes—intense blue washing over her; the trace of wine on his lower lip. Sleep is a welcome escape where it all makes sense—the words, the voice, the thoughts, the smile, the blue.

She finds herself downtown. Running an errand? Shopping? A cancelled date? She will call him because she is two blocks away. He is a busy man, that won't do. She will call him to discuss the corrections to the play. She hasn't touched her typewriter in days. She will call him…

"Where are you?" he asks.

"Down the street. King and Jarvis. I wanted to discuss…"

"Come on by."

It is after business hours. His office is locked. She knocks on the door and he flings it open immediately. Has he stood on the other side and listened to her approaching footsteps? She has no chance to ask. No chance to ponder his unshaven, sleep-deprived face.

Swept up in Luke Garson's embrace, she feels weightless, engulfed and triumphant, flying and falling. He stumbles and she is slammed into a wall, his body crushed against hers. He pins her arms against the wooden panelling. Those lips that played host to trickling wine now split hers open. No longer soft. They are demanding. Tongue—now entreating gently exploring; now thrusting forcefully possessing. Then, again the sensation of swirling levity.

She has no idea how they have ended up in the conference room. He sets her on the table. Steps back. Looks into her face. Almost shyly. Their eyes are locked with a ferocity that moments before their bodies partook in. She smiles, afraid to speak, afraid her voice will come out in a scream. Begging.

He approaches her. His thigh wedges between her knees. Forces them apart. As his hand slips under her skirt, up her stocking, and verges the boundary of lace and flesh, he emits a hoarse groan: "Don't destroy me. Please."

~~~

Two weeks later they are on an airplane landing in Sheremetievo Airport in Moscow. As an ex-Soviet her entry visa should have taken three months. Luke had flown to Ottawa for a day, had lunch with someone and returned that evening with her paperwork in order.

If the man could mould Soviet bureaucracy to his schedule, what might he do with her future?

Her university career is temporarily on hold. Her school's Chancellor had agreed with her that working with Luke Garson was a priceless opportunity, both educational and professional. It would be worth a delay in receiving her degree.

Still above the clouds, sunshine playing off the metal wing, the weight of what is about to happen chokes her. With every second her body is reconnecting to the land of her birth. Will it be familiar to her? Will it embrace her? Will there be understanding?

The airplane dips into the cloud layer. Sunshine erased. A white nothingness beyond the portal. Time too becomes nothingness. It becomes the past as it hurls into the future. She emerges above trees, buildings in the distance growing larger, closer. Clarity of air. World in every shade of grey. MOCKBA—on the side of the terminal as they taxi in. The letters spell out that she has just completed a circle. Moscow.

stage notes

KARINA AND TOLSTOY *stand side by side downstage centre. A loud Soviet song, Kalinka or Moscow Nights sung by the Red Army Chorus, becomes warped as if on a tape that has been left out in the sun. Then it fades out.*

KARINA: Reliving the past, even on a page, is acidic. I am far enough removed. I can almost convince myself that this had happened to some other person, but memories drip painfully onto my armour, dissolving it, forcing me to feel more than I wish. I know the monsters that await around the bend. Why am I going willingly into their trap?

TOLSTOY: In order to affect others, an artist must be searching; his composition must be a quest. If he has already found everything, knows everything and is just lecturing, or entertaining for entertainment's sake, he will not be effective. Only if he is searching, the audience, the listener, the reader will merge with him in the exploration.

KARINA: Search for something new? Yes, there were many unknowns. Mostly "hows" at first. Then the "whys"—a whole *khorovod* of them.

the discreet charm
of the KGB

"YOU CAN ALWAYS tell an American in a restaurant," says their guide, Stanislav.

"How?" asks Luke Garson. "Because they're loud?"

"No, because of the way they hold their cutlery." A smug grin appears on the Russian's face. "Just look at them," he nicks the air in the direction of a table by the window, where several Texans are making fools of themselves in front of a leggy Russian blonde. "Americans inevitably mince their food first, then discard the knives and transfer their forks from the left to the right hand before commencing to eat. Even the most cultured ones! Amazing that a nation that managed to send men to the moon cannot grasp simple table etiquette!"

Luke rolls his eyes. "I would have thought those Stetsons were a bigger giveaway."

Their guide ignores the sarcasm. In 1988, Perestroika or not, wit and official Soviet workers are still not allowed to mix.

Karina, however, understands what Stanislav is doing. He is not trying to be funny. He's engaged in a grown-up version of the game they all used to play in childhood. Finding foreign spies in their midst was deemed an integral skill. Vigilance was a virtue in the world of the progressive "us" and the retrograde capitalist "them." Karina and her friends memorized clues from films and literature, trying to outdo each other with nuances: Russians give themselves away by how they hold cigarettes. Westerners always smile at strangers and look them in the eye. Women scream in their mother tongue when giving birth. Americans all have fake straight teeth.

"What about Canadians?" she asks their guide suddenly. "How do you deduce them?"

Stanislav seems to be caught off guard. "I don't think we've ever had to concentrate on Canadians," he says. Adding quietly: "*Do sikh por.*" Until now.

At that moment their waitress arrives. Luke and Karina had made an attempt to study the menu, but after seven pages of Russian specialties like *"spiked beats"* and *"chicken bifstroganov"* or regional delicacies like *"Georgian testicle soup"* and *"Azerbaijan hash—cow brains and feet in garlic asspick"* they gladly accept Stanislav's offer to order for them.

Karina has assumed that he is a regular here. How else could he have gotten them past the "Restaurant Closed for Lunch" sign, past the liveried concierge, into this opulent hall with starched table linens, crystal goblets and twenty-foot arched windows? Windows with drawn, heavy curtains so that the crowds flowing past them on the sidewalk would not be able to see that this "closed" restaurant is doing brisk business catering to foreigners and communist VIPs.

"What are you serving today?" asks their guide without even attempting to reference the menu.

Of course! She recalls another piece of the Soviet puzzle. Menus are provided in Soviet restaurants for the same reason God provides each human with an appendix. It is a part of the structure, albeit a useless one. None of the items listed are likely to be in the kitchen. To find out what is being served one must ask.

"For starters we have smoked sturgeon and a tomato cucumber salad, borscht for first course and either Chicken Kiev or Siberian *pelmeni* for the second course," rattles off the waitress while fixing her bleached hair. After a quick check with his foreign charges, Stanislav settles on six hundred grams of vodka, pickles, sturgeon, the salad, and three orders of the *pelmeni*—meat filled dumplings served with sour cream.

After writing everything down the waitress announces: "We don't have tomatoes."

"So what's in your tomato and cucumber salad?"

"Radishes."

Stanislav is unfazed, "Fine, we'll take it. Also three of whatever you're serving for dessert, along with cognac and tea."

"It's chocolate éclairs for dessert."

"Made with chocolate, I hope?"

She nods, unfazed.

Karina interjects in Russian: "Excuse me, I'd like some ice-cream instead."

The waitress seems to wake up and observes Karina for the first time. The progression of her thoughts is clear on her face. *I thought she was a foreigner. Her Russian is too perfect. A hard currency prostitute!* "We don't have ice cream!" she snaps.

"I just saw you give those Americans ice cream."

"Listen, young woman," derision in her voice. "I want to have lunch too. It's almost two o'clock and just because you decided to show up here at this hour doesn't mean I need to interrupt my schedule. My break begins in two minutes. I'm setting your food out now, and that's that. The ice cream would melt."

"What's going on?" asks Luke.

"Apparently," Karina switches into English and speaks slowly, boring her eyes into the waitress, "ice cream is served to Americans only. Canadian guests of the Russian government are given a dollop of rudeness."

Their guide and the waitress blanch in unison. Yes, the waitress has understood. She'd have to have a grasp of rudimentary English in an establishment like this. "I'm sorry," she mumbles in Russian. "I didn't know. Of course I will bring ice cream."

With every passing moment Karina is remembering how to play this game on the ever-shifting invisible game-board of the Soviet existence.

She turns to Stanislav, curious now. "So how did you get us into this restaurant? Obviously you don't frequent this place."

"I didn't get you in. You got me in. The concierge recognized you and Luke as foreigners."

"But that 'Closed for Lunch' sign…"

Stanislav laughs unexpectedly. "That sign is in Russian. Most foreigners can't read it, Karen."

Karen. She still starts at this reshaping of her name. It clings to her like an ill-fitting garment. But so many things have been changing since she arrived in Russia a week ago. What matters a name when her whole life, her whole identity are beginning to splinter into unforeseen possibilities?

~~~

The changes begin as soon as they get off the plane.

In the barely moving queue in front of two passport control check-points at Moscow's Sheremetievo Airport she senses the physicality of Russia entering her. As if the years of her absence were a palpable vortex, gathering molecules of herself scattered throughout this land, collecting remnants of thoughts and feelings and hurling them one by one into her soul. Completing her.

Is she unique in sensing this burgeoning bond? She observes her fellow passengers. Clearly there are two types. Most are foreigners—untouched by Russia's energy, remaining in the levities of their foreignness, smiling, joking with each other, stretching travel-weary limbs. A few, here and there, however, are ex-Soviets—suddenly weighed down by the realization that once again they are behind the Iron Curtain, knowing full well its chill, getting ready to face, once again, a forgotten reflection in the mirrors of their psyches—the squashed but never eradicated Homo Soveticus. The ex-Soviets are fidgety, pale, quiet.

Luke must have noticed her discomfort for he chooses this moment to announce, "By the way, it's time you change your name. From now on you'll be Karen Zumov."

Her first impression: Karen? Lacklustre. Zumov is not even a real Russian name. "What's the charade for?"

"Karina Razumovskaya is a tongue-twister. It's impossible to remember."

"Not in Russia."

"You don't live in Russia. Besides, we need a good PR legend. You are the granddaughter of a tsarist officer who had escaped to Canada. Your play came across my desk—true—and I fell in love with it. This project—the first Russian Canadian joint theatrical venture—was born. You are reclaiming, at least artistically speaking, the land that was stolen by the Communists from your forefathers. And Russians, from what I understand, are really keen on meeting the spawn of all those noblemen they kicked out seventy years ago. You'll be a hit here."

"You won't fool anyone. The KGB knows exactly who I am."

"The KGB doesn't write theatre reviews."

"That's what you think."

"They certainly don't in Canada."

That's what you think. This time she doesn't voice it. Instead she says: "If you want to change my name, then it must be Zumoff, with a double "f." That was the accepted transliteration of Russian names at the turn of the century."

~~~

Finally.

For the second time in her life she faces a Soviet border patrol uniform. This one worn by a freckled boy barely eighteen years of age. His smooth face, ruddy cheeks don't look threatening. But his eyes dart impassively from her face to her passport—once, twice… time stretches out. Again, like a decade ago, only her beating heart, only his cold grey eyes exist. This time she is not abandoning her land. She is asking to be let back in. His teeth clench. His lips stretch into a thin line: "Go through."

~~~

Her heart skips several beats. And into that interval an avalanche of noise descends. The screeching of the luggage conveyor belt, the screaming porters, the hubbub of passengers, the laughter of reunions. Luke is already on the other side. He is talking to a man in blue jeans and a leather jacket. As she approaches, the man makes several steps towards her. His movements are nimble, precise. He extends his hand. In it a bouquet of carnations. The flowers of the proletariat. Lenin always had a carnation stuck in his lapel.

"Welcome to Moscow," says the man in excellent English. "My name is Stanislav. The Theatre Union has appointed me as your guide. We are honoured to stage your play." His jeans, she notes, are ironed. His face is almost handsome, almost… but it lacks emotion. His gaze dissects her social mask, sinks into the depths of her fears. She feels something cold and sticky envelop her. Suddenly, a flicker of a smile contorts his features—in it she glimpses a spider confronting a dazed butterfly. He adds, in Russian now: "I trust your flight was comfortable."

~~~

Stanislav's car is a grey Zhiguli. A tin can on wheels. "Where is my black Volga limo?" half-jokes Luke Garson. She knows better. Someone somewhere has written that Stanislav and his ilk are grey men, driving grey cars, wearing grey suits, blending into the grey existence until they bare their crimson-stained fangs. On the highway into Moscow's centre Luke soon gets bored by the monotonous scenery. Mud-streaked cars. Faceless boxes of apartment buildings. Colourless people lining up on identical bus-stops, in front of monochromatic shops. She is riveted by these images. Their repetition is hypnotizing. Soon she is not sure whether she is seeing or remembering.

She becomes aware of her own thought and is surprised by it: have you really not changed?

Whom is she addressing? Russia or herself?

The closer they get to the city the slower the traffic moves. Luke has begun making notes in his journal. Suddenly he asks: "What does that say?" He points to a gigantic banner straddling two apartment buildings. "Communism is Soviet power plus the electrification of the whole country.—V.I. Lenin," Karina reads the Russian phrase to herself. Lenin's disembodied head is floating above the famous words. For the first time she perceives the inanity of the phrase. A bunch of thugs plus electricity equals communism? She giggles. Stanislav studies her in the rear view mirror before translating the slogan for Luke, his steely voice squashing her laughter.

~~~

"Relinquish your passports," says Stanislav when, after parking the car, he ushers them into the hotel lobby.

"What?" she and Luke exclaim in unison. He not understanding the demand. She, afraid that she has understood too well. "Your passports, please. They are required for registration. You will get them returned by dinner time."

Luke checks his watch. "Seven hours for registration?" He hands over his blue-bound document. How easily he surrenders it. How confident he is that a larger truth protects him. Her hand shakes a bit and Stanislav has to tug her passport away. It doesn't matter now. Canada cannot shield her in the land of her birth. The dice have been cast.

"Of course you do not have to wait. I can escort you to your rooms now if you wish." They do.

The elevator is so small that two people would feel cramped. With the three of them inside the experience is verging on unwelcome intimacy. As the elevator jerks and begins crawling up, her forearm brushes Luke's crotch. She feels a distracting bulge. Presses into it. He winks at her.

At that moment Stanislav begins whistling a tune. There is a familiarity about it, a sweet gust of childhood. Words surface through the murky depths of memory.

> *Our steam engine surges ahead*
> *A commune awaits at the end*
> *Out path is determined and set*
> *A rifle is grasped in our hands.*

Why one rifle for multiple hands? she thinks. And then: *dear Lord, what hogwash we used to sing!* Stanislav winks at her.

~~~

As they exit the elevator on the twelfth floor, a hallway attendant greets them. In Russian hotels there is one of these seemingly-cloned ladies per floor. Aged somewhere between thirty and sixty-five, depending on the lighting. Simple names like Vera, Olya, Sveta. Plain peasant faces, and sharp, all-noticing, city-trained eyes. Tight polyester dresses over shapeless bodies. Wool socks over nylons. Slippered feet. A steaming cup of tea on their work table, a pair of black high heels under the table. None of them have ever been seen wearing those shoes. They are probably fixed to the floor—a prerequisite talisman for this post.

The job of these replicated attendants is to mind order, as prescribed by Soviet morality: ensuring that there is no noise, that drinking is limited to a decent number of vodka bottles, that unmarried couples don't share a room, that no visitors of the opposite sex are in the guests' rooms past 23:00. Since homosexuality officially doesn't exist in the Soviet Union, and those who dare challenge this dictum find themselves behind barbed wire in Siberia, no rules are known to exist for guests of the same sex. And don't bother asking which forbidden acts can be performed only after eleven p.m. and are unmanageable before the pumpkin hour. Soviet morality prescribes rules, not explanations.

Stanislav announces their names and in return they are handed two keys. Rooms 723 and 727.

"Why do room numbers begin with seven on the twelfth floor?" wonders Luke.

"Why not?" Stanislav and Karina reply in unison. She is beginning to remember the illogical logic of this land.

"Can't we have adjoining rooms?" asks Luke.

"It is not possible," unexpectedly this Valya-Toma-Katya replies in English. "Room 725 is closed for renovations." Her accent is identical to Stanislav's—a blend of British pronunciation, Russian intonation and arrogance—that, Karina is beginning to suspect, spells out KGB training. She also is beginning to suspect what awaits on the other side of her room's door. She had been briefed about it prior to her trip. She hadn't believed it until now.

When her uncle, Yury, a former gastroenterologist at the Kremlin Hospital, found out that Karina would be staying at the Rossiya Hotel near the Red Square, he sat her down for a little chat. Apparently, Yury used to be invited regularly to the elite Sandunov Baths in Moscow by a patient of his, a general in the KGB, who after a few beers liked to boast about the impregnability of the Soviet system.

Once, after adding vodka to his beer, the general detailed the techniques for surveillance on foreigners: Soviets and foreigners never mixed in a hotel. Either they had separate hotels, or, in the case of huge establishments like the Rossiya, they had separate wings for citizens and for foreigners. In the foreign accommodations every other room was an observation post. In the guest rooms at least one wall was a two-way mirror. There were microphones in the chandeliers and in the telephones. The bathrooms never had shower curtains and at least one camera, usually hidden in the exhaust fan. If a foreigner was a "person of special interest" the observation was conducted live, in real time. If a foreigner was less than exciting, his movements were merely recorded and the recordings scanned randomly throughout the day.

Now, as Karina walks into her room she is not surprised to find almost the whole right wall covered by a mirror. It is ridiculously large, especially compared to the small desk in front of it, and a single narrow bed. On the dresser next to the bed she sees a bright green telephone.

She lifts the receiver and listens to silence. No, not silence, there seems to be a faint echo of breathing. "Allo, allo," she says in Russian. "Stop breathing, I need to make a phone call." She hears a distinct click and a dial tone. She hangs up.

The bathroom yields no surprises. And, of course, no shower curtain. She decides to make an attempt to regain some civility. She goes back out into the hallway, almost colliding with Stanislav. Ignoring him, she marches right up to the slippered Cerberus. "I'm missing a shower curtain in my bathroom."

"So?"

"The floor will become a swamp."

"We will clean it up."

There is no arguing with hostile servitude. Karina returns to her room, shuts the door, and jumps when she hears a man clear his throat. She hadn't noticed Stanislav sitting on her bed.

"I hope you weren't startled," he says, his voice betraying no such hope. "I needed to warn you not to leave the hotel without your passport." He doesn't budge. "Please relay this to Mr. Garson as well." His stillness and intensity force her to focus on him. He does have a charm, a magnetism of sort. A vampirish sort.

"Anything else, comrade?" she smiles, trying to break through the suddenly tangible air between them.

"I will come to fetch you for dinner around seven o'clock," his speech is measured, mesmerizing. "Is that agreeable to you?"

She nods and suddenly imagines what the two of them must look like from behind the mirror. A man on a bed. Relaxed. Poised. A woman leaning on a desk. Flimsy support. He speaks again:

"Do you have any requests for me? Anything you need meanwhile?"

Requests? She wonders if the camera behind the mirror is on a tripod or hand-held. Requests? Get the hell out of here. But she can't say that. There is a din in her head. Thoughts jumble up, break apart without ever arranging into a coherent meaning.

He waits.

Requests? Needs? For some reason the phrase "electrification of the whole country" passes through her mind's eye and Lenin's head...

"Yes!" she remembers gratefully. "Lenin's head. I mean, bust." Stanislav's eyebrows slide up. She rushes to explain: "Luke asked about it and I have no idea where to buy such a thing."

"How big does it need to be to satisfy you?"

Me? she thinks. *Satisfy? Why is he...? Why am I...?*

"Like this," she says raising her fist. Damn, that didn't come out right.

He is not looking at her hand. He never once takes his eyes off her face. The pause stretches, stretches past the borders of comfort and still he says nothing.

"I'm sorry," she breaks the silence. "I'm very tired. We had a nine-hour flight and I need to take a shower and rest."

"Of course." Did he allow disappointment into his voice? "I shall see you in a few hours." He stands up and steps towards her. She presses into the desk. She has no place to go. He attempts to shake her hand. She hadn't noticed that it is still clenched into a fist. Their touch is awkward.

He leaves and Karina listens by the door attempting to ascertain which way he walks. But the carpeted hallway muffles all trace of his retreat. She has no idea whether he is now breathing inches away on the other side of the door, or has already flown to his dark observation lair. She thinks that there is a sound of a door opening and shutting. She certainly doesn't hear the elevator.

She lifts the telephone receiver to call Luke. This time there is a dial tone almost immediately.

Luke picks up on the tenth ring. "I'm in the shower, what's up?"

"Need some company in there?"

"I was wondering what was taking you so long."

"Leave your door open."

As she grabs a change of clothes a surge of anger chokes her. She observes the room. Life in a fishbowl? Mirrors and cameras? Who the hell gave them the right? Then abruptly anger dissipates and Karina is left with the sensation of a body that had been sinking and is suddenly buoyed up by the density of water, propelled to the surface, a breath of air entering its lungs. She has caught the whiff of this game. For the first time since landing in this country she feels a sense of control.

Luke's room is an exact replica of hers. Exact, down to the green telephone and the orange and black chequered bedspread. The sound of running water from the bathroom mixes with Luke's off-key baritone: "If you want a lover, I'll do anything that you want me to…" He is a delicious male specimen, he exudes power and talent, but he can't sing. Still, there is something carnal, irresistibly sexual in the timbre of his voice, which has been widely described in Toronto's theatrical circles as "clit-balsam." Karina steps into the bathroom, checks for the position of the exhaust fan, stands directly beneath it and begins peeling off her clothes.

The mirror is fogged up. The reaction of Luke's body reflects the efficacy of her striptease. When he is sufficiently aroused she wiggles out of her panties and joins him. He presses her against the wall, hand slipping between her thighs, water streaming warm down his hair onto her skin. "Wait," she says loudly. Loudly enough to stop his insistent invasion. Loudly enough for any microphone to pick up over running water. "You have to wash me first." He grins. "Really? Is that what you want?" She nods, doing her best to ignore the fluttering of his fingers. He picks up a bar of soap. She clings to him, and as he slides it down her back she whispers: "We are being watched."

"You are being paranoid," his voice instinctively matches her quiet tone.

"Keep soaping," she instructs and as he lathers her body and washes away the suds, in a hushed voice between kissing his neck, nibbling his ear, she relays the KGB general's tale.

"Well, fuck the KGB, what are you concerned about?" he asks. She knows what he is thinking. They are single. They have nothing political to hide. They look damn good so any pictures would be flattering, not compromising.

"Not concerned. I was thinking that since they're into watching, we should give them something to watch."

"That's my girl," Luke laughs loudly.

"In that case," she raises her voice too, "let's get comfortable."

Karina exits the bathroom trailing water. That Galya-Masha-Klava wanted something to clean, she can have it. She hears Luke turning off the shower.

Placing a chair before the wall-to-wall mirror, she sits and spreads her legs. There is a sound of crashing glass from the bathroom. "Damn, I just broke my aftershave bottle!" curses Luke. Karina checks the play of light on her skin and smiles at herself: "Come here, dry me off. I'm getting cold" she calls out, examining her own reflection. She licks a finger and glides it around an erect nipple. Shuts her eyes as her finger travels down, circling the plane of her stomach, traversing a hipbone onto the sensitive skin of the inner thigh. She feels him come up to her. In the darkness behind the eyelids he can be anybody.

"I prefer you wet." Luke's voice forces her eyes open. He is observing her in the mirror. "That's quite a view."

"Just a preview. Get on the bed," she commands.

She straddles Luke, her back to the mirror now, begins sliding onto him, slowly, teasing the very tip of him. "Is this what you want Mr. Garson? Should I let you all the way in?" she whispers. Luke's fingers dig into her flesh, pulling her down. She relents, and in a swift movement accepts all of him into her. As her lover moans she looks over her shoulder, into the mirror, into the eyes behind the mirror. *Getting a good view?* she thinks. *Wishing you could, like Lewis Carroll, go in through the looking glass?*

What if he could defy the solidity of matter, squeeze his molecules between those of the mirror? What if he could ooze into this room, grab her from behind and plunge into her too?

"Oh God!" she climaxes suddenly. "God, God, God..." the waves of the orgasm undulate through her body. As they begin subsiding, shreds of thoughts peek through the crests: *Are you noting down that... during sex a woman does not... scream in her native tongue...but in the language of her first sexual experience?... Is the prodigal daughter... helping the Motherland?* She feels the swell of another orgasm.

This gives a whole new meaning to "fuck the KGB," she thinks and surrenders to it.

stage notes

Karen meanders upstage, *examining the empty frames, pushing them, forcefully or softly, until each swings like a pendulum. TOLSTOY stands still downstage.*

KAREN: I have entered into a multitude of sins. I have prayed. I have lived a life full of emptiness. Yet this carryall version of my reality is littered with bodies. No, not humans but almost. And more than characters. I turn away from them but there is no turning away from oneself. They seep out of me, demanding that I shine a light onto them, give them a moment centre stage. Again.

(She walks up to an invisible "person," caresses his cheek, then pushes him away. Walks up to another one, takes him or her by the hand and approaches TOLSTOY.)

TOLSTOY: The Gospel's bidding 'judge not' is profoundly applicable in art: recount, illustrate, but do not judge.

KAREN: *Judge not* is the most difficult concept to apply to one's own life. I judge myself for being too Russian. I judge myself for not being Russian enough. I judge myself for not knowing, even now, where I belong.

a golden chain

THEIR FIRST NIGHT in Moscow. August 17, 1988. After having dinner with Stanislav in the hotel restaurant they bid him good-night at ten p.m. and watch him leave the hotel lobby. He still hasn't returned their passports, claiming that the unscheduled arrival of a Bangladeshi basketball team had thrown the hotel administration into a state of confusion.

"I'm going for a little walk," Karen turns to Luke and plants a kiss on his lips. "Care to join me, Mr. Garson?"

"It's late…"

"I've waited my whole life to see Red Square. It's around the corner from here. I'm going."

"What about our passports? Stanislav warned us not to go anywhere without them."

Karen shrugs. "Is it our fault that the so-called registration is taking longer than usual? What's going to happen if we take a stroll through night-time Moscow?"

As they leave the hotel, the doorman holds the door open and rewards them with an obsequious smile. Only his eyes prick their faces with cold calculation.

Minutes later, in front of St. Basil's cathedral, Karen stops, unwilling to move further. How surreal, this moment! The famous multicoloured domes towering over their heads, the granite ziggurat of Lenin's mausoleum, and beyond it, the Kremlin's Spassky Tower with its green steeple and clocks that she used to watch on TV every New Year's Eve as a child. She feels like she is standing in a postcard, her body a tiny pixel of colour, a splatter of blood mixing in with so much spilled blood. This square has earned both its names. "Krasnaya" used to mean "beautiful" in old Russian and has come to mean "red." Phantom events flitter by— parades, assassinations, market days, holy days, monarchs, proletarians, the life and deaths of a country. Karen tries to catch her bearings in the swirling images. Somewhere on this square a would-be usurper of the Russian throne, False Dimitry, was murdered by an angry mob. His mutilated body abandoned on Lobnoe Mesto, a stone platform from which the tsars announced their proclamations. She looks around. There it is, a circular dais, much smaller than she has imagined. Just past it, the monument to Minin and Pozharsky, a peasant and a prince, heroes who liberated Russia from the Poles. Another gust of history makes her dizzy, threatens to sweep her away.

Karen does what she used to do as a child whenever anxious or overwhelmed. She sits down in this playground of passions. Except now there is no use in shutting her eyes, for the assaulting images are born in her own mind. The quartered body of the Cossack rebel Stenka Razin, the crawling columns of tanks and goose-stepping soldiers, the toppling two-headed eagle... Cross-legged in the middle of Red Square she continues gazing at this ever-present past. Her hands caressing the cold cobblestone scabs over the heart of Russia.

"Are you okay?" asks Luke.

Karen says nothing as she looks up at him. The light of the projectors lends a flatness to the surrounding landmarks, pasting them onto the black sky where the only stars visible are the red pentacles over the Kremlin towers. She has never before experienced such acute hatred for this land with its penchant for self-mutilation. She has not, in years, felt as comfortable as she does in this place. Tears blur her eyes.

Rapid footsteps approach from behind and halt. She looks over her shoulder and identifies the two young men in uniform as a militia patrol. Soviet police. Old knowledge resurfaces. Nobody is supposed to sit, drive a vehicle, laugh, shout, play music, run or smoke in Red Square. The militiamen hesitate, recognizing the miscreant and her hulking accomplice as foreigners.

"Mademoiselle," ventures one of them. Then turns to his partner and swears under his breath: "Fuck, how do you say 'get up' in French?"

"I only know 'Hände hoch.' Any chance these two are German?"

It takes all of Karen's strength not to burst out laughing as she imagines some poor German tourists meeting up with this guardian of peace whose only offering would be to tell them to raise their hands. It's 1988 in the rest of the world. In Russia, as always, 1945 is a mere memory away.

"Mademoiselle," says the first militiaman again, and mimes that she should get up. Karen complies. Emboldened by his success, the young man continues: "No, no, no..." his arms spread as far and wide as he can, to indicate all of the gently sloping square. Here he stumbles again. "Koroche, nelzya zdes sidet," he says in Russian with a French accent, hoping that it will help relay to these "Frenchies" the gist of his message: "In short, you can't sit here."

Karen nods, smiles at the boy and taking Luke by the hand leads him back towards the hotel. When they're out of earshot Luke asks: "Why were you crying?"

She squeezes his hand. How can she explain? What's there to explain? Staring straight ahead at the ugly monolith of the Rossiya Hotel she says: "I wonder what we destroyed to build this monster."

"Tears over lost architecture?"

"Architecture too. Did you know that when St. Basil's was built in the 16th century it was all white with golden domes? It took nearly a century more, before these new more intricate onion domes acquired their many colours. It's not the original design but I can't imagine it any other way."

"It looks garish, if you ask me." Luke is not impressed with her story.

"When Ivan the Terrible saw it, he was so amazed that he had the architects' eyes gouged out so that they would never build anything as exquisite again."

"Look on the bright side," says Luke. "At least he didn't cut off their hands."

"Who knows, he may have," she mumbles.

As they enter the hotel, the same doorman smiles at them. This time there seems much more cheer in his demeanour. The first thing they see in the lobby is Stanislav's pale face.

"Please sit down," he says through clenched teeth.

As they do, he hands them their passports. "How do you think you would have gotten into the hotel if someone asked for your papers, how would you get into your embassy if there was a need?" He is speaking in English but looking at Karen.

She rolls her eyes, "We walked around the corner to pay tribute to Uncle Lenin."

Stanislav is not amused. "What if something had happened?"

"What could happen? Nobody recognizes me as a Russian. I just had a militiaman try to address me in French."

Their guide looks confused: "You don't speak French."

"Neither did he. Anyway, as far as anybody here is concerned I am a foreigner. Nobody would dare ask questions."

"Give it time," says Stanislav.

~~~

He is right. Exactly one week passes, and the change comes. Suddenly the proto-businessmen on the Arbat stop harassing her with "Khello, laydee, you have Levee jeans?" and "I change dollar for good rate." Suddenly in the establishments for foreigners Luke passes and she is halted. Even her Canadian passport seems like a barely adequate defence. Did the Secretary of State for the External Affairs of Canada, who on behalf of Her Majesty the Queen requested that the bearer of this document be allowed to pass freely without hindrance, ever imagine that he was addressing restaurant security guards and store managers? Why are Russians suddenly not convinced of her foreignness?

The days of that first week had all been identical. So what has served as the invisible pivot?

~~~

They had commenced work on the production. They had conspired to get rid of Stanislav, whose presence at first was a mere nuisance— yes, an open-air heated swimming pool is an impressive feat of Soviet engineering, Stanislav, but why don't you tell us about the Cathedral of Christ the Saviour that had to be dynamited seven times before it crumbled, to create space for the swimming pool? Now Stanislav has become a hindrance—murmurings of underground clubs and illicit poetry readings keep melting away when Luke and Karen's ever-present shadow appears. But no snide remarks, sarcasm, unsubtle hints and polite requests can force their faithful guide to part from them.

~~~

Beginning work on "Fragments," however, has been worth the temporary KGB shackles. Her play, her words are going to be heard in one of Moscow's famed venues—the Lermontov Theatre, which Luke had procured during his previous visit to Russia. She is going to be working steps away from the Patriarch's Pond, one of Tolstoy's favourite meditation spots in Moscow!

Having satisfied all the requirements of the Union of Theatre Workers, which included a mandatory Sony double cassette deck for the Union's head of the Foreign Department, Luke and Karen have embarked on tweaking the official translation of "Fragments," interviewing designers, and casting the actors.

How fast she has fallen into the role her Pygmalion has chosen for her! Their days are spent watching the words born in her imagination eventually becoming solid, three-dimensional. In the evenings they attend complimentary performances in theatre spaces consecrated by Stanislavsky, Tairov, Chekhov, Meyerhold. An unknown theatre student just weeks before, she is now a rising star in the birthplace of modern theatre!

~~~

Day seven in Moscow. The day when that mystical boundary into Russianness is crossed. Over the years she will examine it carefully to pinpoint that moment. Over the years several possibilities will appear as likely catalysts.

They enter the theatre by 9:00 a.m. as usual. As usual, the space, lit by prosaic house lights, reminds her of an old whore caught in the glare without her make-up. Karen sits between Luke and Stanislav, partly to use every opportunity to annoy Stanislav and partly to allow Luke to concentrate on the auditions without having to listen to Stanislav's running commentary: "I suggest you pay attention to the next actress… Very talented this one… He is not too bad, I think… He was a hit last season in… You cannot be serious, this one is an embarrassment…"

After several faces come and go, reading lines with the AD, reciting monologues or poetry, a hopeful for the role of Tolstoy enters the boards. The man's appearance is haggard. Thin, drawn face. Heavy bags under his eyes. Clothing hanging off his frame. Strands of greying hair, once thick, now scraggly and carefully combed over a bald patch. It is his eyes Karen recognizes at first. Then when he begins reading lines, his voice too. It forces Karen to the edge of her seat. Both Luke and Stanislav seem to be surprised by her sudden excitement. "Isn't it Bozhenov?" she whispers.

Stanislav nods, frowning.

As Bozhenov reads his lines—half memorized, for he has prepared diligently for this audition—Karen sees another face superimposed on this old man's features. A handsome face staring out over sea waves, as his ship sails towards the horizon. Bozhenov played the Count of Monte Cristo around the time when she first read the book. She fell in love with the noble and brilliant Edmond Dantes and she fell in love with his cinematic alter ego, the handsome and gallant Nikolai Bozhenov. Her first love. She fantasized about growing up, going to Moscow and meeting him.

Now she turns to Luke: "He is going to be my Tolstoy."

"As long as you're sure." Not much to object to. The audition is brilliant.

She is about to throw decorum to the dogs and plant a huge kiss on Luke's lips when Stanislav intervenes: "No, no, no. Absolutely impossible! The man drinks."

"Everybody in this country drinks," says Karen, and Luke smirks.

"Not like that. He is unreliable. A real *alkash*."

Ah, one of those. A slave to the bottle. A victim of the "Russian epidemic."

Karen looks again at the man on the stage. He is now standing quietly. Eyes boring into the people in the front row. Asking for a lifeline.

"What if we talk to him, make a bargain, make him promise?" suggests Luke. He too has understood the prayer in Bozhenov's face. "The money should be a good incentive not to drink…"

This production, financed by foreigners, promises each actor ten times their usual compensation.

"I know he can do it. I know it in my gut," adds Karen.

Stanislav takes out his thermos and begins pouring himself some tea. It must be noon. Like clockwork this man has his snack at this precise hour. Tea and chocolate, which he claims he needs to eat because of his plummeting blood sugar. "A habit my mom got me into as a kid," he smiles and mumbles every time. Now, instead of the habitual phrase, he blows onto the surface of the dark brown liquid and states: "I advise against it. He might have been a decent actor once, but…"

Karen turns to Luke, anger constricting her throat, "What's in the contract? Who decides on the casting?"

"I do."

"In that case…"

Luke places his hand over her fidgeting fingers. "Don't worry."

"Thank you Nikolai Alekseevich," Karen breaks the ritual of the auditions and addresses the actor directly. "That was excellent! Please leave your telephone number with the assistant. We shall let you know by the end of the week."

She hopes that in her smile he can read her promise. And at that precise moment an idea occurs. Triggered, likely, by a silver wrapper she glimpses in her peripheral vision. A flash of sweet inspiration.

Catching Stanislav's wrist before he finishes unwrapping his chocolate, she smiles coyly at him. "How about sharing it?"

There isn't much to share. Before the look of alarm leaves his face, she adds: "Better yet, why don't we swap? I suddenly have a craving for Russian chocolate."

"Is it so different?" asks Stanislav, hesitant.

Karen pulls out a large bar from her shoulder bag, making sure that she removes the outer wrapper while her hand is still sunk in the bag's cluttered depths. Stanislav's hesitation gives way to anticipation.

She can almost hear his thoughts. *Sure it's said that Western chocolate is not as good as ours, but it can't be that bad.* Besides Karen's offering is much larger than his.

He nods his assent. An exchange is made. Karen bites into the chocolate before Stanislav can reconsider. He unwraps the thick gold foil from the foreign bar and examines the logo stamped into each small square.

"Ex-Lax?" he reads.

"Yeah, have you heard of Kit-Kat?"

He shrugs noncommittally.

"Well, this is the Canadian version."

Stanislav takes a big bite. A slight grimace contorts his lips before training composes them into a smile of gratitude. Karen winks at the Russian. He winks back. "Do you like it?" she asks, demonstratively biting into the bittersweet porous chocolate Moscow is famous for. Stanislav nods and after a gulp of tea crams another large chunk of the Ex-Lax into his mouth.

Karen wonders how long it will take him to digest it, plugging all the variables into the time equation—the amount of laxative eaten, the size of the man, the bullet-proof Russian stomach accustomed to being bombarded by much worse agitators.

It is another hour before they break for lunch. The whole bar of Ex-Lax has been gulped down with tea. Stanislav is still unperturbed. As they enter his car to go to a restaurant, Karen remembers:

"By the way, have you found out where to get Lenin's bust?"

Their KGB escort looks from one Canadian to another. "I thought you were joking." Then seeing Luke shake his head, he asks: "Why would you need one?"

"Not one," Luke joins the conversation, "twenty or so."

"Twenty Lenins?"

"For gifts."

Stanislav raises his eyebrows, "You have so many Communist friends in Canada?"

"You wish! These busts make great paperweights," Luke laughs in that unrestrained manner of his that makes sombre Russian passers-by turn their heads and hasten their steps.

Minutes later their car dives out from one of Moscow's narrow side streets onto what must be the vastest square in the city. Except in this one, pedestrians are relegated to narrow ribbons of sidewalks wrapped around the perimeters of the surrounding buildings. The enormous open space is a traffic turnabout, several lanes wide. In the middle of the constant stream of cars is an island with a giant statue on it.

"This," Stanislav pulls up to one of the buildings in the square, "is Moscow's Children's World. The country's biggest department store for children's supplies—clothes, toys and such. They sell Lenin's busts."

"Lenin is a childhood supply?" even Karen is confused, although she is familiar with the store. There is a Children's World in every city of this empire.

"He is educational material."

"And who is this?" Luke points to the gargantuan stoic statue in the middle of the square. "Lenin before he lost his hair?"

"That is Iron Felix," Stanislav replies and then clarifies with a hint of a smile, "Felix Dzerzhinsky."

Karen is rooted to the spot, knowing full well where she is now, staring at the yellow brick building behind this bronze despot. Luke, having done his homework on Russian history, needs no biography on Dzerzhinsky. However some things do require an explanation: "Why did they place a monument to the guy who founded the KGB in front of the Children's World?"

"Because that's KGB Headquarters," she points out the building behind the Iron Felix. "This is Lubyanka."

Technically it's the Dzerzhinsky Square, known as the Lubyanka Square before the Revolution, but Russians simply call it—Lubyanka. One word. Conjuring visions of a terror that for decades crept like a poison gas through Russia's nights. All caught within those fumes became either cripples, monsters, or memories. Russians joked that the Lubyanka instantly improved one's vision: from there one could see all the way to Siberia. Beneath this square, Karen takes in the vastness before her, beneath the ground they're standing on, there are tunnels and torture chambers, a labyrinth of terror.

Luke is still confused, "They built the largest children's supply store in front of the KGB? Why?"

Karen and Stanislav exchange glances of understanding. How do you explain? Can you explain?

"Russian sense of humour," Karen turns away from the men and walks into the store.

She approaches the first counter she sees—this one selling plastic green rocking horses—and asks where she can find a bust of Lenin. The saleswoman, not looking up from filing her nails, in a bored voice directs Karen to the third floor. Soviet customer service.

Rage begins to simmer as she takes the stairs two at a time: What would it take to shake them out of their complacency? That bronze Minotaur in the middle of the square and this woman, metres away, calmly doing her nails. *Thank God I am no longer one of them*, thinks Karen.

Soon she spots the desired location. A counter with two gossiping saleswomen who are ignored by milling crowds and who ignore the one, obviously stupid, foreigner staring at them. Behind them the shelves are lined with heads. Like a cannibal taxidermist's display. Young Lenin and mature Lenin. Bronze and plaster. A foot tall and smaller. The glass display of the counter illuminates more Lenin memorabilia—buttons, posters, banners, flags, postcards, booklets of famous speeches, biographies.

Karen smiles at the saleswomen, knowing that Russians are unnerved by smiling foreigners. One of them, a pudgy blonde camouflaged with an annual supply of rouge and eye-shadow steps forward hesitantly, preparing to do battle with her arsenal of four French words and two English expletives. Her surprise is palpable when Karen addresses her in Russian: "Would you please show me that bust of Lenin over there? No, the one to the right, the bronze one." As the blonde mutely hands her the bust, Luke and Stanislav catch up to Karen.

"Boy, did you take off running fast! Stan and I barely found you. Ah, look at all the Lenins," Luke's voice booms out and snags the attention of several passing shoppers.

"Will this one do?" Karen hands him the bronze bald head she is holding.

Luke bounces it in his hand. "Heavy enough. That's fine. Let's pay and go to the restaurant."

Karen turns to the blonde, who is even more confused by the foreign woman's male escorts. One, her husband she presumes, is a foreigner. Or is he? Can she be certain? Or are these two spies? But then, why are they accompanied by this third man, with such an obvious stamp of KGB approval on his demeanour?

"How much is this bust?" asks Karen.

"Six rubles, fourteen kopecks."

"You can't pay here," intervenes Stanislav. "The saleswoman will write you a slip, you go pay at the cashier and then come back here with a register receipt to pick up your merchandise."

Karen nods, remembering this routine of Soviet shopping. "So how many should we get?" she addresses Luke. "They come to about sixty-two cents each."

"Two dozen. Christmas is going to be fun this year."

Karen turns to the saleswoman again. "Please write me a slip for twenty-four of these busts."

"How many?" the saleswoman looks at Stanislav for support. Are these two foreigners on a day trip from an insane asylum? Their guide just shrugs.

"Did you say twenty-four?" the look of pity and incredulousness on the woman's face makes Karen laugh. *You're missing a few pieces from this puzzle,* she thinks. *You won't solve me.*

~~~

The laxative catches up to Stanislav's guts just as they are finishing lunch. Suddenly he blanches, excuses himself and runs towards the head waiter.

"Stanislav, we'll walk to the theatre or we'll be late for the next round of auditions!" Karen shouts after him and then, turning to Luke she beams, "Come on. Freedom at last."

"Do you know how to get to the theatre?"

"We'll find our way to the Kremlin and from there it's easy."

"How about catching a cab?"

"I lied. There are no auditions this afternoon and our meeting with the set designer is not until half-past five. Plenty of time. Let's go!"

Step by step, block by block, exhilaration replaces her anger. The ornate buildings, the street names, the histories are being grafted onto her senses, incorporated into her. They are losing their strangeness, becoming beautifully mundane. She begins feeling cajoled by this rumbling colossus of a city. *Don't succumb. You are not a part of this scene. You're invisible. They see you but they don't see into you. You, however, understand them perfectly.*

All over the city, when least expected, faceless modern architecture lifts its coat flaps to reveal hidden architectural gems. This section of Moscow, Zamoskvorechie, was least mutilated by Stalin's demolition crews. Here lovely old buildings abound. Turning the corner onto Bolshaya Ordynka, a road that used to lead out of Moscow to the stronghold of the Orda—the Mongolian Horde—they soon pass the Church of St. Nicholas with its silver onion domes, exquisite fretted cornices. Such beauty. Such ruin.

There once was so much splendour. Why destroy it? What prompts Russians to obliterate, to mutilate? She does not see the answer in the faces passing her. Just tiredness, just a resolve to suffer. So she taunts them. She taunts them because if she escaped, so can they. And someday, perhaps, that Iron Felix will fall.

She picks her "victims" randomly. When Karen inquires in flawless Russian how to get to the Kremlin, there is a split second of almost panic on their faces. Russians don't expect foreigners to speak their language any more than a Westerner might expect a stray cat to begin a discussion. There, in that split second when their bearings are rattled, she wonders what label they are affixing to her—an Intourist guide? A prostitute? A capitalist provocateur?

What clues are revealed to this woman? Early thirties, furtively eyeing Karen's strange outfit—Karen's high-waisted black jeans synch her like a corset and end at the knees, revealing her toned calves; a cropped red denim jacket; red high-top sneakers; a long mesh black scarf wound around her neck and trailing below her waist. Karen's hair is worn long. Moscow's breezes playing in the silky strands. Her make-up, uncharacteristically for Russia, is subtle, almost not there. Except for bright red lipstick. No Russian would dress like that, decides the woman. Definitely a foreigner. "Just continue on Bolshaya Ordynka. It will lead you right to the Kremlin Embankment," she mumbles. "Thank you, so very much." Karen smiles at her. Go ahead. Wonder. Am I so foreign?

Or this man—his reply is a wave of the hand in the general direction of the Kremlin as he lances Karen with an acrimonious look before lowering his gaze to his worn-out sandals over black thinning socks. What will it take to break through his defences? Nothing. If the Iron Felix will ever fall it shan't be for long. This man and his like will raise him again.

Soon Karen and Luke see the Kremlin's red walls, and before they know it they've passed Red Square—a familiar sight now. As they head up Gorky Street their discussion shifts from that morning's auditions to set design and costumes.

How apropos discussing this on a street that was so drastically redesigned in the 1930s. All buildings razed, the street itself widened by over forty metres. And then, Stalin ordered some buildings reconstructed just as they had been but in new locations. Others were replaced by modern apartment blocks. How different a world can look on a whim of a headstrong artistic director.

They pass an old man, who seems like a barely moving dirigible among the billowing throngs on the street. A cane in his left hand. Right arm missing at the elbow, his jacket sleeve sewn up. His sports coat is covered in World War II medals.

Luke slows down, turns his head and observes the old veteran's slow progress.

"What do you think of setting the play in a contemporary setting?" he says.

"Sure," Karen is not at all pleased. "While we're at it maybe Tolstoy can be unwrapping a Bolshoy Mac. I heard the golden arches are going up around the corner from the theatre."

"But it might work. Tolstoy is all in his head, in his ideas. Like this old man who is living in his memories."

"That's just it. Tolstoy at that point of his life is living in the future. The past doesn't much concern him."

"All the more…"

"No! It's way too unsubtle for Russians…"

"Ha! Russians and subtlety! Ha-ha-ha!"

Karen mock slaps him. He intercepts her wrist. "Paint your fingernails red."

"When?"

"Tonight. Come to my room wearing nothing but red nail polish."

"And if I don't?"

"You will."

"Hold it, Luke, what about Tolstoy? You've changed the subject."

"I always do what I damn well please." Suddenly Luke grabs Karen and hoists her over his shoulder.

The world flips upside down. The sidewalk rushes up at her—cigarette butts, cracks, shuffling feet, calloused hands carrying woven string *avoskas*—the "perhaps" bag carried by everyone, as in "perhaps I will find some food today". No faces, just snapshots of Russia.

Laughing now, Karen begs: "Luke, set me down."

Luke walks on, whistling. She knows the Russian crowds are parting for them. She can hear them grumbling. "Oh my… What is he doing? Get a load of her outfit. Foreigners, what do you expect."

A shrill militiaman's whistle sounds close-by. "Luke, we're going to get arrested. Set me down."

"Arrested for what? I'll tell them that I have an unruly girlfriend. Your shrieking will only confirm this."

He has never called her his girlfriend before.

"Luke, enough! I'm getting dizzy from hanging upside-down!" she hammers him with her fists.

"Hey, what did this guy do to deserve a statue?" Luke asks calmly and again the world spins, rights itself, as Karen is carefully lowered to the ground. Blood rushes out of her head; for a second everything goes black and quiet. She has a distant sense of Luke's arms encircling her, not letting her fall. Through the quietness she hears a voice. A child's voice: "Mama! Mama! Look, it's Pushkin."

Slowly light returns. Indeed they're standing in front of a monument to Pushkin—Russia's greatest and most beloved poet. Where did the voice come from? Karen looks in its direction and sees a boy, no more than five years of age, and with him… a young woman. But Karen can swear that she is looking at herself. At herself wearing a modest cotton dress with blue daisies and sensible sandals. An invisible vortex pulls her towards this woman who might be her twin, her sister, her alternate self who never left Russia.

At the same time she feels fear pressing her into the ground. Repelling her. Whispering for her not to look. It's an illusion! The eyes of the two women meet. But eye-contact in Russia is short-lived. Karen's Soviet twin turns away without a spark of recognition. For Karen, reality moves in elongated seconds of crystal clarity.

The young woman walks over to a flower vendor, carefully counts out several coins and is handed three white carnations wrapped in newsprint. "Mama! Can I do it? Please?" the boy is hopping from one foot to another, looking up at his mother. She smiles: "If you can recite something from Pushkin…" Before she finishes her sentence the boy stands still, raises his chin and proclaims:

> *An ancient oak upon a sea shore*
> *Around that oak a golden chain*
> *A learned cat, from eve till morn,*
> *Walks round the tree, by gold restrained.*

The mother ruffles his hair, hands him the flowers, and watches him skip up to the monument. Hugging the meagre bouquet, the boy clambers up the four steps to the base of the statue and gazing up at the poet he carefully places the flowers. Pushkin's face is bent down, as if looking back. Karen sees the boy's lips move but the hubbub of the street drowns out the words. The child then makes one more step towards the monument, spreads his arms and embraces the cold stone. A plump cheek pressing into the granite, eyes closed.

And suddenly Karen knows what the boy has been whispering. She knows it as certainly as if she had heard it. It could be only one thing: "Mama, he smiled at me."

No, not all is lost in a country where in every city monuments are erected to writers and where common people, unprompted by holidays or television cameras, spend their hard-earned kopecks on flowers to honour those, who have forever touched their minds with beauty. "He smiled," whispers Karen. She saw it.

summer snow

To L.N.T.

The second time I glimpsed you seems even less real. But all of it seems like a dream: the youthful sense of harnessed time, my two Russias—the lost Russia of my childhood and my adult Russia, the Russia of my greatest loss.

A dream, then. Why not? I dreamt you, as I dreamt my success, and the smell of greasepaint and sawdust in the theatre during rehearsals, and the flights back and forth between Toronto and Moscow. I dreamt it all and I am still dreaming.

~~~

It is the first week of June, 1989. I am alone in Moscow. My business in Russia is over but I have extended my stay on a whim.

I tell myself that my idle strolling through these streets has a purpose. I'm recording life in this changing Russia. A Russia of discontent and empty store shelves. A Russia of crumbling structures and a populace looking for meaning and hope. A Russia where government-run street kiosks still offer communist propaganda leaflets and pins with hammers and sickles, but the subway underpasses are filled with budding private enterprise—young men peddling cheap icons—postcards decoupaged onto wood—and worn copies of Playboy.

My observations are coalescing into a new play. I even have a few scenes jotted down.

~~~

A face from that dream. A man's face—rosy-cheeked, lined. White clumps of thin hair stick out from under his grey doorman's cap. He should be in some distant village, carving wooden roosters for his grandchildren, or downing glasses of vodka while exchanging war stories with his only remaining friend. Instead he is here, in the middle of Moscow blocking my way into the building, staring at me with disdain. I have business inside. My friend, Olya, who has given me a lift here, has nervously grabbed my upper arm.

I step closer and reach for the door handle. The man's obsequious smile, also part of his uniform, remains on his face as he hisses at us, *"Kuda poperlis'? Nu-ka valyaite devki. Zdes' tol'ko dlya inostrantsev."* His rudeness makes me stumble. *Where the hell are you going? Go on, scram broads. This is for foreigners only.* I've instructed Olya to keep quiet no matter what transpires, so when, after a moment of indignant silence, I remember my own role of a blissfully ignorant foreigner, I smile and say in English, as if I hadn't understood, "Oh, hi, I have to go to the Canadian Airlines offices to change a ticket. They're in this building, aren't they?"

Usually English works like "open sesame," oiling the squeaky rusted cogs of Russian hospitality. This grey man is not so easily flustered, though. "May I see your passport and ticket, please?" he demands in flawless English without missing a beat, politeness forced through his clenched teeth. Olya's grasp tightens on my upper arm. He examines the proffered documents for a long time. I'm not worried. I really have nothing to worry about. To me this is only a micro power struggle. A test of my acting skills. Olya begins shivering, gently tugging me away. Finally he steps aside, but as he opens the door for us, he scowls at me and says in Russian, "go on, pretend all you want, but I know that you understand Russian perfectly well." Once we're out of his earshot I giggle to release the tension, "His English was really excellent."

"Sure," says Olya. "He is third generation KGB."

~~~

This is another segment of the dream.

"What's this queue for?" asks a middle-aged woman in a blue gingham dress. She has just taken her place in a human chain stretching from a basement store all the way around the block. After receiving her answer she says, "Uh-huh," tucks a loosened strand of bleached blonde hair behind her ear and now settles into the uniformity of the waiting shuffling snaking mass.

I'm observing this from a bench in a tiny square. It is a tucked away corner of central Moscow—could be somewhere on Ivanovskaya Gorka, Zamoskvorechie or Arbat. My legs are stretched out, relishing the warm afternoon sun. I'm on my second ice cream of the day. The sweet rich milky flavour is straight out of my childhood. As is the setting—the park bench with its peeling green paint, the smells of exhaust fumes and the hot asphalt of the sidewalks, the shade of a linden tree, the apartment buildings with sloping 19th century rooflines and ornate cornices, the open windows with pink, white, black drying laundry, the glass sign of a bakery with the "b" missing, a haberdashery with a permanent "Closed For Restocking" sign, an office supply store with a dusty globe and an antique typewriter in the window. A tiny church with unassuming grey domes, dwarfed by the surrounding buildings. And the long heaving, grumbling, slithering, mutating, thousand-faced snakes that are the ubiquitous human queues of Soviet Russia.

These unending lines are traps. Catching passers-by before they are aware of stopping. There is one, shuffling along, black socks peeking through worn brown sandals, clutching his briefcase held together with electrical tape. He crosses the street and walks into the tail of some queue. He stops, never once lifting his head. He shuffles in place for a few seconds as if his feet have not yet caught up to the command of his brain—*stop, goods have been "tossed out" at the distant unseen end of this human file.*

Tossed out. That's a peculiarity of the Soviet lexicon that is, most likely, the first to be forgotten by us, émigrés. Goods don't enter the marketplace in the USSR, they aren't "sold," but, in the proper lingo, are "tossed out" to the ravenous masses. People don't claim to "buy" things but to "procure" shoes, tomatoes, frozen fish, children's winter coats, pork, onions, bookshelves. A nation of scavengers.

Finally the man looks up, and without addressing anyone in particular asks the question that one hears uttered in high and low, tired or shrill voices, days, mornings, evenings in all the cities of Russia—

"*A chto dayut?*" Literally, *what are they dispensing,* or, in other words, with what have the mighty rulers decided to bless us proletarians once we fulfill our solemn duty to waste one or ten more hours hobbling along towards the dream reward of… "oranges," "toilet paper," or "calf liver." Once he hears the answer he never leaves. Even if he doesn't need the "Mongolian high-heeled boots" he'll buy a pair and then sell it to a friend, an associate's wife, a neighbour.

Lulled by the steady rhythm of the "A chto dayut?" I watch the queue move at a brisk pace. At the other end of the file, the end hidden in the basement store, they're meting out cheese. There used to be many different types of cheese—the Swiss-like Sovetskiy, the salty string-cheese Sulguni, the nutty mellow Gollandskiy, the creamy Kostromskoy. But now food supplies are scarce, a rationing system has been reinstalled for the first time since World War II, and variety has become an unnecessary luxury. A generic "cheese" has been tossed to the people and they queue up, grumbling that before long they'll be trading their rubles for three hundred grams of nonspecific "food."

The swift pace, I know, can be explained by an absolute lack of anything else in the store and by the arbitrary pronouncement of the salesperson that is passed down the line like a judge's sentence: "No more than half a kilo per person." This queue will disperse only after the supply runs out and angry voices will confirm to the unlucky hopefuls that there indeed is nothing else to wait for. Then the uniformity of the queue will shudder and sigh and break up into its individual components—each regaining his or her face, fate, direction.

I once again see the woman in the blue gingham dress. She has just emerged from the basement store, and slipping her new oil-spotted paper package into her string *avoska* she crosses the square. I watch with interest.

She stops in disbelief. Another file of people, and only steps away from the one she has just successfully navigated. What luck! She finds the end of the new queue, positions herself and once again rearranges her packages before finally lifting her head and asking, "What's this line for?"

"Baptism," mumbles the young man in front of her without turning and embraces his girlfriend. The woman in the blue gingham dress looks around, bewildered for a moment, and realizes that this line leads to the front door of the church. "Uh-huh," she says and, tucking an escaped blonde tendril behind her ear, settles into the homogeny of the queue.

~~~

The scenes from my dream: the doorman with the face of a simple peasant who speaks such perfect English; the shopping list that includes buying cheese and getting baptized. Glimpsing you happened among these scenes. One more stroke on the canvas of that distant dreamland.

~~~

Night. The steps of the Moscow Art Theatre. I am saying goodbye to a group of friends. We had just watched a new production of Three Sisters.

The weather is balmy; the streetlamps lend a quaint nostalgic atmosphere to these old Moscow neighbourhoods; I decide to forego the subway and to walk to the apartment the Theatre Union is renting for me. Moreover, the streets at this time of year are covered by what the locals call "summer snow"—white fluffy poplar seeds. To me it seems magical. The warm air, the green trees and these white ever-shifting weightless tufts blanketing lawns, caught in the filigree of the wrought iron fences, twirling in the playful breezes.

I tie a scarf around my shoulders against the playful gusts of summer wind and extend my bare forearms, delighting in the soft poplar "snow" brushing against my skin. My gypsy skirt billows in the breeze. I'm glad that I didn't wear heels. Now the rubber soles of my espadrilles render my footsteps springy, light. I feel like one of the poplar tufts, about to take flight, present and not on this Moscow sidewalk.

My thoughts, however, weigh me down. I had had a very disheartening meeting that morning with one of Russia's most eminent playwrights. After an hour of hot tea and small talk he got down to business.

First it was the business of trying to place his hand on my ass with studied nonchalance. When I, courteously, told him that I was hoping to get a serving of advice without a side of sex, he got down to the business of destroying my ego.

Page by page he analyzed my new play and laid bare the mediocrity of my supposed talent: characters converge on stage but their relationship doesn't grow; observations are trite; philosophy is unnecessary; the dialogue is stifled. The whole annihilation took ten minutes or so. It felt endless.

He ushered me out of his apartment with a long tirade that basically amounted to "your writing is as overwrought and useless as Chekhov. And yes, young lady, in my humble opinion Chekhov's plays are overrated. The Emperor's new clothes. Now his short stories are a different matter..." His voice trailed after me as I ran down the stairs.

What if I don't have any talent? The thought haunted me through the day. If I can be "as useless as Chekhov" I could live with that. But what if I'm a one-shot-wonder? By the pond outside the Novodevichiy Convent I looked over my notes. Scenes that had seemed quite good only the night before now appeared awkward and amateurish. I called a girlfriend and begged her to get me tickets to see some Chekhov production. And so we ended up in this theatre, on this lovely early summer night, watching Three Sisters.

Scenes from tonight's production emerge in my memory. Do I have any talent, I ask myself for the umpteenth time that day? One thing I know for a fact—Chekhov did have it. And yes, Chekhov is usually botched on the stage, but his talent is unmistakable. I compare tonight's Three Sisters to all the productions of the play I have seen in Canada and the States. Chekhov's popularity in the West baffles me. They know it says "Comedy" but they can't find the key to making it funny. Chekhov in the West is either forced slapstick or meandering melancholy. I always suspect that people stage him because they've been told that Chekhov is a genius, but I've never seen a justification of that label until tonight. Chekhov is laughter through tears, abandoned mirth after downing a bottle of vodka. Comedy in a minor key.

But what if my creations are simply off key? Or worse yet, Muzak? I must stop obsessing, I tell myself. If I can analyze Chekhov, I'll be able to learn. If I can learn, I'll be able to improve. If I improve, perhaps someday I'll know for a fact whether I have talent. Chekhov, Chekhov, Chekhov—what's the key to Chekhov?

If Chekhov's plays were melodies, in the West they'd be staged with full orchestras, blasting out the lines in full symphonic outburst. But Chekhov should only be performed on a single piano with one hand, gently tapping out the notes.

I imagine that hand on the black and white keyboard and when the fingers descend I hear once again the leitmotif of Three Sisters—Moscow, Moscow, Moscow. The city symbolizes childhood idealism, and yearning, and unfulfilled dreams.

As I navigate Moscow's maze of streets, it strikes me that Chekhov must have imagined a Moscow very much like this one with its buildings still warm from the day-long sun, its mature trees, ornate streetlamps spilling ochre puddles of light, the white poplar tufts falling like giant snowflakes, the horse-drawn carriages lining up along the sidewalk...

Carriages?!?

I stop. Where am I? I must have taken a wrong turn somewhere. Nothing looks familiar. Except the white poplar seeds that have stopped their whirling dance and are now suspended in mid air. Of course they can't be suspended, I tell myself. It's an illusion. The wind has died down. They appear motionless because the air... Well, the air does feel more humid. It is permeated with a fresh scent I hadn't noticed before—linden and something else, something musky. The night seems darker. The light from the streetlamps is different. It flickers, imparting a quivering life to shadows. I'm not afraid. Moscow is a safe city. I'm just disoriented. I try to recreate my steps. I went up Gorky Street, then through the arch to the quaint Bryusov Pereulok. I remember the neoclassical building of the Conservatory on Gertsen Street where I turned towards Nikitskie Vorota. But then... what streets had I taken? And how long had I been walking?

The street before me is abandoned. The city is inert. Its motorized pulse of automobile engines has disappeared. A faint piano melody rises from the silence and floats over the low rooftops. In the distance a dog barks and is echoed by other dogs. Every one of my footsteps resonates with a dull thump against the ground. Like a heartbeat. Otherwise the entire world seems asleep. Even the horses look like they're sleeping. I am about to approach one of the carriages, hoping that a coachman might help me find my way back, when from behind a wooden fence I hear a sudden burst of laughter. It's muffled at first, then a door bursts open and laughter splashes out into a courtyard that must be on the other side of the fence.

I can't see the gate, so I cry out, "Excuse me!" but my appeal is drowned out in another wave of laughter. Then a voice rings out. A voice that trumps all the other voices and my heart somersaults. I heard this voice not too long ago in a small bookstore on a street lined with cobblestones.

Once again I have somehow found you amid our disparate times.

I press my face to the smooth wooden planks of the fence, trying to catch a glimpse of you. The sharp earthy aroma of pine resin envelops me. On the other side of the fence I see a house. Light falls from its windows in long amber rectangles. A crowd of men is on the front porch. In the dark, the lit ends of their cigarettes are coppery bopping moths. I try to discern which of the men is you, but against the brightly lit doorway the people are anonymous silhouettes. All I have to guide me is your deep measured voice.

"Agafya Mikhailovna, our housekeeper, has had trouble sleeping for as long as I've known her," you say, and everyone grows quiet, hanging on to your every word. I don't dare interrupt. "She has always described her insomnia as a birch tree," you continue. "A birch tree that is growing from her belly, spreading out, pressing against her chest, hindering her breathing. And the other night she says to me that she was lying in bed, all alone, feeling the birch tree spreading its branches. All was quiet and only the clock was ticking as if repeating: What's life… What's life… What's life?"

A man on the porch shifts, turns his face towards the light. It's you: the same beard, the same unhandsome but unforgettable face. Ilya Repin, the painter, once said that it seemed to be roughly hewn by a zealous axe, but the summary effect of its plain, crude features was so interesting that after glancing at it, even for the briefest moment, all other faces appeared forever boring. You continue, "When Agafya said this I began to think: What is life? And I spent the whole night thinking about it."

"My, my!" someone replies. "We have another Herzen in our midst."

"Herzen?!" someone else picks up and laughs. "Nay, we have Socrates."

"Have you heard about Beltsev's latest escapade?" shouts a third voice. "It's positively precious. You know his passion for attending balls. He never misses one, especially at court. So he goes to a grand ball all decked out in a new helmet. Have you seen the new helmets? They're fantastic, much lighter. So he is standing around… well, to make a long story short, the Grand Duchess is passing by with some ambassador or other, and, as his ill luck would have it, they begin discussing the new helmets.

The Grand Duchess wants to demonstrate the new design, and what do you know, Beltsev is standing right here. The Grand Duchess asks him to hand her the helmet, but he doesn't. Everyone is in utter disbelief. What is he doing? Everyone is winking at him, nodding, grimacing—go on, give it to her. He doesn't. He is frozen. Can you imagine? Then, what's his name… well, he tries to take the helmet. Beltsev won't give it up. So it's yanked out of his hands and given to the Grand Duchess. 'This is the new model,' she says and flips it over. And out of it—can you imagine?—plop a pear and candies. Two pounds of candies. Beltsev had stashed them in there from the table, the rascal."

After the laughter dies down I hear the strain of another conversation. You're speaking again, and I catch the latter part of your response to an unheard question: "… and therefore it is a grave mistake thinking that something beautiful can be senseless."

The air around me has acquired a texture, a soft yielding density. My movements, the shift of hip, the twist of neck to get a better view are slowed down by this concentrated air. My very breath seems suspended in resin, and the only life, the only movement in the world is over there where you are, in the patch of light behind the fence.

"But first and foremost there must be purpose in art," says another voice, obviously belonging to a very young man. "It must explain, unravel…"

You interrupt, "It is not an artist's duty to irrefutably solve any issue. His aim must be to rouse a love for life itself with its countless permutations. If I were told that I could write a novel in which I would irrefutably prove some social viewpoint that I hold to be true, I would not dedicate even two hours of effort to such a novel. But if I were told that what I write today would be read by today's children, say twenty years from now, and that they would cry and laugh over its pages; that they would grow to love life through it, then I would dedicate my whole existence to such a project, all my strength."

"Twenty years from now?" Someone whistles. "That indeed would take talent. Do you think you're up to the task, Lev Nikolaevich?"

"Talent?" you guffaw. "Do I have any talent compared to modern literary masters?"

A horse neighs, startling me. I turn towards the sound, suddenly aware of the booming racing beating of my heart. When I again look through the fence boards everyone has gone back inside the house. All is dark on the front porch. Dark and quiet.

My forehead aches from pressing so hard into the wooden surface of the fence. Your last phrases permeate the white flurries of poplar seeds, the scent of resin, this whole amber-tinted night before dissolving in silence: "Do I have any talent compared to modern literary masters? Absolutely not."

stage notes

LIGHTS COME UP *on KAREN sitting downstage. She is surrounded by old books and as she talks she builds a structure— stacking books one on top of another—creating a rickety house of books.*

KAREN: You doubted your talent infrequently. And you vehemently protected the fragility of that certainty. Had you met Luke Garson, I wonder whether his talent was great enough to touch your jealous streak. Would you, perhaps, have challenged him to a duel, like you once did Turgenev? It was all your ego's doing.

(TOLSTOY enters)

By the time you entered St. Petersburg's literary circles, Turgenev, a decade your senior, was widely considered the greatest living Russian author. This shy, soft-spoken man with exquisite European manners and extraordinary erudition took you under his protection. You were flattered by his attention. You were also exasperated by it. He was your match and you couldn't handle an equal. Your journals at the beginning of that long contentious friendship are so revealing. You sound like a capricious lover. On February 7th, 1856 you wrote...

TOLSTOY: Had a fight with Turgenev.

KAREN: February 10th

TOLSTOY: Had dinner at Turgenev's. We're friends again.

KAREN: March 12th

TOLSTOY: I believe Turgenev and I have parted ways once and for all.

KAREN: July 5th

TOLSTOY: Turgenev has arrived. He is a completely discordant, cold and difficult person and I pity him. I shall never befriend him again.

KAREN: October 28th.

TOLSTOY: I have read Turgenev's Faust. Charming

KAREN: November 10th

TOLSTOY: I read all of Turgenev's novellas. Horrible.

KAREN: And you know what Turgenev always said about you? "I have grown to love him with a strange, paternal kind of affection." Turgenev was known, to his last breath, to be your staunchest supporter, announcing to everyone who would listen that your work is the future of Russian literature. How did you repay his love? You insulted him on his methodology of educating his daughter, calling him a hypocrite because "a little rich girl mending the clothing of paupers is a farce." He called you a genius, you called him a bore. You picked fights. Wishing to preserve your friendship he apologized for infractions he wasn't aware of committing. You called him a coward and challenged him to a duel. It's a good thing you realized in time that it would be a sad day for Russian literature if two more of its sons ended their careers with a bullet match. You recanted on the duel but didn't talk to Turgenev for 17 years. And all for what? Ego.

(Karen stands up, tugs on a book at the bottom of her structure and the whole thing collapses.)

You would never again allow your ego to be perturbed. You would never again allow yourself to get close to another person whose talent's magnitude even remotely approached yours. When Dostoyevsky came onto the literary scene you refused to meet him. Instead of dealing with your ego, you suppressed it, but during the writing of Anna Karenina, your ego exploded. From then on, instead of writing fiction, you became obsessed with creating a religion. At some point between creating the woman you loved on the page and pushing her under the wheels of that train you stopped being a writer and started being a prophet. Were your physical urges easier to deny this way?

TOLSTOY: I can no longer do artistic work, just like I can no longer play with toys.

KAREN: On his deathbed, Turgenev wrote to you.

(TOLSTOY takes a letter out of his pocket and reads.)

TOLSTOY: "I write to you actually to tell you how glad I was to have been your contemporary, and to express my last sincere request. My friend, return to literature."

KAREN: The letter broke off in the middle of a line: "That's it. I'm tired..." were Turgenev's final words.

TOLSTOY: I keep thinking about Turgenev. I do love him, and I am so sorry... I keep reading him. I've just re-read his Notes of a Hunter. It is somehow difficult to be a writer after him.

KAREN: But the writer in you is precisely what he loved. That's what he begged you to be. But you were too far gone. By then you were hell-bent on achieving divinity. Alas, you no longer saw it as hypocritical that you, a man with the blood of princes in his veins, a man who spoke seven languages fluently, a man who owned lands and people, would dress in rough burlap garb and ramble through the countryside, carrying on philosophical conversations with bewildered peasants. All too often we become caricatures of our fears.

blindsided

To L.N.T.

I WROTE SOMETHING last night. The words escaped in a flow of anger and pain. If I hadn't had a piece of paper I would have carved them into my desk, or smeared them on the wall with my lipstick. Cherries in the Snow, my favourite lipstick. Red on white:

> *I have not touched the when of that affair. The when of conversations through the night, of endless solitudes colliding. The shadow he trod on, the former "I," has been suffused with light of him-less memories. I've been unwrecked by others.*

It was an exorcism. The emptiness left by the escaped words filled with peace. But why this outburst, you ask?

Remember Robert, the second AD I told you about? During the production we had begun to hang out, going to an odd movie together, sharing a coffee in Loz Feliz while listening to impromptu poetry readings—pleasant, non-obligating stuff. Robert had never made a sexual move. He must have felt the boundaries within me and skirted them, offering only kindness. I had started to relax into a belief that I might have made a friend. For the first time in years.

Last night he invited me to a wrap party for some movie he'd worked on. We didn't stay long, the schmoozing and the limelight-grabbing too incongruent with our need for tranquility. After the required round of smiles and shaking hands with everyone Robert and I headed for the door. Since the party was on Melrose there would be no shortage of restaurants for two people to have dessert and a cup of tea. Once we were out in the cool air of the Los Angeles night, the comparative silence of the street swathed me. I stopped, relishing it. The sidewalks were almost empty. The purr of engines from passing cars was as relaxing as sounds of cicadas after the stifling noise of human swarms.

"I want to give you something," Robert said, pulling a wrapped package out of his canvas messenger bag. It was obviously a book. "The title character reminds me of you."

I didn't like where this was going and I didn't know how to stop it. He spoke faster and faster, as if fearing that I might disappear before he finished what he had wanted to say. His blond surfer-boy hair glistened under the street lamp as his head bobbed to the rhythm of his words. "It's not that she just reminds me of you, it's like she is you but somehow imprinted in literature under a different name."

Somehow imprinted in literature, is a silly phrase, I thought. He folded my fingers one by one around the package. "Open it. Please." My fingers obeyed the gentility in his voice.

Before I could turn back the time it was before me. Your "Anna Karenina."

The book itself might have been fine. It was the words that Robert said next about me and Anna.

"She has your essence," he said.

With this phrase the *when* of a distant affair indulged, again, upon my life. The when of *Him*. The echo of a similar conversation. Then the end of *Him*. What happened? Banality. The unthinkable made solid. A party. Heavy drinking. Cocaine. Maybe heroin. He had said that he needed some air. Stepped out onto the balcony. No, I cannot ever think of him again. I don't want to do this. Instead…

excerpts from a heartbreak

LIKE TRANSPARENT BLOOD, red light fills the hotel room. Her naked body is submerged in it. The clock ticking, her beating heart—the only sounds she is aware of. That and a growing scream within her: Enter me! God damn you Luke, enter me! But her lips don't move. Her throat remains parched with silence.

It's a game Luke Garson likes to play. She has no choice but to follow. She has to lie still, voiceless, apathetic, as he does whatever he wants to her body. Whatever, except the one thing she craves. His whatevers are exquisite, practiced, but she is forbidden to surrender into enjoyment. If a glimmer of it appears on her face, an involuntary sigh of pleasure, Luke stops. Leaves the room.

The first time he did it, she laughed. It's a joke; a man needs sex, he'll soon tire of this, she believed. But Luke needs his games more than plain sex. Or perhaps the plain variety he is getting elsewhere.

It is usually thoughts like these, thoughts of anger that stop her from yielding to the movements of his tongue and fingers. If she can only hold out! It *has* to happen tonight—it's Valentine's Day.

She has failed to be his perfect marionette for eight weeks now. For eight weeks she has been discarded by her master, only anguish entering her. No! Don't think of it. Concentrate on something, anything, like when did it begin? When did she miss the first sign that the road with Luke Garson was going to be Misery Lane?

~~~

September of 1988. A week after they returned from their first trip to Russia, Luke was leaving again. This time to Montreal, where he was to work on a new production at the famed Centaur Theatre. The telephone rang on Friday morning.

"Meet me in the lobby of the Royal York at noon," Luke's voice gave no hint of a request. A romantic tryst in one of Toronto's most glamorous hotels before separating from her lover? She wouldn't think of declining.

"Wear that red miniskirt and fishnet stockings," added Luke.

In the gilded lobby of the hotel, dodging the disdainful looks of the Royal York's starched and prim clientele, Karen searched for Luke.

"May I help you, Miss?" The concierge with a pseudo-British accent and without a hint of British politeness tried to edge her closer to the door.

"She's with me," Luke materialized from behind a gargantuan vase of flowers, and, grabbing Karen by the forearm, manoeuvred her outside. "Where are we going?" Karen's fantasy of down pillows, champagne, and chocolate-dipped strawberries was vanishing behind the smirking porter boys.

Luke didn't reply as they crossed the street towards Union Station—Toronto's central railway hub. Finally, when they passed the towering limestone columns that in 1927 made the Prince of Wales exclaim during the opening ceremony, "You build your stations like we build our cathedrals," Luke pulled out a train ticket. "You're coming with me for the weekend."

"But I haven't brought anything with me," objected Karen.

"We'll buy whatever you need in Montreal."

The rhythmic rattling of the train wheels carried them further and further away from the downtown skyscrapers. And as the bland monotony of suburbia began flickering past the windows, Luke handed her a gift-wrapped oblong box. She flushed, not used to receiving jewellery from men. Inside was a pair of wire-rim eyeglasses. Clear lenses. "I don't get it," Karen looked up at Luke.

"Try them on."

"I don't need glasses," Karen objected while doing as he requested.

Luke smiled, obviously pleased with his choice, "They make you look studious. Just the right touch. I want the cast and crew to take you seriously."

"You don't think the fishnets and my staying in your room will give them a different idea?"

"You're not staying in my room."

~~~

She learned then that Luke Garson always rented two adjacent rooms. "I need breathing space to work," he explained. He needs his lair of unmolested independence, she now realizes. Her eyes are fixed on the red silk kimono draped over the lamp. She wishes it would catch fire— anything to break through this slow torture. The ticking clock is driving her crazy. Why had she agreed to come to Montreal with him again? Still hoping for an introduction to his mother? "She's too Canadian—all ice and white bread. You won't like her," Anoush had warned.

~~~

Anoush. Three months into their relationship Luke picked Karen up, wearing a tie and looking somewhat nervous. "I want to introduce you to someone tonight," Luke said. "This person is very important to me." Karen speculated who it might be: His children? His ex-wife? A theatre producer?

It was Anoush, a crusty old Armenian woman. His self-appointed surrogate mother. They had met when Anoush was a music instructor and Luke Garson a theatre student at the Royal Canadian Academy of Dramatic Arts. What Luke loved about her was her unwavering sense of self. Anoush had survived the genocide in Turkey at the turn of the century. She had never seen the need to assimilate into the bland Canadian politeness.

"How are you, Miss Apparently-Brilliant-Playwright?" Anoush greeted Karen in the foyer of her Cabbagetown bungalow and stood on tippy-toes to kiss Luke on the cheek. "And don't you dare utter 'fine' or I'll kick your skinny little ass out. I mean, really, how are you?"

Luke's glance told Karen that the hostess wasn't kidding. "Hungry," Karen hoped that would pass for an appropriate response. "And terrified," she added.

"Hmm..." Anoush gave her the once-over and again turned to Luke. "At least this one's got tits and a personality. Unlike that cold fish you used to hang out with."

~~~

The cold fish was Lettie. More snake than fish. An eel, perhaps. Lettie—a professor of theatre history, the mother of Luke's younger daughter, Grace.

Luke was married when Lettie slithered out of her mouldy university moat and into his life. Under the pretext of doing research for a scholastic treatise, she fed Luke's ego. When it was sufficiently bloated she confessed that her biological clock was ticking and since there was no man in her life, would Mr. Garson agree to donate his illustrious sperm? Oh, no, blush, blush, she wasn't averse to the traditional method of insemination. She would be discreet and she would never ask for child support.

When Grace was born, Lettie called only once, to inform Luke that to honour him, she had given their daughter his mother's name. Seven months passed. Then Luke came home one day to find Lettie sitting on his front steps, the baby in her arms. His wife was in the living room, crying, trying to stuff her ski-jacket into a suitcase overflowing with photo albums, shoes, and her grandmother's lace tablecloth.

Lettie had shown up an hour before, claiming that a fire had destroyed her apartment, and that she had no place to go with the baby. She asked to stay for a couple of weeks until she would find new accommodations. Luke's wife didn't need to ask why a strange woman wanted to stay in her house. She took one look at the little girl and she knew.

"Don't even bother denying it," his wife screamed. Luke tried to calm her down. He tried explaining that she was overreacting. This woman would stay for a few days, where was the harm in that?

"Why can't she go to her friends, her relatives?"

"Her family is in Vancouver. Look, she is writing a book about me. I can't just throw her out."

"That's what I figured. She can stay all she wants. The children and I are going to my mom's."

Lettie swore that causing a family fight was the last thing she wanted. This was temporary, she promised Luke. Lettie was certain that his wife would come to her senses and return.

Weeks turned into months. Finding an apartment in Toronto proved an impossible task for Lettie. Luke's wife filed for divorce. Lettie stayed in the house to lick his wounds. Her search for an apartment permanently abandoned.

Luke moved out of that house two years later, right after he and Karen came back from their first Moscow trip. He claimed that his relationship with Lettie had been platonic since she conceived Grace, and that they had lived together purely out of convenience. "But it's time for a clean start," he said as he showed Karen around his newly leased condo on the Lakeshore.

~~~

How happy she had been the first time they made love on the floor of that apartment amid stacked boxes, empty bottles of Upper Canada Lager, and Styrofoam containers of hot-and-sour soup. The scent of lemongrass mixing in her nostrils with the musk of their sweat.

No, no! Can't think about sex. If she shudders-squirms-sighs now, it's over, he'll leave. And she has held out for so long this time. Perhaps a few more minutes. "Do as I say," he tells her, "and you'll get what you want." Perhaps tonight…

Think of something horrible. Concentrate on the red light and think of blood. Imagine the tragedies happening right now somewhere. Who knows, maybe on this very street. People howling like wolves, shrieking like hyenas, wailing like the Polar wind. If she tries she can hear them. They are on the periphery of her world, in the pulse of this city beyond the windows. They are the fibres of her nightmares. There! An ambulance siren. Someone, somewhere in pain. Like she had been that night. Strange, almost a year has passed.

~~~

How nightmares begin… The dialling of a telephone number.

As she did so, she thought that she would always remember this date. March 8, 1989. *Good portent,* she noted—*International Women's Day.* She was calling Luke, asking to see him. He also had a pressing issue to discuss. They agreed to meet in his apartment.

She hadn't felt well all day—cramping, cold sweat. She changed her outfit four times, finally settling on a long corduroy skirt and a red cashmere sweater. Luke liked her in red. She rehearsed her speech in front of the mirror for an hour. She would never get a chance to utter it.

That night, while the skyline of Toronto with the famous tower glittered in lieu of stars against the black sky, she stared at Luke. Tears burned her eyes, blurring his face. Can words hurt? Oh yes, they hurt exquisitely. Scorching pain. Her one hand on that throbbing knot in her stomach, her other hand flailed behind her seeking a wall, a chair, anything for support.

"Did you hear what I said?" his voice was very even. Unbearably calm. Yes, she nodded, she had heard. She had stepped through the door, noticed the bottle of Scotch on the coffee table and had time to wonder why he was still standing with his back to her, looking out the window.

She walked up close behind him. "What's wrong, hon?" She smiled, wrapped her arms around his waist.

"This relationship is over," he said and only then turned around pushing her away. Karen felt nausea and something imploding in her stomach.

"I don't ever want to see you again," he continued. That pain! Like a hot knife stabbing again and again. Bile was rising in her throat. Between shallow, hurried breaths, more barbed phrases reached her: "not my office…" "don't telephone me…" "behind my back…" and "your career is over" but none of it made sense.

"God-damn, you made me look like a fool!" suddenly Luke's voice was shrill. The bottle flew past Karen, and disassembled shards rained down the opposite wall. "Silent now, are you? Afraid to admit it to my face? Why? You've been saying it all over town! Just using me to get into the business? Beating the aging—what did you call me, libertine?—at his own game?"

It was a nightmare. The floor was spinning. The air was too pungent with malt. Karen's legs felt like they were deflating. She would have fallen had she not grabbed the back of the couch and slowed her progress to the floor. She wanted to tell him that this was a preposterous lie. She wanted to ask him who said all this, but there was an invisible hand on her throat. It only let out a hoarse: "Who?"

"Lettie."

That woman had treated Karen with contemptuous chill the one time they had met, but Lettie had nothing to do with theatre. Not with the live, passionate business of theatre! She was a mortician embalming dead productions in some university dungeon a city-space away. She didn't know anybody who could have... Suddenly everything made sense. The grip on Karen's throat was released. Words flowed. Words, and anger and righteousness.

"Lettie? Lettie?! Have you considered that this useless amoeba's social orbit has never intercepted mine? Where would she hear something like this? From whom? How could you have believed her?"

"She has no reason to lie," he was less certain now. How fragile his ego, but, oh, how overbearing his egotism.

"No reason? Are you daft? You're ready to destroy me, us, because that thin-lipped bitch..."

"She respects me. She only has my best interests..."

Karen didn't let him finish. "Respect? Where is my respect? Have I ever asked you for introductions, for help, for sponsorship, internship, nepotism?"

Silence. Karen forced herself to stand up. Although the twisting knife in her gut was making it difficult to breathe, she stepped towards Luke. "It was you who contacted me," her finger jabbed his chest, "you who needed my play, you who seduced me!" She took a deep gulp of air, trying to calm her voice. "And you believe the ranting of that pretentious, stale..."

"She would never..."

"And I *would*? Think about it. If I were using you, would I be stupid enough to brag about it?"

"I'll sort it out."

"Lettie is a lying slut!"

"She's the mother of my child, so watch your mouth!"

Another thrust of pain. "I'll call that dried-up pallid cunt whatever, whenever..."

Luke slapped her. It must have been hard because she would have a bruise on her jaw for days. But at that moment she didn't feel the pain on her face. The impact of his hand made her body lurch, stumble backward, trip over a rug and fall.

She wanted to rise; she wanted to leave, to slam the door. Her sense of dramatic structure demanded this next action, she even flashed on a great exit line. Something to the effect that "libertine" was a word used by Lettie's generation, not hers. But life doesn't follow neat dramatic structures. Comedies become melodramas and farces turn into tragedies within a blink of an eye.

Karen had managed to get up on all fours but every movement caused the vice of pain around her stomach to tighten, driving in that blade, which had replicated and was now a claw of daggers. She prayed just to reach the door, she didn't want to be anywhere near Luke. Something warm was trickling down her leg. She opened her mouth to say "help me up," but all that came out was a scream. And with it, she couldn't control it, more warmth was flowing down her legs, the trickle becoming a stream.

The pain obliterated vision, sound, touch. The pain was a whiteness, an almost oblivion. Almost, because later she remembered some images that had seeped through. The red and white flashing lights of the ambulance. Blood streaks on Luke's shirt and a red hand print. Hers. The doctor's first words: "I'm very sorry."

~~~

Why has she taken him back? Because he cried, sitting hunched over like an old man on her hospital bed? He whispered "forgive me" over and over again. He kissed her so tenderly. He said that they could have another baby together. "Please," he said, "you must take me back. You must!" Why did she not walk away when she had the chance? Because she wanted to finish the work on Fragments with him? Because she loves him? She loves him. Doesn't she? She loves watching him sitting in a darkened theatre, biting the tip of his pencil as the actors try on shades of personalities, explore scenes. "Hey, Laura," he jumps up, "why don't you try…" and then, like magic, with a subtle flick of his one idea the elements of the scene line up, the thoughts of the playwright rise to the surface, actors become breathing characters, and Luke, he smiles sitting at the edge of his seat. Two facets of his personality coming through in that smile: a kid on Christmas Eve, ready for the magic and the surprise, and a god, pleased with his creation. Now he won't even let her watch the rehearsal process. Says she is too distracting. Even dynamite couldn't distract him from the rehearsal process. So why, why, why when their relationship was just beginning to mend did he not take her to Calgary back in October? She'd never been out West…

~~~

Time trickled so slowly while Luke was away. For two days she barely got out of bed, surrounded by characters out of 19th century Russian novels—the only friends who could abide by this listless rhythm. Not even all of them. Raskolnikov, too busy with his own neuroses, begged to be put back on the shelf, and Prince Myshkin was too cerebral in his desires. But Vronsky understood. He longed for Anna with every fibre of his soul. He fought for her to the bitter end. Vronsky, Karen decided, is one of the most misunderstood characters in Russian literature.

When she tired of reading she attempted writing but nothing was coming out. She hoped that pacing, which felt like crawling from wall to wall, would spark an idea. She had to come up with something. She had to prove to Luke that she wasn't a one-shot-wonder.

She didn't want to think about the abandoned draft of her new play, "Uncast in Stone." It seemed promising but when she showed it to Luke, he shrugged it off: "Try again. This is trite."

Is that why he hadn't invited her to Calgary? Was he disillusioned with her?

The telephone rang. It was Anoush inviting her over for dinner.

"Luke is out of town."

"Did you hear me invite Luke? What, are you two attached at the groin? Just come over to have some food. Keep an old woman company."

It wasn't Anoush who opened the door when Karen knocked. It was a man whom she had never seen before. A man who took her breath away. He was tall and lean. "Angular" was the word that came to Karen's mind when she scanned his face. His hair was long, once black it was now streaked liberally with silver, although he couldn't be much older than forty. His goatee outlined a sensuous mouth and Karen forced herself not to look at it, to concentrate on his eyes. Black pools a woman could drown in.

Anoush peeked out from behind him.

"Come in, you're letting in the cold. This big oaf is my godson Vahe Pogosian. You'd think he would have introduced himself by now instead of just blocking the doorway."

Why did that name sound familiar?

"He is Luke's best friend," Anoush volunteered with a sly smile.

"Luke never mentioned you," Karen blurted out. "I mean, he has never mentioned a best friend in the city." Why was she flustered?

"I live in Montreal and he has certainly mentioned you." Vahe's voice was a baritone with gravel mixed in. A voice that grazed her skin.

Where did she know his name from? The question continued haunting her through dinner. A dinner during which Anoush took centre stage, recounting stories of her life as old people are wont to do when there is a willing audience.

"The Turks dragged my sister Tamar out of the laundry trough where my mother had hidden her. I didn't know it at the time but my mother was already dead, her hacked-up flesh lying at the bottom of the ravine, two feet away from our dog whom the Turks beheaded. There was nobody to stop the soldiers. My sister was a big girl, nine years old and she kicked and shrieked as they pulled her by the hair into the middle of our yard. Her hair was long and shiny like a raven's wing. It was her pride and joy. An ugly man with a big red scar on his cheek hit her on the face with the butt of his rifle. He hit her so hard that his fez fell off his head and rolled towards the tree where I was clinging to a branch, trying to melt into the bark. I prayed that nobody would look up, but I needn't have worried: they were too busy with Tamar. She was no longer wiggling as they threw her to the ground. Her lovely black hair spraying into the dust and chicken shit. They tore her clothes off, laughing. I thought how ashamed she would be afterwards. I thought that I shouldn't look, but I couldn't force myself to turn away. They spread her legs and the ugly man sprawled on top of her and bounced several times. Then another, and another kept lying on top of my sister and bouncing. When they were finished, the ugly man leaned over Tamar and made a movement like slapping her. Then he walked away and a ribbon of red bloomed on my sister's neck. I thought it was a present the scarred man had left her for lying so still while they bounced on her."

"You were four at the time?"

"Almost five. I learned the lesson of loyalty when I was almost five. Loyalty is as important as love. Perhaps it is the flipside of love. My sister could have given me away. She didn't."

"And all your relatives perished?"

"All but my uncle Vartan. I found him in the relocation camp…"

Karen and Vahe had heard these chilling stories before and their thoughts were free to wander with only a rare interjection. Their eyes tried hard not to connect. Yet every time Karen glanced at his face she got a distinct feeling that it belonged on a Byzantine icon—high cheekbones, narrow aquiline nose—not in downtown Toronto. He made her uncomfortable.

After dessert Anoush begged off. "But you kids stay on. Have fun. I have a bottle of nice cognac in the pantry."

They drank watching the dying flames in the fireplace, saying nothing.

Karen broke the silence first: "Why didn't Anoush tell me you were here when she invited me?"

"Anoush likes throwing people into the mix without warning and then watching what develops."

"So what conclusion did she reach tonight, do you think?"

Vahe shrugged. "You were staring during supper," he touched Karen's arm and she recoiled, jumping up. To cover up her awkward reaction she put another log in the fire and returned to the couch.

"Yeah, I couldn't decide whether you should model for an icon of Jesus or Saint Gregory."

"Why not John the Baptist?"

"There is too much mischief in your eyes."

"So what's the verdict?"

"Saint Thomas."

Vahe laughed, "I can see why Garson is so smitten with you."

"So smitten that he chose to go away for a month without even inviting me to visit him."

"He is afraid of you."

"Afraid? A grown man afraid of a girl half his age? No, I'm his typical mid-life crisis honey."

"There is nothing typical about Garson and there is nothing typical about you. He is afraid because he is in love with you. In love for the first time."

If that was true, Luke had a funny way of showing it. Karen shook her head, trying to dispel images that proved anything but love.

"Believe me," Vahe leaned towards her and reached for the bottle that she had placed inadvertently almost out of his reach. "Garson's told me himself."

She was flushed, whether from Vahe's proximity or from what he had just revealed. "I guess Luke is very selective about what he says and to whom. Like why has he been hiding you from me? Also afraid? Whatever he said about love is a pile of bull."

"It's the cognac talking. I'm sure you love him too. It will just take time to iron out the glitches." Vahe smiled. An infuriating smile. A smile that forced her to look at his lips; forced her to consider what would occur if she only moved two feet closer to him.

"What are you, a shrink?"

"I'm a priest."

Karen felt a cold draft, gulped down her cognac and got up to draw the draperies. Anoush hated to wake up knowing that strangers might have looked into her house at night.

"What kind of church lets you wear your hair this long?"

"I've taken a leave of absence."

The clock on the mantle showed five minutes to midnight. Still plenty of time before the subway system shut down for the night.

"When did you take a leave of absence?" Karen sat back down but somehow ended up much closer to Vahe than she had intended.

"Fifteen years ago."

"Spiritual crisis?"

"Addiction."

"Women or wine?"

"Theatre."

"You're an actor?" He was handsome enough, though not Karen's type at all.

"No. I tried directing, but I wasn't that good at it." And then, after a pause as if confessing something that might diminish him in her eyes: "I'm a critic."

That's why the name was familiar! She had read his articles but for some reason she always presumed that Vahe was a woman's name. Karen suppressed a giggle. This six-foot body in faded jeans, a tailored sports coat and cowboy boots was one hundred percent testosterone! Nobody could mistake him for a girl.

Their conversation began flowing freely as they discussed the differences between the Montreal and Toronto theatre scenes, the universal phenomenon of misunderstanding Chekhov, argued whether Michel Tremblay's plays would ever gain popularity in the States, what with their themes of incest, homosexuality and the like, and speculated whether Anne Marie Macdonald would ever write anything to rival her Goodnight Desdemona (Good Morning Juliet). And somehow she ended up lying down with her head in his lap, and him softly stroking her hair. When Karen looked at the clock again it was past two a.m. and the bottle of cognac was empty.

"I guess I'm crashing here tonight." She felt neither drunk nor sleepy.

Vahe offered her the guest bedroom. She considered it for several moments but a bedroom would present much temptation and little room for retreat. She declined and curled up on the couch, away from him, becoming acutely aware of the absence of his scent.

He brought out a quilt and tucked it around her. They were friends now. There was no reason why she shouldn't have taken pleasure in his gentle touch. As he turned to leave she grabbed his hand, "Don't go yet. Let's talk some more."

He looked at her for a long time and then, twisting his hand out of hers, he said: "If you were dating anyone else, anyone but my best friend, I'd kiss you right now."

"Priests don't kiss women."

"Priests don't kiss and tell."

~~~

The humming of the radiator brings Karen back to her less-than-satisfying present. Damn Luke and his penchant for Victorian bed-and-breakfasts! The red light, the monotonous crawl of minutes, and now the annoying sound. Her clitoris is sore from too much friction. No sign of Luke ever letting her surrender into enjoyment. Anger is percolating, held back only by fear of losing their potential happiness. "Happiness?" she almost laughs at this folly. Is that why Anoush introduced her to Vahe? Could she have wanted Karen to leave Luke? But leave him for his best friend? And then there was that odd thing she said the next day when Karen woke up to find that Vahe had already left for the airport: "Vahe is very loyal, so tread carefully. He is like a son to me," was the reply to Karen's flippant "Vahe is a good man," which was meant to elicit gossip.

Was Anoush's remark a threat or an admonition?

"Luke is also like a son to you, right?" Karen asked.

"I love them both. But Luke is like a wolf and Vahe is like a dog. You understand?"

Karen nodded. Then Anoush handed her a folded piece of paper. A note: "If you're ever in Montreal..." followed by Vahe's address and phone number. Over the next weeks, while Luke was in Calgary and she aimlessly crossed the empty days off the calendar, Karen memorized Vahe's note as she replayed "their night" over and over in her head. In her head, she allowed herself to inundate her face in his hair, to trace her finger over his lips, to allow his long fingers to trace her body. She almost called him so many times, but always chickened out. That night, if she had dared one tiny gesture she would now have a delicious secret stored in her memory. Instead, just a note: If you're ever in Montreal...

Suddenly Karen hears a sound that makes her shudder. Laughter. And it is not in her head. It is coming from her, spilling out of her guts, out of her lungs, out of her mouth. Her body is racked with laughter. How stupid can she be? She is in Montreal. And this game of Luke's has gone on long enough.

"You moved," Luke rolls away from her and gets up. "That's it for tonight. Game over."

Karen also jumps out of bed. "You bet it is," she begins pulling on her sweater.

Luke, about to exit her room and go into his, as he always does when she "loses" this game, now halts, watching her by the door. "Where are you going?"

"None of your business."

"It's three in the morning. Get back into bed."

"I'm done taking your direction, Mr. Garson."

"You don't know this city; you don't know anybody here," Luke grabs her by her forearm as she passes him. "Get some sleep and we'll talk in the morning."

"I'm not in the mood for sleeping," Karen yanks her arm out of his grip. "Or are you going to convince me with your fist?"

The February night in Montreal is so cold that the air seems solid. Shards of crystal, not oxygen, scrape her lungs. The full moon has a halo around it. Toronto, Luke had once remarked, is a city where the bars are open from 4 p.m. until 1 a.m. and everybody thinks about money; Montreal is a city where the bars are open from noon until the last customer leaves and nobody thinks about money. Karen walks aimlessly through this city whose pulse is barely muffled by the nocturnal tides. Her initial resolve is frozen by indecision. What if Vahe has a wife, a girlfriend, a boyfriend? What if he is not home? What if, what if, what if…

She stops and looks around. Across the street is a hotel with a row of taxies in front of it. What has she got to lose?

~~~

Vahe opens the door, wearing a bathrobe. His long hair is dishevelled—a silver and black mane around his perplexed face.

"May I come in?"

He steps aside to let her in and she waves the cabbie off.

"You look like hell," are the first words out of his mouth. God, his voice—deep and soft and raspy—it abrades the ice from her cheeks. They burn and the warmth begins to spread through her body.

"You want a drink?"

She nods but neither of them moves. She can't because this is as far as her plan goes. Beyond is a looming reality she doesn't know how to leap into.

"Karen, stop crying. What's wrong?"

She is not aware of crying.

"Is it Garson? Has something happened?"

Ah, yes, the warmth on her cheeks is water. Salt water that now trickles onto her lips. "I can't stand it anymore," is all she is able to squeeze out before she feels her throat constrict and a wail rise like bile—a histrionic reaction that she so hates in females. She turns away. Faces the wall of his hallway, so that he doesn't see her face contorted. She attempts to control her body but it trembles from suppressed sobbing.

His hand is on her shoulder.

"Hey…"

She should turn around, smile and ask for that drink. Her body refuses to cooperate. The tears flow harder.

"Come on, look at me. It can't be that bad," Vahe's arm encircles her waist. He pulls her away from the wall, manoeuvres her around and embraces her, whispering all the while that "everything will be okay." She wants to bury her face in his bathrobe, the terry-cloth feels good on her skin, but instead, somehow, he shifts or she miscalculates, her face slips through the opening, resting on his bare chest. At that very moment, Vahe kisses the top of her head and in response, without thinking, she also kisses him. She kisses the skin that is under her lips.

And then, because he doesn't shrink back, because the faint scent of musk is intoxicating—she does it again.

He steps away now, but his hands remain on her shoulders. Their eyes lock, the unspoken conversation more tangible than any words. He unravels her scarf, unbuttons her coat, and still their eyes are connected.

"Come on," he says in a half-whisper as he takes her hand. "I'll get you that drink now,"

She leans into him, tilts her head up, attempts a smile and Vahe kisses her. He kisses the tear trails on her cheeks, and gently tastes her lips, and this moment, the first in months when Karen has felt desired and desirable, does not feel like betrayal. Her body tingles with long suppressed pleasure.

The night falls into a slow rhythm. The clanking of glasses filled with rye whiskey, the murmured conversation, the unhurried exploration of each other's bodies. An exquisite sexual meditation. There is time to savour the foreignness of accepting another man into her, time to imprint the unfamiliar sensations onto her synapses—his body fits hers differently; their scents mix into an alien perfume; the touch of his hands trails electricity over surfaces that are used to another charge and pressure; his voice doesn't demand performances from her, doesn't order her to scream in gratitude when she climaxes. Vahe nurtures and whispers her beauty and cradles her away from fears and pain.

It is dawn when she curls up in his embrace and feels the last kiss on her neck.

They are awakened seemingly immediately by insistent banging on the front door. The clock reads 7:07 a.m.

"It's Garson," says Vahe after glancing out the window. "Please stay here," he kisses Karen on the forehead. "We'll figure out what to do, but I don't want to hurt him..."

She nods, pulling the blanket up to her chin. In the light of day the repercussions of their night don't seem so clear.

"Bro, I'm sorry to barge in on you like this," Luke's voice booms through the house, words stumbling over one another. "I'm afraid Karen has left me. I was going to… fuck, it's Valentine's Day and she just walked out. I stayed up waiting for her, but she's gone. I need a drink."

"Calm down, you've had enough to drink." Vahe's voice is almost inaudible and Karen has to strain to hear. "I'll make us some coffee."

"She probably took the first train back to Toronto…" Luke's voice trails off and becomes a burble as they move into the kitchen. At first snippets still reach Karen—"don't understand" and "can't lose"—but soon Luke takes a cue from Vahe's calm timbre and she can make nothing out.

She watches the sky grow lighter and lighter, ice-encrusted branches tapping the window—a grey-on-grey world. She cannot sleep, her heart is pounding. She cannot very well go into the living room for a book. She notices a manuscript on Vahe's nightstand and reaches for it.

The title page says: "Through Angel's Eyes." And underneath: "A play by Luke Garson." Luke's handwritten note scribbled on it: "Give me your honest opinion. My agent says it's great. I want to workshop it at Stratford next season."

As Karen reads, curiosity turns to disbelief and then to ice-cold anger. This is her play. This is "Uncast in Stone," the one he had called "trite." The bastard has plagiarized her work and didn't even bother to rewrite her best lines!

Anger is a brief lunacy, but while in its grip Karen dresses hastily, grabbing Vahe's sweatshirt, which hangs down to her knees. Her own sweater is probably in the living room. A few minutes before she would have worried about Luke spotting it. Now, script in hand, she marches into the kitchen.

Silence. Both men stare at her in shock.

"Karen!?" Luke's face is as pale as the frigid dawn light.

"Anoush introduced us. You were in Calgary." Vahe's voice is almost a whisper. His eyes don't leave Karen's face. As if there he might find the reply to her betrayal.

"How could you?" Luke turns to Vahe.

"How could you?" Karen shoves the manuscript into Luke's face. He glances at the title page and turns a shade paler.

"It's not what you think…" Vahe and Luke say in unison.

Karen doesn't see Vahe. Her eyes are filled with disdain, aimed at Luke. Vahe grows quiet. Luke continues: "Often two writers come up with the same thing. Ideas float in the ether…"

"Ah, so this trite little idea floated around in the ether begging to be snatched up? In the middle of a snowstorm a woman, obviously hurt, shows up on a reclusive man's doorstep. As they talk through the storm, the story of his transgressions comes out. And we gradually learn that this woman is an angel—but is she an angel of death or an angel of redemption? That is up to the man and how he treats her. What a common story!"

Vahe looks from one to another, comprehension and disbelief mixing in his expression.

"I was going to give you credit, Karen," Luke's voice is tired. Suddenly he looks old. Much older than his forty-six years.

"Really? I don't see my name mentioned anywhere."

"You slept with my best friend. I think we're even."

"We're far from even, Mr. Garson."

stage notes

THE STAGE IS *fully lit. KAREN and TOLSTOY are sitting at the table, facing each other.*

KAREN: So I said: we're far from even, Mr. Garson. And then…

TOLSTOY raises his hand, stopping her.

TOLSTOY: It is necessary to destroy without sentiment all the passages that are too long, lack clarity or simply don't belong. In other words, cut anything that is not satisfactory in the whole context even though in and of itself it may be good.

Sound of shattering glass. Then footsteps crunching over glass shards. The curtain falls. Dead silence. KAREN steps out from behind the curtain, comes up to the very edge of the proscenium.

KAREN: You are right. Again. As usual. Enough about Luke. Let me condense the rest of the tale. Luke begged me to "be reasonable," and let him make amends by putting my name on the play along with his. I was firm. He had seven days to give me written proof that the play has been pulled from Stratford's Young Company where it had already been accepted for workshopping next season. Otherwise both he and the festival would be hearing from my lawyers. I also told him that my friends at the Toronto Star would love to get their hands on the scandalous details of Canada's theatrical darling caught red-handed in plagiarism.

"What am I going to tell them at Stratford?" he pleaded. I liked the supplication in his voice. Vengeance is sweet.

"I don't care."

Within a week he complied. I never learned the details. Just knew that he was fined for breach of contract. He began drinking. We saw each other less and almost exclusively in preparation for the next round of work in Moscow, or while pretending to be a happy couple at social functions. We did look good together and the press loved us.

I also made sure that Luke knew all the particulars about my submitting "Uncast in Stone" to several theatres in Toronto— Tarragon's Extra Space, Passe Muraille, Factory Theatre. It was eventually accepted by a company that was relatively young at that time. Necessary Angel. Now it is quite synonymous with groundbreaking productions.

Luke never congratulated me.

I feel guilty about Vahe. I tried calling him. He never returned my calls. I wrote him a letter of apology. It went unanswered.

stage notes

THE CURTAIN RISES. *A section downstage is lit. In the lit section, there is an old wing chair—The fabric is worn, its colour indeterminate, with pale outlines of what once might have been flowers or vines. The wooden legs are intricately carved. A few feet away is a large free-standing mirror. Behind the mirror, a "soft wall" of scrim runs diagonally across the stage. Behind it everything is dark, so at the top of the scene the scrim appears opaque. KAREN walks to the chair and sits down.*

KAREN: The window in my bedroom affords the loveliest view from my apartment. The small side yard of our building. Tall bougainvillea hedges and a camellia tree, heavy with pale pink flowers. And far, far away, visible only when the air is free from smog, which is rarely, the tops of three skyscrapers on Wilshire Boulevard.

A few months ago, in a thrift store on Fairfax I bought this wing chair. It looks like an object from the nineteenth century, though it might be a reproduction. I'm not an expert. I placed this chair under my bedroom window and now like sitting in it when I have no idea what to write. I sit there often. From time to time I glance in that mirror over there. I adjust my posture and imagine myself sitting in a similar chair but in a different century.

(As KAREN continues talking, lights gradually begin to come up behind the scrim, revealing a dark shape.)

Today is a day like so many others. Empty of meaning. I have not been able to add a word to it. I observe the neighbour's children playing hopscotch under the camellia. The little girl, Leah, stops, balanced on one foot, and looks up. Her eyes meet mine. How mature she seems. Infinite age in a small body. And compassion. How different from those children I grew up with.

Those of my generation are the fucked up ones. The fallen stumbling ones. Born amidst morality's collapse in the '60s, growing up in the fantasy land of the '70s, coming of age in the hedonistic '80s, maturing in the neo-puritanical '90s. We are fucked up and we are dreamers, knights errant who dismember paradigms and reinvent individual certainties. Unlike these children's generation. They are the enlightened, the unfettered ones. They enter a world where Jesus Christ and Kafka are two sides of the same coin and Einstein is sitting on the throne in the lap of the gods. Their reality shimmers with shattered slivers of truths. They are to weave something we can't quite see yet.

Leah smiles at me and resumes hopping. Her smile hurts me. The smiles of prophets must have the same harshness.

I miss you.

(At this point the lights upstage behind the scrim are bright enough to make it almost transparent. Through its gauziness the figure of a man can be seen. He is leaning on an object that appears to be a chair.)

I turn my eyes to the mirror and concentrate on blurring the periphery of my vision. I invite the haze to move in until it covers my face, my body. I have no use for my own reflection. The chair is good. It's an anchor. I will myself to dissolve in the mirror. I'm summoning you. This chair should feel familiar. It might even be an object found at your house. I stare at the glassy surface and push everything else out of my sensory perception. The breeze flowing through the window slows down. The clock's ticking grows distant, then silent. I stare.

Eventually a shape begins to appear in that mirror-chair. It wavers and solidifies. First a hand, then a dark sleeve. I follow the details, not rushing them. Appear at your own pace.

(The scrim rises. An amber light washes over the dark male figure—it's TOLSTOY. He is leaning on the back of a chair. It looks identical to KAREN's but the fabric is brand new.)

There you are. Still and solid on the other side of the mirror. My own world however, has lost its certainty. It flutters, begs my attention, beckons me back. I shake it off, staring only into your eyes. They shine so brightly. Like grey-blue water.

Thus we look at each other. I'm afraid of speaking, keeping up the concentration of seeing you is all the strength I can muster. I hope my eyes transmit my need for camaraderie.

(TOLSTOY walks around and makes himself comfortable in his chair. His hands cross, fingers interwoven, under the chin. When he speaks his voice is quiet but every word reaches the audience as if etched in the cottony silence of the stage.)

TOLSTOY: I haven't seen you in a long time and I especially enjoy our meetings when I am in my winter mode, which I am entering now. The creative juices are beginning to flow. I keep setting out receptacles for them. Whether the juices are good or bad, it doesn't matter. It is utterly joyful to let them course through me during these long, wonderful autumn and winter evenings.

KAREN: How delightful, this reality of you. There was a time when I could predict every word, every sentiment you would express. But now! Every meeting is a surprise—when I need your commiseration you force me to face a fear head on; when I expect a rebuke you are gentle and understanding.

TOLSTOY: There comes a point in every composition where we, the writers, stop inventing the characters and begin simply recording what they do and say.

KAREN: Like that time with your game of solitaire? You had stopped gambling years before, but continued indulging in the small tinge of guilty pleasure afforded by a good game of solitaire. It helped you think when you worked on a story, you said. One evening, as usual, you were spreading the cards, considering the principal question of your "Resurrection." Your wife happened to walk in and joshed you about your dedication to the *Devil's deck*. "I'm not playing cards," you said. "I'm deciding my characters' fates. If I win, Katyusha Maslova will marry Nehlyudov."

TOLSTOY: If I win, Katyusha Maslova will marry Nehlyudov. Yes, I remember that. "Once a gambler, always a gambler," shrugged my wife. Later that evening she asked, "So, did you win?" Yes, I replied. "So they will get married?" No, I said. "Why not?" Sofia Andreyevna was genuinely surprised. (TOLSTOY laughs.) You see, I told her, once a character is born they become real. As real as any person living on the Earth, except their Earth is the page. The author can only record a character's action and comment on it. The author cannot command characters what to do or not to do.

KAREN: So if you understand this, then you must know why I am stalling. Right now this tale still lives in possibility. One more step and it enters inevitability. And with it—pain.

(TOLSTOY walks downstage and stands before KAREN. The bright light makes his face at once luminous and ruthless.)

TOLSTOY: Go deeper into your pain to surpass it. You have to bring yourself into the condition of a child or Descartes and tell yourself: I know nothing, I believe in nothing and I want only one thing— to grasp the true essence of the life I have lived and which I still must live.

KAREN: And if I lose the remaining wisps of faith?

TOLSTOY: Writing is the best prayer.

KAREN: All right. I'm scratching the scabs off. But be warned. Once He enters my memory's stage other things will fall into the wings. They will have to. Other events will stop mattering, will almost cease existing. Only their shadows will touch down as markers of passing trickling life. See? I'm procrastinating, weaving a verbal veil to hide from the glare of Him. From that bog, that intoxication, that... No, no. Just a man. Did you know that Russian theatres are always filled with flowers? Are they in your day? Flowers after the performances, flowers in the dressing rooms… Again procrastinating. Oh, here goes nothing. Luke and I were in Moscow. It was… Gosh, we went there so many times I'm losing track now… First in '88 for casting and production meetings, then December of '88 and spring of '89 for rehearsals… That was a difficult trip—right after the miscarriage. I stayed in Russia longer to sort my thoughts out, to be away from Luke. That summer we worked on our relationship, and then when Luke returned from Calgary we went back to Moscow for more rehearsals in November of '89, so this must have been our fifth trip. A few weeks after that disastrous Valentine's Day. Spring of 1990. I had no more illusions about Luke. I was there only for the final round of rehearsals for "Fragments." I mustn't forget the flowers.

(Blackout.)

such stuff as dreams are made on…

Early May. Moscow. Spring still uncertain of her hold on this ancient city. The air sometimes yellow with sunshine, sometimes colourless, tired, surrendering to the sulking rain and the short-tempered wind. Karen's mood reflects this ambivalence. It's their fifth trip to Russia and the relationship between her and Luke has deteriorated into a pseudo-polite nothingness. He is probably too busy to observe the formalities of breaking up. She is too superstitious to do it before the play's opening. But Karen feels a peace here in Russia. A peace that doesn't exist in Canada. A part of her regained. The city's wide boulevards are awash in familiarity. It is a different flavour of familiarity. Not at all a prelude to assimilation. She is a foreigner in Russia. She no longer shares its gripes and its sorrows. She will never again partake in its pain. Yet only through her foreignness can she appreciate her closeness to this land.

Having earned her nostalgia, she basks in its opiate rays as she strolls through the sounds, the almost intimate speed of this city. She loves this land with the greatest devotion a foreigner can afford. She loves it more, for she knows that she will leave it. Geographies of the heart, however, are harder to map. Unwittingly she ventures into uncharted territories on that May evening.

~~~

Alla, their stage manager, invites Karen and Luke to a production at one of the new "studio" theatres—the budding movement for theatrical freedom and a beacon of political change. This one features a recent addition to their troupe—an actor who had begun his career with the illustrious Lenkom Theatre but was lured away to this new establishment by a promise of risky roles and unlimited theatrical exploration.

"Is the show any good?"

"It is different," says the Russian. Still afraid to commit: the Soviet Union is dying but not yet dead.

Luke refuses to go. He scoffs at Russian theatre. Like all Westerners, he is enamoured with Stanislavsky whereas so much of modern Russian theatre has outgrown Stanislavsky's realism and embraced Meyerhold's symbolism. Only in symbols can truth live on the Soviet stage. Luke does not understand this. He doesn't try to.

Karen has begun to see through his genius that is all too involved in its own greatness. The self-consuming, self-centered self-adulation. She imagines his evening. Alone with his tape recorder, glorifying for posterity the day's anecdotes and his directorial trials in this country where promises are given out freely but fulfilled only once upon a miracle, or a powerful political connection.

Months before Karen wouldn't dream of spending an evening away from Luke Garson; now it is a welcome respite from the tension of their togetherness.

He must feel that tonight will forever close the door on the two of them. Painful words lead her out the door. She slaps him instead of a good-bye. He slams her against a wall. Hand raised to slap her back. Her eyes challenge him. Go ahead. Hammer out your own demise.

Does he hit her? She doesn't remember now. She doesn't remember leaving the apartment. She doesn't remember the subway ride to the V.I. Lenin State Library where she is scheduled to meet up with Alla.

Her memory begins to clarify as she stands in front of the stone effigy of Dostoyevsky. Hunched over on a bench, uncomfortable, he too must be pondering the irony of being erected in front of the USSR's State Library, which might have borne his name but instead sports the name of one ultimately responsible for the deaths of so many writers.

The outlines of Karen's memory become more solid as Alla appears, another subway train is boarded and unboarded and they join the stream of an eager crowd coursing into the basement of an apartment building in Moscow's South-West borough.

She finds herself in a small makeshift theatre. A perfect modern space—a black box. Everything—ceiling, floors, brick walls, rafters, light casings—all painted a matte black. Black folding chairs. An almost empty black raised platform—the stage. Almost, except for a backdrop of black torn-scorched scrim.

She looks around and notices no fire exit, no safety precautions. Why does she do that? Why does she not succumb to the swell of urgency, the heedless need to drink in theatre? Why is she thinking of practicalities? Is this a precognition of imminent disaster?

Murmurs hush. The play begins. Hamlet.

With detached amusement she watches the first scene. She has never liked it. The tiresome and confusing "hark" this and "who goes there" that. The unlikely and crude introduction of the ghost. An element of the supernatural that suggests a mystical play but never delivers on the promise.

Tolstoy, she remembers, hated Shakespeare. He thought the playwright was tedious and grossly overrated. Once he told Chekhov that his playwriting was as bad as Shakespeare's. Tolstoy knew of no worse criticism. Chekhov was elated.

For the first time now Karen is watching Shakespeare in translation. The archaic words usually demanding concentration suddenly too clear in modern Russian. A disorienting, un-Shakespearean experience.

Shakespeare is language. Certainly there is no surprise in the plot lines after almost four centuries. His plays are familiar maps from one famous line to another. Shakespeare allows millions to join the hallowed theatrical rite. There is a thrill of dissolving in timelessness within a darkened theatre, within innumerable rising whispers in rhythm with the players on the stage, intoning the long ago memorized:

"Romeo, Romeo wherefore art thou Romeo…" "Frailty, thy name is woman!" "Why, then the world's mine oyster…" "If music be the food of love, play on…" "Lord, what fools these mortals be!"

Shakespeare—a collection of brilliant aphorisms tied together by an improbable and often ludicrous plot.

Scene two. We are about to meet the principal characters. A boisterous crowd of revellers. Noise. Merrymaking. Musicians and acrobats. A stark contradiction to the uneasy serenity of the previous scene. The only homage to the slain king is the attire of the musicians—they all wear black.

Karen scrutinizes the actors. Time slows down. Enough for her to peer into every face, to scan every energy. This is the moment in Hamlet that she treasures. Will she feel the force of the actor who must play the title role? Will it be a great performance?

Talent is a sexual energy, a maelstrom that Karen senses viscerally. A simultaneous jolt to the solar plexus and the groin, releasing a tide of simmering honey.

But tonight none are present to trigger that delicious sexual tingling. The stage is filled with able thespians doing their best to eke out their two-three minutes of inconsequential posturing before the meaning-feast of Hamlet's meaty words. Karen is not listening to the prattle of King and retinue. This isn't even Shakespeare. Whose translation, she wonders. Pasternak? Probably. His is considered the best in Russia.

A few discordant musical notes jar her out of contemplation, momentarily directing her attention to the blah-blah-blah of whoever is on the stage. Laertes? Polonius? Has Hamlet spoken already? She doesn't care. This play will not be anything exciting. An opportunity to think amidst words.

Again that sound! She realizes that its discord is tactile, anachronistic. A guitar strumming off stage, scratching into the fluidity of flutes and fiddles. In the next moment another musician appears. The guitar player. Dressed in black, as are the others. He stands against the backdrop. Stage left. He is almost obscured by the crowd.

A ball of electricity pummels into Karen, exploding behind her rib cage. She digs her nails into her wrist, opens her mouth but when a wave enters her lungs it is not air but something scorching, evaporated lava. A force emanates from Him, enveloping the stage, the audience. He is almost completely still. Just plucking his strings. Looking down at his hands, as if he is not aware of anything but the random chords of his guitar. The world keeps slowing down and speeding up in rhythm with the waves of heat surging through Karen.

She is convinced that He must be Hamlet.

He glances, casually, at the King. This relaxed turn of his head zooms her focus on the words that are being spoken: "What say you, Laertes? You've a request for us?"

Ahead there is still the whole exchange between the King and Laertes. A whole era before He speaks. A whole era for her to comprehend the ramifications of this man on this stage. To chase them away.

This cannot be happening! He is but an actor. She probably will never see him again. Absurd, impossible. He is of this land in a way she can never be. He is a part of her in a way no-one will ever be. She senses it. The pain of separation is blossoming already.

She cannot wait to hear his voice. Perhaps then the spell might be broken. She is whispering his first line, prompting him to speak.

"A little more than kin, and less than kind. A little more than kin…"

The King is still talking: "Take opportunity of this auspicious hour, Laertes…"

"A little more than kin, and less than kind."

The King is loquacious: "Make use of it and relish it!"

"A little more than kin, and less than kind."

The moment approaches. The King turns to Him. Yes, instincts are indeed the voice of the soul. Her face tingles with heat. "And you, our friend and son, most gracious Hamlet…"

They speak in unison.

He, a mandatory aside in Russian: "More than a son, less than a friend."

She, an involuntary whisper in English: "A little more than kin, and less than kind."

A theatrical incantation. A vow. He doesn't know it has been made. She doesn't know how to keep it. But now inevitabilities are beginning to swarm over her. Over him. Over this basement theatre in the heart of Russia. Over two lives that have crossed. One has already been scored, scorched.

As the minutes tick on, for her Hamlet becomes a one-man show. The structure of the scenes and acts is a blur. Only He exists. Her awareness surfaces when Osric, at the King's behest, has goaded Hamlet into a duel with Laertes. He laughs quietly and begins singing. Words not of Shakespeare. Not even a reflection of Shakespeare. This wrenches her into attention completely. She knows these words.

It's Pasternak's Hamlet from Doctor Zhivago:

Murmurs hush. I walk onto the stage...

Horatio interrupts him: "You will lose this wager, my prince."

"I do not think so," He replies. "I have been in continual practice. I shall win. Although, you would not believe what heaviness I feel within my heart. But it is nothing."

With fierce determination he yanks the strings of his guitar but again Horatio interjects.

"No, my good lord. If your soul dislikes anything, obey it."

"Precognition is foolery," He rejects his last chance to escape fate. Again his fingers pluck he strings of his guitar. Karen wants to shriek, to beseech him to change the unchangeable. Just like in her childhood she used to shout to the prince on the stage not to go into the forest because the wicked witch was waiting there for him.

He answers Horatio, her, the gods: "If not later, then now; if not now, then later. One must be ready, that is all." He pats Horatio on the shoulder, and now surrenders to the song with a force that is unstoppable.

> *Murmurs hush. I walk onto the stage.*
> *Leaning on a door-post, I can glean*
> *What will happen in my day and age*
> *From an echo's distant stream.*

Why is he singing Zhivago's poem? she wonders. It's a bad omen. Zhivago, Lara...

> *Dimness of the night is being aimed*
> *At me through a thousand opera glasses.*
> *Abba, Father, if you can, detain it*
> *Take this cup from me, make sure it passes.*

She listens to the familiar words as if they were being written anew. For her. *Somehow, somewhere*, she thinks, *that's exactly what's happening.*

I admire your obstinate conception
And I do consent to play this role
But this once I ask for an exemption
As a different drama now unfolds.

Miraculously, through these verses that have nothing to do with Shakespeare, the experience becomes intrinsically Shakespearean, as the whole audience whispers along with these words they all know by heart.

But successive acts roll on, unshaken.
The established ending cannot yield.
In this Pharisaic horde I am forsaken.
Life, indeed, is not a romp through fields.

The established ending cannot yield. One more scene. The famous forced finale. An artificial drama. The darkness following THE END is filled with the ice of loss—this is over. As lights come up He takes his curtain calls—once, twice, thrice. Tired now, vacant. Karen is shaken. She cannot pluck one solid word out of the two languages swirling in her brain.

She is aware of nothing: not of the applause, not of the women of all ages rushing to the stage with bouquets of flowers, not of the crowds buzzing and surging about her. Not of the mad dash to the stage door where she is told that he has been whisked away already. Gone. Melted into the amorphous vastness of the city. Now the two of them are swirling in a protoplasm of otherness. Will they find each other again?

stage notes

THE STAGE IS *raked. The stages of life are always raked, distorting the perspective. Train tracks run from the proscenium in a straight line towards the back wall. There, on a large screen, is a head-on image of a speeding old-fashioned locomotive. It looks like it's about to come down the tracks, but the image is frozen, puffs of steam escaping its chimney are petrified in the anaemic grey-on-white air. KAREN and TOLSTOY enter the stage from opposite sides. They stop a few feet apart, facing each other. The train tracks separate them. There is a hushed clickety-clack of train wheels, like a heartbeat, throughout the scene.*

KAREN: What I'm about to tell you will paint a less than flattering portrait of my morals. But I will hide nothing.

TOLSTOY: In order to be a wordsmith, one must be innately predisposed to rise spiritually to lofty heights and to fall very low. Then all the stages in between are known, and one can live in the imagination, live the lives of people who inhabit these various stages.

KAREN: This is both—the highest high and the lowest low. To be fair, you tried to warn me. But I don't know whether agonies can be averted by a well-timed word. Still, you tried. It was about a month later. On the train to Leningrad.

(The sound of the train wheels grows louder. Then a train whistle sounds, piercing, pervasive. Suddenly, for a brief moment the theatre is flooded by a blinding white light. Then darkness. Silence.)

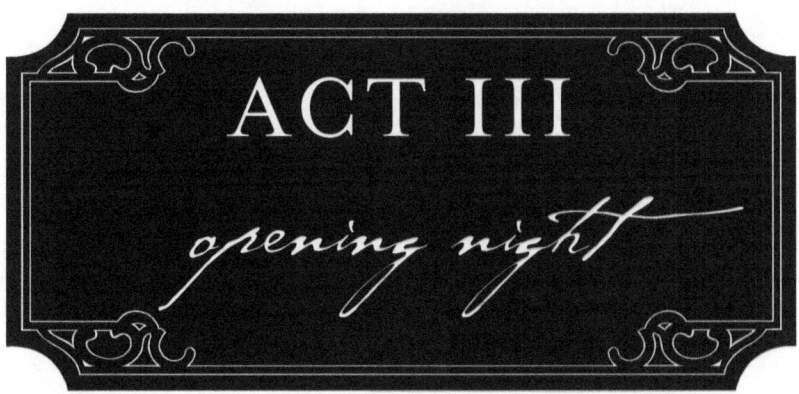

ACT III

opening night

the joke

To L.N.T.

T HUMP, THUMP, THUMP—my heart is pounding against my rib cage. Thump thump thump the train wheels are even faster. I shouldn't have gotten on this train. What the hell possessed me? I'm Canadian. We play by the rules. We don't break laws.

But I had. My heart had been beating just as loudly when I stood in line earlier that day to buy the train ticket. I tried to blend in, affecting a gloomy demeanour. *I must pass for a Soviet; otherwise they won't sell it to me*, I kept repeating to myself.

~~~

Luke had already gone back to Canada. Another round of rehearsals finished. One more trip left, and then, in September—the opening night of Fragments. I extended my stay in Russia, deciding to see Leningrad, where my grandmother had faced her darkest decision. One glitch in my plan was my business visa. It allowed me entry to only one city in the USSR—Moscow.

Soviet travel visas were issued for specific cities, but on this night I was planning to stray 700 kilometres outside my permitted area. Flying wasn't possible because I would have had to present my passport with my very limited visa stapled right in. The train was the only option—no identification needed, leave at midnight, arrive in the morning.

~~~

The Leningradsky Train Station.

The movement of my queue had no rhythm. At times it advanced relatively fast, at other times it seemed to barely stir. To distract myself I recited the names of the three sleeper car classes, lest I mix them up accidentally: *Spalnyi vagon*, usually shortened to *SV* (1st class, two-person compartment), *kupe* (2nd class, four-person compartment), and *platskart* (3rd class, communal-style coach with open bunks). I was hoping to get an SV seat, or at least a kupe. In Soviet trains you have to share with strangers. *The fewer people,* I thought, *the better.* The nomenclature kept getting jumbled in my mind, so I devised a memory aid: SV—two letters, two people; kupe—four letters, four people; *platskart*—many letters, many people.

I was absorbed in my anxiety when a man, whom I had peripherally noticed, leaned in very close to me and said, "I wonder if these will ever be taken down."

I had no idea what he was talking about. His tone was jocular, and, assuming that he was addressing me, I smirked and nodded knowingly. Smiling at a stranger wasn't an appropriate response for a Soviet. For the first time I really looked at him. He was small, dressed in a crumpled grey suit. His face was ruddy and plain, his shoulders stooped, like a man who had spent his life bent over a desk. He looked as if any minute he could dissolve into the pervasive greyness of Soviet life. "Do you imagine they will ever be taken down?" He was in the mood for talking.

My eyes followed the direction he had indicated with a bob of his head. Over the ticket windows, half of them shut and the other half sporting long human lines, like unfurled tongues from tiny mouths, there was a huge red banner: "The Party is Our Helmsman!"

I smirked again, louder this time, and shrugged. My queue swayed and shuffled one more step forward. The Uzbek woman in front of me moved to the ticket window. I would be next.

"I hope someone more competent than the Politburo is operating the train," the grey man's voice trailed after me, surprisingly resonant.

I giggled. The mass of people around me seemed to breathe a sigh of relief. The monotony cracked.

Someone else picked up the tone, "Did you hear the latest one about Ronald Reagan, Margaret Thatcher and Gorbachev? They are in a plane and suddenly they see the Angel of Death flying behind them. Reagan throws the Angel of Death $1,000,000 but it continues to follow them. Thatcher hurls £2,000,000 but it continues to follow them. Gorbachev flings him a piece of paper. The Angel of Death recoils in horror and immediately flies away. 'What did you give him?' ask Reagan and Thatcher. 'A Membership to the Communist Party,' Gorbachev replies."

The nascent laughter was cut abruptly by a shriek of the ticket vendor in front of me.

"No, absolutely not! Get out of this line and go to Intourist."

Intourist was the state-run travel agency for foreign tourists, in other words, a petri dish for the KGB. I didn't hear what the customer replied. I had presumed her Oriental features plus drab Soviet clothing spelled out her Uzbek origin, but now it appeared that she was from beyond the Soviet Union. Korean perhaps?

Everyone stopped talking, listening to this disruption.

"No! Rules are rules," the ticket vendor's voice was rising. "These tickets are for Soviet citizens only. You have to travel on the Intourist train."

Now the woman's voice was rising too, shaky, almost crying. She had a pronounced foreign accent, "But I work here. The Intourist train costs over ten times… and in dollars…"

She was cut off, "Don't shove your passport at me. I am not selling you a ticket and that's that. Next!" And she peeked from behind the Oriental woman, her eyes locking onto the next customer. Me.

Intourist wasn't an option for me. I didn't have a visa for Leningrad. In my head I auditioned the best, most Soviet-sounding opening lines: Should I go with a brusque Soviet style? *One ticket to Leningrad.* No, perhaps, try the intelligentsia approach. *Please be so kind…* No, that won't work at all. Not as a lead. Too obsequious.

When I approached, the ticket vendor was still incensed and began talking before I got a word out, "Can you believe the gall of those foreigners?"

I rolled my eyes in commiseration, "One for Leningrad. Preferably in the SV car."

"For what day?"

Thank goodness she didn't ask for my passport.

"For tonight."

"Young woman, we are all sold out for tonight. We have no kupe, no platskart, no SV."

"None?"

She shook her head, "You could stick around. Maybe someone has an extra ticket to sell. Next!" Dejected, I stepped away. I didn't move more than a metre before the grey jokester intercepted my path. In a surreptitious voice he inquired, "I overheard you asking for an SV ticket to Leningrad?"

I nodded, hope rising.

"For tonight?"

I nodded again, "How much do you want for it?"

"No, no, no!" he flapped his arms around for emphasis. In their ill-fitting grey jacket they looked like wings of a baby bird. "Just the face value. I'm selling it for a friend. He had an emergency and can't go. But SV is too costly for most people…" I didn't hear the rest of what he was mumbling, for indeed he mumbled when he wasn't declaiming his jokes. Eagerly I pulled out the cash. Twenty-four rubles. Almost a quarter of an average monthly salary. For me, $2.40.

Must be my lucky day, I thought.

~~~

I was the first to enter my compartment. My watch showed 11:45 p.m. I had rushed out of the subway, dashed into the train station, tripping over my skirt several times and nearly falling, raced past the crowds on the platform, and stood trembling and catching my breath as the conductor checked and rechecked my ticket. To the last minute I didn't believe that it was true. I had gotten a place in a luxury car on a sold-out midnight train. I was breaking Soviet law. I was going to Leningrad.

If I got caught, what was I risking? Siberia? No, too dramatic. Deportation, if I was lucky. Jail, quite likely, and no lawyer, no phone calls home, and no adopted government would be able to protect me in the land of my birth.

As I settled on one of the two bunks, wondering who my travelling companion would be, I looked out the window at the crowds. That's when the chilling realization crept in. Almost everyone I saw on the platform was in uniform. These were not the usual meandering bands of two or three soldiers in their khakis. No! There seemed to be a platoon of officers in dress uniform milling about every which way, smoking, talking in groups, laughing, and... trickling into my train.

I jumped up and stole a glance into the hallway. More uniforms. Men, men, men. Uniforms, uniforms, uniforms. A military train?! Frantically I started to climb the small ladder to grab my knapsack from the luggage rack above the bunk . There was still time to run!

No, there wasn't. My compartment-mate entered. He looked like an inflated version of the grey jokester who had sold me the ticket. Same ruddy face, same nondescript features. But taller, fatter, older, and dressed in a meticulous uniform. "Hello," he nodded, took off his cap, wiped his sweaty brow with a starched white handkerchief, hoisted a bulging attaché case and a plaid suitcase onto his luggage rack and said, "I was expecting... a friend of mine. This is a pleasant surprise. I'm Ivan Olegovich. Let's get acquainted since we're to spend the night together."

He laughed. A quiet chortle that made me scamper down my ladder and press myself into the farthest corner of my bunk. "Natasha," I blurted out the first ubiquitous Russian name that came to mind.

~~~

The rest, like an unwanted memory, resurfaces with vivid details, morphing into a nightmare.

The train moves off. Ivan Olegovich's comrades one by one file into our compartment. One, two, three, four of them. I'm sitting with five uniformed men. The small table between our bunks grows crowded with one, two, three vodka bottles, a loaf of black bread, a camping knife, hardboiled eggs, salami, boiled potatoes, and one large pickle that is now being sliced into long delicate strips. A box of "Bird's Milk" chocolates. I used to love these as a kid. The thinnest of dark chocolate shells and a creamy marshmallow center.

But this is no child's play. I'm a foreigner illegally leaving Moscow, surrounded by high ranking officers of... I try to figure out what branch of the military they're from, but I'm clueless. A real Soviet would have been able to glance at the royal blue of the ribbon and piping on their olive uniforms and immediately identify whether they're airmen, infantry, or navy. But I no longer remember such minutiae. Perhaps I never knew it. If my father were here, he'd know. He also could look at their epaulettes and tell what rank they are. One big star is a general.

That's the only thing I seem to recall. This Ivan Olegovich has three stars. He is a big shot, that's for sure. But not a general. Or maybe he is a three-star general. Sweat trickles down my spine. The supply of oxygen is dwindling.

His comrades had asked to sit on my bunk. That's a formality. "Do you mind?" and plop. They're down. It's Russian train etiquette. People party, sitting on strangers' beds, until one of the legitimate occupiers of the compartment declares that they wish to retire. Then the party disperses or moves elsewhere.

I'm too afraid to tell these officers to leave. I don't want any attention drawn to me. I can't avoid it, being the only woman in the compartment.

"To beautiful ladies!" announces Ivan Olegovich. All the officers stand up, turn to me, raise their glasses and down their vodka. This is the first of many toasts. I lose count. Russian drinking is always accompanied by toasts. This is the only aspect of decorum in a ritual that usually unravels into sentimental morass. They're getting drunker and drunker. "Come on Natasha, drink with us."

"No, thank you. No, no. Really."

"Come on, let's drink to Gorbachev," says Ivan Olegovich, winking at me. Everyone laughs. Yeah, funny. Gorbachev and his anti-alcoholism campaign.

"Have you heard the latest joke about him?" asks one of the men with one star on his epaulettes. Kind of a small star. I'm pretty sure he's not a general. Besides he is too young. He launches right into his joke, "A man is standing in line for vodka. One hour passes, two, three, four. Finally he can't take it any longer and tells his friend, 'I've had it. I'm going to the Kremlin to kill Gorbachev.' A short while later the man comes back. 'What happened?' asks his friend. 'The line over there is longer.'"

More laughter. *This can't be good,* I think. *A foreigner illegally on a train, overhearing high-ranking officers making fun of the General Secretary of the Communist party.* Ivan Olegovich turns to me, "What do you do, Natasha?"

"I… I work in theatre."

"You're an actress?"

"No," *think fast, think fast! Pick an understated profession!* "No, I'm an assistant director."

"Which theatre?"

Is this line of questioning normal or is it really turning into an interrogation? Best lies are veiled truths.

"I'm at the Lermontov Theatre." *Please stop questioning me. Please! Please.*

"The Lermontov?" one of his buddies pipes in. "Aren't you rehearsing some foreign production there now?"

My heart stops.

"Yes, I heard that too," says another. "You're working with Canadians, right?"

My heart resumes beating but so fast and so loudly that my whole body vibrates.

"Canadians! Ha-ha-ha! So, Natasha," asks Ivan Olegovich, "do you think it's possible to build socialism in Canada?"

I manage a shrug, and he continues, "It's possible, but why destroy such a beautiful country?"

Laughter all around. A joke. I cannot take any more jokes. I force my mouth to stretch into a smile.

"Excuse me," I grab my purse and head for the compartment door.

"Don't be too long," Ivan Olegovich shouts as I step into the hallway. "It's not the same without a woman." As I shut the door I hear them breaking into a song, words slurred by alcohol.

I want to run, but there is nowhere to run. I cannot lock myself in a bathroom. The urine-saturated air would suffocate me before morning. I could sit on one of the pull-down hallway seats but that would look all the more conspicuous.

My feet carry me forward. I move from one sleeper car to another to another to another. Everywhere in open compartments I see uniforms and drinking men. And as I move down these narrow train hallways my heart beats wildly—thump, thump, thump. *I shouldn't have gotten on this train,* I'm thinking. *What the hell possessed me? I'm Canadian. We play by the rules. We don't break laws.*

I yank open the door at the end of yet another railway car. The train must have sped up, and as I'm about to enter the narrow gangway between the carriages a gust of air rushes up from the tracks to meet me, with gleeful whistling it tries to knock me off my feet. I struggle to open the door in front of me. But I enjoy the struggle. It gives me a purpose. In the darkness beneath the massive jiggling railway car connectors, I don't see the rails or the cross ties. But I can feel their presence, their rushing endless indifference.

I cling to the cold door handle and hold my skirt down. With enjoyment I draw deep breaths of the cold night air. Here, between the carriages, the rattle of the train wheels is pervasive and soothing. I'm finally anonymous. In a dark space between two well-lit dangerous expanses, I'm en-wombed by the train and its rhythms, familiar to me from childhood.

I don't know how long I stay like this, clinging to the door handle. Filling my lungs with the rushing air. Listening to the song of the train-wheels.

When I finally pull the door open, I find myself in the restaurant car. It is unexpectedly luxurious for a Soviet train—a plush, green runner stretches the length of the floor, brown leather semi-circular booths, tables with vases of fresh-cut lilacs, starched table cloths, dark green velvet curtains on the windows, the walls covered in peach damask, and a flickering amber glow coming from frosted glass lanterns. If I didn't know better, I'd presume these to be kerosine lamps.

At this late hour there is only one occupant in the car—a man sitting with his back to me. He is not in uniform, but in a brown suit. I make a few steps forward, relief flooding the cells of my body. I don't intend to intrude. I just want to take in this welcome sight of a regular man in regular clothing. An unthreatening man.

I slide into one of the booths and open a hard-bound menu. Inside, the single page is covered in typescript that, at first glance, I presume to be in some foreign language. It takes a moment to realize that it's simply old Russian with the obsolete, pre-Revolutionary letter ѣ sprinkled liberally among the descriptions of smoked-sturgeon open-faced sandwiches, wild mushroom julienne, eggplant caviar, tea-cured rabbit loin in aspic...

"Would Mademoiselle care to order anything?"

A waiter has approached me without my noticing. He looks like a character out of a picture book—in a traditional red *kosovorotka* shirt buttoned all the way up to his jawbone, wide-legged trousers tucked into knee-high polished boots, and a long apron. A picture book on working-class life at the turn of the twentieth century. Every detail is meticulous, from his clothing and his servile expression, to his hair, neatly parted down the side and slicked back with something glossy.

"Perhaps some tea," I mumble, pushing away the thought that this might very well be the Soviet train equivalent of Air Force One. Even the service staff, notoriously rude in the USSR, here has been drilled into flawless obedience.

At this moment the only other occupant of the restaurant car demands in a rather tipsy voice, "Waiter, I'll have more wine."

As the waiter dashes off and leaves the car, the man turns and glances at me. Our eyes meet.

It's you.

My body stirs but I am not controlling it. The shift of muscles is slow and arduous, as if fighting with the weight of a suddenly dense air. My body moves towards you. Finally you are only inches away. Somewhere within my rib cage a heart beats. Its sound is dulled, as if I'm hearing it through layers of insulation. Somewhere under my skin veins are coursing with blood and my lungs are taking in this heavy air. They must, because I still live, but I am only aware of a fizzing current of excitement washing over the skin of my arms.

"Lev Nikolaevich, I'm sorry to intrude, but… I know you," I finally manage to mumble.

"Everyone knows me," you curl your lips into a rueful smile, shake the last drops out of a crystal carafe into your glass.

"May I sit down?" I motion to the seat opposite you.

You shrug and swill your wine. I take it as assent.

You are quite drunk and not very hospitable. Having drawn open the green curtain you are staring out the window into the darkness. Your eyes seem to be studying your own features reflected in the black mirror of the glass.

"Lev Nikolaevich," I finally dare to interrupt, "I've been such a great fan of your work…"

"Ha!" you cut me off. "Blind faith in the so-called experts results in the experts' mistakes being put forth as examples," you say while still looking at the darkness outside.

"Well, it's not blind. Blindness implies a lack of basis for my admiration…" I'm speaking fast, afraid that I won't be able to say what I need to say. "I can appreciate what you've done. I'm also a writer." There! I've blurted it out.

"Do me a favour—don't," your voice is tired.

"Don't what? Write?"

You nod.

"That's not an option."

You sigh and finally look at me, "Then you'll suffer. There is no such thing as a trouble-free, self-satisfied thinker or artist. Spiritual insight and its expression is the most difficult vocation for a person—the cross, as described in the Gospels. Without suffering no spiritual fruit can be born."

The waiter appears with a small tray. Noiselessly, he sets a glass of tea in an ornate silver holder in front of me, refills your carafe from a bottle swathed in a red satin napkin, and then tops up your glass. His movements are graceful, dance-like. Even the ruby glitter in the dark liquid feels choreographed.

"Will you be desiring anything else for the moment?" he inquires smoothing down a wrinkle in the tablecloth. You wave him off.

When he leaves I resume the conversation, "Are you saying that you're miserable?"

"I just got married."

I'm puzzled by this response, "You don't love her? Is that why you're unhappy?"

"I love her, but so what? An artist can find happiness only in his work or in death."

"But love feeds art! In love we find salvation."

"What a female delusion! For an artist love is fodder for work or an instrument of death. If you remember nothing, remember this."

Tolstoy or not, I don't buy it. Yes, my last relationship didn't work out, but I still believe in love, don't I? "This is wine talking, Lev Nikolaevich. Throughout millennia artists have extolled love…"

"Fodder for work."

"…have sacrificed everything for love! Take Pushkin, for example…"

"Pushkin?" You smirk and shake your head, "Like I said—an instrument of death. If you're an artist, forget love as the end goal. When the delusion of love fades, and it always fades, every artist has to face his destiny—work, or death."

I don't know what to reply. We sit in silence. You, once again staring out the window. I, wishing that there was a second glass so that I could have some of that wine.

"I've seen death, you know," you say.

"You mean in the Caucasus, when you were in the military? I don't doubt it. You must have seen comrades fall in battle…"

You interrupt me, "Death is a small man with a plain, creased face, in crumpled worn rags. He appears when you least expect him and he mumbles, mumbles things. And you're fascinated and disgusted at the same time. You want to lean in, to catch his words, but there is such a strong repulsion!"

Your words are an ice-bath. I remember the small grey man in the crumpled suit at the train station who had sold me the ticket. And I remember something else. When I was packing for this trip I had taken my passport out of my purse because I didn't want anyone on the train accidentally glimpsing the foreign blue document and gilt Latin lettering. I had hidden it in my knapsack along with my return airline ticket. A knapsack that is now on the luggage rack in a compartment full of drinking Soviet officers.

The train jolts, and everything begins spinning. My heart races as I jump up. "I'm sorry, I must go, this is urgent…" I turn to run. Everything grows dim and wobbly around me. My knees buckle, but I force myself to move, move, move towards the only object I still see clearly—the door. Then there are more doors and hallways and I feel like I'm going to throw up and yet I run, and run, and… I collide with a man in uniform who has just exited his compartment.

"I'm sorry," I mumble and want to move on but he grabs my arm and holds it tightly.

"Karen?"

I look up at his face. I've never seen him in uniform, but the handsome cold features are unmistakable. "Stanislav!"

It has been several months since our paths have crossed. As Perestroika's crescendoing liberties corroded the Soviet system, the KGB finally gave up the sham of insisting that Luke and I needed interpreters on our trips to Moscow.

But if Stanislav is KGB and he is wearing this olive uniform with the royal blue piping, then the whole train...?

"This is a very pleasant surprise," he says, gripping my arm tighter and leaning into me.

"I... I have to go," I mumble but even to myself I sound unconvincing. "Is Luke here?"

I shake my head.

"So you've amended your visa and you're going to Leningrad for...?"

"Look, I'm in a hurry," I repeat and feel tears rising. I bite my lip to prevent full-blown hysteria.

"What's your hurry at two o'clock in the morning? We're not scheduled to arrive for another six hours," he begins pulling me towards his open compartment. "Come on, let's have a drink and catch up."

"Stanislav," I hope I sound strong. "Is this whole train KGB?"

He laughs, raises one eyebrow, and steps even closer to me, pinning my arm to the wall. There is one star on his epaulettes. One star, two stripes.

"What does this star mean?" I ask just to divert attention from me. "A major."

"I'm in a compartment with a guy who has three stars."

"Who?"

"Ivan Olegovich..."

"You're traveling with *him*?" Stanislav immediately steps back.

"Well... no... I bought a ticket and ended up in SV with him." I feel a wayward tear tickling my left cheek. I don't want to cry.

"I hate crying women," says Stanislav in a voice that makes me rather doubt the veracity of his statement. Or perhaps he likes crying men better. "What's the problem?"

"My knapsack...It's in the compartment and there are all those men drinking..."

"...and you don't exactly have the right to be going to Leningrad. Don't tell me you left your documents in there?"

I nod.

Stanislav shakes his head but there is a crooked smile on his face, "Well, let's see if we can work something out." He fishes a handkerchief out of his breast pocket and hands it to me. "I think," he continues, "that you'd much rather spend the night with a friend," he emphasizes the word, "instead of a fat drunken colonel."

The train swerves, Stanislav stumbles and his body is thrown against mine. He doesn't hurry to right himself. His fingers trace the drying tear trail on my cheek, and slide down, grazing my lips. "We understand each other, don't we?"

"Yes," I whisper.

"Now cheer up. So where is that bag of yours being held ransom?"

I tell him and he pokes his head into an open compartment door, "Petrov, wake up! Pack your suitcase, you're moving in with Olegych." Garbled grumbling comes out of the darkness. Stanislav raises his voice, "That's an order. Be ready in five minutes!"

Then he turns to me, "Let's go fetch your knapsack and arrange this little, how do you say it in English, *switcheroo*?" He pulls me into him. The brass buttons of his uniform cut into my bare arm. "Oh, relax," he whispers in my ear, his lips brushing my skin. "Let me tell you a little joke. It takes place in a hotel room. You're familiar with our hotel rooms, aren't you?"

His grip on my wrist is tight as he leads me towards my compartment:

"A man arrives in a provincial Russian town in the middle of the night. There is only one hotel, and in that hotel the receptionist tells him that there is only one bed left—in a communal four-person, dorm-style room. He'll have to make do. On his way to the room he decides that he might as well make friends with the three strangers he is about to meet. He stops by the floor-attendant and asks her to bring four cups of tea to their room.

"As he enters the room, he finds the other three occupants having a fairly obnoxious party with drinking, smoking, singing, and empty vodka bottles strewn around. He asks them to pipe down but they ignore him. So after a couple of minutes he nonchalantly grabs a table lamp and speaking into the light-bulb as if it were a microphone he says loudly: 'Comrade Colonel, we would like four cups of tea to Room 727 right away!' In a couple of moments there is a knock on the door and the floor-attendant delivers the tea. In horror, the drunkards fall silent, pack their bags and scurry out of the room. Alone at last, the man opens the window to let in some fresh air and finally falls asleep.

"The next morning, as he's checking out, the desk-clerk winks at him: 'By the way, Comrade Colonel said to tell you he had a good laugh at your little joke last night!' "

a picture's worth

June. Leningrad. Almost white nights. The sun sets around midnight. Soon it will barely tease the horizon, allowing the air only a brief repose into dusk.

The ordeal of the train ride to Leningrad is all but forgotten. All the fear and thoughts of death feel ridiculous in the light of day. Stanislav can be crossed out of memory and if he will ever surface he will take on the guise of an exotic one-night tryst.

Karen is now visiting a friend she had met at a theatre party in Moscow. A set designer named Svetlana. Russian melancholy clings to this woman like perfume, seems woven into her mermaid hair. Svetlana is able to create fantasies out of nonexistent budgets and even more scarce materials. She is in high demand. Great theatres are vying for her services. But she takes on no more than one project at a time. Set design is her second love. Painting is her true passion.

To commemorate her first visit to Svetlana's home, and her first visit to this legendary city, Karen has purchased a bottle of Canadian Club whiskey and Swiss truffles from the state-run Beriozka store—an establishment open to foreigners and diplomats only. The cost, $30, is three average Russian monthly salaries, if converted at black market rates. The Russians are usually embarrassed at such displays of largesse but not Svetlana. She looks at the objects before her as if they were only half there. As if this world's substantiality does not convince her. Svetlana contributes boiled potatoes, black bread, red caviar, fresh tomatoes and pickled cucumbers to the foreign refreshments.

The small kitchen table is laden. No room for dinner plates. Just saucers. Two chairs. Two young women. One pale almost-night.

They rapidly skip through the events gapping their meetings. Soon they enter the deeper pasts and more distant futures. Svetlana talks of the royal French blood that flows in her veins, of her two great uncles escaping Russia soon after the last tsar abdicated and finding refuge with long lost relatives in Paris. She talks of her own grandmother, who had the misfortune of falling in love in the midst of the Revolution. Love: the wrong route of escape. Her new husband, a nobleman, sympathized with the cause of the Bolsheviks. He wanted to fight on the barricades. He believed that there should be no poor people in Russia. Nineteen years later he would be executed by firing squad, because Russia's new regime believed there should be no rich people in Russia. By then, 1936, he was no longer rich, but he once had been. His ancestors had been noble. That was crime enough.

Svetlana talks of a man she loved when she was attending theatre school in Moscow. She describes a one-night-stand, the first and last night when she experienced bliss and when her daughter, Tanya, was conceived. Her lover went on to become a famous actor. He never learned that he had a child.

"Is he someone I know?" asks Karen.

Svetlana smiles and shrugs, turning the conversation to her guest.

Karen recites the stories ingrained in her personality. She even broaches the emptiness looming in her future, after her play opens in Moscow.

They clink glasses. "To our pasts and futures converging in this moment of friendship." Ah, yes. The prerequisite melodrama of a Russian evening.

Unexpectedly: "I'm a witch," Svetlana says.

Russia, Russia—a land that a thousand years ago chose its religion for its theatricality. Paganism and magic are the underbelly of its grey sombreness.

"What is your brand of magic?" inquires Karen half seriously. She expects a metaphoric melancholy yarn that Russians are so apt to fall into when they forget that she is a foreigner.

"Whatever I paint comes true."

"Like what?" Karen wants proof.

"My friend wanted a baby," says Svetlana, "so I painted her holding a large egg, the ancient Slavic symbol of fertility. She conceived the very next month."

"Is that it?" Karen doesn't hide her disappointment.

Svetlana smiles. Rifles through thick ranks of paintings that are lined up, faces hidden from the room, ten, twenty deep all along the walls of this small two-room apartment shared by four people (Svetlana, her parents, and Tanya), and two pets (a dog and a cat). She pulls out a canvas finally, careful not to dislodge any of the paintings it had supported. On it: a blond girl, obviously her daughter Tanya although several years younger, is looking with amused curiosity at the artist, head cocked, giggles awaiting to burst forth beyond the flatness of the canvas. On her lap a curled up cat. Their cat, a black and white shorthair named James. Next to Tanya sits their dog Bond, a mutt of indeterminable pedigree but whose colouring is almost identical to the cat's. Both resemble a tuxedo, hence the names.

Karen waits to hear how this painting explains Svetlana's magical gifts. She can't see what is so special about this picture of Tanya with James and Bond.

"This was painted," Svetlana confides slowly, "before we got the animals."

"What...? Seriously?!"

Svetlana nods. A quiet assent. When Karen's incredulity is about to peak, she continues with the story. Several days after the painting was completed the night watchman at a theatre where she was working was giving away kittens. By the time Svetlana arrived there was only one left. She points to James.

Karen is intrigued: "And Bond?"

"As soon as we got James his favourite sleeping place became the rug by the front door. We didn't think much of it. Except several weeks later, he started meowing very loudly quite early in the morning. I tried to calm him, pick him up, but he kept wriggling out and running to the door. Finally I opened it. Bond was sitting there, like his long lost brother. We tried finding his owner but no luck. And from that moment on, James never again slept at the front door. He only slept with Bond."

Karen knows that her friend is not joking. She doesn't know how to respond to this story. She laughs. Then, taking a gulp of the whiskey, she gets an idea. "Could you paint something for me?"

Svetlana smiles. She is fond of Karen. It is one of those rare friendships that blossom immediately and last a lifetime. She nods.

"Paint me a man," says Karen.

"What about Luke Garson?"

"It's over," as soon as Karen utters it she knows that it is. No regrets. They had just been postponing the inevitable. Now she says more resolutely: "Paint me with my perfect man. My soul mate."

"There are consequences to magic," warns Svetlana. "Grave responsibilities when you make demands of it."

Karen is not listening. Now she wants to taste that giddy childhood belief in the impossible. She wants to make a wish and have it appear. Have him appear.

"Do you have a particular person in mind?" asks Svetlana. Her voice is solemn.

Karen almost says the name of the actor who had played Hamlet and had inhabited her dreamscape ever since, but her superstition flares up and lest she jinx an improbable future meeting she only suggests the physical characteristics: "He is about this tall, lean but muscular—a dancer's body. His hair is shoulder-length. His eyes …"

As the minutes are counted off by the pre-Revolutionary grandfather clock, Svetlana's canvas responds to her wish. He appears. Half hidden behind Karen's quickly sketched face. He leans into her hair. Only his eyes shine an intense blue through the shadows. Karen's face is in the foreground. What is that look Svetlana has captured? Surprise? Disappointment? Grief?

As Karen sips the remainder of the whiskey she wonders if that indeed is what her face shows to the world. She resolves to hide it better.

The painting shimmers into life three days later. Karen's birthday. Friends take her to an underground club just off Nevsky Prospect. The watering hole of Leningrad's artistic elite. The evening promises to be perfect. Only Svetlana is not there, forced, at the last minute, to stay home with her daughter who has fallen sick.

Her friends have already raised a couple of toasts to Karen and alcohol is running warm in her blood. She has already danced a lively jig with Maks, one of the handsome actors she met recently, and it felt liberating and intoxicating—no burdensome love, no responsibilities, no promises or entanglements, just two young bodies moving in unison. Surrounded by beautiful people who seem genuinely determined to show her a good time in their beautiful city. Now a gypsy in a purple satin shirt is singing one of her favourite songs.

When he finishes, the emcee walks onto the stage and whispers something to the gypsy guitar player, who nods and leaves. The emcee takes the microphone:

"Tonight we have a surprise appearance by an award-winning actor, a beloved bard…"

A bard! Excitement buzzes through the crowd. A singer-poet, a *chansonnier*. Bards are the soothsayers of modern Russia. Adored by the intelligentsia, idolized by the millions of lumpenproletariat, their voices transcend social boundaries and plant their thoughts into the souls of the people. Who will it be tonight?

Murmurs hush. He walks onto the stage. Her Hamlet.

stage notes

Darkness. We only *hear voices.*

KAREN: I can't see anything. My imagination has become clogged with silt. Emotional silt? Metaphoric silt? I can still hear her voice, though. Hers. Karen's. The one who lives in third person.

TOLSTOY: Beware, in art there are two departures from the true path— vulgarity and affectation.

KAREN: Am I departing from the truth by hiding behind her voice? No. There is, however, one major difference. In third person apologies are not needed.

TOLSTOY: The most common and widespread reason for lying is not trying to deceive others, but to deceive oneself.

love of course

THE WORLD OOZES omens, prickles with portent. Why does she disregard all the warnings? Why not notice the air growing chilly and the waiters rushing to close the windows? Or the gust of wind swinging the door open with a loud bang? Or the young woman running in and loudly complaining of a sudden summer deluge, while rain drops stream down her face like tears?

Why does Karen surrender so completely and so obliviously?

Perhaps because she has invited magic into her life and it is already weaving a cocoon around her. Filaments of inevitability. Strands of tangible yearning. Fibres of loving caresses. Yarns of despair.

In this basement bistro, its vaulted ceiling and thick stone walls dating back to the founding of St. Petersburg, amid people born in the Soviet Union but destined to see its demise, amid tables laden with chilled carafes of vodka and small plates of pickles, herring, devilled eggs, crudités, slices of black bread, she is recklessly falling in love.

He is singing on the stage. Dressed in nondescript blue jeans and a thin black sweater accentuating lean, athletic muscles. A man of average height. With an average Russian face—high cheekbones, dark blond hair. Only his stance has the relaxed confidence not given to the average. Only his eyes flash with a blue intensity that no man should wield. An intoxicating power. Again like when she saw him in Hamlet she is caught up in the maelstrom of his energy. Again an incantation. This time she is mouthing his name. Tasting it. Andrey. Andrey. Andrey Vorontsov.

Vorontsov is close to Vronsky, she thinks, but cannot decide whether the echo of Anna Karenina's lover is a good or bad omen.

What does she feel? Trite phrases ever-present at such moments in literature: electric, drawn, hypnotized, breathless, flushed, dizzy, tingling, numb, smitten, pierced by Cupid's arrow?

No, somehow her experience is simpler and thus less prosaic. Only one phrase circles in her mind: There is love of course. And then there's life, its enemy.

He sings, and she wonders if he can see her. His eyes seem to travel more and more often to her table. She wants to believe that his eyes question her, ravish her space. She is acutely aware of her body, alive with a foreshadow of his touch. Her hand reaches into the future, brushes the unruly strand of hair off his forehead. Pauses upon his cheek. Anticipation and certainty, an elixir of knowledge beyond knowledge. A new reality unleashing itself with every note, incorporating his music, his soul, his voice into every minute of existence henceforth.

His songs are delivered in a baritone, sometimes brusque, spitting out the harsh Russian consonants, sometimes soothing, like a woollen throw on a cold winter night. Scenes of the hidden ugly Russia alive, rhymed, dissected. Forbidden words. History forever recorded in three verses and a chorus.

He sings a set—four, five songs? The audience is on their feet, demanding more. Andrey sing… Andrey how about…?

He nods. His hand rakes the guitar strings, and the instrument wails in response. The room grows still. It's not a song, really. It's a cry set to a few angry chords:

> *I feel somewhat threatened in havens of concrete*
> *I feel somewhat naked in mass masquerades*
> *I feel somewhat blinded by brilliance of mockery*
> *I feel somewhat frozen in flames of betrayal*
> *I feel somewhat scared in a gale of indifference*
> *I feel somewhat blue in an ocean of red*
> *I feel somewhat puzzled inside of a mystery*
> *I feel somewhat living among all the dead.*

Andrey stops just as suddenly as he had begun. The guitar strings reverberating with a dying wheeze into the microphone. "I just wrote that last night," he says.

His guitar hanging across his body like a shield, he smiles, "A short break now." The shield is discarded. Defenceless he jumps down from the stage and heads towards Karen's table.

She wants to stand up, but her legs don't obey. She wants to smile but her facial muscles are frozen. He walks past Karen and embraces Maks, the man she had danced with all night long. Someone pulls up a chair for Andrey and sets it at the table next to Karen. Someone else pours him a glass of vodka. All amid a seemingly endless stretch of back-slapping, hand-shaking, and compliments until finally, she hears some voice introduce her to him.

For an instant doubt scalds Karen. Will he feel what she is feeling? He kisses her hand. "A playwright?" His voice sounds more confused than impressed. "From Canada?" Something doesn't add up for him. As if she better fits the image of Mashka the Milk Maid. Somewhere a flash goes off. He turns away from the photographer and sits down.

Their knees touch.

Around them a hum of voices.

Adoration is meted out to him, people coming up, asking for autographs.

"Here is a glass of vodka from director ... actor... minister... How long will you be in Leningrad, Andrey? I hear you will be playing Astrov in Uncle Vanya, Andrey. Is it true that ...? A friend of mine, you know... It would be a fabulous role for you... Your new song about the..."

"Thank you... Of course I will... Perhaps next week... That is very kind of you..."

Through this they continue the heady surrender into certainty. They have not exchanged a word. They are sitting so close that looking directly at one another would be brazen. Or indicate a lack of interest. Just fleeting glances, hand brushing hand, knees are the only body parts afforded free will and honesty.

He has to go up again, the pressure from the crowd too insistent.

He puts his arm around Karen possessively and leaning over to her ear, lips touching skin, he whispers: "Do you know..." he pauses. She looks at him, inquiring, inviting. Their eyes have now locked in dangerous proximity. Something tangible passes.

He doesn't have time now, his audience is waiting. She cannot abandon propriety and taste his lips.

"Do I know what?"

He shakes his head. First thought abandoned. "How long will you stay in Leningrad?"

"I leave tomorrow night."

"I will drive you to your hotel tonight."

Anywhere else in the world this might have sounded presumptuous, but in Russia there is an understanding that this is just an overture of chivalry. Had she been staying in a hotel, he would not be allowed up to her room, a fact both know.

Time oozes and rushes at once. Its texture has become incomprehensible to Karen. His voice, his words, the force of his gaze are not just anchors in a shifting existence, they define the very parameters of existence. *If this is infatuation,* thinks Karen, *it is the sweetest poison.*

Eventually the last set is sung. He rejoins her at the table but barely tastes the food. Two obligatory toasts later, one to her birthday, one to Andrey's health, they exchange a complicit look. Time to go. Karen is pleased that he is so indifferent to vodka. Rare for a Russian man. A welcome change from Luke, who has been drinking so much lately.

They exit the restaurant at half past eleven p.m. but the sun is still high in the sky. An eerie sensation, these white nights. Surreal.

Karen has read that the closer to the summer solstice the shorter the night. Right on June 21st it won't get dark at all—just dusky for an hour or so. The solstice is still a week away. Although it is hard to imagine at the moment, ahead, sometime soon, she will have to live through darkness.

"I grew up in Leningrad," Andrey says while snapping the windshield wipers onto his car. Karen vaguely recalls that people take them off to prevent theft because spare car parts in Russia, even for domestic Zhigulis, are the weight of gold. He has a Toyota, which he now caresses lovingly. His hand runs over sleek black metal and she suppresses a shiver, as she imagines this hand running up her thigh. "This is my favourite time of year," he continues. "I always try to visit my mother in Leningrad during the white nights." He holds the door open for her. "What hotel are you staying at?"

"I'm staying with a friend on the Petrogradskaya Side." Then she adds, just to keep talking. Anything to extend the precious minutes with him in this magic night when the sun reigns, "My grandmother is from Leningrad. She left after the War and never wanted to come back. It's my first time here."

"Your first time in Leningrad?" He shuts the door. "Then it will be my birthday present to you. This city is my first true love. You ought to meet your rival."

They begin with a tradition. Watching the raising of the bridges at midnight on the Palace Embankment. Around them many couples are just as mesmerized. Nobody pays attention to two more people falling in love. Andrey has picked the most picturesque view. The Trinity Bridge and beyond it, on the other bank of the Neva River, the Peter and Paul Fortress where the city's founder, Peter the Great, is buried. Karen has seen the open bridges on post cards and posters. Nothing has prepared her for the experience. A multi-lane highway rears up like an untamed stallion, its immensity defying gravity, soon almost perpendicular to the ground. And beyond it, magical and fragile, a golden needle jutting into the unnaturally bright night—the steeple on the fortress Cathedral—one of the most enduring symbols of this city.

Karen is stranded. She cannot get to Svetlana's apartment until the bridges are brought down. On the embankment she finds a telephone booth with a working telephone—another good omen—and makes a phone call. Giggling she tells her sleepy friend that the magic painting has worked. She has met *him,* and will be home in the morning. Svetlana begins asking who it is but at that moment the line goes dead. Karen doesn't attempt to call again. She will tell Svetlana all about it soon enough.

"The city plays with you," Andrey begins her introduction to Leningrad. "It is a unique experiment. The whole historic center is one cohesive architectural ensemble. Conceived and built at the behest of Peter the Great. A man who single-handedly challenged nature and created a jewel where only swamps and disease reigned. A man who yanked Russia out of xenophobic exile onto the European stage. A man who died at forty-two, leaving a legacy that is unparalleled—a city at once reflecting the dark, unyielding willpower of Russia and its beautiful artistic nature."

There is a scar on his face—a thin white line stretching from his left eyebrow to his temple. Karen's need to know the origin of this scar is physical. But she must concentrate on his words. They too are an intimate revelation. "Leningrad," Andrey says, "is the only unbastardized Russian city. By a whim of fate the Bolsheviks did not mutilate it like they did Moscow."

"The Bolsheviks changed its name," Karen smiles, but Andrey shakes his head.

"They couldn't change its heart. To the natives it will always be Peter's city. Petersburg."

Pale incandescent air. Sweet scent of linden blossoms. Time stands still. Andrey's love for this city drips like a transfusion into her soul. As they explore the alleys and squares, parks and avenues, canals and bridges bridges bridges of this imperial capital, their lives are bridging.

Here is the Winter Palace. She'd always imagined it would be icy-looking, white and frosted, carved of crystal and fantasy. But the real Winter Palace turns out to be a sea-foam green building, albeit accented with white detailing. She thinks that if she focuses her eyes just so she can glimpse the 19th century St. Petersburg under the mask of Leningrad. She thinks that most of the year, when the sky is overcast and hangs low over the city, its brightly coloured buildings—yellow, green, orange, turquoise, red, pink—must look dramatic, like vivid jewels against nature's neutral backdrop

She answers questions without thinking—yes, no, my play is about... But mostly they don't converse. To her surprise he takes his role as tour guide seriously. His his low, raspy voice lectures while she memorizes his scent, gets branded by his smile.

From this vortex of details little will remain, it is too rich. Yet some landmarks surface with startling clarity. She has seen them in innumerable images but now she is learning their significance. Akhmatova's house on the bank of the Fontanka River, a place of pilgrimage where the goddess of Russian poetry lived in a palatial manor subjected to utter poverty by the disapproving government, receiving alms from her fans... the shrapnel wounds on buildings, left unrepaired, so that future generations would always be aware of the horror of war...

"Dostoevsky lived in this building," says Andrey, "come, I'll show you Raskolnikov's neighbourhood."

The buildings, like ancient courtiers, are decrepit and proud. She feels as if she were standing in the middle of a novel. The air is literature.

No, poetry.

"Petersburg is poetry in stone," she says, and this phrase sparks something in him. She is certain that he has now almost kissed her. Why doesn't he just do it? Will his lips be soft or press hard into hers? "

He smiles, "You're humming."

"What? I don't hum. I never… I'm tone deaf."

"You're humming my song," and he begins singing. He serenades her through the finally dimming air.

The darkness doesn't last long. Light infuses the sky as they emerge from a narrow side street and are engulfed by the empty vastness of a square. Across from them, seemingly on the horizon, the golden dome of a majestic cathedral reflects the early rays of the night-time sun.

"This is St. Isaac's," Andrey stops, as if awed by this view he must have seen hundreds of times. "It was the largest church in the Empire when it was built."

So this is it, thinks Karen. *This is where in the cold winter of 1942, my grandmother released a desperate prayer.*

Her grandmother had been neither the first nor the last forlorn woman appealing to the cold granite of this building. Karen wonders if it is haunted with the memories of these cries. But perhaps memories don't linger here. Perhaps church bells scatter them when they summon the faithful to service. Karen feels an overwhelming urge to enter the Cathedral and to light a candle in front of an icon of the Virgin.

"Is St. Isaac's an active church?" she hopes that although there are few operational churches in the USSR, this might be one of the exceptions.

"No. It's a museum," he says and adds after a pause, "At least it's no longer the Museum of Atheism, which it was in the 1930s."

In the centre of the square at the foot of the monument to Nicholas I in his equestrian finery, a group of drunken revellers stops laughing when Karen and Andrey pass by.

"Aren't you Andrey Vorontsov?" calls out one of the young men.

"No, I'm a private tour guide," Andrey winks at Karen.

"You are Vorontsov," squeals a woman. "I would recognize your voice anywhere."

"The statue is a technical wonder," Andrey says loudly. "The tsar's horse is balanced only on its rear two hoofs."

"Can I have an autograph?" the woman comes up, undeterred by the lecture. Her face is flushed and beautiful. She sizes Karen up with a look of envy. Andrey quickly scribbles a banal phrase on her proffered address book, as Karen leans into him possessively.

As soon as he is done, he grabs Karen's hand and they run towards the Cathedral. Away from this group of people who had no right to enter into their night.

They're both out of breath when they reach the church steps, smiling at each other, panting, gazing up in awe at the enormous structure before them. "How could they have built something this huge on a swamp?" she says between gasps of air, but she thinks, *Now! He will kiss me now.*

He steps away. "It's fragile, just like this city," he says softly. "Elegance amid harsh northern winds."

"The city plays with you," Karen whispers. She suddenly knows what he had meant by this phrase. "It toys with your emotions."

The immensity of its squares outlined by majestic palaces is awe inspiring, and when you are dwarfed into near numbness, the city lures you into the intimacy of its winding streets. Narrow but not claustrophobic, intimate, allowing for a meditation of the intricately carved porticos, perfectly spaced windows.

Yet just as the respite is becoming comfortable, excitement turning to contentment, the end of the street is in sight. The heart begins pounding in anticipation. What awaits there? More grandeur? A palace or a cathedral? The unexpected delight of a park? A solid sidewalk giving way to the silvery surface of a canal? Will graceful bridges entice you into exploration? Will the phantoms of yesteryear lure you into contemplation? Will there be a monument? Pushkin? Dostoyevsky? Gogol? Writers who could not live without this great city. Now the city cannot be imagined without them. Will it be a well-known symbol like the Bronze Horseman with its laconic "To Peter I from Catherine II" or a less known horseman in front of the Mikhailovsky Castle inscribed simply "To Grandfather from Grandson." No names needed. The tsars knew what intentions were implied. You reach the end of the street. And enter what you hadn't had time to consider, a pageant of a wide boulevard bustling with people, shops and restaurants.

Towards the morning, strolling along the shimmering ribbon of the Griboedov Canal, they stop by the famous golden-winged griffins of the Bank Bridge. Legend has it, that if one rubs the foot of one of these mythical creatures one would surely make a fortune. She doesn't stir. She knows that she has already won the jackpot.

Karen and Andrey haven't exchanged a word in a while now, enjoying the intimacy of silence.

"Back in the restaurant you said 'you know' and stopped," she suddenly remembers.

He looks so deeply into her eyes that she is afraid he can read her thoughts. His voice is quiet, "When I saw you I felt an incredible familiarity... and a fear. Something dark. I wanted to express it somehow, but," he shrugs, "how can I? I don't understand it myself." His hand reaches for hers. Fingers brushing fingers. Palm accepting palm. The light reflects off the golden wings of the sculptures flanking the bridge. "It is so beautiful, your city," whispers Karen.

He draws her gently to him as if afraid that speed will cause her to disappear. He draws her into himself, into his body. His hand grazes her cheek, tilts her chin up towards him. Something shines in his eye. Is it the non-moon light? The white night light? Is it a tear? He lays a triptych of soft kisses on her face—eye, eye, lips. Everything seems to stop: the flow of the water, the breathing of the city, the gentle breeze in his hair. Only Andrey exists, the lions with upraised golden wings, the night that refuses to don darkness and a transparent timelessness.

"I wish I could marry you right now," he says.

"What is stopping us?" she asks hoping to put some mirth into her voice, but it is no joke.

"I am married," he says.

splintered

To L.N.T.

Do not condemn my actions. There is nothing you could say that I have not said to myself a million times. But in the end, we could not resist the force that drew us together. From our first meeting things began to go wrong. But when we were together everything felt so right… The next few months are a blur through which brief scenes appear with startling clarity, like a passion play's tableaux.

Andrey and I… the tender-violent embrace by the Griboedov Canal in Leningrad as he whispers the details of his predicament. Married too young. Apartment shortage in Moscow. He doesn't love the wife. They lead separate lives. Hasn't seen any reason to upset her. His father-in-law is a high-ranking apparatchik. A definite reason not to upset her. None of this matters now. Now he has to leave. That's what he says.

Later that morning, stumbling into Svetlana's apartment, hungry, dazed, elated. Svetlana's face becoming paler than the pale night we had just lived through when she sees Andrey by my side.

"Andrey Vorontsov," he extends his hand.

"We've met," she says.

As soon as he leaves, Svetlana begins a quiet monologue. Talking to the air, the walls, the whiteness outside the windows. Her eyes refuse to acknowledge me.

A one night stand. A man she had loved once. A child growing up without a father. Svetlana taking frequent jobs in Moscow, hoping he would notice her again but being too proud to approach him. Missteps that stitch together the patchwork of a broken life. I have heard this story before but now it takes on a different meaning.

"You mean, Tanya is Andrey's daughter?"

"It's irrelevant now." Svetlana's voice is cold. A tear rolls down her cheek as she looks through the window at the man whom she has loved for so long leaving her apartment, watches him turn around and blow a kiss at her window. But not at her.

Svetlana never forgives me for falling in love with Andrey. Worse, for his falling in love with me. I find my soul mate that night in Leningrad. I lose a friend. The consequences of resorting to magic.

I thought that was the end of the payback. It was only the beginning. But even now, in hindsight, knowing that the price for that love is pain and darkness, I would gladly pay it. Andrey and I were each other's reflection, we felt alive only in each other's presence. When separated we felt like ghosts.

We did and we did not begin our affair that first night. How I wish I could just skip the banal explanations. Could I not move with the speed of memory from one enchanted moment to another? But then, who would understand the impossible? The lot of the prose writer. Some poet once said that the reason he could never write prose was that he would be forced into writing trivialities like "the baron stood up and walked to the door."

I'm procrastinating, can you tell? A blank page before me. On it... no... through it... aided by it, memory replays images.

Two months in Canada where time thawed only as the telephone rang. Where colours only existed in the night as I dreamt. Days were de-saturated, impossibly bland. The air gelatinous. And through it, Luke sometimes pleading, looking like a sorry shell of his former self, sometimes angry. Banging on my door. Once the cops are called.

Back to Moscow, September 1990. The opening of my play and the night when Andrey and I became lovers. What ensued was delirium. A euphoria that wielded so much pain. I ought to analyze it but all I can think of are his wife's tears as she begged with me to stop seeing him. She said that I had everything in my posh western life. Why did I need her man?

To me her man was everything.

Was our time together fast or slow? Or does time exist at all when love enters the equation? I am afraid of reliving it but I must in order to understand the rush that engulfed me. Again the lot of the writer. Resurrect dramas that have long ago dispersed into the chaotic dance of memory. Infuse life into blankness. The past. We have the power to make the past a forever present. Do I dare? Will it lose its poignancy in the new attire of solidity? Do moments condensed, slowed down, trapped on the page become less real?

Yes, dragging my feet again.

Isn't it weird how we can clinically summarize decades of pain, but delve into one perfect night and we are inept? Words cannot recreate perfection no matter how powerful the writer. I am afraid that I won't do it justice. Therefore why recreate? Reinvent. Relive.

the theory of happiness

OVER THE SOUND system she hears the first bars of music. Her play is about to be launched into the world. Opening night of Fragments.

Karen crouches on the floor of an unused dressing room. The pre-curtain jitters have escalated over the past two hours. Her stomach is aching. She can hardly breathe. Her hands are over her ears. Her heart expands with each desperate thump, hardening into a boulder that pushes against her oesophagus. "Please let it go well," she prays under her breath. "Please!"

She wishes she could faint to bypass this terror.

How do actors do it? Night after night so... naked in front of all those people.

"Get up off the floor," says Andrey and tugs at her arm. "You'll ruin your dress. Come on, sit in this chair."

She lets him pull her along to a wobbly wooden chair in front of a make-up station. The small table bristles with brushes, scissors, razors, glue sticks, and tubes of greasepaint. The face staring at her in the mirror is almost foreign in its stiff paleness.

"Here, drink this," he says, crouching down beside her.

Karen downs a small glass of medicinal-smelling liquid and grimaces. "What is this?"

"Valerian and water. It will calm you down."

She is trying not to listen to the sounds happening on the stage. The pace seems all off tonight. It is so unbearably cumbersome. How can they still be doing the first scene?

"My acting teacher, Krasnova the great character actress, had a theory of happiness," says Andrey in a gentle tone. "She said that life exists only in one moment. You know, like the song" he hums, "There's but a moment between the past and the present. That moment is what we call Life." He stops singing, tugs Karen's chin and turns her to face him. "Krasnova used to say that in any given moment, if we concentrate on something good around us we will feel happy. So concentrate. There must be something good around you right now." He smiles.

Karen buries her nose in his hair willing her nerves to unwind.

"Don't you want to watch?" he asks, as a few excruciatingly slow minutes pass. She shakes her head. She is not ready yet.

"Relax. The dress rehearsal was fantastic." His voice is genuine.

"Really? Then what do you make of this?" Karen produces a greeting card from her purse. "Luke gave this to me earlier tonight."

Damn Luke. All calm, sitting out there now in the VIP box with the honchos from the Theatre Union. And she is here, backstage, not able to face anything, not able to think of anything but keeping down the horrible bile of fear.

Andrey twists the card in his hands, "What does Edvard Munch have to do with your play?"

"Oh, the Scream is Luke's favourite painting."

"What does it say?"

Right, she has to translate because his English is not that great. "It's a quote from Tolstoy: ' *It seems to me that a good actor can give a wonderful performance even of the most frivolous work.*' And then Luke wrote on the other side, 'Let's hope that we have the best actors in Moscow.' "

Andrey throws the card in the garbage can. "This is what I think of your Luke Garson."

Karen nods and forces a smile. These should be the greatest minutes of her life. So far they are the most frightening. Suddenly there is a burst of applause! Dear Lord, could they actually like it? And everything begins to change.

Her fear thaws more and more with each reaction from the audience. That place occupied by its cold heaviness is now starting to surge with a trilling, tickling current. Sounds crash into her heart forcing it to beat faster—the words of the play, the laughter, the applause, even the silences are heavy with meaning and approval now because Tolstoy, her own Tolstoy, is suddenly alive on that stage and all of Moscow is hearing him and loving him.

Time speeds up and she is swept up in a gale. It is the gale of her dream. Success!

~~~

After the performance, at the opening-night party clarity begins to seep in. Clarity, thanks to her third Canadian Club whiskey and ginger ale. Waves of elation sweep through Karen. Her mouth is parched. She asks the bartender for another drink. She wants to laugh out loud, to dance. She loves everybody.

Even Luke cannot spoil her mood tonight.

They are in the theatre's café, the usual intermission fare of white bread with a thin smear of butter and red caviar, salami sandwiches, dark chocolate and champagne is now replaced by a feast of *zakuskas* catered by Luke's favourite restaurant "Chez Margarita." They are doing their best to approximate the West's friendly service. Karen recognizes Luke's touch in the selection of dishes—smoked sturgeon, cabbage *pirozhki*, and their famous *satsivi*—a cold dish of chicken, walnuts, cilantro, garlic and a bouquet of aromatic spices.

Another sip of the CC-and-ginger. Better stay close to the bar; let Luke deal with the handshaking and back-slapping. Andrey and Karen are making an appearance but they have to leave soon. At midnight they're taking the Red Arrow, Russia's most famous train, to Leningrad. Andrey is going to introduce Karen to his mother.

She downs her drink too quickly. There is no ice in it: the The Canadian Embassy staff, who provided the alcohol, forgot to bring ice and no Russian establishment ever has it—it is not in the national character to dilute alcohol.

She doesn't feel drunk. She doesn't feel anything except Andrey's arm protectively around her shoulders, encroaching calmness, and, yes, sheer unadulterated happiness. Every time someone approaches to congratulate her, Andrey beams as if tonight is his personal triumph.

She looks around, recognizing a reporter from the CBC, a couple of hockey players, a sprinkling of Eastern European pundits who always appear on The Journal whenever questions arise on the ever-shifting landscape behind the crumbling Iron Curtain.

Andrey excuses himself and heads for the bathroom.

Without him she is vulnerable, unsheathed. She forces her thoughts away from this man who has become an indispensable layer of her being in just a few short weeks.

Glancing around, Karen notes many famous faces from both of her lives—the Russian and the Canadian. She has stepped into a dreamscape where both of her worlds have united. The dim lighting and thick cigarette smoke through which faces emerge and dissipate only add to the dreamy illusion. There is Nikolai Bozhenov. She had been right. He is perfect in Tolstoy's role. As if to confirm her thought, a bright light flares up, illuminating Bozhenov—the local TV crew has arrived. Too bright. Karen turns to the bar and continues to study the faces in a wall-sized tinted mirror.

There is Andrei Voznesenskiy, one of the grand maîtres of Russian poetry. There are the actors, like a roll-call of her childhood idols—Dzhigarkhanyan, Karachentsev, Tabakov. There is Vera Alentova who was so wonderful in "Moscow Does Not Believe in Tears," a film Karen watched over and over when it first came out, for it gave her an intangible sense of belonging.

The television light flares up again. This time Luke is caught in the glare. "Karen!" his voice booms over the hullabaloo of the crowd. "Come, translate!" slurred words.

Before she has a chance to respond, a secretary from the embassy appears by his side and Luke shoots Karen a hateful look before turning to the camera and donning his famous disarming grin.

"Mr. Garson has had too much to drink," a voice says behind Karen. She turns and faces a stocky man with a receding hairline and keen eyes behind wire-rimmed glasses.

"I'm Michael Stephens," he says extending his hand, "the new Canadian Cultural attaché." His voice has a breathy-hissing tone, like dry leaves being scraped against pavement by autumn wind. Karen has to lean in to catch his words.

"Yes," she shakes his hand and nods toward Luke, "unfortunately Russia doesn't agree with him."

"Russia has a way of not agreeing with foreigners."

"Spoken like a Russian, not a Canadian, Mr. Stephens," says Karen. She'd always presumed that "Cultural attaché" was a euphemism for "spy." Then again, does Canada even have spies or does it contract the dirty work out to the CIA?

"My grandfather was a Doukhobor."

"One would never know it, with a name like Stephens." No, he doesn't fit the spy mould. He looks like a bank teller—soft, neat, nondescript.

"The family name was Stepanov. My father changed it during the Cold War."

"So you're actually Mikhail Stepanov?"

The Cultural attaché nods, smiling, then says, "I came over to thank you for mentioning the Doukhobors in your play. Few remember Tolstoy's selfless generosity. Which celebrity today would use their own money, and lots of it—what would 200,000 rubles be in today's currency, eight, ten million dollars?—to buy the freedom of persecuted people? He saved thousands of lives, literally, by paying for their passage to Canada. I hadn't thought of it in years, but tonight I suddenly recalled a camping trip with my grandfather when he first told me…"

His words continue to rustle by her, but Karen pulls back, no longer aware of their meaning.

She thinks about how little it takes to impact another heart. Stephens/Stepanov has latched onto two lines in the play and now Karen's work has given him back a whole night of his life with its moonlight, the fragrance of pine needles, and an old man's eyes glistening with tears as he stokes a dying campfire. Is that how it is with everything in life? A dropped smile, a casual gesture, a phrase—all can become monumental building blocks in another person's world?

When Andrey returns, Michael Stephens curtails his lecture on Tolstoy and the Doukhobors and says in excellent Russian: "Andrey Vitalievich, I saw you in Hamlet last season—a brilliant performance." Then turning to Karen again, he adds, "I won't take up much of your time, but I was deeply touched by your play. Thank you again and if there is anything I can ever do for you, don't hesitate to call."

Andrey leans over and murmurs in her ear that it's time to leave for the train station. The scent of his cologne shocks her with joy. She wants to nuzzle his neck, to slip her hand under his shirt and feel the beating of his heart… but she must wait. Wait just a little more. Before them is a whole night in a private compartment on a train. Their first night together.

An errant thought obscures her elation: if life exists only in the moment, and she is living through moment after moment bursting with happiness, how many of these moment-lives filled with misery will she have to live through to compensate for this almost unbearably glorious spell of bliss?

But then she chases the cloud away. It's merely superstition. How Russian of her to distrust pleasure.

a promise in the night

Beyond the horizon in every direction stretches Russia. Beyond the train compartment stretches a starless autumn night. Beyond their bodies nothing exists. Each touch is a creation. His fingers create the skin over her hipbone. Her lips create the hollow under his Adam's apple.

A candle in a clip-on holder is breathing out an amber light over a bottle of sweet Soviet champagne, two paper cups, sliced Borodinsky bread, it's dark malty sourness perfectly laced with cumin, and a half-eaten jar of Beluga caviar.

Minutes tick on long past midnight. The train car is rocking over invisible rails. They are going on their last trip to Leningrad. Neither knows that "last" is an adjective they should attach to it. To them it's a night of firsts. The first surrender. The first unhindered flesh melding into flesh.

And later, listening to the lullaby of the train wheels, Karen refuses to sleep. Not while she can still collect memories. She watches the shadows their bodies are casting on the ceiling of their compartment. A sense of déjà-vu overtakes her. A line of poetry come alive. *The well-lit ceiling was awake with swaying shades of crisscrossed arms, and crisscrossed legs and crisscrossed fates.*

Where is that line from? The candle sputters. More poetry flitters through her thoughts: *Explain to me the depth of vice, and death, and sulphurous fires, and horror, when unashamed of many eyes I clung to you, like quivering vines entwine a tree in endless sorrow.*

She whispers this out loud, and the moment she does, she remembers where it's from. As if echoing her memory Andrey murmurs back, "Ah, The Magdalene from Doctor Zhivago! Your favourite book, I presume?"

"I don't have a favourite. It's just the candle, the night, you..."

"My Lara," he smiles.

"Not funny," she says, the analogy of being in love with a married man too close for comfort. "What's your favourite book?"

Andrey's reply is unexpected. "Anna Karenina. Come to think of it, Anna suits you better. She has your essence more so than Lara."

"You sure know how to cast me in cheerful roles. If I have to stick to literary characters I'd prefer Margarita." Karen is referring to Bulgakov's masterpiece "Master and Margarita," which has only recently been published in the USSR, after nearly 50 years of being banned.

"Tolstoy's work is grander; it has more potential." Andrey's voice is solemn.

"Come on!" Karen tries to recapture their suddenly-departed carefree banter. "Woman cheats on husband, feels guilty and kills herself versus witches flying naked over modern cities, the Devil's grand ball at the stroke of midnight, Margarita's flooding the apartment of that literary critic who condemned her lover..."

He sits up and the candle flame reflecting in his eyes gives them a fevered look. "Listen to these quotations. Tell me who said these. One: *Everybody makes plans, yet nobody knows whether he shall live to see the evening.* Two: *Time passes but the written word remains.* Three: *To love is to immerse yourself in the life of the one whom you love.*"

"That's easy. It's all Bulgakov. That thing about plans is what the Devil tells that editor whose head gets cut off. The written word remains is a paraphrase of his famous 'manuscripts don't burn' and the quote on love describes Margarita's behaviour. She totally immerses herself in the Master's life. Am I right?"

Andrey runs his fingers along her jaw line and tugs her ear, "Wrong. It's all Tolstoy. He first came up with all these thoughts. He ushered in the age modern literature. And in many ways Anna Karenina is the first modern character."

Karen hasn't given great thought to Tolstoy's influence on the modern world. In her mind he has always been "the great classic" and an old man at a train station. An eccentric.

"Tolstoy was emblematic of the 19th century," she objects.

"Yet all of 20th century Russian literature is an answer to Tolstoy. Either an argument with him or a paean to him. Bulgakov's novel is merely the flipside of Tolstoy's. Tolstoy uses God and his morality to kill Anna as punishment. Bulgakov uses the Devil and his gentility to kill Margarita and the Master as a reward, because by then the world is no place for true love. Bulgakov is only cleaning up what Tolstoy has wrought. If only Tolstoy hadn't killed Anna. If only he had created a world where great lovers can live, not die. Where great artists can find salvation in their work, not succumb to society's conventions."

"Tolstoy didn't create a world, he described his world…"

"Every writer creates a world. Eventually all of them seep into ours," says Andrey.

This observation claws at Karen's heart. The sensation is fleeting but a scratchy discomfort remains. She shudders, pulls the blanket over her knees and says the first thing that comes to mind: "What world did Tolstoy create?"

"A world where great love can't survive."

"And Bulgakov?"

"Just reinforced it."

"I don't understand. They're so different! Tolstoy lets one of the lovers live. At least Vronsky survives. Bulgakov kills off both the Master and Margarita."

"But in Tolstoy, the lovers are separated. Love doesn't survive. In Bulgakov love survives, but both lovers have to die to preserve it. Both writers say the same thing—in this world love can't survive. Don't you see? Tolstoy himself suffered through the death of love. It changed him forever. Before the book was born, he fell in love with Anna's prototype, Maria Gartung.

"Did you know that in the first draft of the novel, a draft completed in eight weeks, Anna Karenina does not die? Yet in the process of rewriting this book over the next four years Tolstoy-the-writer reaches a spiritual crisis. One that leads him onto the path to killing Anna, and by doing so—killing himself. In experiencing the death of love, Tolstoy-the-writer dies. When that happens he loses his only source of happiness. For the rest of his life he stumbles in misery through a reality full of words but lacking… lacking in muse song. A couple of times he tunes into the self-forbidden melody—the Kreutzer Sonata, the Resurrection—but mostly it's just words, words, words. Not love. Not happiness. He makes his choice and what he chooses is not literature. Morality, yes. Religiosity, certainly. Rigidity, alas. And hollowness. Perpetual hollowness. But it could have been so different."

"Who was Maria Gartung?"

"You don't know the story? I'll tell you if you promise me something."

It is on that night, a candle dripping wax on a table, a northern rain storm crashing into the window of their train compartment and wailing its timeless song, that Karen makes a solemn promise to Andrey. She will create that world where great love can live. She will write a modern rendition of Tolstoy's novel where Anna doesn't die. The one he had intended to give the world in the first place.

ave maria

To L.N.T.

Y OU HID YOUR passion on the pages of a book. Then you used those pages to smother it. Don't bother denying it. Now that I've revealed so much of my life to you, let's speak honestly about yours.

Love is energy. Energy cannot be destroyed, it can only change form. After you killed your Anna, the reality you created in the novel spilled into your reality. You became increasingly restless, miserable. Anna's real life twin suffered dishonour, the suicide of her husband, a long life of abject loneliness.

Andrey was right—nothing created on the page is ever entirely fiction. Real life plagiarizes the words and worlds we write.

But first... You had a premonition of her existence, her perfection. Long before your fatal mistake, you glimpsed her on the pages of a book. Her father's pages. Alexander Pushkin was the only writer whom you unabashedly idolized. Just yesterday I overheard you talking about his Belkin's Stories. Do you remember how transparent your excitement was? "Pushkin is my spiritual father. Every writer must learn from him," you had exclaimed, your voice choked by tears.

Years later many will believe your wife's version of how Anna was born. That you were reading a short story by Pushkin and were struck by the elegant precision of the prose, by the thoroughly modern structure. "This opening sentence is incredible!" you allegedly told your wife, pacing up and down the dining room, refusing your morning cocoa. "'The guests were getting ready to leave for the country house.' That's the way for us to write! Anyone else would start by describing the guests, the rooms, but he jumped straight into the action." You began work on Anna Karenina that night.

It was the version you had to give your wife, but you and I know better. It was Pushkin's other creation that had ignited your imagination.

For years you had sought a paragon of womanhood. You had put off getting married, praying that a woman would walk into your life and would enchant you as powerfully as the impeccably wrought lines of Pushkin's poetry always did. One day you found her—a woman who played both the piano and chess exquisitely, a woman who could hold her own in conversation with Europe's luminaries whether the topic was literature or politics, and whether the conversation was conducted in Russian, French, English or German. One day, alas, years into your marriage.

Even her name was perfection—Maria. Maria. Maria. Maria. Pushkin's daughter.

You were not unique in being smitten by her. Everyone who met Maria Pushkina Gartung found her stunning. She looked like her father but her features were softened, refined by her mother's famous beauty, for which Pushkin fought in his fatal duel. Only unlike her mother's coldness, Maria's beauty was accentuated by an infectious laughter and a piercing intellect inherited from her father. There was no trace of her mother's vanity. Only serenity mixed with a glint of sadness in her luminous grey eyes. It was said that just like her father, she had a gift for conquering people's hearts. You were doomed to love her.

You met her soon after she married your neighbour—General Major Leonid Gartung.

One dreary weekend at the end of February, the Governor of the Tula Province threw a ball on the occasion of a visiting dignitary from St. Petersburg—Count Dmitry Alekseyevich Milyutin, Russia's Minister of War.

The evening was young. Your wife, excited to get away from the monotony of a provincial winter, dragged you to the Governor's estate at the earliest decent hour. She had wanted to see what the courtiers from St. Petersburg would be wearing.

You were bored and frustrated. You had always hated these large festivities, and you sat in a corner on an uncomfortable French settee, frowning. Your bad mood was compounded by the fact that you hadn't been able to write anything for over four months. Everything dripping off your pen was trite, flat. Then, amid twirling couples, notes of a lively waltz, and flickering candlelight, you saw her. The people and the music seemed to stop, the light around her grew brighter.

She wore a low-cut, black velvet gown, showing off her throat and shoulders that looked as though they were carved of ivory. The whole gown was trimmed with Venetian guipure. On her head amidst black hair—her own, with no added fashionable chignons—was a wreath of tiny blue pansies. Wilful tendrils of curly hair broke free about her neck and temples and arranged themselves into careless perfection around her pale face, her graceful neck and one simple string of pearls. Neither her coiffure nor her outfit were ostentatious. They were only the frame, and all that was seen was she—simple, natural, elegant, and at the same time cheerful and spirited.

She was standing, holding herself very erect, and when you drew near her group she was speaking to the guest of honour, Count Milyutin, her head slightly turned towards him.

"Who is this woman?" you heard your own voice ask and were surprised at the calmness in it. And when you learned her identity you mumbled, already bewitched: "Those curls!" you were referring to Pushkin's African ancestry, "Yes, now I understand their pedigree. Magnificent!"

You demanded to be introduced to the Poet's daughter immediately. For the rest of the evening the two of you were inseparable, to the indignation of the other guests. You ignored the loud whispers of "This is indecorous," hurled at you by couples passing a tad too closely. You ignored the scathing looks of everyone in the room. Nothing could force you to separate in those first drunken hours.

Maria Alexandrovna, at your request, talked about her father, shared her opinions about literature and art. You were mesmerized by the tender expression of her face. Amid the flow of waltzes and mazurkas, surrounded by rustling crinolines and tapping heels, you admired the subtlety of her taste, the individuality and boldness of her views but all through this, you could not ignore her shining grey eyes that looked dark from beneath her thick lashes and rested with friendly attention on your face, as though she was recognizing you too. As though she too had searched for an ideal man and had finally found him. You noticed a suppressed eagerness, which played over her face and flitted between her brilliant eyes and a faint smile that curved her lips. It was as though her nature was so brimming over with exhilaration that against her will it showed itself now in the flash of her eyes, and now in her smile.

Oh, there is no point denying it. You were love-struck. You even told your wife that evening that Pushkin's daughter resembles her father not only externally, but that she had inherited his brilliant mind. You bit your lip, because you had almost revealed so much more. You leafed through a worn-out volume of Pushkin until the early hours of the morning, reading nothing and everything—a stanza from Onegin, a chapter from the Captain's Daughter, a poem, an opening of a play. Through this you were haunted by a vision, as you described in your journal, of "a bare exquisite aristocratic elbow." And then, after a brief, fevered collapse into sleep you began writing Anna Karenina.

Eight weeks later you had finished a draft. Anna lived. She had escaped the sanctimonious shackles of society that forced couples to live in loveless marriages. Anna dared to embrace the truth of love with Vronsky.

Your passion engulfed you with such fierceness that it frightened you. You began searching for an antidote. You had always struggled between being a great man and aspiring to be a humble saint. Now, in combating the growing "demons" of lust, you snapped. The more Maria, and now her paper twin Anna, obsessed you, the more you forced yourself to take the antidote—religion. When you imagined your fingers running through her hair, you forced yourself to read Christ's words on humility over and over again. When your hands longed for the weight of her breasts you gripped your pen with a fury and thrashed the lives of your characters. When Anna found rare moments of genuine happiness with Vronsky you forced yourself to live on bread crusts and water for days on end. More and more you adopted the life of an ascetic, you eventually gave up all property, all attachments and lived in self-imposed celibacy. Eventually nothing mattered any more—not literature, not your family, and certainly not your passion for a woman who came into your life too late. As you finished rewriting Anna Karenina four years later, you had declared the character to be "unbearably repulsive."

You had killed passion. But at what cost to yourself, to literature? At what cost to us all?

chapter without a name

THERE IS A famous poem by Alexander Blok. The rhythm, at first, reminds one of flickering still images.

A night. A street. A lantern. A drugstore.

Then the camera of the mind's eye comes alive. The rhythm wakes up, begins a slow movement.

A meaningless and meagre light.

That night when Luke was finally erased from Karen's life she now remembers to the rhythm of this poem.

A night. Her home. A bath. The doorbell.

She slips into a bathrobe. Heads for the door.

Karen is expecting a contract to be delivered from her agent. Instead of a courier she is surprised to see Luke. He is holding a large box.

"I brought some of your things. Aren't you going to let me in?"

He appears calm. His eyes, though bloodshot, look more tired than imploring. Karen leans in but cannot smell alcoholic vapours emanating from his skin. The box looks heavy. She steps aside.

He enters. "Where should I set it?"

"Kitchen counter is fine."

Karen peeks into the box. A photo frame, the picture of her and Luke in the Red Square. Several VHS tapes. Books she had lent him. Earrings he had bought her in Montreal that she must have left at his place. A serving platter they picked out together on a stopover in Zurich. A summary of a relationship in several objects.

She lifts out her first gift to him. On one of their early dates they had finished a bottle of an exquisite cognac. The bottle itself was so beautiful, made out of thick cut glass, that Karen kept it and several days later filled it with Luke's favourite snack, jellybeans. She snuck into his office and was positioning it on his desk when he walked in, catching her in the act. Without a word he had shut the door, pushed her onto the desk and began making love to her.

"Karen!" Luke's voice, suddenly close to her ear, startles her and she lets go of the bottle. It shatters on the kitchen's tile floor, releasing a rainbow of candies in every direction.

"Karen, I want you," he attempts to kiss her but she averts her head.

"Are you drunk again?" She knows that he is not.

"We can't just drop it," he seizes the lapels of her bathrobe.

"Let go of me!" She pushes him away. "Leave, Luke."

He steps towards her again. "You can't be serious."

"Quite. We're over. Leave, or I'll call the cops."

He grabs her by the waist, drawing her close, "All right. Let's just do it this once. For old times' sake."

"No!" she struggles free.

"Come on. You'll remember how good we were together," he attempts to open her bathrobe.

He is never this persistent. She slaps his hand away and steps backward into the kitchen. Karen's eyes search for the phone but it's on the other side of the room. She'd have to get past Luke to reach it.

Glass shards crunching under his shoes, Luke corners her between the stove and the shattered bottle. Her feet are bare. He has blocked her only possible path of retreat. She tries to push him out of her way but he doesn't budge. Luke tugs at the sash of her bathrobe and it comes undone.

"Luke, this is not funny. Get the hell out of my apartment." Her robe is swinging open now. He presses his six-foot-two body into her slight frame, pinning her.

"You don't understand," his voice is hoarse. "I want to marry you." His breath scorches her neck. "I forgive you."

She struggles, but cannot move away from him. He is too strong.

"I'm in love with you, Karen."

"Luke, please stop this," she forces her voice to be calm despite her rising panic. "I'm in love with someone else."

He laughs. A sinister, cold sound. He releases his grip on her. She wants to slip away towards the door, wrapping her robe around her. But she moves slowly, afraid to cut her feet on the broken glass. Before she makes two steps, Luke grabs her by the wrist and pulls her back into the kitchen.

He is still laughing. "You're in love? With whom? That guitar-strumming actor?" The word "actor" is full of naked disdain. Luke's face is ugly, contorted. "That pathetic cokehead?"

"What are you talking about?"

"Cocaine, baby. The big C, gutter glitter. Your troubadour is a junkie."

She wants to scream, *it's a lie!* but all she says is "No," and even that comes out in a whisper. She is beset by images. The glassy sheen in Andrey's eyes when the essence of him seems to suddenly disappear and he looks through her as if he, or she, were dead, but maybe he is just creating at that moment? He eats surprisingly little, but he has to keep in shape for the theatre. His nosebleeds, once, twice, too many times, but he laughs it off as weak blood vessels, or lack of rest. Yes, his rest patterns are erratic. He writes at night as she curls up in the empty indentation on his side of the mattress. Should she think it peculiar when after this maniacal work for several nights followed by days of rehearsals and evening shows, he crashes? Then he can barely get out of bed by mid-afternoon. Everything coalesces into... Into what? Are these symptoms? How can she be sure?

Luke shrugs, "Come on, it's obvious."

It's obvious obvious obvious echoes a voice inside her. But is it? How can she know for certain? She doesn't run in cocaine circles—beer is more her crowd's flavour. Her wrist is still trapped in Luke's tight grip, which is probably bruising her, but she can't feel the pressure of his fingers. An icy disgust oozes into her veins, courses through her.

"You can't be that naïve," Luke's breath scorches her ear. "Or are you? My little misguided, sheltered Russian princess..." Again he yanks at her bathrobe, and the terry-cloth begins slipping off her naked skin, but she isn't aware of it as much as of the growing chill. *Stupid, moronic, love-struck imbecile!* Luke continues talking but his words barely reach her through a jumble of images. *How could I have missed it?* Andrey's frequent disappearances into bathrooms. His lack of appetite for food or vodka. His spurts of maniacal energy. Something forceful is pushing her down. *Oh, God! What if I'm just his ticket out of the country?* Her legs buckle under an unbearably heavy weight. Something dark comes between her eyes and the light overhead. As dark as those nights when she'd wake up, finding Andrey's absence next to her. He'd be scratching away on a notepad, quivering amber candlelight caressing his clenched jaw. And when he'd see her awake he'd want to talk, talk, talk. *No!* she thinks. *No, it can't be!* And she hears, a distant cry repeating it. Calling out—"No! No, no, no, no!" It grows louder and louder until she realizes that she herself is screaming. At that very moment Luke's hand slaps down onto her mouth, "God, baby, you're getting me so hot. But don't scream so loudly. This is good. This is all good." With his voice she surfaces into full awareness. The pain! He is thrusting into her, ripping into her, his massive frame blocking out the light. Again and again his body slams into hers, rhythmically crushing her into the floor. A million knives seem to be tearing, slashing her back. She arches it to escape the burning agony, but Luke shoves her down harder. Hot tears are rolling down her cheeks and there is something warm and sticky under her shoulder blades. She strikes Luke with her fists, claws at him, tries to bite him, desperately attempts to push him off, but it merely increases the pain. "Good girl. You know how much I love it when you resist," he moans and climaxes. The movement on top of her subsides. A few more interminable seconds and he pulls out.

Karen scrambles out from under him and looks at the place where she has just lain.

Blood. Glass shards. Jellybeans. Discarded robe.

Luke's mumbled whisper, "Damn, you're hurt."

She doesn't look at him, walks to the telephone, dials 911.

stage notes

Darkness. Only voices *are heard.*

KAREN: I know what must be written next but will I be able to convey to you the breadth and depth of it in meagre words? What if I get mired in minutiae? What if you never understand?

TOLSTOY: I can sympathize with the fear. As I am writing and editing sometimes everything is clear but the amount of work still ahead of me instils absolute terror. It is good to clearly define future work. That way, in anticipation of paramount and important passages you don't try to perfect and work on the minutiae ad infinitum.

KAREN: Yes, just continue... The last time I saw Luke was in court. He was convicted and served some months in jail. He was also fired from the Dominion. Toronto's theatre world was scandalized and tantalized. I got offers to write two plays. But all that seemed like a gauzy veil—vaguely there, distracting my focus from where it needed to be—Andrey, cocaine, addiction. I wish I could say I have forgotten the next few months of bitter revelation and clawing through the bureaucracies of two countries to get Andrey out of Russia with its stresses, destructive fame, shackled artistry, sycophants with free flowing poison. The few months during which innocently, blindly, I decided I could save him with my love. He believed me... I wish I could say I have forgotten, but memories are always written down—on pages, on faces, in cuneiform scars on our hearts. Am I getting ahead of myself?

dysphoria

WHILE IN THE hospital, examined by doctors, questioned by the police, all Karen can think of is the telephone. Through the haze of questions and drug-induced torpor the telephone appears to her a Kafkaesque machine through which Andrey's voice is going to scrape off the last vestiges of hope. Would he deny it? Would that be a lie? Would he admit it? Which is worse?

She keeps thinking about their last outing, the day before she left Russia. Andrey drove her to New Jerusalem, a monastery not far from Moscow. On the way there he described how in the 17th century Russia's patriarch Neekon decided to convince the world that the centre of Christendom should be in Russia. To achieve this, he embarked on an ambitious project of recreating the Holy Land's sacred sites outside Moscow. The New Jerusalem monastery was the heart of the project, with its replica of the Church of the Holy Sepulchre, its forest, renamed The Garden of Gethsemane, the river Istra, renamed Jordan in the stretch that passes through the monastery's domain.

As Andrey spoke, transporting Karen back into the time of wilful patriarchs and obstinate tsars, his voice had the gentility and pride of one speaking of a loved-one. He loves Russia, she kept thinking. This land is entrenched in his being.

Then, at the monastery they walked past the once-magnificent churches now blown-up, plundered and desecrated by the retreating Nazi army in 1941 and left in partial ruin by the Soviet regime. There didn't seem to be another person among all these overgrown stones, just chirping birds and utter peace. In the forest they spread a blanket on the bank of the Istra-Jordan. Andrey told her that he wrote a couple of new songs. He sang them, a cappella, to her. Bitter lyrics about the loss of love and faith, about Russian young men dying in Afghanistan, about mothers once again burying their sons, about another generation of children growing up fatherless.

Karen was intoxicated with pride. She was the first to hear them. He laid his soul bare for her alone. The late afternoon sun filtered through the branches of the surrounding trees and touched the faded scar on his temple.

"How did you get this?" she ran her finger over the pale long mark.

"First love," he said. "I was fourteen. She was sixteen. Oksana. She lived in the neighbouring building and didn't know I existed." He paused. "Are you sure you want to hear this?"

Karen nodded and he resumed his story, "All the girls wore their hair braided, or cut into some fashionable short style, but she always had hers flowing free, waist-length, like a sheath of heavy ivory satin. Her skin was translucent, never any make-up, and amid all this lightness her eyes, in contrast, were dark and very serious. Her parents were always away, I think they were diplomats, so they spoiled her with expensive, foreign clothes, unlike any of us could afford. Other girls tried to shorten their skirts or unbutton their blouses as low as possible. Not Oksana. Her outfits were modest, almost always pale icy colours, but those foreign fine wools and silks accentuated her full breasts and long legs subtly, making them all the more alluring. Many boys were in love with her, but she never went out with anyone, not even the guitar-playing dashingly brooding Sashka, the neighbourhood Casanova. Sashka tried to pick her up but was rejected. He composed a song about it, calling Oksana the Snow Queen. I was obsessed with her; I needed to see her daily. So every evening I sat by her building entrance, watching as she went out, following her until she entered the subway station or the car of her woman friend. It was always the same woman and always the same car. She parked it a couple of blocks away. It was a silver Toyota and at that time, I think, the only one in Leningrad.

"One night I waited for Oksana to come out of the building but she didn't at the usual time. Then the silver Toyota drove past the entrance and the woman driver craned her neck, looking at Oksana's building. Something was wrong. I ran up to the entrance and entered. It was dark. Somebody again had unscrewed the light bulb, a common enough occurrence since household supplies were at a deficit. There was the usual smell of urine and stale cigarette butts. I was about to leave when I heard a muffled moan. It seemed to come from a door under the stairwell leading to the building's furnace room. The door, usually locked by Uncle Grisha, the maintenance man, was slightly ajar. I heard that noise again. I pulled it open and looked in. A low-wattage light bulb was hanging over the furnace in the far corner. Beneath it was some heaving mass. As my eyes adjusted to the light I heard Sashka's voice. 'You bitch,' it said. 'You spread your legs for all those foreigners but you won't put out for nice Russian boys.' Then under him I recognized a long slim leg and next to it a delicate white high-heeled shoe.

"She jerked and he hit her. 'One more move and I'll kill you, slut,' Sashka hissed. Her face, wrenched to the side by the impact, was now in the light, those dark eyes wide open in horror, her porcelain skin dirtied by soot or maybe blood, some rag stuffed into her mouth. She couldn't scream so I screamed for her. I ran at Sashka, grabbing him from behind, choking him, dragging him off her. It all happened so fast. I hit his head against the furnace and then something flashed. He had been pressing a knife to Oksana's throat but now it was directed at me. I ducked but he slashed my face. I felt no pain, just heat. I rolled away to compose myself and readied to attack him again. Then I heard him scream. A horrible, animal sound. Oksana had had the time to scramble to her dropped handbag, and armed with some sort of spray she was now dousing his face with it."

Andrey rubbed his scar. "She visited me a few days later. 'Thanks to you,' she said, 'Sashka didn't... do what he wanted to. He just roughed me up pretty badly.' I asked her whether it was true about her and the foreigners. She looked at the floor, 'I came to say good-bye,' she mumbled. 'My parents are sending me to live with an aunt in Voronezh.' She asked me if I wanted a kiss to remember her by, I said no."

Karen embraced Andrey. That chivalry made him even more perfect in her eyes.

~~~

Now Karen's body is in a hospital bed in Toronto. Her mind is in Russia. Her soul feels depleted. But can one actually feel a soul? Perhaps she just senses the withering of that innocent happiness spawned on an afternoon mere weeks ago. Perhaps she senses a looming, horrible revelation. She gives free reign to tears. "Crying is normal," says a rape counsellor, who happens to be sitting by her bed at the moment. "So is anger."

Karen doesn't remember her getting there. A gaunt woman in a grey turtleneck, with grey, closely cropped hair. Karen feels utterly alone. She cannot call Andrey and ask him straight out whether he is using cocaine. Telephone calls are monitored by the KGB. But she needs to know!

The rape counsellor, glancing at the clock is starting to show her frustration. Karen hasn't uttered a word. There are only a few more minutes left of the session. "Is there someone you can call? Someone who can help you when you are discharged?"

In the pandemonium inside her head—scraps of lyrics, faces, cobwebbed scenes—she remembers someone saying, "If there is anything I can ever do for you, don't hesitate to call." Who was it? Where? It was on a night of many people. Alcohol, laughter. A theatre café. She had been happy... The opening of "Fragments" in Moscow. She focuses on one face in the memory crowds. Wire-rimmed glasses, balding round head and a sibilant rustling voice. Something about the Doukhobors. The name emerges: Michael Stephens. The Cultural attaché.

~~~

So Karen calls in that favour. She reaches him at his Moscow apartment, introduces herself.

"Is this line secure?" she asks.

"I'll call you back from the Embassy."

Two hours later Karen stumbles over words, embarrassed, unsure of herself but gets her message out—her fears, suspicions, angst. "Get Andrey to the Embassy," she begs. "He and I have to have an uncensored conversation."

Stephens, true to his word, arranges an invitation for Andrey to the Canadian Embassy under the pretext of a "cultural exchange evening."

When Karen hears Andrey's voice on the line, panicked, yet so full of tenderness, her throat dries up:

"What's going on? Why didn't you call me at home?"

She can't say anything. What is he imagining? That she is breaking up with him? That she is pregnant?

"Please, Karinushka, say something. Are you hurt? Did something happen?"

"It's about cocaine," she finally blurts out.

Now it is his turn to be silent.

"Is it true?" she asks. Please, let it be 'no.' Please,—no, no, no, no.

"Yes."

Her chest is in a vice, and it is being squeezed with a terrible force.

"I have tried to quit," he continues. "But someone always offers it," his voice trails off and then resumes with resolve. "I know it's not an excuse. I need you. Only when you're around am I strong enough to control myself."

"You've never done it when you were with me?"

He hesitates, but when he speaks his words hurt, "I have, but in moderation. I think I can quit, but I need your help."

At least he is honest.

"I'm not qualified to help. You need a program."

"That's such a Western concept—programs, psychiatrists. I need you. I need your love."

~~~

She is flattered by his trust. She cannot ignore this plea. She gets an official invitation to come to Russia, an entrance visa, an airplane ticket. She goes to Moscow and approaches cocaine the same way she approached her own cigarette smoking two years before. Cold turkey. She stocks up on food and water and locks herself and Andrey in a friend's apartment. She hides the key. She expects screaming, begging, threats. She expects tantrums, vomiting, violence. What she is faced with when his body "crashes," exhausting its supply of the drug, is agitation, irritability, pacing around the apartment, cold sweats, eye-splitting headaches, and paranoia.

"What are you writing in that notebook? Show it to me!"

"What's in this soup?"

"Why have you hidden my scarf?"

On day three, as the abstinence continues, he lapses into a depression. Nothing Karen does can make him get up from the bed. Still she is hopeful. Curled up in a foetal position he has asked her for a cup of tea. They're dealing. They're fine.

Day four. He begins to talk about his hatred for this regime, where nothing is straightforward, where rules and fates are warped. "We are all victims here. All these uncountable millions who grow up in this country that is the antithesis of civilized norms. Just think of it! Here in this farce of developed socialism or communism or whatever other inanity the Party is building, religion is outlawed, the present is inconsequential, the future is a solid certainty, and only the past has been continually revised, rewritten, reinvented. How can we be normal here?" He talks of his love for this land, for his work, for Karen. He is purging. She listens.

That evening the telephone rings. Andrey gets up to get it. She sees it as a good sign. He's moving. As he talks she falls asleep, exhausted, finally allowing herself a full surrender into rest, lulled by the sound of some television program he has turned on in the other room.

Karen wakes up. There is silence in the apartment. The television is still on, but the programming has stopped for the day. Its screen a bluish-grey blankness. It is past 2:00 a.m. Andrey is not there. He has found the key and has escaped. She cries. She cries until the sky begins to turn pale. Then she puts on her boots and coat and goes searching for him. She doesn't know where to look so she drifts through the maze of courtyards between buildings, winding side streets, wide boulevards. By the time she returns to the apartment he is there. He has showered. His hair is still wet, combed back. His face is pasty but otherwise he seems unharmed.

"I have made us breakfast," he says.

Karen is silent.

He falls to his knees. Embraces her. "I'm sorry. Denis called. He is one of my friends from the theatre. And just his voice. The craving came so suddenly… he said he could give me some. Honest, it was just a little… I was sucked in. I couldn't… I'm so, so sorry. "

"I waited all night."

"We were just sitting at his place, talking…"

"I thought something had happened to you."

"Then this poem came. I lost track of time. When I got here you were gone. I was scared. I thought you'd never return."

Again she locks the apartment. Again they go through days of agitation, bad temper, anxiety, headaches, restlessness, confusion followed by catatonic depression, lack of appetite, nightmares. After a week he starts to come out of it. He calls her his guardian angel. She believes him. He begins gaining confidence. Another week passes. Another. Then, a few days before she is supposed to go back to Canada he relapses again. Then, again, the remorse, the pain and shame in his eyes. She forgives him. He is sick. He needs her help. She changes her ticket and once more they lock themselves in an apartment.

Karen learns then that abstinence isn't enough. To break the vicious cycle he needs to escape any possible contacts with conditioned associations—people, objects, places, situations—all can be cues, triggering a new overwhelming urge, leading to a new binge. She knows then that Andrey has to be taken out of Russia.

longitudes and platitudes

IT'S NIGHT-TIME. The windows in their newly rented apartment off Queen Street are open to a pleasant summer breeze. The illumination of downtown skyscrapers leaks into their bedroom. They are in bed, not sleeping, fingers touching.

Karen had tried to prepare Andrey for the shock of the move. She honestly told him to forget theatre and concentrate on his music. He has been in Canada five months now. Although he still hasn't said anything, Karen senses that his initial euphoria at being in the West, being free, is becoming stale. He hasn't written in weeks. He tries but nothing comes out. He has asked Karen to translate some of his songs and has begun to attend English classes. But he misses the stage, she knows. She has arranged several concerts for him in the Russian immigrant community, twice here in Toronto and once in Montreal. He blossomed temporarily, but he needs a wider audience; he cannot be satisfied with a pickled glory.

Now they lie awake most nights. He is shutting in, searching for that ever-evasive bit of his soul that had allowed him to create. She tries to invent ways to keep him going, keep him afloat, here, with her, until he finds his own role in the West. Only towards morning do they fall asleep. Andrey first. In sleep he always embraces her, wraps his body around hers. He still needs her. Thus cocooned she too surrenders into dreams.

~~~

But this night in August of 1991 is destined to be different. The telephone rings. Its peals splintering darkness usually herald misfortune. Karen grabs the receiver. It's Olga, Andrey's wife. She usually doesn't talk with Karen when she calls to discuss the details of the divorce or the splitting of property with Andrey. If Karen picks up those calls, she just hears a disdainful silence in response to her "Hello." She knows to pass the telephone to Andrey. She doesn't blame Olga. She too wouldn't want to speak to a woman who had robbed her of a husband. Now, frantically, Olga demands to speak to Andrey.

Even with the receiver a few feet away Karen can hear Olga's shrieking voice. The telephone call lasts but a few seconds. Andrey seems shaken.

"She said something is wrong in Moscow. There is nothing but Swan Lake on TV. She heard shots on the street. Then the line was cut off."

"Swan Lake? The ballet? Why?"

"They only do it in time of war, or a big political upheaval."

They rush to the living room. Over the next few days, with shock they watch television images of tanks rolling through Moscow's streets. As if in a dream, the television being their only window into their vanishing homeland, they witness the Iron Felix being toppled in the Lubyanka Square. And the faces, smiling openly into the Western cameras recording this unthinkable event, announce to the world months before Gorbachev would—the Soviet Union has disintegrated. Not under a thunder of Nazi bombs, but with a sigh and a rumbling implosion.

Its death casts a shadow over their lives. Both realize, though neither verbalizes it: Andrey now has nothing political to run away from. Now everything will be allowed in Russia. Now it will become a land of vast creative opportunities. Here in Canada, he only has her body to cling to. Will that be enough?

~~~

One day in January, just after the official dissolution of the Soviet Union, she finds him standing on the balcony in his shirtsleeves. His glazed eyes are turned towards the famous skyline of Toronto—the jutting needle of the CN Tower, the half globe of the Sky Dome. He is focused on something deep, deep inside, where only his loves exist. On the floor, neatly stacked next to the railing, a pile of cigarette butts.

"We must talk."

"I'm listening." She knows what's coming and steels herself against the pain.

"I have to return to the theatre. To Moscow. This language… this foreignness… I'm suffocating."

Theatre. No matter how honest she had been—the scarcity of work, the rivalry—Andrey believed that with a year or two of English lessons he could enter the Canadian boards as an equal; he dreamed of acting in plays forbidden or undiscovered in Russia. Now it was clear to him that a foreigner with a heavy accent would at best be relegated to small character roles. Foreignness. Suffocating.

Karen had hoped to fill with love the emptiness where theatre's jealous muse Melpomene once lived. Humans should never compete with goddesses.

"Of course I understand. I too will go there. I can write… anywhere."

"You would return to Russia?"

"I would return to you… as soon as…"

"Yes, of course."

"I just have to…"

"Without question."

"I love you."

"No doubt."

~~~

They hold hands in an airport bar. Share a beer between kisses. Share promises among stray tears. Press body to body. Wallow greedily in each other's scent until…

Canadian Airlines flight 348 is now ready for boarding. Would all passengers…

Then the long nights of disembodied voices. Toronto—Moscow, Moscow—Toronto. Longing zipping along cables buried beneath the ocean. Love lines. Lifelines. Whispered words melding merging uniting … days, weeks, months.

Day 98 of their separation. On the 2367th hour the first ray of hope: "Our theatre has been invited to perform Crime and Punishment in Paris."

"I will be there."

~~~

Paris. After 151 days apart. Almost 5 months. 3624 hours. Here they are, together in Paris! The city of her imagination is superimposed on the city of their rekindled love. For the first time in years she cannot write. Everything seems too clear for words. Her Paris. Not her Paris. Yes, pockets of the old Paris she has inhabited in literature still exist. The mansards, the palaces, the cobblestones, the melodious elegance of its language. It is a delight discovering the perfectly set jewels of its squares—all individual in humble or ostentatious splendour. All connected by twisting strands of streets. Paris. The thrill of glancing out of the hotel window and awakening into the realization that yes, this is the Rue de Richelieu and no, not a dream away but ten meters away is the time-steeped enchantment of the Palais Royal.

She is delirious to be lost in the streets consecrated by innumerable literary pages. Delirious to be among the clichéd love-struck couples. Delirious to see Andrey's face framed by this city.

"Was the artistic director angry at you for leaving the theatre? Abandoning him for me?"

"He was. It's good for him to be knocked off his certainty once in a while."

"Has he finally given you back your old roles or are you on probation still?"

It is almost the question she truly wishes to ask. Are you happy enough to stave off your addiction? Is there someone you can lean on? But she is afraid of the likely answer. And she can see no sign of cocaine use, so surely asking him would undermine his efforts. More than anything she is afraid of hurting him.

"Well, I have Porfiriy back," he refers to his role as the detective in Crime and Punishment, "and a couple of other old roles," he says slowly as if himself not believing his own words. "It's getting better. I can handle it."

"Are you happy…" she bites her lip and continues, "being back on the stage?"

He smiles. Something is different but she does not probe. Perhaps the difference is only the air of Paris. He picks her up, whirls her on the very spot where the Bastille once stood. Giddiness sprouting where horror once reigned.

"How is your new play?" he asks.

"It will be produced this fall at the…"

"I am proud of you."

"There is a great part in it for you. I'm working on the translation…"

"I'm still taking English lessons, so perhaps…"

"After the opening night I will book the first flight to Russia."

"That will be…?"

"November… probably. I mean, most likely. Unless The Dominion will want to workshop 'Cocktail Hour.' Remember, my new…?"

"Luke Garson's theatre?" He orders the third bottle of wine.

Drinking, she thinks, *is better than cocaine.*

"Luke is no longer there. It has nothing to do with him. It's just a marvellous opportunity. The largest dramatic theatre in Canada…"

He grabs her hand. Says nothing. He's done that often on this trip. Grabbing her hand and staring at this union of fingers. Interwoven hands. Interwoven lives. As if he needs to feel the solidity of this truth. In those moments his face betrays a battle. A battle so incendiary, so faraway in his soul, that she cannot reach it. He resurfaces. Breaks into a smile: "My understudy is on tomorrow afternoon. I've always wanted to have a picnic in the Luxembourg Gardens…"

Again they are amid the magic vortex of Paris. Truly, where does this fabled city exist? In a solid reality? In one's mind? People write in their travel journals: today I climbed the Notre Dame or today I went to the Place Pigalle and visited friends who live in a refurbished former bordello. But does that make it tangible? No, Paris lives in the soul. In the sounds, the smells, the memories engendering the ever-present synaesthesia of love.

Then another airport. The tears more weighty this time. Separation forcing itself onto the scene before their bodies have parted. Earnestly she promises to attempt a quick jaunt to Russia before the rehearsals start. "Three, four days together is better than nothing, right?"

He kisses her. Hungrily explores the taste of her mouth, plants gentle good-byes on her eyes.

Neither suspects how long the separation will be this time.

~~~

It is December 26, 1992.

They have been apart 5 months and 6 days. Karen decides to surprise him with a visit. It will be the first New Year they usher in together. A fax to the head of the Union of Theatre Workers in Moscow generates an expedited entry visa. A swift credit card transaction eases the sticker shock of a decadent last minute ticket.

She packs haphazardly. Clothing is irrelevant as long as there is one elegant gown for New Year's Eve.

It is the most important holiday in Russia. The only festivity that hadn't been artificially prescribed by the Communist regime. The only honest holiday. And it is celebrated with gusto. In the weeks leading up to it, all in Russia is permeated with the promise of newness. Hope reigns. As if stepping over the imaginary threshold of time will cleanse off tiredness, disillusion, despair. As if there, on that first day of the next year as the sun's rays weave prismatic rainbows upon the snow, magic will be woven into a hitherto bleak existence.

With elation Karen anticipates the taste of sweet Soviet champagne on Andrey's lips as the clocks in the Kremlin's Spassky Tower strike midnight.

While she is en route she knows that he will telephone, so she records a message on her answering machine in Russian and in English: "I have an urgent business meeting in Montreal. Will stay there until January 6th. Talk to the machine."

She is pleased with her subterfuge.

Twenty-two hours and forty minutes later the mud-caked taxi halts in front of Andrey's theatre. It is early evening. She hands the cabbie a handsome tip. They exchange the customary felicitations for the upcoming New Year.

She inhales the exhaust-tinged Moscow air. It is already dark. Catching, as she did in childhood, a falling snowflake onto the back of her hand she makes a wish. A woman laughs with abandon, startling Karen. Across the street a crowd of revellers breaks into "Moroz, moroz"— a folk ditty about frost, accompanied by an accordion. In that momentary distraction Karen does not notice whether her wish got out before the snowflake melted.

The guard at the stage door knows her. Nods. Lets her in without a word, as if she were expected. She runs up a dim staircase to the greenroom as fast as her garment bag will allow her.

A fleeting note of surprise—surely by now actors would be doing pre-show rehearsals or warm-ups. She hears nothing through the intercom.

The theatre is silent. But it is such a brief thought. Her heart's pounding fills the soundless void.

Already she is imagining how he will look in the navy cashmere turtleneck she has bought him at Holt Renfrew.

In the greenroom she finds Oleg, the set designer. She drops the suitcase, runs to him. They embrace.

"Where can I find Andrey?" she asks.

Just warm breath in her ear.

Oleg holds her tight. His body is trembling. She disengages his arms. Steps back.

"Oleg, where…?"

Tears running down his face: "Don't you know? Yesterday Andrey…"

Flight

Poised
On his iceberg
High above
The boisterous avenues,
He mastered solitude...
Amid decaying residue
Of scoffed,
Rescinded
Longitudes and platitudes
That mapped his life
The artist gazed within.

The corner
Of his mouth twitched
Into a smile. Wry and frayed,
It cracked the glacial
Surface of the lakes
Within his eyes,
Unlatching
Salty water which
Cascaded
To his feet
He mourned a talent
flayed.

Wind slapped him
Through this daze
With murmurs
Of indifferent crowds,
Akin to transitory

Thunder of ovations
He used to get on stage.
Then he recalled
Another, long ago,
Who, strapped to wood,
Disgraced,
Was forced to haul
The perfidy of destiny
Through droves of raging
Philistines, informers,
And disciples -
Spurned by all.
As bold resolve
Unfolded in his breast -
The artist vowed
That this, his final role,
Would be his best.

His naked body played
The wavering refrains
Of cold December rays.
He knew, he made
A striking sight
Up on his bastion's
Topmost ledge.
The open window
Bound him
Like an unsightly frame
Around a painting
Of Saint Sebastian
At the Hermitage
Or a proscenium
Suddenly too tight
For the immensity of spirit
It enclosed.
"What slighted
Beauty blazes

In this static moment,
plucked from the fainting
stream of mundane days!" -
He mused.
"What beauty still remains..."

The full white curtains flapped,
Beseeching,
Tempting him
To trip the clouds.
Spurned on by breezes
Of the drab
And leaden day,
Bewitchingly
They danced, caressing,
Covering his face.
And he was certain,
Something was familiar
In their folds
That, like a shroud,
Diluted light
To a hypnotic haze.
"Of course," he thought,
"My cue. When curtains draw,
I take a bow.

I'll wait
A second more, not yet,
Not now..."

The purity
Of lace before him
Parted. A sigh
Escaped his lips.
A tiny sound,
A ghost of a cry,
Reaping

The essence of this script.
Relaxing
In a practiced swing,
His torso drew
A smooth
And sweeping arch
Toward the ground.
In rumbling
Of the street
He heard applause.
His fingers reached
To make a humble
Sign of the cross...

He felt a piercing jolt.
A brilliant flash
Of colour blasted
Through the abysmal
Grey, igniting cobalt fires
In ashen skies.
Cajoled
And cradled
By boundless air,
He noticed he still clutched
A strip of white,
And waved a last good-bye
To all his fans.
He knew
What they did not—
That he could fly.

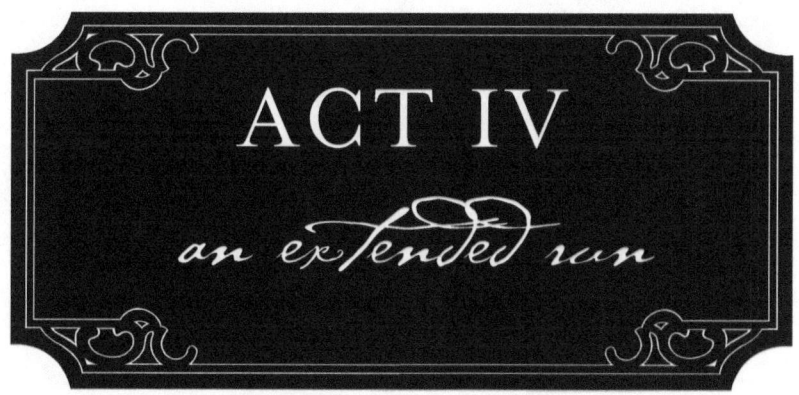

ACT IV

an extended run

in the ruins of a prayer

Suicide or accident? There were many hushed stories in the days that followed. Rumours of a big fight with Frolov, the theatre's artistic director, who had belittled him during a rehearsal. Then Frolov appointed another actor to the role Andrey had dreamt of playing since his student days, a role he had studied and rehearsed for five years. A role taken from him three weeks before opening night. There were rumours of cocaine, and wild parties and a fling with Frolov's mistress that had driven the director into a jealous rage. There were revelations of a failed, embarrassing performance where Andrey was either drunk or stoned on the stage and had to be replaced half way.

Karen chose to believe all those rumours. They were all better than knowing that she had abandoned him. That she hadn't kept her word. She willed herself to believe in the one reality where it was not her fault. But she was haunted by a vision.

~~~

He is standing on the ledge. The abandoned telephone receiver has just finished, for the fifth time, relaying the same recorded message. Her voice. So cheerful, so full of life. That foreign life. Business. Montreal. But its subtext making it clear that she will not be here, by his side, where he needs her most. Again. Snowflakes carouse in the darkening air.

Down below traffic flows on the wide avenue. Headlights and taillights white and red like sparks from train wheels. The full moon over the rooftops seems to wobble, grow larger. No, it's not his tears, must be the smog over Moscow making it appear like an approaching projector of a locomotive. Suddenly under a street lamp he sees her. A woman. Black hair spilling from under a knitted red beret. He wonders for a brief moment whether it's Karen, come to be with him after all. But his thought is cut short by the woman's movement. She is standing too close to the train tracks. She is about to jump or maybe she just wants to cross but she will never make it. The train is moving too fast. He must stop her. He must rush. He must...

~~~

The funeral is held on the third day, in accordance with Russian tradition.

There are crowds but no sound. Somebody has turned off the volume to the world. Everything has become deaf and mute. There are faces and colours. Coming into focus, dissolving into a wave of pain. Flowers, obscenely bright. The sky aptly grey. Black black black. Moving fabric. Suits, dresses. Must be people. White, too. Pallor. Faces? Erased dreams?

Vagrant thoughts enter her mind. Unhindered by reason they fail to form a cohesive chain. Silly thoughts, like: Why must funerals be on the third day not on the first or the fifth? Something to do with Christ's resurrection. A gust of wind invading through an opening door slaps Karen, briefly, into focus.

Amid a sea of flowers an open casket in the theatre lobby. A long line of faceless people shuffling up to it to lay a final kiss on Andrey's waxy forehead. Andrey. This pale effigy cannot be him. This sallow membrane cannot be the same skin she had longed for. Sentries around the shell of the man. Already guarding his memory, moulding it into a legend. His sobbing wife, mascara trails on her cheeks, casting glances of searing hatred at Karen. Frolov biting his lip, pulling out a handkerchief and dabbing his dry eyes whenever a camera points in his direction. Andrey's mother composed, pale. Grief clings to her frail, stooped figure like a viscous mist, creating a chrysalis that nobody dares transgress. In her stillness she seems to be listening. Listening... the theatre is filled with her son's voice. Spilling from the loudspeakers.

It's the song, Karen remembers, he performed in Leningrad one night long before her prayer came crumbling down around her:

I feel somewhat frozen in flames of betrayal

Then the pain takes over.
The world swirls again into incomprehensibility.

queen of the angels

To L.N.T.

GRIEF LASTED ONE day. One heart-rending suffocating blinding day. One day composed of countless unchallenged dawns and sleepless nights.

I ran away as far as I could from my life. I ended up on the other side of the continent. They call this the city of angels, but I've always heard in it the original designation. It is a city named for a grieving woman. El Pueblo de Nuestra Señora la Reina de los Ángeles—The Town of Our Lady the Queen of the Angels.

Here everyone moved at the speed of some fantasy life. It didn't match my speed. I and they were mutually unrecognizable. They were mere echoes of humans to me, as I must have been to them. Finally I was anonymous, deserted. Perfectly alone among all these foreign fates. Yet there was so much sound that I would never be haunted by the echoing footsteps in the empty theatre. The manicured rows of palms against the smog-tinged sunsets would never remind me of that snowflake that melted before the wish got out.

Only rarely, when a grey shroud obscured the blue sky, when rain pounded on the louvered windows of my apartment and dripped off the camellia leaves outside, the emptiness around me took a shape. A ghostly shape of a man, long buried and wilfully pushed out of my mind. This phantasm whispered of a pledge once made. "You promised," it said. "You promised."

~~~

One evening a rain storm brought with it strong winds. The electricity went out. A downed power line somewhere. I could already feel the coalescing accusing shape. The chill in the air. The smell of tears. Sleep was out of the question. Curling up on my couch I lit a candle. At first I could barely make out the familiar voice through the loud rapping of water fingers on the window. But it grew more insistent. "You promised, you promised, you promised."

And then it added something I'd never heard before. "You promised. Rewrite Anna's fate. Bring her back to life."

I looked up in surprise. Directly before me the large window, turned to a black mirror by the night, reflected a scene I did not immediately recognize. The candlelight lent an aura of a Dutch painting to the surrounding darkness. A woman lit by an amber glow. Knees drawn up. A gaunt face—deep shadows under prominent cheekbones, eyes rimmed by dark circles. She is no longer young but far from old. A patch of wall is illuminated above her. Its blankness is interrupted by dark outlines. Rectangles, ovals, squares, large and small—empty picture frames.

"Rewrite her fate," the voice repeated. And immediately I was racked by a long suppressed memory of a night on a train. The flickering candle casting shadows of entwined bodies on the compartment walls and ceiling. The musk of perspiration. The last sweet drops of champagne. Murmuring voices. A promise.

I jumped up, scattering the fibres of the painful vision. I pulled your Anna Karenina off the shelf and that night, by candlelight I began fulfilling Andrey's wish and my promise.

~~~

After the first reading I knew Andrey had been right. There was a sense of the unfinished about the work. Or perhaps, overfinished. Overworked. This was not what you had originally intended. Of that I was sure. The pages of the novel are crammed with ideas that, although politically interesting in your time, are irrelevant to the dilemma and the juxtaposition of the three central relationships, the Levins, the Oblonskys, and the triangle of Karenin, Vronsky and Anna. It's as if you were trying to define the essence of yourself with this book and in seeking the definition you rambled on and on. In your search you created a pulsing, live world on the pages of *Anna Karenina*—a mark of true genius—but what did it reveal to *you*?

~~~

Early morning hours. Sleep was evading me. I got into my car and drove aimlessly, all the while thinking of your book and what it was about Anna Karenina that made you change your values so drastically in the years of creating it. I drove as far as was humanly possible, reaching the end of the earth, the rim of this continent. There, in Malibu, I strolled up and down a small beach, pushing my body through the anaemic light of early morning. The air was briny and cold and I walked fast, measuring the rhythm of my gait against the hypnotic syncopation of crashing waves, waiting for full comprehension to float up. It was so near the surface, I felt. And as the sun rose behind the Santa Monica mountains and sand granules glittered with fire under my feet, it burst into clarity.

Up until the moment of embarking on this novel you had lived with a soul divided. Man vs. genius had been the battle you'd skirted your whole life. Will I toil through life in the realm of men, and if so, what is my role in it, or will I dare the divine solitude of genius?

Anna Karenina was your soul's grand battlefield. In it you examined these issues through a clash of archetypes.

You couldn't pick a side in the end. You committed yourself to a no-man's land. And from then on you were forever in turmoil.

~~~

Levin is the idea of a pure man. Adam. Everyman. Oblonsky the debaucher and Karenin the puritan are the devil of temptation and the angel of virtue. The forces of darkness and light, the two polarities of Christianity. Nothing else is supposed to exist in a Christian paradigm.

Yet there is Vronsky.

Vronsky doesn't fit into the Christian mould. He starts ostensibly like Oblonsky but he is not tainted by falsehood (he genuinely doesn't realize that Kitty might be hurt by his ardent flirtation) and hypocrisy. He has affairs with women but he hasn't given marriage vows to be faithful to one. He is an innocent sinner but a sinner only by definition of society, not of honour. A passionate adventurer. He is a pagan primal god. Pan, the frolicking seducer. Dionysus, the carouser. The dark well from which all passions and creations are born. He is the quintessence of the creative (and therefore destructive) energy. He is the embodiment of an artist's soul. A true artist has to step outside the society and to create to the rhythm directed only by his muses, rhythms more primal and delicate than anything that can survive within constraints. Vronsky is an outsider, a gypsy, a foreigner to the Christian mores of your time.

Vronskyism is where you were drawn and yet Levinism is what you were forcing yourself to desire.

Where there is a pagan god there must be a goddess. Vronsky's true nature blossoms when his counterpart, Anna appears. She is the moon, the nymph, the Muse. She is defined by her passions. Both Anna and Vronsky are driven by primal, ancient, dark and powerful, forces. Forces outside the Christian mythology. Vronsky and Anna are a pair. In pagan mythology, unlike in that of the Christians, the male and the female are in an inseparable dance. Anna is so much more dimensional than the women inhabiting the flat Christian universe—the Kittys, the Dollys, the Betsys. The virgins and the martyrs and the whores.

Is this why the book is called Anna Karenina and not Three Families or something? The muse is the fulcrum to unlocking the potential of a soul, launching it into brilliance?

Your nature blossomed too when your perfect woman appeared. Your Muse. Your goddess. Suddenly you felt your soul soar and you felt acutely your incongruence with the Christian mould. I don't think you fit into it ever. Religion and society are delineated spaces and an artist cannot be anchored within delineations.

~~~

The sun rose higher and more sounds entered the waking world— cars on the Pacific Coast Highway, seagulls squawking for morsels of food, even the waves lapped with more vigour. The sparkles under my feet merged into a wash of peachy-ochre over the sand and I slowed my momentum to catch my racing thoughts.

After defining your archetypes, you failed to embrace them and then you punished them for your own inability. You yearned to experience Anna and Vronsky. Your life, though, resonated with the mundaneness of Levin and Kitty. Stifled in the dark gap between their two realities, you couldn't bring yourself to accept the most important themes of your own life, those areas where your artistic nature was most drawn. So the characters of Anna and Vronsky, though meticulously executed… *in the end are not fully realized.*

Electrified by this "forbidden" thought, my mind reeled and I sank down to the sand that, although now fully coloured crimson by the sun, still bore the damp chill of night. I barely registered the discomfort. My face was burning. I *felt* the error you had made and its palpability gave off heat. There is an oscillation in your portrayal of Anna and Vronsky, like you couldn't make up your mind where to take them, so you killed her and pushed him off into oblivion. There is an undercurrent of desperation, not in the narrative but in the writing itself. In you. You were deserting a crucial part of *you* and that excruciating process of fission produced an unbearable heat that consumed you for the rest of your life.

Sometimes religions are nestled within societies. Other times societies are nestled within religions. Russia has always been the latter. It is defined by its brand of Christianity. When in the writing of Anna Karenina you felt your soul repelling this Christianity, and therefore Russia, you panicked.

Instead of surrendering to the paganism of your artistic soul you set out to reinvent a Christianity within which you thought you could exist. It became your raison d'être.

~~~

Over the next days, weeks, months I turned to your journals for clues, and through them met the real you, grew closer to you. To the you before 1873, the year when work on the novel commenced, because in 1877 after completing your final draft of Anna Karenina you emerge a different man. A man I barely care to know. And in between those years—a void. The years of writing Anna Karenina were the only time in your life when you didn't keep a journal. You said in a letter to a friend that everything was poured into this work. Indeed, in retrospect, Anna Karenina is a portrait of your soul going through turmoil.

Day after day, I analyzed each sentence of your Anna. I took it apart strand by linguistic strand. I discovered the turning points in your mind, the earlier drafts peeking through the later additions, the spirit of the woman you first conceived through the shape of the character you eventually released into the world. I then rewove your words and your initial meaning into a tale full of your passions but not your debilitating doubts.

Days aggregated into weeks, weeks into months, and months into years. Four years to be exact. Finally, my Anna, like your original heroine, lived.

I thought it would redeem us all.

stage notes

Darkness. KAREN's voice.

KAREN: I watched it flutter in the barely perceptible air current. Almost alive. Almost needed. I wanted to erase the almost. It gave off barely any heat and even less light. The room was getting darker by the moment. It took courage to do what I did. With a quick exhale I blew out the flame to my dream... Now I lie in bed. Facing the future is so much more frightening than regretting the past. I will continue lying here. Breathe in, breathe out, as desire trickles out of me at the speed of one second per second.

(Lights come up. The desk centre stage is now set-up as a bed. KAREN is curled up on top, her head resting on a thick manuscript. A Russian scarf covers her like a blanket. TOLSTOY crosses the stage to the table/bed, sets a few sheets of paper on top of KAREN. He caresses them, then bends down, blows hard and white sheets flutter down to the floor.)

TOLSTOY: I have abandoned, quite permanently, I believe, all literary activity. Why? It's difficult to say. Mostly because everything that I had done and feel I am capable of doing is so far from what I envisioned I should have done.

KAREN: I have abandoned, quite permanently, I believe, all literary activity. It is too fast my "now." Imagination has been usurped by flickering cinematic images. Thinking itself is regimented into two-hour slots. It is too fast for literature.

TOLSTOY: The decline of literature is the most certain sign of the decline of civilization.

KAREN: *(sitting up and turning to TOLSTOY)* You are the only island of sanity I have left. What more do I need when I have you, this stage?

TOLSTOY: (taking her hand and helping her down from the bed/table) Perhaps the stage is an ideal environment.

KAREN: Andrey said that once. Those exact words. The stage is an ideal environment where reality can be moulded and replayed, disregarded and reinvented until perfection is found.

TOLSTOY: When I was a child, I was taken to the Bolshoy Theatre. We sat in a box and I didn't see any of the show. I didn't know that I was supposed to look off to the side towards the stage and I kept looking directly in front of me into the boxes across.

KAREN: We all do that, don't we? We forget to look at the stage of our lives. We get distracted by the velvet of the chairs, the cherubs painted on the ceiling, the hairstyles and incidental faces around us. While there, on the boards, we are being taught the lessons of being and dying.

once a gypsy

To L.N.T.

WHERE DO I go to escape this time? Once a gypsy always a gypsy. Leaving a place has solidified into a habit. Searching for the home that will never be found. Allegiance sworn to only one geography—my heart.

I left Russia for Canada, then left Canada for this... this snowless purgatory. I've no doubt that some day I will leave again. But for where? My Russia, the land of my childhood, no longer exists. Childhood lands exist for no one. Even for people whose lives are forever centered around one patch of the planet.

Never having a place in the world where I belong. Is it a curse or a blessing? I am Canadian; I will always be Russian. Yet somehow the mathematics of wandering and assimilating has defied arithmetic. One plus one equals zero.

Solitude and loneliness—two sides of the same coin. Both experienced by a gypsy. And a writer. Alone among many. Always. Understanding many, misunderstanding many more.

Beyond my window rain is cascading in slow motion, each drop descending lentando. With a force of will even gravity can be slowed down. If raindrops can decelerate to contemplate their fall, can I not do so also?

Where will slowness seep into my pores, weigh me down with happiness, cleave to my senses and saturate them with a certainty of belonging?

Is this why I write? To delve into a world that is created by me and thus irrevocable? Is this my land, my nationality? Words. My worlds. Do I belong? Can I enter and never leave?

drama is conflict

To L.N.T.

I woke up with a start. A crash of thunder drowned out the hushed rapping of rain on the open windowpane. I had fallen asleep at a desk. The throbbing muscles in my back confirmed as much.

A flash of lightning momentarily shredded night, which rushed to seal itself again. Ozone-charged air wafted into the room.

The desk was not my own. It was large, made out of dark polished wood. On it a malachite inkwell, several quills lined up like soldiers, a kerosene lamp emitting a soft glow.

Where was I? A doubt crept in. Maybe I wasn't awake after all. Maybe this was all a dream.

The room was cajoled in soft nocturnal shadow. No light seeped in except the harsh flashes of lightning and the circle cast by the desk lamp.

If it was a dream, I was aware of it and I began examining the perfectly wrought details, which, at that time, I still believed to be the manifestations of my imagination.

It all felt very real. Even the texture of the air, the soft coolness of a summer night. I turned away from the light of the lamp willing my eyes to rend darkness. With childish delight I waited as darkness slowly released the shapes of the quaint nineteenth century furnishings—the massive wardrobe, the narrow bed with a metal headboard, the pitcher and wash basin on top of the dresser. The squares and ovals of picture frames splattered on the wall.

Not my picture frames, for these were populated by faces.

The armchair…

Then I saw you.

You were sitting in the chair, feet propped up on a footstool, covered by a knitted throw, probably tucked in by a servant. A quill rested neatly upon a book on the floor.

Stepping cautiously so as not to wake you I walked over to the book on the floor. It was your diary. The last entry read:

"In the beginning there is a superb description of nature, it's raining. The way it is described even Turgenev could not have done it as well, and as for myself I couldn't even come close. But then, there is a young lady, pining away. And that's about it. This whole set-up with the girl's trite feelings, the rain, were simply needed for the writer to write something, anything down on paper. As usual, when there is nothing to talk about, people talk about the weather, same with writers. When they have nothing to write about, they write about the weather. So, it rained, so what? It would be just as well if it hadn't rained. It's time we stop this."

And then, after a line viciously scratched out "…drama is conflict."

My heart began racing, my breath came in fast. This whole room enveloped in a swirling darkness and I was pulled away rapidly, violently, with a snap awakening on the floor of my own apartment, miles and years from you, the smell of ozone still in my nostrils.

I stayed on the floor for a long time, willing myself, unsuccessfully, to breach the unyielding distance between us. I watched the sky outside my window grow grey, then a yellowish white and finally orange with sunrise.

Conflict. I've been in conflict with my whole world, with its tempo. I've had my fill of drama. I want peace now; I want peace in your time, with you. And I know what should finally make me happy. Helping you rewrite Anna one more time. You will succeed where I failed. One more draft. All I have to do is meet you before you encounter Maria Gartung. Yours and mine will be a different love. It will save Anna. She will live.

So now I light candles; I listen for your voice; I practice the speed of your life.

ACT V

closing night

pleasure without repentance

"Happiness," you said once, "is pleasure without repentance." Where have I always found my pleasure without repentance? On the blank page. As have you. It is what bridges our two lives.

The blank page is never empty. It is white with promise. We find it irresistible. We enter the blank page. We enter its everythingness and we live there. For an hour, for a day, forever. The marks left on the page are tracks of that other life.

So now I approach yet another blank page. I embrace its whiteness. I breathe it in. I don't try to imagine you, your world, your face. I don't try to imagine anything. I feel the hammering of blood in my temples. I force the beating to slow down.

Nothing else exists. The expanse of the blank page and the slow, ever slowing beating of my heart. And the wind. Yes there is wind now. And a sharp-edged, dry frost. The whiteness around me moves, dances. I'm in an endless white flurry. Snow. Winter. The white swirling snow whitewashes the world. Is this a steppe? Slow down. Wait.

Gradually the wind dies down. Shapes begin to emerge through the whiteness. Trees. Buildings.

Moscow.

Of course, it's Moscow. The place of our first meeting will become the stage of our re-acquaintance. Here I am in this snowy city where your wife drags you now more and more. You agree, grudgingly, because indeed, it is the only possible solution to give the children proper education, but you miss the peace of your estate in Yasnaya Polyana. Rest assured, I will take you away to the calmness you crave soon after our meeting. Moscow is too full of noise and responsibilities for us to rework Anna's fate.

~~~

The zoo and its ice-rink is where I will find you, as all of Moscow's *beau-monde* gathers there to see and be seen. Let's pick a date. Any date as long as it's before your meeting with Maria Gartung. I have to intercept the sparking of the idea. So, our re-acquaintance.

January 27, 1872. Two o'clock in the afternoon. Conscious of a pounding heart I turn the corner of Bolshaya Gruzinskaya Street towards the Zoological Garden and head down the wide path towards the hills and the skating rink. I know that I will find you there.

It is a brilliant, frosty day. The passing men's top hats are gleaming in the sun. At the entrance there are rows of carriages, sleighs, cabbies and policemen. "Clean" crowds—a delightful old term for the upper classes, but so precise for indeed they are clean, contrasting with the pervading dirt, mud, and squalor in most side streets—swarm around the entrance and along the neatly swept paths between the little Russian houses adorned with intricate carvings. The garden's old birches with all their branches weighed down by snow, appear bedecked in new ceremonial robes.

I do not feel the nipping of the frost. Nervousness heats up heart and senses, threatens to accelerate me, to propel me into the swirling emptiness of a later age. I walk along the path towards the skating rink, mumbling to myself, "Stop shaking. Calm down, take a deep breath. Beat gently, gently my heart. " The image of your face, of all your faces, before, now, later, demands to be made flesh. I advance towards this vision. One precarious slippery step after another. Into your time. The more I try to compose myself the less I succeed.

I must not look well. I think a passing man asks whether I need assistance. This comment is like a shadow seen out of a corner of the memory's eye. Maybe nobody has spoken. Maybe it is a detail my imagination has added later. Maybe...

Time to enter certainties. I progress towards the sledding hills that resound with a cacophony of merriment—the clanking of chains as sleds are being dragged up the hill, their rumbling as they whoosh down, laughter, screams, excited din.

A few more steps. The ice rink is before my eyes. A whisper of intuition and my eyes are drawn to the left. Immediately amidst all the skaters I see you.

You are talking to a lady—your sister, I'll learn later. There is nothing immediately striking either in your dress or attitude. Yet for me you are as easy to find in that crowd as a rose among nettles. There seems to be a glow about you. A glow of greatness.

I am rooted to the spot by doubts. I seem to fear that which I most want—my salvation. You, who are obsessed with saving humanity and the fate of Mother Russia, are about to be invited to be my own personal saviour. Yet now I am afraid of that final step. If I am to come to you, I will have to absorb your world completely. I will have to invite into me the full force of your genius.

The place where you stand seems bright and dangerous like a holy shrine. There is a moment when I almost consider retreating. Into the familiar rapid madness of my world. Into the familiar misery. No! There is no turning back.

I have to make an effort to master myself. I concentrate on the brittleness of frosty air entering my lungs. I slowly walk down the hill, avoiding looking in your direction as if you were the sun itself.

Below, on level ground I allow myself a glance at the ice rink. You are obscured by other skaters. I sit on the closest bench, realizing that my legs are shaking. It seems that on this day of the week, at this time of day the ice welcomes only people of a certain circle. They all appear to be acquainted with one another, using the ice as an outdoor meeting place. There are expert skaters here, showing off their skill, and novices clinging to chairs with timid awkward movements. There are young boys and there are old people who come out not for enjoyment but for the health aspects of exercise. All of them blissful idiots. To be in proximity with true genius and retain self-possession out of sheer ignorance! Here they are skating around you, near you, toward you, by you. Some have probably spoken to you and have gone on, unperturbed, enjoying the glorious weather and the pristine snow.

I shut my eyes and compose myself momentarily. The inevitable is about to become the inescapable.

Suddenly I feel as if the sun were coming near me. Invisible fire drenching my face. I turn my head and collide with your reserved smile, your eyes, serene, frank, sharp with intelligence. You are standing not three feet away.

"May I offer you my assistance on the rink?" you ask but your voice betrays a curiosity, a hesitant almost-memory.

"I haven't brought my skates," I reply marvelling at how easily words skip over the barriers of emotions and fears.

You seem transfixed, demanding information from my eyes, from my soul yet somehow, seemingly, skating around the heart of the issue.

"We have met, have we not?" the smile is still upon your lips, yet I can feel that you are already falling into the inevitability of us.

I only nod in response.

"Allow me to formally introduce myself. Count Lev…"

"… Nikolaevich Tolstoy."

You look befuddled. No, not surprised that I know who you are. You are straining your perfect memory and only bringing up a shadow of a not-yet memory. "And you are? I'm sorry…"

Of course you do not know yet.

"Karen." Then anticipating further inquiry, "Just Karen." I extend my hand and your lips press into it. I can feel their heat through my glove's thin wool fabric.

"Do you live in Moscow?" you ask, still believing that information will equal solution.

"I don't know. It depends upon you." My reply is honest but I do not know whether it has been formulated clearly enough to reach you. I do know that these words seal the commitment. At this moment the solidity of your world becomes the strength of mine. The rhythm of your breath becomes the lifeline to my sanity. All at once we have become a universe onto ourselves. The conduit of energy between us is tangible, maddening, transmitting information on the molecular level that may take years to transmit in words and experiences. The birth of passion.

No, don't even think it. Don't confuse a spiritual fire with a corporeal itch. Don't tempt me with momentary pleasures. We are brought together for creating something much more sublime than the merging of two bodies. We shall merge our minds.

You are no longer smiling. Yet you are still misguided. If there were no people around us I know beyond knowledge that I would be swept into your arms. You would demand to possess me right here on this bench in this snow. Yes, this current is strong.

My God! What have I done! Merciful God, help me, guide me! I say a silent prayer. Luckily we are in a public place. I have time to explain my purpose. I know there is an echo of this knowledge in your heart. You are about to embark upon the true path.

"I have been thinking about you for many years now," you say quietly half conscious, half entranced. "I am glad you came."

There! You too have jumped head down from this cliff of certainty and have committed to flight!

"Shall we continue…?"

"To a restaurant?" I finish your thought, and laughing out loud at your surprised expression I explain, "I have read something like this scene in a book once."

"Will it be the Anglia or the Hermitage?" you try to sound casual but there is a note of exhilaration in your voice.

"I have no preference."

"All right, then, the Anglia it is," you say.

first impressions

I EXPECTED THE streets of 19th century Moscow would be quiet. That had been my impression when I briefly glimpsed them before. Not so, actually. There is noise—bustle, outcries, wheels striking paved stones, metal clinging, dogs barking, laughter, song, hansom cab drivers giddyapping the beasts, peddlers pushing wooden toys, scraps of fabric; street vendors promoting sugar candy, boots, fresh chicken, hats; a beggar-woman soliciting alms, boys playing *salki*, and the *garmoshka*, the precursor to the accordion, wailing out a simple tune—prodigious noise. But noise outlined in silence, punctuated by lack of a mechanical hubbub.

There are also smells. Smells that assail the nostrils: sweat and frost and manure and food and wisps of rosewater and burning wood and all this unclouded by petrol.

Everything is clearer. Everything still has its own place. Before the mad tempo of the next century whips everything into a sensory scramble.

The sled runners glide over the compacted snow on the street. The horses whinny. We float through a wintry postcard. Impressions percolate in me, rising and exploding on the surface of my thoughts. I've seen these streets in old books about Moscow. The white snow, the black filigree of fences and tree branches look just like the photos. But gradually colours begin to seep through. The azure, pink, yellow, red, salmon, green walls of the ornate building facades, the towering gilded steeples and cupolas of churches, the yard keepers in their long aprons wielding brooms, their faces red from frost and alcohol.

Most streets had been renamed in Soviet times. Only pages of old books preserved the historical names—Varvarka, Tverskaya, Volhonka,

Mohovaya. I used to repeat them as an incantation, never imagining that one day I would be traversing this ancient maze.

We turn a corner. The elegance of this street is painful. My heart begins to thaw, its rhythms unsteady. Such charming buildings. Such sense of harmony and history. Up ahead, in the trembling frosty air, I glimpse but can't seem to focus on one of the Kremlin towers. Familiar elements in an unfamiliar Moscow. Islands of sanity amid looming destruction. Destruction that, like an irreversible phantom, is already built into the unsuspecting bricks and fibres of these streets.

Where are we? I want to ask. Maybe I do, but I don't hear my voice. The street and its buildings seem to be made of gelatinous translucent glass. Through it I am glimpsing another street—stripped, eradicated and rebuilt. That street is wider. Much wider. Its buildings, different buildings for the most part, are so far away, pulling at these structures. "What is this street?"

"This is Tverskaya," you say. "I hope you don't mind but I have to call on the Governor-General before…"

I don't hear the rest of your explanation. Tverskaya—Gorky Street in my time. The street that Stalin widened from sixteen to fifty meters, razed and rebuilt at his whim.

Fast, it was oh so fast that transformation. A city that was built drop by drop, building by building, street by street, century by century was reconfigured in a handful of years. Fast—buildings that were meticulously designed were demolished and replaced by uniform boxes. Fast. Some transformations happened in one night. Like the widening of Gorky Street.

The few buildings here that weren't destroyed by Stalin were moved with all their inhabitants inside. The tenants, being aware that their buildings were scheduled for "relocation" begged the authorities to be given advance warning, so that they could take precautions and get out of the heaving creaking colossal structures. But Moscow authorities were only concerned with beating records set in the decadent West. They worked in the middle of the night, when a huge winch smoothly lifted the buildings and rolled them on temporary rails to their new locations. All utilities remained functional, since they were connected via flexible temporary connections. The buildings were moved so smoothly that many tenants learned about their relocations only in the morning.

You continue talking but I have a hard time catching your words through a suddenly unsteady air. As if the weight of all those destroyed and moved buildings is muddying my senses. I am trying to catch a semblance of familiarity, something to anchor myself to but all I keep seeing are the buildings, slowly being dragged back, the narrow street before us widening then narrowing again as I desperately struggle to keep focus on the pedestrians, the shop signs in front of me. "The Great Tverskaya Pharmacy," "Fillipov's Bakery"… Something about this bakery, a shadow of a memory snags my racing thoughts. I know something about Fillipov's bakery. Yes! The buildings grow more steady and opaque, this is where Moscow's famous sweet raisin rolls were invented. I inhale, trying to catch a whiff of sugary sweetness in the air and run my finger on the sleeve of your *tulup*. I concentrate on its supple texture and chase away the images of wobbling shifting buildings, growing tall and shrinking again, crumbling and rising. Just surrender, I tell myself. The faces of cities change even more than the faces of people. Nothing stays the same. Clinging to images of what is to come only invites this mad holographic dance of architecture. Just get your bearings in these surroundings, I tell myself. Take these streets, and these names, and these faces as the only possible solid fact. Surrender. Surrender.

"Where are we now?" I ask.

"Gazetny Pereulok," you reply. And thankfully, before my brain begins to audition this lane's possible names a century hence, before the mad swirl begins again I hear someone call your name.

The voice is so loud, so cheerful that I cannot help but turn around and focus on it. Slow down on only one detail. One element of this reality. One man.

He is standing at the corner in a short overcoat and a low-crowned hat, jauntily askew. A smile of red parted lips shows a gleam of white teeth. His cheeks are red from the frost, or perhaps his cheeks are always red. He has a rosy complexion, a well-fed round face. Radiant, young, beaming.

"Obolensky," you mumble.

Obolensky calls out again. Vigorously and urgently, insisting that you stop. He has one arm on the window of a carriage that has halted at the corner and the heads of a lady in a velvet hat and two children are peeking out of its window. Obolensky continues smiling and beckoning to you. The lady smiles a kindly smile and she too waves her hand at you.

"That's my cousin Katya," you say. "Ekaterina Vladimirovna Obolenskaya. I didn't particularly want to see anyone in Moscow," you add raising your hat in greeting. You would have instructed our coachman to drive on, but Obolensky runs across the snowy street towards our sleigh.

"Oh, shame on you for not letting us know you are in Moscow. Been here long? I was at Dussot's Hotel yesterday and saw 'Tolstoy' on the visitors' list, but it never entered my head that it was you," says Obolensky, knocking one foot against the other to shake the snow off his gleaming black boots. "What a shame not letting us know," he repeats.

"Yes, fancy running into you, Pavel Stepanovich," you respond dryly. "I have meant to call on you but have had no time; I am very busy," Obolensky glances at me, then at you and smiles. He thinks he understands and raises his hat to me, ever so slightly. A non-committal gesture. Just polite enough to register my presence in case I turn out to be important. Just fleeting enough to be an inconsequential twitch, should I prove to be a momentary visitor through your life.

"I'll tell you what we'll do," Obolensky beams at you and casts furtive glances at me. "We are throwing a dinner tomorrow night. Just an intimate circle of friends. Do come. The crème de la crème will be there: Fet, Pestov, and Grigorovich is visiting from St. Petersburg. You will have a thoroughly delightful evening. You shall, shan't you? We will expect you at five or six o'clock if you like."

"Well..." you begin, but he shakes his head. "No, no, no. I won't hear any excuses. It's settled," and before receiving your reply he begins a brisk trek back towards the carriage with his wife and children. In the middle of the street he turns towards us again and shouts, "Katya will be thrilled. We shall see you later on."

As we pull away, I turn around, watching Obolensky kiss his wife's hand and walk jauntily along the sidewalk up Tverskaya.

"Paul, Paul!" suddenly calls out his wife remembering something.

He turns around. A figure out of an illustrated 19th-century novel. A costume from some movie. But this is real. There he is, a 19th-century dandy standing in the middle of a 19th-century wintry sidewalk. She shouts something else but I don't hear it. The words are swept away by the wind. And the same wind raises a flurry of snowflakes, and these white magical dancing flakes twirl in the air, erasing memories of what is to come. They outline this figure in a short winter coat. An oblivious satisfied smile on his face.

bliss

Y OUR WIFE AND children are in Italy this winter. You are in Moscow attending to the sale of family lands and are, indeed, staying at Dussot's Hotel.

When we arrived last evening you graciously offered to rent me a separate room but I insisted on staying in the servants' quarters. I must cause as little interruption to the flow of your life as possible. Now my first night here, so close to you, is almost over. My body is buzzing with sheer euphoria. I am acclimating to this time. I don't try to swim in its stream. I float, feeling the buoyant waves lapping through my soul. I feel, as you once said, "absolutely extricated from the restrictions of material life."

Unable to sleep, I open the window and let the freezing air flood the room, but I feel fresh and strong and energized. In the next room you snore and moan a command about feeding horses in your sleep. I resist the temptation to open the door and sneak a look at you. I hear you, that is enough. It is really you, tossing in a quaintly narrow bed only a few feet away, and the sheets grow warm with the weight of your body.

I feel that anything is possible, that I could fly. When dawn begins to release the shapes of buildings from the black backdrop of night, I dress hastily and slip outside.

I absorb the details about me. The silence and crackle of frozen snow under my feet, the milky puffs of my breath in the cavernous transparency of the morning air. The sky turning from inky to pale blue to blush and finally a vibrant triumphant orange. The day promises to be glorious. Everything seems extraordinary: the group of young boys rushing to school, the grey doves flying down from the roofs to the pavement, the bakery shutters thrust open and the loaves sprinkled with poppy seeds pushed out by an unseen hand.

Those loaves, those doves, those boys with their timeless faces and archaic military-style uniforms, all seem like enchanted creations. And this magic converges in a single moment—one of the boys runs towards the doves and glances, smiling, at me. The dove with a whir of its wings darts away, flashing iridescent in the sun's rays, rising higher and higher amid snowflakes whirling in the currents of the brisk morning wind. The aroma of fresh-baked bread escapes from the window where the baker is setting out his wares. A word comes to mind. It describes what I am seeing, what I am feeling, what I am breathing. Bliss.

in candlelight

Slowness. This is the flavour of your time. Not so in the impending century. We will become accustomed to running throughout the day, continuing our mad dash toward the night. A constant frenzied tempo that will cloak from us the fleeting subtleties of life. But here, in a world that pulses to varied rhythms, you have managed to seize nuances, to savour them. Your daylight is so slow compared to ours. There is no traversing continents in five hours. There is no racing to work at a hundred and ten kilometres within sixty minutes. No, you move through space with more contemplation. The speed of life is delineated mostly by muscles. Human muscles, horse muscles. Whereas soon we won't even notice the transition between day and night, in your era the passage of time is excruciatingly present in every moment. Dusk is a separate sensation from day, from night. Sunrise is not the same as morning. Noon and late afternoon entertain very different shadows and aromas. And night is even slower. Holding a candelabra, moving from room to room demands deceleration, guarding from gusts and drafts the glittering feeble source of light.

In candlelight one walks tentatively.

The world around is more elusive. Objects fade into the darkness releasing their outlines into non-existence. The ambiguity of edges, flickering boundaries, mutating certainties.

Time creeps through the shadows, sighs with the creaking floorboards, quivers between the hoots of the barn owls. Then stops, wavers.

One breathes slowly. One lives slowly in candlelight.

an intimate circle

"All the guests have arrived," says Matvey, the Obolenskys' butler. "His Highness, Pavel Stepanovich is running late." It is well past five and as we hand our coats to the butler, the host himself is finally heard in the entryway.

He walks in with the same big smile that he had sported yesterday when we met him on Tverskaya. "Ah, Lev Nikolaevich!" he embraces you and bows to me.

"May I introduce you to Mademoiselle Zumoff," you say.

"Ah, delighted," Obolensky kisses my proffered hand. "So, we reached the door almost at the same moment," he continues without missing a beat, without asking who I am or even indicating in the slightest that your bringing a woman to an intimate dinner party might be questionable.

"Aren't we having perfectly stupendous weather?" he goes on, not in the least bit deterred by our silence as we follow him. Thankfully we are spared a discourse on the weather, because it is apparent as we step into the candle-lit expanse of the drawing room that things are not going so smoothly without the gregarious host.

"Oh, Paul, thank God you're here!" Obolensky's wife Katya—Ekaterina Vladimirovna—wearing a lovely gray silk gown, is rushing past us. She pauses just long enough to explain to him in a soft tone, "I was starting to get worried. I shall be right back. I'll only check on the children. Grisha was starting to come down with a sore throat and Mademoiselle Dufis will surely not know how to goad him into eating his dinner."

With a rustle of her silk skirts she leaves the room. The rest of the guests are sitting like so many priests' wives at a social gathering, obviously wondering why they are there and forcing out remarks simply to avoid being silent. Pestov, a small jovial man in a military uniform, feels unmistakably a fish out of water, and the smile with which his thick lips greet Obolensky says, plainly as words: *Well, old boy, you have plopped me down amidst all these learned folk, whereas a drinking party, or a gypsy restaurant, now that would be more my style!*

A heavyset man with a thick beard and thinning hair jumps up. "Ah, so here is our guest of honour," he exclaims while embracing you.

"Yes, Afanasy Afanasievich," you mumble while earnestly returning his embrace, "here for your consumption. Fine Baltic sturgeon over there. Fine provincial writer over here."

Afanasy Afanasievich? This hulk with an arrogant glint in his dark eyes is the celebrated poet Fet?! I have never seen pictures of him and for some reason I imagined that all those romantic impressionistic odes to nature and beauty would be written by a delicate waif of a man.

Obolensky apologizes, explaining that he had been detained by prince so-and-so. You lean over and whisper to me that this particular prince is Obolensky's constant excuse for all his absences and tardiness, and all his friends know that when he invokes the prince he has usually spent time with Rezhkina, a dancer at the Imperial Theatre whom he patronizes.

Whatever his faults, Obolensky's social graces are immaculate. Within moments of the host's entering, the drawing room fills with voices.

I stay off to the side, my attention wandering from some political discussion on the Russification of Poland to examining the sombre oil portraits of ancestors in military regalia and powdered wigs, the heavy burgundy damask of the draperies, the delicate china. We move into the dining room and stand around a side-table laden with carafes of various liquors, six types of cheeses, all with little silver spades, caviar, herring, pickled mushrooms and cucumbers and plates with thinly sliced French bread.

Through all this, the portraits and the cheese and the pickles and Poland, your gaze shimmies over my face with thousands of unspoken questions.

You make a few steps towards me but Obolensky intercepts your trajectory: "Lev Nikolaevich, there is someone you should meet." You nod, squinting nearsightedly at the new figure entering the drawing room. "Yes, of course!" Obolensky takes you by the arm and leads you away to that new man.

The room grows quiet with the new entry. Everyone is assessing the value of the addition to their illustrious company.

"Count Tolstoy, allow me to introduce you to Dmitriy Vasilievich Grigorovich, a writer from St. Petersburg…"

"Very glad to see you again," says Grigorovich shaking your hand vigorously.

"You two are acquainted?" Obolensky is surprised.

"We used to run in the same circles in St. Petersburg, back when I just returned from military service," you say.

"Indeed," nods Grigorovich, "the literary community is small and the young Count Tolstoy caused quite a stir then. It was impossible not to be acquainted with him."

Fet approaches your trio and shakes Grigorovich's hand, "Welcome! Welcome to Moscow. You know, this reminds me: it was around that time I was visiting St. Petersburg and decided to call on Turgenev, who used to get up and take his tea in the St. Petersburg fashion, very early. When his butler opened the door I saw a dress sword with a ribbon of St. Anne in the hall. 'Whose sword is this?' I inquired. 'This is Count Tolstoy's sword; his Excellency is asleep in the drawing room. Ivan Sergeyevich is having his tea in the study. If you please, come this way,' said the butler in a hushed voice, pointing me down the hallway. During the hour I spend with Turgenev, we all but whispered, being afraid to awaken Tolstoy, who was asleep in the next room. 'He came from Sebastopol, straight from his artillery unit,' said Turgenev, smiling paternally, 'stopped here at my place, and straight away plunged into debauchery. Carousals, gypsies, and card-playing all night; and afterward he sleeps like a log until two in the afternoon. At first I tried to talk some sense into him, but after a while I gave it up.'"

"I didn't know you had stayed with Turgenev," says Grigorovich, turning to you. "If my memory serves me correctly, you lived on Ofitserskiy Street, on the lower floor?"

You nod, "Well, I couldn't impose on Turgenev's hospitality indefinitely."

"Wasn't there another writer renting the apartment next to you?"

"Yes, Mikhailov. A strange fellow. A Freemason, I believe. He liked to keep to himself."

"Couldn't say that about you. Mikhailov, yes, of course. I believe he was the one who introduced us," Grigorovich laughs, "although your reputation preceded you."

"Lev Nikolaevich," Obolensky joins the conversation, "Your keeping permanent lodgings in St. Petersburg is rather incomprehensible to me. I've known you for years and you not only dislike St. Petersburg, you are irritated by everything connected with it, present company excluded," he bows slightly to Grigorovich.

"Oh, no offence," says Grigorovich. "Count Tolstoy's views of our Venice of the North are notorious. Everything that bore the cachet of St. Petersburg infuriated him to no end. You should have seen him the first time I brought him into the offices of 'The Contemporary' to meet the editorial staff."

"Hah! That has nothing to do with St. Petersburg," you interrupt, frowning. "They were simply talking such rubbish at that newspaper of yours..."

Obolensky cuts in, "Lev Nikolaevich, do let Grigorovich finish the tale. Surely no harm can come now of his exposing your youthful escapades."

You cross your arms and bow to Obolensky, as Grigorovich continues:

"If memory serves me correctly at that time you, my dear Count, had already had a few stories published in 'The Contemporary,' but you had never met any of the staff face-to-face. I agreed to make the formal introductions. On the way there I warned you to be careful, diplomatic, shall we say, and not touch certain topics and in particular not attack Georges Sand, who at that time was the idol of most of the editors and quite a few of the contributors. The meeting was going smoothly, tea and cigars and all, and you were rather taciturn, but toward the end you could no longer control yourself. Hearing yet another round of praise bestowed on a new novel by Georges Sand, you jumped up and loudly declared your hatred for her, adding that her shameless heroines, if they existed in real life, ought to be tied to a hangman's cart and driven through the streets of St. Petersburg as a cautionary example."

Everyone finds this highly amusing. I bite into a pickle and the bitterness of the brine squirts into my mouth. Is it Sand's characters you object to or the woman herself? A woman who had dared to step outside the corral of societal mores? If so, all is lost. I swallow hard, forcing the acrid brine and masticated remnants of food down my throat.

"This cheese is quite lovely," says Ekaterina Vladimirovna, who has returned from attending the children and is again playing the gracious hostess. "Do try some."

I force a smile, "Thank you. I shall a bit later."

"Well, I for one, don't believe in the slightest that Lev Nikolaevich had such a harsh opinion about Miss Sand," says Fet loudly. "In those days it was just his tendency to contradict and challenge everyone. The greater the authority of his interlocutor, the more he would insist on defending an opposite view."

"Contradiction? Nonsense!" you say. "I merely insist that if one has an opinion one ought to be able to defend it. If it falls apart under a bit of scrutiny…" you shrug, but Fet interrupts.

"And what about Turgenev? You used to drive him into a fury and then just sit back, enjoying yourself, throwing out sarcastic remarks as the poor man paced back and forth, stuttering and pressing his hand to his throat with a look of a dying gazelle."

"Ah, poor Turgenev," Grigorovich laughs wholeheartedly. "Do you remember the time when you two engaged in one of your famous arguments until Turgenev, voice hoarse, clasping his throat began pacing up and down the room declaring, `I cannot talk any longer! It will give me bronchitis!' At which you, Lev Nikolaevich, sneered, `Bronchitis! It's an imaginary illness. Bronchitis is a metal!'"

"Well, come, come," says Obolensky. "Isn't that in a writer's nature— you all bicker and mull over this or that—but in the end thoughts tempered in these arguments end up on the pages of your work? It is all for the best. We should be proud that we live in an age where so many great Russian writers have the opportunity to argue with one another."

"I never thought you were such a patriot, Pavel Stepanovich," bows Grigorovich.

"Patriotism?" Pestov, who had been quiet amid all this literary talk, finally has a theme to latch onto. "I'll tell you who the real patriots are.

Married men, especially you, Lev Nikolaevich. As I was saying, there is but one method for the Russification of our foreign populations—to bring up as many children as one can. My brother and I are terribly remiss," he gulps down the wine he has in his goblet, "but not for lack of trying."

Everyone laughs and Obolensky with particular gusto. "Oh, yes, that's the best method!" he says munching cheese and refilling Pestov's wine glass. At this the conversation drops as the host and hostess lead the guests to the table.

The meal is as fine as the china it's served on. The asparagus soup is splendid; the flaky dough of the potato *pirozhki* is impeccable. The two footmen and Matvey in white cravats do their duty with the dishes and wines unobtrusively and swiftly. The dinner is a success, both gastronomically and intellectually. The conversation, at times general and at times between individuals, never pauses and towards the end the company is so lively that everyone rises from the table without interrupting the lively chatter.

Everyone takes part in the conversation except you and me. At any other time you might have been quite interested in the topic of Russia's imperialistic ambitions. But there is a dreaminess in being in each other's presence and all other concerns dissipate. You and I have our own conversation. Not a verbal one but an inexplicable communication, which brings us closer moment by moment, igniting a giddy terror at the sense of the unknown we are both entering.

moscow waltz

How MUCH TIME has passed? I don't know. Time seems to have stopped, while you and I move through a meaningless gyration of light and darkness, urged on only by our heartbeats. We visit the homes of your friends. I am all but invisible to most. It is easy to get lost when a friendly impromptu gathering might involve twenty, thirty people. And when someone does happen to focus on me, you call me your "young protégé." The men believe they know the nature of our relationship. They tend to be reserved. The women prefer not to know anything and are therefore cordial.

I enjoy the anonymity. I am mostly left to my own devices and observe. The faces astonish me. Such refined features. Such dignity and poise. It will be decades, if ever, before Russia sees the likes of these expressions again.

A proclivity towards grandeur has become ingrained in all of you. You are all counts, princes, barons. You are all on the verge of extinction. I must be vigilant. I cannot allow any blunders, any knowledge of my other life to speed up your curiosities. That would jar them out of their charming tempo. I know this lifestyle of philosophical conversations, capons with asparagus, gilded mirrors on silk-covered walls will be pulverized in the quickening cogwheels of civilization. Alas, what horrors will these imposing mirrors reflect only a few decades in the future? Muddied boots scuffing up parquet floors, ball-dresses stained with blood, the pale blue and rich rose silks gutted…

I must not think of that. Slow down. Breathe in the here-and-now and the magnificent slowness reverberating to the tempo of horse-hoofs.

I turn to you. Your nose and cheeks are red from the wind. You tell the sleigh driver to go faster, but I ask him to slow down. The voluminous transparency of this day seems to stretch beyond time, to arrest the senses.

"Would you be able to describe the splendour of this moment in just a few sentences?" I ask.

You love a challenge. An impish spark flares up in your eyes.

"I am astonished today by the poetic beauty of winter weather," your voice is tinged with mock solemnity. "A fog has risen in the sky, through which only the white disk of the sun is seen. On the road there is thawing manure and a damp crispness is in the air."

I laugh; that indeed sums it up.

We are on our way to a restaurant. It is mid-afternoon. I wonder if it will be "Slavyanskiy Bazar," where a journey to your favourite table inevitably takes a quarter of an hour as you stop to greet others of your circle. A half a century ago Pushkin used to frequent this restaurant. You yearn to get close to his spirit and that's why you go there again and again, although generally you don't like the city centre, as if you sense the havoc that it will spawn.

Today, however, we're not going to "Slavyanskiy Bazar." The sleigh leaves behind the last houses of Moscow proper. We're heading past the boundary of this still un-sprawling city. (I mustn't remember what it will look like some day. Now we're going up Sparrow Hills, so forget the syphilitic despot whose name one day these hills will bear.) If you must be in Moscow at all, you prefer the periphery, its gentler pace, its cleaner air. You enjoy strolling through the forest, down the steep embankment to the water.

Then, once you've worked up an appetite, you like relaxing in Krynkin's new restaurant, with its exotic theme—half Moorish, half trans-Caucasian. Waiters standing erect in their elaborate uniforms of *djigits*, the proud warriors from Georgia, greet the arriving visitors. The décor is straight out of Scheherazade's tales. I think this evokes for you a memory of your youth as a soldier in the Caucasus.

There are fewer familiar faces here. We can talk without being interrupted. When we sit here, sometimes for hours on end, I cannot help noticing a certain peculiarity of expression, as it were, a restrained radiance about your face and whole figure. I dare not think that it is I who is imparting a bit of happiness to your life. I believe it is the focus of the conversations. I always stir them towards literature.

Now you take off your overcoat and walk into the dining room, giving directions to the djigit waiters, who are clustered about you in their long dress coats, daggers dangling off their belts, napkins folded over their arms.

Bowing right and left to the people you encounter, you go up to a sideboard for a preliminary appetizer of smoked fish and vodka.

"If you prefer, your Excellency, a private room will be free shortly; Prince Golitsyn is in with a lady and they are about to leave," says a particularly unshakable, red-headed young djigit with narrow hips, and epaulets accentuating his broad shoulders.

You nod your assent. We each down a glass of vodka, its pleasant warmth spreading through our bodies, chasing away the winter chill and relaxing the muscles, when the young djigit returns.

"This way, Excellency, please. Your Excellency won't be disturbed there." We follow him. "Please, this way, Mademoiselle," he says to me, showing his respect to you by being attentive to your guest, as we step into one of the several cozy private dining rooms with a magnificent view of the surrounding forests and the Novodevichiy Convent across the river, its red turrets and gold domes festive in the pale sunlight.

Instantly tossing a fresh cloth over the round table under the bronze chandelier, though it already had a table cloth on it, the djigit pulls up two velvet chairs, and comes to a standstill before you with a napkin, awaiting your commands.

You study the menu.

"Fresh oysters have come in," volunteers the warrior-waiter.

"Ah, oysters!" you shake your head. "I should like some cabbage pie more than anything else."

"Your Excellency means le pâte en croûte de chou?"

You cringe at the pretension but nod, "That's it my friend, you give us the cabbage pie with vegetable soup..."

"Printanière," prompts the waiter. But you do not care to allow him the satisfaction of giving the French names of the dishes.

"With root vegetables in it, you know? Then turbot with cream sauce, and some canned fruit for dessert."

The djigit, realizing that you will not name the dishes in French, does not repeat the list after you but allows himself the pleasure of mumbling the French names under his breath, "Soupe Printanière, Turbot avec de la sauce à Beaumarchais, macedoine de fruits," and then instantly, as though worked by springs, he picks up the menu and sets down the wine list.

"What shall you drink?"

"You can give us Les Nuits. Oh, no, better the classic Chablis."

~~~

You remain silent over dinner, entangled in a mental world you have yet to share with me. The wine makes me light-headed, I feel like bantering. I try several topics before one of them, about contemporary writers, brings you out of your thoughts.

"I am trying to find something redeeming in them," you say, "but it is impossible to read them. Their writing is steeped in literary ignorance, sloppiness. They haven't read anything, they don't know anything."

I wouldn't dare mentioning Turgenev, but I almost slip by wanting to parry your response with the brilliance of Bulgakov. Catching myself in time and now afraid of mixing up my eras, I ask whether you could define what, for you, constitutes good writing.

"The art of good writing is not in knowing what to write, but in knowing what not to write. No ingenious insertions can improve a composition as much as relentless slashing of lines and paragraphs."

You're not in a talkative mood. I let you wander in your thoughts and now I too disappear into mine. I remember the magic of last night. You taught me to waltz. As befits your class, you have been tutored in it by some Frenchman in your youth.

You are quite an elegant dancer, but you do not engage in it often. A silly preoccupation, you scoff. But you were in a silly mood. Alone in the grand ballroom of your cousin's estate, the sun was close to setting. The gardens beyond the window were awash in the lazy amber lull of a retiring day. My thoughts were spinning a tapestry of names, faces, titles, fates that had passed through this room. I too began spinning twirling for the sheer joy of being able to see it, to feel it. I heard you laughing but it was only a reflection of my joy so I spun on. Then your arms quelled the momentum of my rotation. They picked me up. My eyes were shut. I knew you would kiss me there within and among all those illustrious spectres. My heart was beating fast. Perhaps too fast? Is that why suddenly instead of a kiss I heard you counting—one, two three, one two three… only then was I aware that you were moving, slowly rotating while holding me still aloft.

"Set me down."

"Ready to dance?" you asked.

I was. I was ready to accept your lesson of tempo.

As we twirled in a dance without music, you began whispering and your words became the melody that propelled us on and on. You said that you conceived a character of a woman, married, from high society, but one who has lost her way. You said that your aim was only to evoke pity for this woman, not to scorn her, not to judge her and that as soon as this character came to you, various male characters that you had been thinking about suddenly came together and found their places around this woman. "It's all clear now," you said.

essences

THE THIRD WHISTLE sounds. You and I settle on the soft upholstered bench of the compartment. We're going to your estate, Yasnaya Polyana. We're going to begin work on our novel.

As the train shudders and the platform outside the window begins to move slowly, my eyes linger on two elegantly dressed women—one young and beautiful, one old, desiccated with carefully pomaded ringlets and traces of former beauty. A handsome officer approaches them. The old woman steps towards him, smiles with her thin lips and raises her gloved hand for him to kiss and then, lifting his head from her hand, she kisses him on the cheek. The officer turns towards the young woman, bows to her and when his face lifts I register a look of awe and fear and puzzlement on it. Is this what the thunderbolt of love looks like, I wonder?

This all happens in a couple of beats then the train speeds up. The three people disappear from view. You sigh, "Am I glad to be leaving Moscow! Look at this." You nod at the elegantly dressed crowds outside the window, the grey slushy snow, the beggars, "stench, stones, luxury, poverty. Depravity. A gathering of villains, who have robbed the people, have hired soldiers and judges to protect their orgy and now they're feasting."

I have been in an anxious, excited frame of mind the whole day, and now I take pleasure in settling in for the journey. I take off my boots, and tuck up my feet, wrapping them in my long coat. An elderly gentleman across from me is already snoring, and a stout woman with a big mole on her upper lip makes observations about the train's poor heating system. I mumble a few words in response, and seeing that I won't make a good interlocutor she turns to her neighbour. You ask your servant, Yegor, to get a lamp, hook it onto the arm of your seat, and take a book out of your valise.

I cannot help listening to the train sounds, then observing the snow beating on the left window and sticking to the pane, and the sight of the muffled train conductor passing by, his one side encrusted by melting snow, and quiet conversations about the raging storm outside. And it goes on and on—the shaking and rattling of the train car, the snow against the window, the rapid succession of steamy heat and cold and back to heat, the flickering of the same faces in the twilight, the same voices.

The stout woman has fallen asleep, a red bag on her lap clutched by stubby hands in red gloves, one of which is torn. Your book lies abandoned next to you as you look out the window at the darkening air.

"It will be strange if my love for my work will dissipate into nothingness," you whisper and those are the last words you say before we arrive at the small provincial train station and climb into a sleigh for the one-hour ride through the countryside to Yasnaya Polyana. Something about the tempo of our movement awakens ideas in you. Here, in the freezing night, you talk and talk.

~~~

The swaying of the horse-drawn sleigh is lulling. My thoughts sometimes follow your baritone, sometimes the swoosh of wind meandering over the austere winter terrain.

"It's dreadful, dreadful in Russia," you say. "In Saint Petersburg, in Moscow, everybody is screaming something, everybody is agitated and waiting for something or other to occur. Whereas in the backcountry— patriarchal barbarism, theft, and lawlessness reign supreme. Believe it or not, upon my return to Russia, for a long time I had to fight a feeling of disgust, and only now I'm beginning to adapt to all the horrors that comprise the perpetual backdrop of our life."

You had recently visited your family in Italy and are experiencing our homeland with un-calloused senses. But, my dear, it's hitting you so hard because you are an indelible part of it.

"I know that you don't agree," you continue, "but if you could have seen everything I have witnessed in one week: how on a street a gentlewoman was pounding her handmaid with a rod; how a station master demanded that I dispatch a wagon-load of hay to him, or else he would not issue a lawful ticket to my servant; how in a narrow alley not far from the Sukhareva Square a drunk peasant woman collapsed on the sidewalk. From a nearby courtyard a rivulet of dirty water was flowing into the gutter, right under the woman's head and back. She was sprawled in this cold oozing slime, mumbling under her breath, flailing her arms, flopping her whole body in the wetness, but could not get up. A drunken woman is disgusting! She was so foul, so gelatinous that nobody would help her up. A grey-eyed boy crouched next to her. Tears flowing down his cheeks. Sniffling, he wailed in a thin voice, hopeless, exhausted: 'Mom, mo-o-o-mmy. Ma, get up, won't you?' She would wiggle her arms, snort, lift her head and then again, smack it back down into the mud. Horrid, absolutely dreadful!"

You shudder, shut your eyes, and quietly continue: "If you had seen all this and a vastness of other events, then you would believe me, that life in Russia is an infinite toil and conflict with one's own feelings."

A conflict of feelings—a familiar landscape. Alas, what you don't know is that a hundred years hence nothing will have changed in Russia. Nothing will probably have changed in two hundred years either. The essence of a country does not transform with political upheavals, education, or mechanical innovations. Essences are inert.

I must be careful not to slip into too many memories of that persistent world. That world that is looming like a tornado on your horizon. You do not see it yet. You who live at the apex of our civilization cannot conceive of the gruesome abyss the next century will bring. My life is tainted by that knowledge. I see wider: I see further. I see darker.

You have the war of 1812. The great war, you call it. From Russia to France a chain-mail of frozen corpses over cannonball-torn earth; Moscow burned down. Still, a gentlemanly war, I say.

My horrors are more macabre. They reek of German ovens where innocence is incinerated.

Can you conceive of mattresses stuffed with human hair and lamp shades made out of tattooed human skin? Or red torrents gushing through Africa, fed by tributaries from battered, minced, torched bodies? Can you conceive of a woman choosing which of her children to kill for his meat?

You cannot imagine any of it. You will leave your world several years before mine takes a firm foothold. You will miss its introduction fanfare of yellow-green gases rending lungs on the mud-filled expanses of France. You will not hear the wailing Armenians burned alive in their homes, raped into assimilation, bludgeoned into exile. Your feelings won't be conflicted over the uncountable—ten, twenty, thirty million —under the snows of Siberia. Yes, our country will sacrifice its crème de la crème on the altar of a dictator. And what of Hiroshima, mon amour? Shadows of humans burned into the ground and not a bone to bury. Time mercifully will shield you from glimpsing the killing fields of Pol Pot. There the bones remain. Bones bones bones—a sea of them. A monument to yet one more idealistic cannibal. Madmen rule in my distant future. Mad men casting a web of insanity over the whole planet.

Is it a wonder I chose to escape?

I smile indulgently as you bewail the inadequacies of your society. Patriarchal barbarism? The nobles speaking more French than Russian? The iniquity of classes? Do not push your world away too fast my dear. Let it linger a little.

You whisper something in my ear. Maybe just a soft blow. I stir warm in your embrace. We must be approaching your estate. I open my eyes. We are still in the sleigh, wrapped in the sheepskin brought to the train station by your one-eyed coachman Ignat.

Surely I had not fallen asleep. It was a waking nightmare. Thank you for pulling me out of it, back to this night sky and tree silhouettes, snow and stars, black and white reality. Ultimately my grandmother had been right—black-and-white realities are so much safer.

~~~

It is just before nine o'clock when we reach the main house. Light is falling from the windows, etching amber squares into the snow of the front courtyard.

"Agafya, my housekeeper, is still awake," you say.

A grey wool shawl wrapped around her, she walks out onto the porch to greet us. A candle flame shielded by her hand illuminates her smiling, time-creased face and white hair, seemingly spun of snow.

A white borzoi hound leaps out after her, almost knocking her down, and yelping, runs to you, butting his head into your knees.

Nodding politely to me, Agafya says, "We did not expect you so soon, Excellency," as she leads us into the house.

It is a grand old manor, and although you had planned to stay in Moscow for the winter, you demand that the whole house be heated and used. It is a part of you and you cannot bear any part of you being dormant.

"Weekly balls and daily suppers with Princess Volkonsky are all fine, Agafya, but I got an overwhelming urge to write," you squeeze my hand, "and the younger children have a new game that makes it impossible for me to concentrate. Those rascals have found their way into the pantry where we keep spare dishes and when it is too cold outside for them to play, they use our silver serving tray, you know, the oval one with the handles, as a sleigh and go down the front stairwell with such a racket that one can barely think, never mind create amid all that noise."

In the drawing room you settle in an armchair, your favourite as I will soon learn. I stretch out on the chaise by the piano. Agafya brings us tea with cherry preserves, and sighing, "Well, I'll stay a while, Excellency," sits by the window. For minutes or hours, I release my grasp on time, and we each follow the roadways of our own thoughts. The pulse of this idyll is set by Agafya's gossip about how Prokhor, the bailiff, has abandoned his God and conscience, and with the money you had given him to buy a horse he has been drinking non-stop and once beat his wife until he had almost killed her.

Something in her patter suggests a whole terrain of ideas to you and without a word you get up, grab a candlestick and head out of the room. I follow.

You usher me into your study. Nobody dares to enter this room without your consent, not even your wife. Once when you weren't there, your children ran in while playing and you caught them under the desk. You said nothing, but the cold fury in your steely eyes made them tremble. Your eyes, sky blue when you're happy, turn the ominous shade of storm clouds when you're angry. The children scurried out but the sense of guilt and shame at having defiled something sacred would remain with them for the rest of their lives. And here I am, at the entrance to the sanctuary. I feel honoured.

The room's details gradually emerge in the light of the candles you just carried in. Shapes familiar to you, curious to me: the stag's horns, the shelves laden with books, the fireplace, your father's sofa, the walls painted green (your favourite colour), a large desk, on the desk a notebook lined with your bold handwriting, a malachite ashtray (green again, the colour of rebirth you call it). Through it all the comforting smell of old paper—books, books everywhere.

Why would you want to get away from this? Do you really believe that by denying yourself luxuries, by negating your own education, pedigree, knowledge you will coax yourself into the simple happiness of a peasant? The chasm between you and them is not measured in money or stale bread crusts, silks or burlap. You cannot undo your essence. Essences are inert.

There is only one world of normalcy for an artist—the arts, literature, loves and attachments. And in this world nobody—no station master, no bailiff—can get in your way. Sit by yourself. Beyond this frost-filigreed window the wind is howling, there's the filth, the cold. Let your fingers (no they're not at all inept) coerce a gentle Mozart sonata out of a pianoforte keyboard. Allow tears of delight to fall freely. Or read the Iliad or Onegin, which you love so much. When you're ready sit at your desk and invent people—admire or despise them or fall in love with them—live with them, scribbling and "wasting paper," as you call it. And when you need a break surrender yourself to thought as you are doing now, about the people you love. Remember what you yourself once said: your only salvation is in your work.

breakthrough

"Are you in a bad mood?" I ask you over breakfast cocoa, trying to decipher your sullen silence.

"I am melancholy," you say after a pause, as if finding the right words for the explanation is painful. "I'm not writing anything, and when I do it is torture. You cannot imagine how difficult this preliminary work is for me. Ploughing this field that I am compelled to sow to great depths. I must consider and mull over everything that may happen with all the future people of the upcoming composition, which is very long. I must consider millions of possible combinations in order to pick out of them the one-millionth correct one. This is incredibly difficult."

But by the afternoon, it is as if a dam has broken.

You have begun writing in various little notebooks everything that may be needed for an accurate description of mores, habits, dress, and everything that touches everyday life. In other notebooks you are recording everything that comes into your head about characters, plot movements, scenes etcetera. This work is akin to a mosaic. Characters appear to you one by one.

You have attempted the beginning about ten times and are not content with any version. I am so tempted to drop, nonchalantly, "All happy families are alike. Every unhappy family is unhappy in a unique way," but you will come up with it yourself. That part does not need my help.

~~~

What a difference one week makes! This morning you say: "The mechanism is all ready. Time to set it in motion." You promise to name the main character after me. Karen, of course, is not a Russian name, but her last name could be a derivative of Karen, perhaps Karenskaya, or Karenina.

~~~

The tempo is anything but steady at the beginning. I smile at you but you remain grim. You are reproaching yourself for idleness: "Today is one of those days when I have done absolutely nothing. The day has passed and I have left no mark on it."

~~~

My fingers move over your face, trying to smooth out the deep furrows in your forehead.

"I wrote a little bit," you grumble, "but so sloppily and superficially that it doesn't amount to anything. My mental abilities have dulled from that aimless and disorganized life and the company of people who don't want to and cannot understand anything remotely serious and honourable." But there is a glint of hope in your voice and you embrace me tenderly as you say this.

~~~

This evening you declare: "I wrote quite a lot and finished the scene at the Oblonsky household but it is still a very rough draft." You are excited. "Work, work! I experience happiness when I work." You plant a kiss on my forehead and time freezes. You are but inches away. I feel your breath on my face, heat emanating from your body. It takes all my strength not to step towards you. Your eyes search my face for an answer I don't know how to give.

~~~

You look drained and unhappy. "What happened?" I ask, finding you sulking on the front porch. "The work was going so well just a few hours ago ."

You shake your head, "I am always a sap for praise and your kind words about Dolly's character genuinely cheered me up, but I reread everything and it seemed very paltry. I wanted to change things around but couldn't. I felt as if my hands grew limp. Overall today I am very disillusioned with my talent. On top of it all, what I dictated to you this morning is total drivel."

~~~

You avoid me today. When I ask what you've done, you seem distracted. "I got up at eight, corrected the first chapter and wrote nothing else the whole day. … I must get up early and work without stopping on the passages that seem weak. Just keep a smooth busy tempo. I can do corrections later but I can never return wasted time."

~~~

I beg you to go for a walk. Instead you pull me into your office. "I am engrossed in writing," you smile, your face glowing with an idyllic happiness. "I cannot tear myself away. I think that just like nature instilled in people the instinct to procreate, in order to continue the human race," your fingers skim my cheek and tuck an escaped tendril behind my ear, "in the same way it instilled a comparable intense instinct to create art in some people, so that they could conceive works that are enjoyable and beneficial to others. You see, I am being rather immodest, but that is the only explanation of this strange phenomenon that a not so foolish man at the age of forty-seven could be occupied with such a trifle as writing a novel."

~~~

My head rests in your lap. The air is dimming. Soon Agafya will call us to supper. "I rewrote only one-and-a-half chapters," you say. "The conversation between Levin and Oblonsky is a bit strained, but the scene at the ball is wonderful." You begin reading words born just today, bringing the paper close to your eyes, stumbling over your own handwriting. Your other hand strokes my shoulder, wanders onto my neck, sending an army of goose-bumps down my spine.

unforeseen

I HAVE AVOIDED a disaster. I shall repeat this until I believe it.

You were out all day, having left in the morning without a word. It was dark when I heard a horse neigh outside. I ran out to the porch. You dismounted (you rarely ride alone) and brushed past me with barely a nod of acknowledgement. Your face looked haunted. And when Agafya offered you supper you demanded vodka and drowned two glasses.

I waited.

You plonked down onto a settee and I approached, slowly. I sat next to you. Still, not a word. Your finger traced my cheekbone, my jaw. You pulled me close to you. Your eyes were red-rimmed. My lips grazed your cheek and the words spilled out. You told me about an apparition that gashes into your memory from time to time. A cultured, intelligent woman you once knew. A mistress of your friend Bibikov. When she found out that her lover had fallen for a beautiful German governess, she threw herself under the train. And you, as one of the local gentlemen and Bibikov's friend, had been invited to witness the autopsy. You saw that naked mutilated twisted body, like a pulverized slab of meat. You saw that once-beautiful face disfigured beyond recognition. The skull crashed. You said you dreamt of it last night again and couldn't get the images out of your mind all day. Something about that incident is inviting itself onto the pages of the novel we're working on. You kept saying that beauty crushed under the weight of a freight train is appalling.

Images rushed at me too. A train. Sparks. Metal grinding on metal. A puff of breath rising through freezing air from a boy's chapped lips. Specks of blood on a white cuff.

I had to stop them. I had to stop you. I knew all too well what it's like to be overwhelmed by ghosts. I knew all too well how to chase them away. Positioning my face directly over yours, I said: "Don't think of death when there are unexplored pleasures in life." But it wasn't the banality of my words, it was what I did next. I pressed my body to yours. I ran my finger over your lips, chapped, roughened by riding all day, and then, while looking directly into your eyes, I kissed you. You didn't resist. No, you didn't resist at all.

~~~

A wise woman never yields by appointment. It should always be an unforeseen happiness. I can't remember who said that. I don't think it was you. Probably a Frenchman.

I can honestly say that we have skirted and avoided this ever since we met. Never daring to get too close for too long. Until now, this day, this hour. What for months had been my one absorbing, forbidden desire, eclipsing all my old notions and calculations; what for you had been an impossible, unspeakable, and therefore even more entrancing yearning, has been fulfilled.

I kneel before you, my face burning, and beseech you to be calm, though I could just as easily be addressing my own jumbled emotions.

"Lev Nikolaevich," I mumble with a trembling voice. "Levushka, for God's sake!"

But the louder I speak, the more you avert your usually proud and jovial, now shame-stricken gaze. You sink down to the floor from the sofa still strewn with hastily discarded pieces of clothing—a cotton chemise, a silk stocking.

"My God, forgive me!" you say, pressing your hands to your eyes as if trying to reign in escaping tears. "What have I done!"

I embrace you to offer comfort. I try to explain that this has no bearing on your corporeal obligations. I try to kiss you into believing that this is a simple surrender to your art, that Muses demand no less than a blooming wound of passion. Yet I physically sense your shame, and my speech dwindles into silence.

You hold my hand and do not stir for minutes that seem like hours. At last, as though making an effort, you stand up and push me away.

Your face now looks as noble and calm as always, only the corners of your lips betray that part of you that has been forever changed by our act. Something in you has broken.

"Levushka," I try to cheer you up. "Your writing will only be fortified by these few minutes of happiness we allowed ourselves."

"Happiness!" you say with loathing. "For God's sake, not a word. Not a word more!" You leave the room.

Later you will confess that at that moment you could not articulate the sense of awkwardness, terror and rapture at stepping into this new life, and you did not want to speak of it, to vulgarize this feeling by inappropriate words. But this would be much later, for in the next day after this happens, and on the third day, you still find no words in which you can express the complexity of your feelings. Indeed, you cannot even find thoughts in which you could clearly think out all that is in your soul.

I am patient. We are reaching a critical point in the novel. I now have the means to guide you.

between worlds

T HE FULL MOON resembles a spotlight behind the thinning backdrop of clouds. Their tattered edges are shimmering in the relentless cold rays. And thousands upon thousands of stars, like audiences holding flickering lighters, witnessing me in my newly forged drama.

You are a forceful lover, even your tenderness is passionate, hungry. Taking every square inch of flesh to be your own. Possessing and repossessing. Sometimes abandoning yourself, frequently observing. Memorizing. The shade of blush on skin. The scent of perspiration. The reflected candle flames in half closed eyes. Hair, matted, strewn over starched bed sheets. Not white but ecru, the white is not as white here. The black is blacker than our black.

"Stop inspecting me," I say half joking. "Can't you stop at least at night?"

"Recently I read a book," you reply in that relaxed dreamy voice of contentment. "It was poetry by a deceased young Spanish poet. Besides the wonderful gift of the writer himself, I was very much taken by the description of his life. His biographer recalls a story told about him by an old woman, his nanny. Over time she had noticed with great worry that her charge often spent sleepless nights, sighed, muttered some words out loud, walked out into the fields during a full moon, towards the trees and remained there for hours on end. One night she even thought he had gone totally insane. The young man got up, threw some clothes on himself in the dark and walked on to the nearest well. His nanny followed him. And she saw that he drew out a pail of water and began pouring it out onto the ground slowly. Once it was all gone he drew some more water and again began pouring it out. The nanny burst into tears: 'My darling has gone raving mad!' But the young man had a very specific purpose in mind—to observe closely how on a quiet moonlit night a stream of water flows and splashes. He needed it for a new poem. In this case he was testing his memory and a poetic impression that had lodged in it when he once observed nature. Just like painters who, as you know, use models that they place in various poses and dress up in suitable clothing. Whenever I read writers, Russian or foreign, I inadvertently feel which one was true to nature and had realized the task before him, and which one was faking it."

I bite you to bring you back into me. Not me the lover to be dissected and described in many guises on many pages, but me. The flesh, the person.

"Tell me more about her," you say.

"The woman? The modern woman?"

"Yes," you whisper, but I know there is deep concentration in your voice.

"She dares to love. Love with her heart, not her mind, not her ennui but her soul. She dares to follow her love and be honest about it. Once she has given herself to her love, no man-made rules can keep her with another man, her body would never belong to anyone but her love."

You consider it. "The church, society deem it wrong. Sure people have affairs, but is there a reason to break up a family? Two families?"

"Honesty, integrity, fidelity. These concepts are not black and white. Living in a sanctioned lie is more sinful than surrendering to spurned truth." I remember a poem by Anna Akhmatova: "What do you think of Lot's wife?" I ask.

"The pillar of salt? Simple parable. She disobeyed God."

"No. She disobeyed the emissary of God. She disobeyed the husband who followed rules blindly. Her act wasn't idle curiosity. It was her life she was fleeing. The place where she had known love, where she had borne children, where the most important moments of her life had seeped into the very ground, where her tears had fragranced the air, where her laugher had become part of the trees and the flowers. She dared to look back at her life. She has been scorned ever since."

I recite the poem. You ask me to repeat the last four lines.

Who will sing a lament for this woman's demise?
She may seem like the smallest of losses perchance.
But my heart will forever remember and prize
Her, who forfeited life for that one final glance.

You are quiet for many minutes. Beyond the window clouds have dissipated. Blue snow is puffing out and highlighting the geometry of oak branches. Indifferent observing stars. And total silence. Just your breathing. My heart beating. Deafening. I am tempted to imagine a sound. Any sound that might shimmer with the echo of the coming century, a flying machine, captured music. But no, I stop myself, even a memory, a wistful thought might make me move faster, break away into a time I no longer wish to know. I force myself to relax into the silence, to embrace it, to savour its slowness.

"It is very beautiful, this poem," you say finally.

Yes, it will be one day, I think.

"What a person must have experienced to write this."

"A loss of husband, son, lovers, friends. Forced to keep her eyes open while love was slain over and over in front of her."

"A woman? A Russian?"

I nod both times.

"And her name?"

"Anna."

"Anna? That was the name of Bibikov's mistress. Anna Pirogova. The one who jumped under the train. Yes, Anna. A perfect name."

at work

T HE EXTRAORDINARY BEAUTY of spring this year in Yasnaya
Polyana "could wake the dead," as you put it. Two rows of tall swaying
birches flank the "Preshpekt," lending grace, grandeur and elegant
simplicity to this wide lane leading from the gate to the main house.
The morning game of light and shadows through the dense foliage of
the birches, the dark green grass sprinkled with forget-me-nots, the
impenetrable nettles—everything whispers of hope and promise. We
have embarked on the second draft of our Anna.

There is a definite rhythm in our schedule. In the beginning I would
read the manuscript, correcting the punctuation and obvious mistakes
and indicating to you the spots which I felt needed improvement.
Usually, almost exclusively, these were areas where you began straying
from your original image of Anna—a muse, a heroine-victim, a woman
before her time.

After I jotted down my notes you went over them, implementing
some, adding your own modifications. We continued in this mode until
half-way through the novel. It was around that point that you overtook
me, having gradually become more and more engrossed in the work, and
I began making corrections after you had already marked up the draft.

From then on the cadence of the work changed.

Now in the morning, having talked our fill over coffee (it is served
at noon on the terrace), we each go to our respective rooms and begin
to work. I prefer working on the verandah but when the weather or the
mosquitoes become too bothersome I move to the guest room, or the
downstairs library as it is known in your family. Usually when alone you

work here, it is your favourite room, but temporarily you have moved into the upstairs vaulted office. Once it had been a pantry, its thick stone walls making it the coldest room in the house. But you ordered a wood stove to be brought in and now the stone keeps the warmth and doesn't let in any outside noise.

We have an agreement that an hour before dinner (5 p.m.) we are to go for a walk, to get some air and work up an appetite. No matter how much I enjoy this work, I never miss the appointed rendezvous and, ready for our stroll, begin calling you. You, however, almost always procrastinate, and sometimes it is impossible to tear you away from the work. In those instances the traces of intense concentration are very evident: your face is flushed, you seem distracted. Thus we work every day for over a month.

This concerted effort has borne fruit. No matter how much I loved the first draft of the novel, I rather rapidly have become convinced that your corrections are always done with exquisite mastery, that they elucidate and deepen the traits that had seemed clear, and that they are always strictly in the spirit and tone of the whole composition. As for my notes, I am starting to sense a problem, although I don't know that it should come as a great surprise to me. You vehemently fight every deviation from your chosen path. You staunchly defend every small expression and do not agree to the most innocent changes. The Devil is in the details. You and I both sense it. My small alterations will lead Anna in a new direction. Your new additions are beginning to take her down the path of doom. From your explanations I discover how jealously you value every single word that you set down on paper. In spite of, at times, ostensive carelessness and unevenness of style, you consider your every turn of phrase with the punctiliousness of a poet.

~~~

Pale pre-dawn minutes. Glimmers of powder blue among the oscillating, heaving foliage. A moving darkness. Stare at it long enough and it becomes like water. With every minute revealing tinges of deep green but not individual leaves yet. A breathing mass just beyond the window as I listen to your measured breathing. Outside birds are beginning to rejoice. You do not hear that, lost in your dream world. Are the dreams you invent in waking life an extension of what you are seeing right now? You are working so much, teaching me, purporting to be learning from me. But are you? We have had the discussions. Leave Anna be. Do not kill her. She has suffered enough. Yet with each day your speeches are more and more introspective. We work, but is it a we? I have a schedule. You, a passion. A something that will not let you synchronize with the speed of any world. Not even your own.

tea and philosophy

Your birthday. A day like any other, you insist. From dawn we work. I lose track of the leisurely crawling hours and only just have time to go into my dressing room, sprinkle my face with powder, brush it off, fix my hair, and order tea in the dining room, when one after another carriages begin driving up to the house. The guests, mostly local gentry and a few friends who don't mind the long journey from Moscow, step out onto the wide driveway, and a stout doorman opens the door, letting the visitors into the house.

You walk into the dining room from your office almost at the same instant as your guests. It is a large room with white walls lined with paintings. In the center is a new portrait of you by Ivan Kramskoy. It was his gift to you. The guests come up to admire it. I remember entering your office and coming upon two great artists, one writing Anna Karenina, another painting the portrait of the writer. Both of you had the same expressions on your faces—intensity, concentration, seriousness—I dared not interrupt and backed out, quietly shutting the door behind me.

The brightly lit table gleams with the glow of candles, white cloth, silver samovar, and a nearly transparent bone china tea set. You sit at the head of the table. Extra chairs are set by servants moving almost imperceptibly about the room; the party settles itself, people try to get as close to you as possible. The conversation wavers, as it always does, for the first few minutes, broken up by meetings, greetings, offers of tea, and as it were, searching for a topic to rest upon.

Here and there I hear snippets of idle chatter. Your friend and neighbour, Aleksandr Nikiforovich Dunaev—Nikiforych, as you call him—is chatting up a fat, red-faced, flaxen-haired lady without eyebrows, wearing an old silk dress. Nikiforych is telling her about his new doorman, who in Moscow has a habit of reading newspapers in the morning behind the large glass door of his house, for the edification of the passers-by, but who is flabbergasted in the country because there is nobody to impress with his erudition.

Laughter rises from the round game table. "She's an exceptionally good actress; one can see she's studied Kaulbach," I hear the conclusion of some tale there.

A young man with a pale face and pale blue eyes behind thick glasses is standing, his arms crossed, next to you. His excited voice rises above the murmur of the guests. "So when should one write, Lev Nikolaevich? Whenever one feels the need to, or must one force oneself to sit down and approach it in a disciplined manner, like a profession? For example Dumas or Zola force themselves to write for a certain number of hours every day. They insist that with this method they may write ten average compositions but one will come out well."

The room goes quiet, all faces turn to you, expecting your reply.

You are angry: "Lord forbid that you should listen to all these Dumas, Zola and the like! It's not worth writing at all if what you come up with is the drivel of Dumas, Maupassant, and the other French novelists. France is experiencing the same thing we are—the triumph of form over content. A blend of form and content happens very rarely. It takes a genius to achieve.

"Maupassant has become proficient in a certain style and it is effortless for him to sit himself down and produce written words. No different from a scribe, really. Two, three, four hours—whatever the order of the day is. Heed my advice. Whenever you feel like writing, restrain yourself with all your might. Do not sit down right away. This advice is from personal experience. Only when it becomes unbearable, when you feel ready to explode, only then sit down and write. You will certainly produce something good."

I am about to protest that this seems quite contrary to one of the "writing rules" in your notebook. I had just been pondering it yesterday.

You stated that in every composition one encounters spots, which force one to halt. One must either force oneself to write them nevertheless, or put the work aside until a future time. But under no pretence should one allow oneself to write nothing when one doesn't feel like working. The harder and more difficult the circumstances, the more one needs resolve, action, and willpower, and the more dangerous is apathy. Weak souls succumb, you wrote. But before I can object, a woman seated next to you with thin, black, unnaturally arched eyebrows that lend her an expression of permanent surprise, leans over and asks you something too quietly for most of us to hear.

You shake your head and respond with the vigour of utter conviction in your voice: "Contemporary literature is all founded on beautiful style and a total lack of novelty in its subject matter. Read Evgeniy Markov, Maxim Belinsky and others. Their style is immaculate. But who will reap any benefit from any of their writing? All of them by means of effort and habit have perfected their individual craft. They write easily. They have individual styles. But where is the content? Where is that new idea that would move society, illuminate its shortcomings, open its eyes to a new spiritual insight, a new way of moral fulfilment? You read all these writers and ask, 'Why did this person write all this? Why did he waste his time? Why all the work?' The answer is that they did it either for fame or for material gain. Either goal is horribly vile. You cannot use words like inanimate objects. Don't believe poets when they begin telling you that they write 'art for art's sake.' No! It is either avarice, or a desire to be talked about that moves most of them. I have written much myself and if I am telling you this it is so, it's because I myself have been guilty of wanting to be talked about. In my opinion, all these various celebratory anniversaries of so-called 'illustrious masters' are the shame of our nation. For example you know Fet. This person for thirty years has written only grandiose fluff, which is totally useless. However his birthday celebration was something akin to a bacchanalia. Everybody was trying to assure him that for thirty years he has been doing something of paramount importance. And he believes it himself. That's the rub of all these laurel-endowing gatherings!"

Everyone knows that Fet is your friend and all are surprised by this outburst of ridicule. An excited murmur of commentary crackles through the crowd of guests. One of them speaks up, "But people delight in Fet's poetry. It draws a person away from the grim circumstances of contemporary reality."

You interrupt irritably, "That is precisely why it is bad! First of all, nothing should draw a person away from life. He must live and live consciously. Second of all, who can be distracted by poetry for a long time? Of course I'm talking about a person of sound mind. Yes, poetry can delight a crowd, it can even become entertaining, not unlike a street performer, a magician, a hypnotist. But isn't it demeaning to make faces in front of a mob, to turn somersaults in front of it upon one's mental trapeze?"

The conversation is cut short by this observation.

In search of a new subject the pale young man asks: "Why do you think, Lev Nikolaevich, is contemporary literature in decline?"

"First and foremost," you declare sipping your tea, "because reading fluff has become the norm, and writing itself has become a mere pastime."

the little green wand

I CAN PINPOINT the day when our paths begin to diverge.

We are walking through the Stary Zakaz woods. Early autumn, the leaves are flirting with golds, ambers, reds, maroons. After the rains of the past few days, crisp, clear weather has set in. Only weeks before you would have held my hand, you would have been laughing. Now there is a sensation of a coming frost, both in you and in the weather.

We approach a ravine and you stop, leaning against a tree.

You tell me that you used to play here with your brothers when you were a boy. Once, your beloved older brother Nikolai, who was twelve at the time, told you about a grand secret. Should this secret become revealed, he said, nobody would die ever again, wars and illnesses would cease and all people would become "brother-ants." This secret is carved on a little green wand, which is buried at the edge of this ravine. The younger Tolstoy children searched for years for the little green wand. You all played pretending to be "brother-ants," huddling under chairs draped with colourful scarves, feeling cozy and secure, delighting in the love for each other. You dreamed of "ant-brotherhood" for all people. "It was all so very wonderful," you say. "We called it a game, although everything else in the world is a game, except that."

You glance around the ravine. "This is where I want to be buried." You turn and head back towards the house, without looking to see whether I am following you.

Standing still, and looking at the tops of the aspen trees waving in the wind, with their freshly washed, brightly shining leaves in the cold sunshine, I know that I am losing you, that your passion for saving the world, your lofty unattainable philosophies are beginning to swallow you again. Again you are choosing them over the blood-and-sweat, roll-up-the-sleeves toil of creating literature. And again I feel that everything is splitting in two in my soul. "I mustn't, mustn't think of this," I say to myself. "I must get ready."

frou frou

"Y OU'RE GOING, NO doubt, to see Frou Frou at the French theatre?" asks Fet who is visiting this afternoon on his way to his brother-in-law's estate. "All the fashionable world shall be there next weekend. From what I hear, it is a delightful comedy."

You give a hardly perceptible shrug, as if to say that the concerns of the "fashionable world" are of no interest to you.

But to me, the idea of an outing sounds splendid! Perhaps that's what you need to dispel some of the gathering gravity in your thoughts. A French comedy!

"Frankly it's the first we hear of it," I exclaim. "Wouldn't it be lovely to go?"

"Only if it were possible to get a box," you say, "but I am quite sure it's too late now."

"I can get one," Fet offers his services.

"I should be very, very grateful to you," I say. "And, please, Afanasy Afanasievich, won't you dine with us?"

You glare at me, at a loss to understand what I'm doing. Why invite Fet for dinner and why insist on some silly French diversion? You are entrenched in your work now. Every distraction, every divergence from your schedule exasperates you.

"The levity shall do you good," I whisper in your ear, having no doubt that Frou Frou will be frothy, frivolous. "But if you don't want to come, I'm sure Afanasy Afanasievich would gladly escort me."

You grunt and turn away, walking with a heavy step to your office. *Frou Frou*, I think. *Sounds so familiar.*

"Who is this play by?" I ask Fet.

"Meilhac and Halevy. They're quite the rage in Paris."

Never heard of them. Still… Frou Frou.

~~~

We get to the theatre at half past eight. You are sullen on our trip into Moscow and when I attempt conversations you look past me or huff something incoherent. I wonder whether you will even notice what is happening on the stage. For the hundredth time I ask myself whether I did the right thing by insisting you come out tonight. A sense of unease tugs at me.

Fet meets us in the lobby. The play has already started, but, as he explains to me, nothing important will have happened at the beginning. And if it does the actors will make sure that the audience has no trouble catching up. This "civilized" approach to theatre allows the gentlefolk to arrive and socialize at their leisure.

An usher, a little old stooped man, greets us and helps us off with our coats. A couple of servants with fur coats over their arms are listening at the doors to the auditorium that are cracked open. A burst of laughter splashes into the lobby.

Laughter is good. I've done the right thing, I tell myself and, as if to confirm my speculation, I hear thunderous applause.

When we enter the auditorium, which is brilliantly lit with chandeliers and bronze gas lanterns, the applause still rages. On the stage a man and a woman bow and smile. Her bare shoulders flash with diamonds. He, glossy pomaded hair parted down the side, is gathering up bouquets that are flying over the footlights. The audience in the stalls and in the boxes cranes forward, shouting and clapping.

Theatre. Once again I'm here. I'm home. How strange it all is. How familiar—the stage, the noise, the herd of spectators. Things change; things remain the same. A slight alteration of costume, but the people, the people here in the theatre! Familiar ladies in the boxes with familiar gentlemen in the shadows behind them; a familiar dance of colours in the women's dresses, and stern black tuxes, and uniforms. Even the greyness of commoners in the upper gallery is palpably familiar.

Act one is over and we do not go straight to our box, but head to the front towards the stage, where your cousin Obolensky is standing with one knee raised and his heel on the footlights. He catches sight of us approaching and waves, smiling.

"What a pity you were not here for the first act," he says embracing you. "Heloise was superb in the leading role!"

"So what did we miss?" you ask.

"Let's see. Heloise plays Mademoiselle Gilberte, known as Frou Frou, an enchanting, beautiful young lady. She marries the Count Sartorys on the advice of her sister, who is secretly in love with him, although he loves Frou Frou."

"Sounds like a silly Shakespearean plot," you grumble.

"Oh, you're impossible. Just give it a chance," laughs Obolensky. "This Frou Frou is adored by her husband and they have a son, but she doesn't take her marriage seriously and her sister has to step in to help with the household. And then Frou Frou gets it into her head that she is jealous of her sister so she runs off with an old lover."

"And abandons her child?" you ask.

"Well," says Obolensky, "the point is not the child. The point is the impulsive, passionate, young woman's character. Frou Frou. At one point her lover describes how perfectly the name suits her. She is as light as the rustle of silk, a flutter of fairy wings… or something like that. She is simply Frou Frou—a delightful nickname, don't you think?"

"For a horse maybe," you say.

And then I remember. Frou Frou. The horse in the novel. Vronsky loves her. She trusts him. He kills her. Accidentally. The portent of Anna's fate. I feel faint. And the theatre begins spinning. The gas lanterns quiver in a congealing dimness. The air is stuffy; the noise overbearing. I cannot breathe. I don't want to stay. I cannot leave. I cannot let you watch it.

But it is too late. Unavoidable like a slow approach of a precipice in a dream. I press on the breaks, I scream but no sound comes out. Nothing happens. And then emptiness. The curtain rises. Frou Frou is on the stage. Loving, dying. A fine French comedy. And I keep thinking: Frou Frou—the rustle of silk, a flutter of fairy wings… a stroke of a quill and death.

no time to be brief

T HE DESK IS covered with papers. You are frowning. As the weather is turning cold and the sky grows darker for longer periods of time, your mood is growing more sombre. Less and less I can connect with you.

"What are you doing?" I ask, as your hand armed with a quill keeps slashing paper.

"Too long," you say through your teeth without lifting your eyes. "Too long! A story is always improved when shortened. If the reader begins hearing idle chatter, he won't be too attentive. You must grab the reader right away and not let him go from the heights to which he has risen."

I sigh with relief. I so enjoy talking with you about craft! These days, alas, more and more frequently our conversations dead-end into one of your lengthy diatribes against the iniquities of the world. You speak about the redemption of the soul, about death. I cannot help but miss that other you, the one who loves life.

You used to always pick flowers on our walks, gathering them into tight little bouquets—daisies, violets, forget-me-nots, lilies-of-the-valley. As you picked each stem you stripped off the leaves. You don't like foliage on your flowers. "Just look at these colours!" you would always exclaim. "Oh, and the fragrance!" gently, as if cradling hatchlings in your hands, you would bring the blooms close to my face, so that I could smell.

Now, however, although you continue working on the novel, your heart is drifting from this art form. It frightens me. We writers believe so strongly in our own fictions that they become our realities.

Your wife said that one time, while you were writing War and Peace, you were late for dinner. The children began fooling around, the English governess, in an unusually good mood, did nothing to stop them, smiling at their antics. Your wife and her sister, who was visiting at the time, were exchanging society gossip. The room was resounding with laughter, singing, ruckus. Suddenly the door swung open and you walked in. Your eyes puffy and red, tears rolling down your face.

"How can you be laughing at a time like this?" your trembling voice trounced the laughter.

The kids looked up in fear.

"What happened, Levochka?" your wife ran up to you.

"Prince Andrey just died," you said and tears flowed with renewed force.

~~~

Yes, you believe in these fictions you create whether on the page or in life.

The first fiction that you willed to become real was that of being a great writer. In your early twenties you were a soldier, a womanizer, a gambler. Discipline was the farthest thing from your mind until one night you lost your family mansion in a game of cards. To make some money fast you decided, on a whim, to write a couple of short stories. You enjoyed the experience and submitted the pieces to a St. Petersburg literary journal under a pseudonym. You didn't want to be embarrassed should they be rejected. To your surprise, the stories were bought. "I received a letter from St. Petersburg, from the editor, which left me giddy with happiness," you wrote in your journal and began thinking that writing might not be a bad way to spend a life. "My debts are all paid. A brilliant literary career is spread wide open before me. I'm young and intelligent. What else is there to wish for? I must only work and abstain from indulgences and I may yet become very happy."

For a long time your ingrained habits rebelled against the necessary discipline of a writer. Your diary entries are replete with:

"Writing is difficult work…"

And:

"Reproaches today: 1) for laziness, and 2) for laziness."

And:

"I have been in a lazy-apathetic-hopeless depressed state. I have won 130 more rubles in cards. I bought a horse and a bridle for 150. What nonsense! My career is literature—I must write, write, write! Beginning tomorrow I am either working for the rest of my life or I am abandoning everything—rules, religion, morals. Everything."

Eventually, through hard work and much stumbling, writing did become a habit. Being a writer wasn't good enough, you wanted to be a great one. You developed a set of rules to hone your craft.

- don't begin reading or writing new material without finishing the one already begun
- well or poorly—always work
- always write everything precisely and clearly
- don't repeat the thoughts of others.
- avoid routine turns of phrase and literary affectations
- while critically perusing your own work, view it from the point of view of a reader who will seek only entertainment in a book
- whenever a thought doesn't quite fit into the narrative, write it down in the margins and without tarrying on it, go on with the story.
- In writing the rough draft, don't pause to consider the aptness and meticulousness of expressing each thought. In writing the second draft, cut out all that is extraneous and allow each idea its proper breathing room. The third draft is for honing your style and precision of expression

You had made that fiction your reality, but happiness was short-lived. You grew tired of the fanfares and praise. The Bohemian lifestyle of the St. Petersburg intelligentsia began to bore you.

Then tragedy struck. Your brother Nikolai died of consumption. You were 34 years old. You lost both parents in childhood, and your brother had become both father and best friend to you. With his death, you truly felt orphaned. You needed to fill the void. The shock of Nikolai's death gave you your next fiction to manifest into life—you would have a family and become the perfect family man. This is what you thought you now needed to feel happy.

You had never thought of yourself as the marrying kind, quite content with seducing gypsy girls, ballet dancers and the wives of your friends. Now you began searching for the woman who would be your life's companion. You idealized her before you met her. You created her out of your dream fibres and fantasy filaments. You imagined her as a creature of purity, who, with her very presence, would redeem you, the sinner. You wrote in your diary that you were afraid that no woman would love you, since by now you were too old and ugly.

It took two years of searching and misery for you to find her. Sofia Andreyevna Bers was eighteen, intelligent and innocent. An angel straight out of your dreams. The night before the wedding you gave her your diaries, which detailed every single conquest you had ever made. Your allegorical sacrifice of your wantonness on the altar of your future happiness. Your bride was so horrified that she almost did not go through with the nuptials. Of course you did get married. And you had children. And you did find contentment in those first few years of matrimony, for in Sophia you also found a devoted admirer of your literary talent. But there was also an emptiness and long periods when neither the family nor the work were satisfactory. Happiness still evaded you.

Then you met your Muse, the perfect woman, Anna's prototype.

I understand now that it doesn't matter whether it was I or Maria Gartung. The fact of the meeting already carried in it the seeds of your undoing. First the elation, the giddy desire, the creative torrent that engulfed you. In eight weeks you wrote a novel that you were convinced would become your masterpiece. Then the luring sweet opium of this love threatened to break up the carefully wrought fiction of a happy family life. You have worked too hard on this reality. Losing it would be undoing so many fantasies. Losing it would mean redefining yourself, not by building on your established habits, but by deconstructing your very soul and rebuilding it anew. But what force could you find to counterbalance this obsession of yours? What can kill a passion for a woman?

There was an idea that had lodged in you long ago and had been waiting for its perfect opportunity to sprout.

In April of 1857, at the age of 26 you wrote in your diary: "Yesterday the conversation about divinity and faith led me to a splendid, enormous idea to the realization of which I feel capable of devoting my entire life. This idea is the creation of a new religion incorporating the advancements of humanity, based on the teachings of Christ, but cleansed of the contraptions of religiosity, mysticism and church practices that are geared towards corporeal gratification rather than heavenly bliss."

Creating a religion. Yes, I suppose, that could push any woman past the boundary of your life. This perfect religion of yours, however, is just another fiction. In the end, even if you believe in it wholeheartedly, it will not bring you happiness. Have you ever known a happy Messiah?

To serve this God of yours you will have to kill Anna as a symbol of killing your passion. Dead passion is useless to a writer.

And what will you gain? Pilgrims and lunatics crowding Yasnaya Polyana, vying for your attention. A motley throng of wannabe writers, vagrants, and crooks. Your family will call them "the Dark Ones." You will be beset by mathematical proofs of Christianity contrived by drug addicts, and old men running naked through your estate. You will fall under the spell of your secretary, Chertkov, and, to the detriment of your family, you will sign over the rights of your works to him. Ironic, the root of his name, "chert" means "demon" in Russian. Why won't you see that? Your wife, fearing your increasingly volatile behaviour, will be forced to spy on you, enlisting the help of servants, friends, family. Can you even imagine her, sprawled in a ditch, watching the entrance to Yasnaya Polyana through binoculars? She will.

Do you know what you will conclude through your quest? "There is no such thing as love, only the physical need for intercourse and the practical need for a life companion."

That's what you will get for killing Anna.

Right now you still yearn for happiness, but happiness is the ultimate fiction. No human has been able to believe in it fully. Happiness descends on all of us only in brief moments. That is its nature; it is not a permanent state. Your moments of happiness have trickled in only during writing. Do not shut off the source.

a death, a rebirth

I've read your final draft. You've made your choice. Not me. Not Anna. Not literature but God. I must leave you. I don't see eye to eye with your God. The rules of His universe are of no use to me. Just like all my pleading, explaining, hinting, urging is of no use to Him. My parting gift to you is a warning: your every step towards some imagined heaven will drag you deeper into a personal hell. You will never experience the bliss of your early drafts where you allowed yourself a full surrender into love. The love of a woman, and through it, the love of your work.

Once, when I was mired in self-doubt you whispered to me that "a work of art is an offspring of love. Perform an act of love, and we will admire that which holds your affection."

And what were your final words about Anna?

"I am heartbroken. My Anna, which I just reread, turned out to be such a disgraceful vulgarity, that I cannot recover from crushing humiliation. I think I shall never write again."

That was the only note you thought fit to leave on top of your manuscript as you left Moscow?

"There is an element in fantasy that is better than reality. There is an element in reality that is better than fantasy. Indeed, full happiness might be in uniting both." Remember when you said that? It was a velvety late summer night. We had taken a walk after supper and reclined on the river bank a mile or so from your estate. The moon had just risen over the hill and illuminated two small, wispy storm clouds. Behind us the cricket was whistling its poignant, ceaseless song, a frog was croaking in the distance, and near the village from time to time we heard the shouts of the peasants, interspersed with the barking of dogs and then again everything grew quiet. And again there was only the cricket's soft crooning and a transparent storm cloud rolling past the near and distant stars. We talked of literature and realities, and the night was full of promise and possibility. How absolutely inconsequential it all is now. Well, I have learned something you don't know. Reality to a writer is not the grinding cacophony of the world that slams into his skin and scorches his ego, but the malleable landscape on the page. Once I've manipulated life to slow down and sample different paces and places in time, I can manipulate it further. I can fit my life into perfectly defined parameters— between Chapter One and The End. So much more harmonious than the butchered plots of your God.

And in the end you've helped me. In your striving to create a perfectly crafted novel, you've created a viable universe. Those characters of yours, they're real. Except their lives are measured not by ticking clocks but by rustling pages. I cannot help Anna. But I can salvage Vronsky. You abandoned him. The one character who undergoes such an astonishing transformation in the novel. He outgrows the frivolity of his circle and learns to love. I am not sure you even noticed that his affection for Anna, his risking his status in society, his love for his daughter are among the most touching, genuine emotional creations on the pages of world literature. I will pick up where you left off. Once he comes back from his Serbian campaign he and I will have no more need for Russia with its frozen expanses, sombreness, death. We'll head somewhere warm— Greece or perhaps the south of France. Yes, that's what we'll do. We'll take the train from Moscow to Nice. There is a promising writer there, Monsieur Verne, who might benefit from my discreet advice.

a beautiful lie

A FINE RAIN had been drizzling all morning, and now the weather was clearing up. The iron roofs, the flint in the pavements, the wheels and the brass of the carriages—all glistened brightly in the May sunshine. It was three o'clock, and the very liveliest time in the streets.

As she sat in a corner of the comfortable carriage that hardly swayed on its supple springs, in the midst of the unceasing rattle of wheels and the changing impressions in the newly cleansed air, Karen ran over the events of the last days, and she saw her position quite differently from how it had seemed just hours earlier. Now the thought of Anna's death seemed no longer so terrible and so unambiguous to her. And Lev's final words to her, "Art is a lie, and I can no longer love a beautiful lie," before he jumped into the carriage and left to be by his wife's side and to attend his ailing child, no longer inspired anger in her, but pity.

I forgive him, she thought. We do not choose art—it chooses us. There is no blissful waltz with the muses. Creation is an agonizing process. Few survive. Yet while we cling to the maps of our senses, through fear and pain we go on writing, stumbling across tundras of unmeaning, planting words like bloody flags in our wake. Who said that? Certain memories have become quite hazy. Yes, I forgive him. He is dealing with it the best way he knows how. In the end, our fates have rhymed more than I had thought. Can I live without him?

And leaving unanswered the question of whether and how she was going to live without him, she fell to reading the signs on the shops her carriage was passing: *Office and Warehouse. Dental Surgeon.* Again her thoughts begged centre stage:

I am no longer in the mood to extract the vagaries of his one major misstep. Anna is dead without fulfilling her promise as a character. He will die without fulfilling his promise as a writer. In the end each person's passing is only that—a brief flash amid the eternally burning fire of some god. We are not remembered in two or three generations. Often sooner. Anything beyond that is not knowledge of us, not of our flesh our smiles our smells and idiosyncrasies. At most what will survive will be our brief connection with the clockworks of the universe—our art. The Iliad is still being translated and enjoyed. Nobody knows what dreams Homer had in childhood, what songs his mother sang, where his heart first shattered or whether he really existed.

We barely remember the celebrities of a century before. We too will live in somebody's remote past. Evenings with friends will become static spectres; sunsets with lovers—frozen inconsequentialities. We all will become a nothingness, giving rise to other transient heartbeats of humanity. Like those girls, so real in this fleeting now. How illusory.

She turned her head and stared as her carriage passed two girls, no older than fourteen, heads bent toward each other, engaged in some fervent conversation. Both smiling, illuminated by a secret happiness.

What could they be smiling about? Love, most likely. They don't know how dangerous it is. Oh, there is Filippov's Bakery. They say they send their dough to Petersburg. There is nothing like the purity of Moscow's water for first rate bread!

She chased away a memory of a more rapid time, when this water could no longer support life and all that flowed down the oil-slicked surface of Moscow River were ripped newspapers, torn tires and the occasional bloated corpse.

The carriage swayed lightly, rumbling over the cobbles of the road, and again one impression followed rapidly upon another. There's someone who's pleased with himself, she thought, as she saw a fat, ruddy gentleman coming towards her. He took her for an acquaintance, lifting his glossy hat above his bald, glossy head, and then perceived his mistake.

He thought he knew me, Karen mused. Well, he knows me as well as anyone in the world knows me. We can never understand the mindworks of another, yet if we see into ourselves, we see into all. They're singing for vespers, and how carefully that merchant crosses himself! As if he were afraid of missing something. People find God in the strangest places. Sometimes even in churches. They don't realize that Heaven is only a reflection of our desires. Naked, undefined, feared. To reach a desire we must surrender the snug status quo. To reach Heaven we don't necessarily need to bid adieu to life, just to life as we know it.

She was immersed in these thoughts when the carriage drew up at the train station.

Making her way through the crowd in the first-class waiting-room, cradling in her arms a thick package wrapped loosely in newsprint, Karen felt a vague fury rising up within her and lest she speed up and slip out of this time's rhythm, she forced herself to walk slowly and deliberately. She was already sensing her grasp on this particular world growing tenuous. The edges of people seemed blurred, faces came in and out of focus.

Once on the platform, the clamour of the laughing, screaming, peddling, parting and reuniting masses reverberated through her, disorienting her with its physicality. She tightened her grip on the package and concentrated on what she meant to do. Everything had seemed so clear in the carriage but now, among this noisy mass of people which teased her with its seeming insubstantiality, she found it difficult to focus. Was her body faltering in this reality as well?

One moment a gypsy woman approached her, offering to read her palm for a few kopecks, but immediately after that a young man, clacking his heels on the planks of the platform dodged past Karen, striking her shoulder with such force that she staggered and almost fell. He turned around to apologize and stared at her with utter shock. Clearly he hadn't seen her and now wondered how he could have missed an elegant lady in a red dress edged with expensive black lace.

The rapidity of her heart's beating hindered her breathing. Karen walked along the platform. Two maidservants turned their heads, staring at her, and made some remarks about her dress. "Real," one said of the lace she was wearing and then turned away as if her existence was already forgotten. The station-master approached her and began asking Karen whether she was boarding the next train, but stopping mid-sentence he stepped away and addressed the lady behind her. Children seemed to be the ones most puzzled by her. A girl selling kvas never took her eyes off Karen and several times a group of young boys ran by her, peering into her face, and with a laugh shouted something in unnaturally nasal high voices.

My God! I can't do it in front of all these people. Where am I to go? she thought, moving farther and farther along the platform. At the end she stopped. A lady with children, who had come to meet a gentleman in spectacles, didn't even pause in her loud laughter and talking. Only the two little girls in identical yellow dresses edged with blue ribbon stared at Karen as she reached them.

She quickened her pace and walked away from them to the edge of the platform. A freight train was coming in, slowing down. She had checked the schedule in the newspaper ahead of time and knew that this train was only passing by. It would slow down and then speed up as it left the station.

The clatter of train wheels hypnotizes the soul into a different rhythm.

The platform began to sway, and she fancied she was in the train again, leaving Russia, like she had in some very, very distant life. And all at once she thought of the trains of her childhood and her desire to travel. She felt herself drifting from this world and willed herself to hold on, for she knew what she had to do.

Decisively she went down the steps that led from the platform to the rails and stopped quite near the approaching train. She looked at the lower part of the carriages, at the screws and chains and the massive cast-iron wheel of the first carriage slowly approaching, trying to measure the middle between the front and back wheels, and the very moment when that middle point would be in front her.

"There," she said to herself, looking into the shadow of the carriage, at the sand and coal dust which covered the cross ties, "there, in the very middle." A feeling such as she had known when about to take the first plunge into a cool pond at midday came upon her, and she crossed herself. This involuntary gesture, once taught by her grandmother, did not bring a security of some god's protection but a closeness to an integral, never changing part of herself. Karen did not take her eyes from the wheels of the train carriage. And exactly at the moment when the space between the wheels came opposite her, she flung the package onto the railroad tracks. The merciless force of the train wheels struck, ripped and dragged the helpless paper.

White pages with even lines of bold handwriting whirled up into the air in a gale. Some wounded, others torn and shredded and still others barely baptized by the ruthless metal they twirled up over her head, crashed into the sides of the train and took flight again, committing to air the book filled with promises, falsehoods, sorrows and sanctimony. With every clatter of the train wheels more and more pages became airborne, the late afternoon sun piercing them, making them glow in a blinding whiteness until the pages obliterated everything around her, becoming light itself.

The avenues of deceit were finally road-blocked. She plodded through clarity one laceration at a time. She willed her heart to beat more slowly, more fully. She forced her breath to coalesce and seek out a richer time fragrance. And when sounds liquefied into a soothing silence, when the molecules of different pulses streamed at her will, she laughed, "You live your life at the speed of one second per second. I no longer do."

acknowledgements

Writing, especially writing fiction, is a spiritual striptease—as frightening as it is liberating. I have been blessed with supportive friends and colleagues who helped *The Speed of Life* take shape, nurtured timid ideas, and ruthlessly executed superfluous passages. Among them are Tamim Ansary, Darrend Brown, Karen Garber, Stan Goldberg, Carrie Hall, Markus Hoffman, Scott James, Frances Lefkowitz, Viktor Naiman, Ransom Stephens, Gary Turchin, James Warner, and Barry Willdorf. I also must mention my favourite literary playground—the San Francisco Writers' Workshop, a Bay Area institution for over six decades. To everyone there who has ever contributed to this novel, I extend my heartfelt gratitude.

about the author

PHOTOGRAPHY © SILVIA PECOTA

Yanina Gotsulsky is a novelist, poet and translator. She holds a degree in Russian Language and Literature from York University in Toronto. She currently lives in Northern California and is working on a novel, which, to her own surprise, does not once mention Russia. She is also completing a full translation of Tolstoy's diaries that inspired this novel.

Follow Yanina on Twitter @YaninaGotsulsky and visit her website: http://www.yaninagotsulsky.com